Praise and Criticism for Off the X

"Mark McDonald's brilliantly crafted work, 'Off The X,' sets the new gold standard for narrative journalism and historical fiction. He combines Jim Harrison's gift of character development and storytelling with David Halberstam's Pulitzer-winning reporting and mastery of military detail and mindset. McDonald, a renowned war correspondent, deftly sifts the carnage in Iraq's desert landscape to discern the larger truths of America's grandest of misadventures. This book is not to be missed."

--- Phil Karber, Lowell Thomas Award medalist

"A serious and important work . . . the product of high intelligence and passionate conviction, alternately mournful and gripping, and occasionally hilarious. It's also a ripping good story."

--- Soho Weekly News

"The best writing about Americans and war since 'The Things They Carried,' and maybe since 'A Farewell to Arms' and the 'U.S.A. Trilogy.' Yes, that good."

--- Partisan Review

"This is war porn, or war smut, something akin to pictures of flag-draped coffins returning home: colorful and descriptive, but also prurient. This is a mean book, and I defy anyone who reads it not to become incensed. McDonald doesn't show us war. He shows us murder."

--- 'Wüste Fuchs,' the O.B.E. blog, National Defence Journal

"McDonald writes as movingly about love and sex as he does about terror and torture. And there's some occasional overlap there, which can be troubling."

--- Argosy

"In the upcoming film version --- and this book is highly cinematic --- we can imagine Denzel, Clooney or Jeff Bridges as the Army general-in-waiting, pacing inside his Airstream, obsessed with his hand sanitizer and espresso machine. Damon, Depp or Ed Norton as the shell-shocked protagonist Micah Ford. Look for Maggie Q --- amped-up and six-packed --- as Micah's Army colleague Sistine Tran, the first woman to earn the 'triple canopy' of patches for Special Forces, Ranger and Airborne. So many great roles here, small and large and full of possibilities."

--- Notes on Modern Cinema

"The sweep of this book! It opens with the funeral of an American political lion, in winter, at Arlington National Cemetery. And there's the burnt archeology of the 9/11 Pile. And a boozy game of Scrabble in an Alabama motel room. A 200-foot fall from a wall of New England granite. A hurtle of a road trip across the great waist of America. Overcooked coffee at the CIA. A young Army private, tortured on camera by ISIS. An aging West Point colonel, restless in the desert labyrinth of his final mission. Chess tutorials from a shackled and broken-brained Iraqi grandmaster. America's first female Ranger, under fire, tested and measured. We get confusion from love, clarity from violence, and a final compass-reading from valor."

--- Look

" 'Off the X' reverse-engineers the customary arc of combat stress disorder. It is in situ, in combat, during a highly charged mission, that the book's badly damaged protagonist finally locates a deep calm and a new, cold-lighted clarity. The author, although not a practicing psychotherapist, clearly knows his way around traumatic stress syndrome, around its snares and demolishings and its biochemistry. The medical scenes are clinically accurate and carefully detailed . . . Plus, the overall story is gripping, poignant and nothing short of brilliant."

--- Psychiatric Approaches to the Management of Combat Stress,
World Health Journal

"This shows McDonald's peculiar genius at its best. He constructs not only the most ironic but also the most cruelly searching portrait to date of America in her fateful recent decades . . . Witty, modern and puncturing, it happily recalls Evelyn Waugh's 'Put Out More Flags.' "

--- Contemporary Fiction in the Levant

" 'Off the X' defies the quick 'elevator pitch' or a one-paragraph-shouted-across-the-room summation at a cocktail party. When I have pressed the book on literate friends who I know to be serious readers, they typically ask what the book's about, or what it's like. I say read it. Just read it."

--- John Courtney Boot, The Beast

OFF THE X

Red Tongue Books / Hellbox Media
Santa Fe, New Mexico

First Red Tongue edition published 2015.

This is a work of narrative journalism and historical fiction. The characters and events in this book are fictions, and as David Foster Wallace has said elsewhere, any similarity to real persons is not intended by the author. The protagonists and occurrences are constructs, especially the characterizations of globally known persons, companies, security agencies and military and political figures. The techniques of both newspaper reporting and literary journalism are the principal techniques of this book. In the Acknowledgements section at the end of the book, there is an accounting of sources, interviews, travels, aides, reference materials, declassified information, FOIA-requested documents, various accomplices, etc., etc.

A companion section, the Reading Notes, resides online. The Notes are intended to serve several functions: footnotes, backstories, bibliography, sourcing identification and perhaps even as a stand-alone meta-text. They provide attributions for certain excerpts, quotes, lyrics, turns of phrase and ideas that might have originated with other writers and artists. Whenever I have explicity borrowed something, I have tried to identify its source. Anyone can access the Reading Notes for free using this link:

http://tinyurl.com/offthexnotes

Portions of this book have appeared in somewhat different form in the following: *The Little Review, Nobel Nominees Review, Ramparts, Soho Weekly News, Partisan Review, the Saturday Review of Literature, Look, Two Worlds, Carlos Quincenal, Rattle and Clank, Galle Fort Journal, Contemporary Fiction in the Levant, Drop-Kick, the National Defence Journal, Warfighting,* and *The Lone Hand.*

ISBN 978-0-9968776-0-2

Written and edited globally. Printed in the United States of America.

TO THOSE WHO REMAIN IN THEATER,

THE ONES STILL ON THE X

PART I

1. ARLINGTON, DECEMBER 2001

It was late afternoon, the sky purpling to the west, going bloodshot, going the color of Mercurochrome. Forty degrees yesterday, barely 10 now, and too cold to snow. The Tidal Basin had skimmed over during the night. Touch a headstone with a bare hand today, it just might stick. It was winter in America.

From atop the rise of Chaplains Hill, looking out across the whitecapped plain of Arlington, the long and final bivouac of the dead, Micah could just make out the rough edge of the damaged Pentagon, a jagged dit-da-dit on the horizon. No scaffolding yet.

Moving downhill, past the Tomb of the Unknowns and skirting Section 60, he made his way slowly among the graves. The frozen grass crunched underfoot. He passed Montgomery Meigs, Orde Wingate, Grace Hopper, then stopped at this headstone: *Spottswood Poles, Virginia, World War I, 369th Infantry. Born 1887. Died 1962.* At the base of the marker was a Crown Royal bottle in its velvet pouch, holding some plastic daisies. He stood there for a minute, leaning on the gravestone, as if visiting an old friend.

He read the names on the markers as he continued downhill, downhill and down, down down toward his father. Micah hadn't caught many of the details when they called to say they had found Hank in the Pile, found him in some dark seam of the burnt archaeology of the towers. His father, 56, gone, just like that, another 9/11 casualty. It had taken a hundred days for the sniffer dogs to find him.

PARDOE MARTIN...CORNELIUS VANE...PLUMB ARBUCKLE...SHIZUYA HAYASHI...JULIET HOPKINS...SALEM POOR...LORI ANN PIESTEWA...PLEZ YANCEY...URIAH LEVY.

In the weeks since the attacks in September, Micah had been staying at his dad's townhouse on D Street in Washington. Hank's remains had been delivered there by a New York City police captain, shot twice on the job, now retired on full disability. The captain arrived at the door in his dress uniform, spit-shined, courteous, limping and grave. His nameplate said Compass. The ashes were in a baby-blue box, Tiffany-blue, John-John-Kennedy-blue, tied with a black ribbon. Inside the box: a thick plastic bag, the size and heft of a sack of flour, packed tight, heat-sealed.

The bag was labeled EVIDENCE. That was the word printed across the front in bright official orange, traffic-cone orange, hazmat orange. There were spaces on the bag for the date, time collected, weight, item no, agent name, agent badge, case no, and GPS coords. All the spaces were blank.

Inside the bag: pulverized bone and skull and sidewalk. Grit, cellulose, scrapings, ash. Talc and oxides, scoured paint, methacrylate plastic. Captured scorch and smoke. Flakes of Hank. Flecks of him. Calcium phosphate, melamine, dark matter, tau neutrinos, HeLa cells. Blanched asbestos. Filaments, filings, phlogiston, graphite, coprolite, resins, rock-chalk, half-lives, God particles, a pebble, powdered pearls, marble dust, methyl isocyanates, silica stipples, shavings, another pebble. White carbon. Cancers. Bits and soot and dust.

Maybe that was Hank in there, some of it. Maybe not.

How to tell? How to know what was truly in that Gold Medal sack of Hank? It was all evidence, sure, evidence of the day, but it was not credible evidence of Hank Ford. There could be powdered anything in there. Powdered *anybody*. Double helices --- unbuckled, unhinged and skirled aloft. Bits from a Paki cabbie, a Church Street dog walker, a barista working the Monday-morning rush, a feral cat, a MacArthur genius. Grooves of proteins, binding sites and ester bonds from Allah-knows-who. Homeless nucleotides. They hadn't needed body bags at the Pile. They needed tweezers, tongs and sifters. All of this EVIDENCE might have been quickly troweled and broomed into one decent dustpan-load.

And that's what they were burying today --- the granulated evidence of Hank.

Tomorrow they would be burying Namaz, Micah's fiancée. Tomorrow, and tomorrow, and tomorrow.

R.O. SHIPMAN...AMORY BLAINE...IVORY WATSON...ORVILLE JONES...STEPHEN SWAILS...WILMER MCLEAN...EDWARD SALTER...ARCHIMEDES PATTI...JOHN BELL HOOD.

Coming down the long southern slope of the cemetery, seeing the gravesite a hundred yards off with the large crowd of mourners assembled there, Micah went into a kind of weak-kneed stupor that suggested the swing-armed lope of a campus goofball. But that wasn't it. It was the sadness that was beginning to work on him now, working under his father's wool scarf and settling onto his chest. The whole scene, from this distance, it was like looking into a shoebox diorama --- his third-grade Valley Forge or Appomattox Courthouse.

A murmur went through the crowd as people turned to watch him walking up. A pathway opened and Micah moved fully into the gathering, past the priest and the rabbi, past the Arlington Lady and the military escort. He appeared so forlorn and vacant that even the monsignor began to wobble. Here and there, hankies unfurled. Micah looked haunted, as if he might give way and collapse at the slightest word or smallest pressure.

The front row of graveside seats was empty, the cushioned seats reserved for family. Jimmy Bloodworth, Micah's grandfather, was the only real family he had left now, and the old man's doctor hadn't let him make the trip up from Florida for the service.

"Where do I go now?" Micah said to the priest. It sounded so odd the way he said it, with the word *now* emphasized at the end, as if to say without my parents, without Namaz, after today, by myself.

The Arlington Lady put a white-gloved hand on Micah's back. "Come with me, honey. You're in the front. You're alone, are you?"

Yes, Micah Ford was alone now, yes he was, the only son of an only son.

THOMAS RHODES...REMEMBER BAKER...ENOCH BOONE...MARGUERITE HIGGINS... WASHINGTON ROEBLING... WASHINGTON TOIL... VIOLET GIBSON...STIPPO RAKES.

Micah had been to Arlington before, years ago, as a 10-year-old boy. That was for his mother's funeral. But taking his seat today, it somehow didn't occur to him, not right away, that his mother was there in front of him, barely 5 feet away and 10 feet down, just *there*, buried long ago under the black Virginia mud.

The gravestone had her name engraved on the back, which was how they did it with spouses at Arlington, having them come in the back way:

ELIZABETH BLOODWORTH FORD
HIS WIFE
4-15-47 9-17-85

On the front, newly etched, was Hank:

HENRY LOUIS FORD
MICHIGAN
US ARMY CPT
VIETNAM
PURPLE HEART
I INFANTRY
5-8-45 9-11-01

Hank Ford, no wants, no warrants, senior vice president at General Dynamics, University of Michigan Class of 1967, MBA '74, Huey pilot in Vietnam (the nasty years), a legit 4-handicap at Oakland Hills and Congressional, a splendid Tudor home in Grosse Pointe Farms, a lakeside cabin and a new Boston Whaler up on the Leelanau, a Capitol Hill townhouse, lapsed member of Holy Redeemer and Temple Beth El, the son of the late Samuel and Frances Ford. A widower since 1985. One child, a son, Micah Bloodworth Ford.

DENMARK VESEY...ROBERT TREAT...DONALD QUIX...LORRAINE MINOSA...TRUTHFUL JAMES... LOTHAR EISENTRAGER...CHESTER OVNAND...SECKETARY HAWKINS.

The overnight cold had felled or frozen most anything capable of flight --- commercial planes, Marine One, Arlington's resident ravens, even the bugle calls at the cemetery. When it got this cold, the buglers couldn't play. No Taps today.

It looked like several hundred at the service, a big turnout given the weather. The lead escort working the funeral, an Army captain with WOODARD in polite Helvetica caps on her uniform nameplate, told Micah it was "the biggest show" they'd had at Arlington in many weeks. "Four busloads from the Pentagon alone," she said. A dozen or so executives had limo'd over from the General Dynamics offices in Falls Church.

The big-time military men on hand were seated in the rows just behind Micah, the generals and admirals with their heads down, shoulders heaving and the snot freezing under their noses. They were the ones who had bought so much of Hank's hardware over the years. It was full dress uniforms today, everybody sharp and crisp and by the book. They were the drop-forged tip of the military-industrial spear, by God, and this was a time when you trooped the colors. No cutters and runners in this crowd. Most of the Army generals sat together --- Powell, Taguba, Sanchez, Eikenberry. "Murderers' Row," as The Nation's funeral coverage would later call them. Stan McChrystal had flown in from Qatar. Dave Petraeus was in from Bosnia. Hell of a thing, those guys coming all that way.

The Israeli ambassador, a sad-eyed former general named David Ivry, had brought with him a small stone from Yad Vashem. He placed it on the gently curved shoulder of Hank and Lizzie's marker, which itself was a lovely piece of stone, Vermont limestone, just the color of today's cold clouds. Sitting next to him were other yarmulk'd men, friends of Hank's from Shin Bet and the IDF, and the old defense minister Moshe Arens. The Israelis' security perimeter, their obvious perimeter, was being manned by half a dozen rented bulls from GrayWater --- sunglassed men with 18-inch necks and wrist radios, their suits lumpy with weaponry. The extent of the other perimeter, the Mossad perimeter, well, there was no telling.

A Saudi royal, one of the younger Bandar nephews, a member of the three-comma club, had been allowed to drive up to the funeral without an escort. Hank had done a lot of business with the House of Saud. He got them better tanks and fancier look-down/shoot-down radar than they needed or deserved. The family knew they owed him.

Admirable that the prince had come at all, really. Every notable Muslim in D.C. --- the bunch from the Maghreb, Indonesia, the Emirates, Turkey, you name it --- all but a few had gone to ground after the attacks. Everyday Muslims had bolted, too. Lebanese restaurant owners made hastily arranged trips to Beirut. Egyptians beat it back to Maadi and Zamalek. Nearly the entire taxi caste in the District was gone --- the yellow-eyed Yemenis, the spindly Somalis and Ethiopians, the glowering Hausas from Nigeria. All the fugitive types who were normally so nimble in the half-light of unwelcoming countries, they were off the streets and lying low.

JEFFERSON DEBLANC... VINNIE REAM... KAZIMIERZ PULASKI... YOUNGER DRYAS... JOHN QUICK... PAUL HEWSON... MIKLOS NYISZLI... SAM STONE... STRONG BARRETT.

Some of Hank's buddies from Edsel Ford High School back in Dearborn were among the mourners. Slack-bellied and slope-shouldered now, they stood by themselves in a small group, near a thin Arlington sapling gone leafless in the cold. The old Key Clubbers, Honor Rollers and varsity wrestlers --- *Go, you Thunderbirds!* --- they mostly seemed stunned, perhaps from the pre-emptive sadness of Hank's death, or from the larger events of 9/11, or maybe from their own sudden stare-downs with mortality. These Midwesterners, these leafless Americans, they were of no mind just now to autopsy their despair.

Among those in the middle rows of seats: Gladys Knight, Maximum Bob Lutz from General Motors, Bruce Willis (now shed of Demi), Clint Eastwood. Plenty of Pentagon Green Badgers were on hand, plus corporate emissaries from Boeing, Lockheed, Litton and the rest of Big Hardware. Ben Bradlee had come over from the Post and sat with Hank's best friend, the Pimlico trainer Bud Delp. Bud had sold Hank a percentage of Spectacular Bid way back when, and the Bid made millions for both of them.

Cofer Black from Central Intelligence was there, Operation Greystone taking scaly shape in that lizard brain of his. Old station chiefs like [redacted] and [redacted] had come. End of the row was Mike Hayden, already hatching Trailblazer. A lot of secrets in this crowd.

More than a quorum of the Alfalfa Club, the Alibi Club and Bohemian Grove had turned out to see Hank off --- the Beltway Illuminati. Tim Russert brought his teenage son Luke. Seated next to Carl Bernstein (of Woodward &) was a talk-radio gas-bag chewing hard at a stubbed-out, half-frozen cigar. Judy Miller from The Times was discreetly on the arm of Scooter Libby. The Mayflower Madam, without escort. Johnny Apple and Mike Wallace arrived together. Mitt and Ann had flown in from Salt Lake.

In the way-back of the crowd were a couple dozen members of Congress, some of them not on the take. The runt of this litter was little Tommy DeLay, his electronic ankle bracelet shorting out in the cold, giving him fits.

No Kissinger. No McCain. And no Condi, although most of her Vulcans were there. Bush Himself sent Karen Hughes. The old grappler, Don Rumsfeld, was another no-show, understandable really, what with his plate so full right now. Still, Rummy and Hank had long-hauled together many times, including a 1983 trip into Baghdad to meet with Saddam. Hank sold a lot of E-ticket ordnance on that trip, and his bonus from GD Land Systems that year had paid off the Leelanau mortgage and topped off Micah's college fund.

There also was no sign of Hank's good pal Dick Cheney. On the morning of the attacks, Code Name Angler collected his personal cardiologist and they headed straight for The Basement, the federal government's Auntie Em storm cellar. A secret bunker complex buried deep beneath Colonial Williamsburg, The Basement was well beyond the blast radius of a direct atomic kerplunk on Washington.

ISAAC BEDLOE...GEORG ELSER...JOHNNY NEUN...CHARLES THOMPSON IV...ADDISON GRAVES WILSON...OPHA MAE JOHNSON...LIBBA COTTEN...NORMAN BORLAUG...HONOR WAINIO.

The secretary general of the United Nations had planned to come down from New York for the funeral, but his pilot and security people didn't want to risk it, not in this weather. Just as well. Hank thought the UN was a fancy-pants sandbox, lousy with cat mess, poseurs, latent Reds, Third World political tourists and all manner of global fuck-ups. Hank had likewise found NATO to be populated mostly by the bungled and the botched, a sissified soldiery that spent billions every year to prepare for tank-and-hedgerow skirmishes with the Russians. The World Bank? A Montessori kindergarten giving away ungodly sums to well-drillers and abortion-pushers. In Hank's view, the Bank propped up too many purveyors of free condoms, expired medicine and whacko Christianity. Idjits peddling widgets.

Hank had run with that crowd from time to time, but only because of business. He held his nose and circulated. Besides, those people searched *him* out, the generalissimos and defense ministers and the central bankers. They sought *his* counsel. Hank always seemed to know precisely which block to slide out of the geopolitical stack so the thing didn't go all Jenga. He told the Chileans what kind of fighter planes to buy (which they then bought). He knew when Latvia needed a couple of attack subs, and when the Singaporeans could do with some upgraded minesweepers. Hank procured NASA-quality generators for the Vietnamese politburo so they could keep Uncle Ho on ice (and on display) when the power browned out Hanoi every summer. He took meetings inside the Kremlin. Meena cut his hair at the Senate barbershop. He knew the gassy, troubled men in the small rooms, the ones writing the secret history of our world. Hank sorted the smoke. He connected the subatomic to the galactic. He was Stephen Hawking.

Hank had always been skilled at connecting the dots. Hell, he had *invented* the dots, a lot of them, and had put them on the maps. But now the connecting was getting more difficult. The world had gone certifiably asymmetric --- planes as bombs, people as bombs, bombs as diplomacy. Nothing was too savage any more. Explosives sewn into children's stomachs, wired into vaginas, triggered by demented pilgrims. The usual political equations, when multiplied by the square root of fundamentalism, were ever more difficult to solve. Put another way, there were now just too many dots.

Hank understood the spaghetti-bowl map of Caspian pipelines, the mother lodes of conflict minerals, the zig of carbon, the zag of solar and the zorg of wind. He kept files on uppity coup-plotting colonels and corruptible U.K. journalists. He could get Z-Cuarenta and Shorty Guzmán on the sat phone. He knew the Cypriot doctor treating Putin's erectile dysfunction and he knew the guy who had cuckolded VVP with Lyudmila. (Same guy, actually --- the penis doctor from Nicosia.) Hank had a GPS on the FSB's hard assets --- its black prisons, pre-teen brothels and polonium-poison mills. He monitored loose Stingers, wayward centrifuge tubes, the nuclear and chemical bunkers most in need of a B-1 deep-vein thrombosis. Syphilitic gin-soaked archbishops, some of them secretly married --- he knew a dozen of those.

What else did he know about? The Iraqi billions bunkered in Beirut, the most promising shale plays, the profiteering folly of the F-35, the rust spots on Iron Dome. He knew Hafez by name, the gatekeeper at the Club d'Alep, and he had Leah Rabin's handwritten recipe for kibbeh. People liked Hank; they told him things. He monitored yellowcake bakeries and weaponized madrasas. He knew the Likud paymaster who ran the slush fund that kept Bibi Netanyahu in pistachio ice cream (and his missus in French vanilla). For years he had known about the Strom Thurmond funny business and the Laxalt-Domenici spawn. Hank had solid leads on Jimmy Hoffa, D.B. Cooper and the missing cosmonauts from 1989. He had been to Dimona, Bushehr, Khushab and Yongbyong, by invitation.

But for Micah now, looking so grave at his parents' graveside, Hank's remarkable skills and reputation were beyond remembering. His father and his fiancée were gone, that was Micah's sad arithmetic. Any number to the zero power is one. Micah was, yes, just as he had told the Arlington Lady, yes, he was alone.

PEREGRINE SESSIONS...JOSHUA ZENO...JAMES LEAVELLE...RICHARD CROOKBACK...BOGGY JORDAN...SOLOMON BIBO...PLINKY TOPPERWEIN...CHARLES GOODNIGHT...WAYLOO HOLMES.

The blood began to chug, to pulse behind the ears. Lips chapped. Feet stamped. Tears froze in their tracks. On a day this cold, attending a funeral was not a coin flip. Purely on gut and heart, you were in or you were out.

So many of today's mourners had attended Hank's parties and drunk his Margaux. They let him spring for the veal oscar at the Old Ebbitt Grill. They sat at his table at the annual Gridiron dinners, angled for his Redskins tickets and played plenty of rounds as his guests at Congressional.

Hank had been a rare one --- old school without being a fogey, and he didn't play the cranky boozy crackpot widower after Lizzie died. A midlife crisis was merely a lack of imagination. He still considered bankruptcy to be original sin, not a bona fide. He was a cloth handkerchief, cuff links and cap-toe lace-ups. He was a Barbasol-and-a-blade man, two hits of Right Guard and a smart slap of Clubman in the morning. Medium starch, box, no hangers. Every watch he ever owned, you had to wind. He still called them dungarees. He missed soda fountains and an afternoon paper. He and Micah would drive a hundred miles on a Sunday for a good church supper. (Micah especially liked the trips when Hank had to stay handcuffed to his black titanium briefcase.) They had a standing rule while driving that they'd stop at any place where the sign said "E-A-T." Even better if the sign was neon.

Hank had been appreciated and he had been enjoyed, to use the passive-aggressive syntax of the day. (It was a way of speaking, by the way, that Hank actively detested. At congressional inquests, for example, nobody ever just stood up and took their medicine. "My fault, totally. Guilty as charged. Guilty as hell. Bring on the penalty phase.") Instead, people used the black art of the subjunctive: *Corners were cut. Documents were shredded. Triggers were pulled. Pussy was eaten. Dicks were sucked.*) That was not Hank's kind of language, this dissembling and mewling. He was, best word to use, authentic. That's why so many people were out there in the cold, squinting those squinted smiles at each other, grimacing and crying, fumbling for Kleenex and feeling such heartache for the broken young man in the front row.

HECTOR XIBALBA…ERNEST TROVA…MARCEL GAUTHIER…PAUL NIPKOW…GEORGE STEVENS…AGRIPPA HILL…BALDWIN FELTS…LAURIE PRITCHETT…HOUSTON HARRIS.

Micah was 10 when his mother died. After that, the things and the people that Hank could really count on, they got whittled down. Hank, of course, became everything to Micah, first a father, capital F, and not a pal, not an equal. That came later, sure it did.

Hank taught Micah to sail and shoot and drive a stick, to cast a fly line, and to hit what he spit at. Helped him with his geometry and algebra --- Hank called it "doing your sums" --- and he demonstrated the delicate trigonometry of a proper double Windsor. He drove Micah to the doctor for weekly hormone shots when Testicle No. 2 didn't drop on schedule, and he drew a diagram to show the boy what was going on down there: no hysterics, no drama, no tee-hee. He also drove Micah to confirmation classes, Wednesday nights, at Holy Redeemer. Lizzie, before she left, had told him she wanted that.

There were flash cards, vocabulary drills, a borax-and-vinegar Vesuvius for show-and-tell. They played pinochle, poker, hearts, gin. Winters, farther up the Mitten, up on the Leelanau, they played pond hockey with the local guys and split their own firewood. Summers, Grandpa Jimmy B, the old major leaguer, he worked with Micah, an earnest Little League catcher, on making the throw to second and blocking pitches in the dirt. They worked his mitt with shaving cream and Neatsfoot oil, just like they did in the bigs. Micah learned to grill a steak, clean a walleye and handle the big Remington 12-gauge. Hank had him do laundry and cut the grass and clean the gutters. Girls and women were not skirts, broads or bitches, not sluts or dykes or cunts. Not ever.

This was teaching straight from the good book, the Book of Hank, the hands-on American canon of bankable knowledge. If Hank had ever thought about his methodology of raising his son --- *My methodology? Great Caesar's ghost!* --- he would have said that a young man is educated, not revealed. The genetic and cultural alibis wouldn't wash with Hank. Boys were built, they were schooled, they were *brought up*.

Hank was firm with Micah, and sometimes stern, and perhaps too often he invoked the therapeutic no. But he was also careful and patient. He never spanked Micah, not once, not ever. He figured Lizzie's death was spanking enough. Enough for a lifetime.

Truth is, from the get-go, Micah was a swell kid, uncomplicated, earnest and quiet. He had a sweet and commendable nature, a correct handshake and a shy laugh. He stood up when adults entered the room and was quick with his sirs and ma'ams. The walls of his bedroom had a map of the world, the Periodic Table and a poster of mountain climbers on the Jungfrau. He didn't microwave kittens or make his own napalm. He was not a slacker. None of that whatever attitude. So, yes, he was a bit of a square peg, and he certainly lived too much in his own head. He was maybe a little too good at alone. But he didn't come home with STDs or spider-web neck tattoos. Sneaked some beers from time to time, but never needed bail. All of this, Hank reasoned, was due entirely to the good-hearted, one-decade influence of Lizzie.

BENJAMIN KOPP...LILA GARREAU...HIRAM REVELS...JAMES MCGOVERN JR... VERNE ORR...BOOKER TALIAFERRO...RONALD HAEBERLE...PETER DEWEY...HYMAN MINSKY.

He dropped the flag when the rifles cracked. The report startled him, that first loud burst from the honor guard, and the flag slid sideways off his lap. The stiff, starched triangle, so correct and compact, so impossibly bright, folded just so, delivered with the thanks of a grateful nation, blah blah blah. It landed in the cold stiff mud, just there at the lip of the grave.

When Micah didn't move to retrieve the flag, an Army three-star quickly came forward and placed it back on his lap. Can't let her touch the ground, the general said, or something like that.

People were gathered all around the grave, six, eight, ten deep in places, many of them standing unawares on neighboring graves, trampling Hank's wingmen, an Air Force colonel to the left, a Marine gunnery sergeant to the right. The mourners pressed in next to each other, shoulder to shoulder and dress-right-dress in a kind of impromptu close-order drill, as if they were somehow trying to get warm. Not just physically warm. A deeper warm to warn away the harm.

Micah, in the front row, held the muddy flag to his chest. He rocked almost imperceptibly forward and back, the way a young boy might sit and stare into a late-night campfire, listening to a ghost story. The priest from St. Stephen's came up and touched his shoulder, as if carefully waking a child from a troubled, murmuring sleep. The priest asked him if he wanted to say something.

Micah stood up, and for the first time seemed to take in the large group that had gathered around him. He placed the flag carefully on his chair, stepped forward and stood at the very edge of the freshly opened grave. He dropped to his knees there, and the icy mud wetted the knees of his pants and the bottom hem-edge of his overcoat, like blood leaking upward. The crowd groaned and moved toward him. They moaned and moved as one, leaning toward him in unison. Several of the women began to cry, loud, horrible, wailing-gasping cries that sent out mad bursts of frosty breath.

He slowly pushed his right hand into the soil, held it there a long moment, then pushed harder into the ooze, as if reaching down, as if feeling for movement or a pulse or a heartbeat. He drew back the hand, coated thick with the mud, and slowly pressed it to his face. He rubbed the mud into his forehead, almost as if it was a balm, then worked it more forcefully with both hands onto his face and throat. There was mud in his nostrils, his ears. His hair and eyelashes were thick with it. The women's crying grew louder. Generals Powell and Petraeus hurried forward to get Micah to his feet. It was all confusion and worry and sadness.

But no one moved away. No one fled. Strange, very strange, but after a few moments there seemed to be no more horror to the scene. The horror just bled away. It bled away in the bitter air, erased like the desperate woeful exhales. This was not ghastly or obscene, and everyone seemed to quickly understand: It was the full and unsurprising arrival of grief, the yoking-down of grief upon this mud-faced young man. Many in the crowd, strangers, unknown to each other, they grabbed for one another out of reflex, even the famous ones, hugging each other tightly or putting arms around shoulders.

Woodard, the military escort, stepped forward. She was feeling shaky, which wasn't at all like her. She had done dozens of these funerals while TDY at Arlington, and she wondered just what in God's name had come over her. The Holy Spirit, maybe. Hmmm. She stood behind the headstone and announced in a loud but wavering voice: "Ladies and gentlemen, thank you for coming today. I have been informed that a reception, yes, excuse me, yes, um, a reception has been informed. I mean, it has been arranged. A reception has been arranged" --- she was reading now from her notes --- "at the Monocle restaurant, located at 107 D Street, Northeast. Immediately following the service. Everyone is invited to attend." She paused. "And may God bless you all. May Almighty God bless this young man and his family. And may God bless our beloved country."

This last bit, those vibrato'd lines of God-blessing, this was a deep breach of Arlington protocol. Escorts at the cemetery didn't say such things, never ever. It was not part of the official narrative. God, Jesus, Allah, religion, no. This could be cause for an official reprimand. This was way out of bounds. And, of course, it wasn't out of bounds at all.

2. SHOOT THE MOON

Zubin Nouri had tortured plenty of men, sure he had, early in his career, back in Iran. Toes, pliers, teeth, hammers. He was dealing then with *kheeyanat kaar,* the traitors, the violent underminers of Shahanshah. These were the ones he had been happy to break. They were the schemers. He was the blunt instrument.

Zubin always dressed nicely for the job, sometimes in his military uniform, but mostly not. His civilian suits ran to drab-gray-government-proper. He wasn't stylish like some of the Shah's more debonair young adjutants. But he liked to keep a sharp crease in his pants and usually wore a white shirt to set off a favored Hermès tie --- a deep arterial crimson, rich but modest, with a subtle cross-hatch.

Some men, yes, he had tossed them naked and squealing into troughs of boiling water. Sometimes, yes, squeezing a drop from a loaded syringe, he would threaten a prisoner with an injection of radiator coolant, liquid bleach or a venereal virus. Using lamp cord, he had whipped innocent wives across their bare breasts in front of their treasonous husbands. (He disliked this approach, largely for its failure of nuance.) He had also used the water cure --- waterboarding is what the American advisers called it --- although Zubin used buckets of dark green ink instead of water. The stain would last for months, on the face, in the gums, in the ears, down the neck.

Colonel Nouri sometimes sympathized with the men strapped into his chairs or laid out on his tables. But he never pleaded or debated. He never shouted. He merely spoke in his low and serious voice. *You will tell us now, please.* His lieutenants would sometimes gather to watch this part, which they admiringly called the *joeedan*, the chewing.

The suspects could answer truthfully, or not. It was their choice, part of the *mosalehe*, the souk-bargain between questioner and accused. It was the understood haggle and kabuki of the bazaar. The arrangement. They all knew precisely the forces and undertows that had brought them together, to this unfortunate and messy point under a bare bulb. Weak, strong, soft, hard, break, resist. These words meant nothing inside the hard gray chaos of Room 101, Zubin's atelier. No one could resist. Pain and fear do not work that way, and fear was the most elegant weapon of all.

He once had a senior political man in one of his chairs --- a worldly gentleman, cultured, and proudly defiant. Before the chewing began, Zubin made a point of lighting a cigarette for the man using a Dunhill lighter that belonged to the man's wife. It was engraved with her initials, a tender anniversary gift. The colonel placed the lighter carefully on the table between them, said nothing, and the man immediately confessed his treachery. No chewing necessary.

Everyone broke. Was broken. Every one. In Zubin's experience (and under his direction), no one suffered very long for an idea. No one ever died for a movement. Of this he was convinced.

Zubin did not want to end these men's lives, not necessarily, but he did endeavor to rearrange those lives. He was no executioner and took no pleasure when interviews by his fellow officers went bad. That meant people had to be buried, unmarked and quicklimed, in Ebne Babooyeh or Tapeh-yeh Boot. At home he caressed his wife. He rubbed her calves and ankles with almond oil if they ached after a long day. He watered the gardenias in front of their house in Niavaran, arranged family hikes and braided his daughters' hair as they sat in his lap before school --- first Namaz, because she was the younger one, then Nava. Sometimes the girls teased him, pulling curlicue hairs from his ears and calling him Uncle Napoleon. When he hadn't shaved, they squirmed away and said his kisses felt like punishment.

After a number of years of this enforcement work for the Shah at Evin Prison --- before he was promoted to liaison duties with the Americans --- Zubin Nouri came to believe that he could see men's souls departing their bodies, as surely as he saw the Room 101 evacuations of their bile and blood and urine. The soul's leaving appeared to him as a heavy breath, a filmy vapor, a sigh of steam that would rise softly off a person. In Zubin's memory he had never cried, not even as a child, not from pain, joy or sadness. But he was close to tears now, standing inside the doorway on D Street, standing there with Micah, his would-be son-in-law, on the morning after the funeral of Micah's father. They would now be heading off to bury Namaz, what little bits had been found of her. A grotesque duty for a father. He could see a soiled American flag on the table in the foyer.

His heart went out completely to the boy, this American boy who his so-strong second daughter had chosen so strongly. He was hoping now that he wasn't right about what he was seeing --- the rising breath. He sensed it, as he had sensed it one recent night in himself. The Iranian father, the hard military man with the proper line in his slacks, the professional harmer who slept so well. When the news had come to them about Namaz, and later when the policewoman had arrived with the plastic bag in the blue box, Zubin had felt a deep, a deep what, a deep rupturing, a thick turning inside himself as if a key was being broken off in a lock. With a dread metallic snap, a snapping off, a breaking.

• • • •

After the funeral sevice at Arlington, Bud Delp, carrying the folded flag, walked the muddy-faced Micah back to the cemetery parking lot, and he told the General Dynamics driver they wouldn't be needing the company limo any more. They drove back to Hank's townhouse in Bud's battered red Suburban. There were two bales of hay in the way back, some bridles, a pair of muddy green Wellingtons, a cooler for vaccines and beer and bute. The windows of the truck were milky with frost. The heater was bust.

Inside the apartment, Bud warmed his hands around a tumbler of bourbon while Micah went to his bedroom to clean up --- what had been Hank's bedroom. When he came back out, he seemed surprised for a moment to see the old horseman standing there, but then, without Bud having asked, he said, "Yes, sir, I'm OK. Thanks for the help back there, Bud. Thanks a lot."

"There's a thing now, you know," Bud said. "Drinks. At the Monocle. The wake."

"Right. OK."

They slow-walked down the street to the restaurant. It was even colder now, coming onto dark, the twilight grave and violet. The streetlights around the Capitol were winking on. Hank had bought the Hill House apartment in part because of all the Congressmen who lived and concubined there, and it was a short sprint to the back entrances of the Hart and Dirksen buildings. But mostly he bought the place because it was two blocks from the Monocle.

Micah had been to the Monocle dozens of times with his dad, usually after they'd gotten haircuts together in the basement of the Senate. The Monocle's owner, John Valanos, a second-generation Greek, always made a loud, favorite-nephew, bear-hugging fuss over Micah. Nick, the maître d', did the same, and when Micah came in now for the wake, John and Nick both went to him and hugged him hard, all together, the three of them clutching onto each other. The two Greek men smelled of their saloon --- strong cigarettes, onions, anise, lavatory soap.

John had reserved his back room for the wake, and it was already noisy with well-connected Washingtonians intent on being part of the sendoff. Laughs were laughed. Lies were lied. Flashguns flashed. Bud went into the back room, but Micah held back.

"You wanna go in?" Nick asked Micah, who seemed unsure. No answer. "OK. You're right. Lessgo other room."

The other room was the kitchen. Nick did a setup at a small round table, poured Micah some ouzo, and in a few minutes Chef Juan-Pablo brought over the same meal that Hank had always ordered. Lunch, dinner, way past closing, weekend brunch, no matter --- Hank always had the Paradise salad, the crab imperial and a bottle of Liberty School syrah. (When the Bay crab was out of season, in the months without an R, Hank went with the gorgonzola sandwich.)

Micah looked through the porthole window in the waiters' door while he ate, and he thought to himself: What a nice quiet bar. A moral pub, is what his father had called it once. A place to just drop in, get a tip on a horse, have a sandwich and a glass of red. And he noticed the wooden bar, the deep color, nicely planed. He liked the way it curved there.

When he finished, he nodded his thanks to Juan-Pablo and asked Nick for the check.

"Come on, Micah, you are being crazy. God bless you. I am so much sad for you. And sad for me. Your father. Such a friend for me. This was a man. My God."

Nick, hard burly Nick, he grabbed Micah's shoulders and pressed their foreheads together. Then with his Gitanes-breath he kissed the younger man softly on the cheek.

"See you, Nick. Thank you, Nick," Micah said, and he edged out of the restaurant.

After a few steps down the sidewalk he stopped and blinked at the cold, surprised, as if he had walked into the place on a boggy-humid summer afternoon and now here it was winter and dark. He walked back to the apartment, stripped to his shorts, pulled on Hank's plaid-flannel bathrobe and was soon asleep on the couch.

Now a bell was ringing. He grabbed the phone, nothing, then reached the alarm clock, no. Still sleeping he went for the phone again. No, the doorbell. It was Zubin, standing there all in gray, with a black beret. It was morning. Today was Namaz.

"Oh, Micah. Oh, son. Why you are not ready? Hurry. Please. The car."

Micah nodded, but halfway down the hallway to the bedroom, he stopped. He clicked awake, noticed he was wearing the bathrobe and walked back to Zubin. Mr. Nouri, who was alive and standing there in the doorway, so anxious and gray and so destroyed over his daughter and now he had the car idling outside in the cold.

"Mr. Nouri."

The old colonel had seen this kind of surrender before, in his other life. Oh, son. He put a hand on Micah's chest and lightly kept it there. The young man was crying. "I know, Micah. I understand. You cannot come. With your father, and Namaz, there is so much sadness on you now. You come to us when you can. You come to me. We can talk and remember together Namaz. She was our star."

"Our star. She was my whole sky."

"I know, Micah. It is OK. Nothing for worry. The family, I am explaining them. Do not lose us, Micah. *Pesaram*. My son. You are my son now."

• • • •

Zubin Nouri had gotten his family out of Iran in 1978, just before the turbans got in.

The Carter people brought the family to Washington, among the very first Argonauts, and Zubin was given a job deep down in the deep state. His departure was covert and important enough that the entire Nouri family received hurry-up U.S. citizenship. They got passports, a lightly used Chrysler Imperial and a house in Chevy Chase with an old bomb shelter buried in the backyard. They were Instant Americans, no questions asked or answered.

Namaz and Nava had places waiting for them at the National Cathedral School, two little Muslimettes among all those High Episcopalians. Namaz developed into an All-Met swimmer, scored twin 770s on her SATs and landed a half-ride scholarship to Michigan. Victors valiant. Her third week in Ann Arbor, she was invited to a rush party at the Delta Gamma house on Oxford Road. The DG sisterhood thought she was so exotic. And a swimmer! They'd never had a scholarship athlete in DG before. Kewl. When she told them her best event was the breaststroke, everybody giggled.

At the rush party, that's where Namaz Nouri first came across Micah Ford. It was a warmish Thursday night, pretty late, and the party was crowded, what with Thursday being the new Friday on every college campus in America. Micah was pretending to be passed out on the front lawn of the DG house, face up, arms folded corpse-like across his chest, laid out like a 10th-century pope. The house mother, as a kind of test for Namaz, asked her to go out and shoo the boy away.

Micah was a junior math major in the School of Information, an intramural rower, a numbers savant and computer whiz, a climbing nerd, a renowned Diag chess player and a virgin. It was a busy life, even without all the knucklehead schemes he had been devising to meet girls. He was a good-looking kid, in a dirty-blond, tousle-haired Midwestern way. He stood right at 6-feet and was a couple cheeseburgers short of 180, with a lean frame that had V'd up nicely under three semesters of crew at Cranbrook. He already spoke six and a half languages --- his brain was nicely wired that way --- but he couldn't seem to get laid in any of them. He could program everything but a love life. It was the one site he couldn't hack.

This phony-blackout stunt he was pulling in the front yard of the sorority house, this was his latest tactic, and Namaz found it both foolish and cute. She looked him over and liked him right away. It wasn't introduction. More like recognition. But still, under orders, she ran him off. That is to say, she peeled the *Hello!* name tag off her sweater and wrote her phone number on it. Then she ran him off.

Micah stalked her around campus after that, from a distance, in a polite, I'm-so-not-worthy kind of way. She always knew when he was trailing her, and they started going out. Football games in the Big House, tailgates, late-night runs to Big Ten Burrito, study dates at the Ugli, all the customary rituals of an undergrad courtship in Ann Arbor. One night he rigged up some climbing harnesses and they rappeled down the side of Burton Tower. Two hundred feet, give or take. That was not so customary.

Despite carrying a full load in computer engineering, math and informatics, Micah began auditing classes in Farsi and Arabic. And to Namaz, in no time, he surrendered his virginity.

They had quickly become close, nearly inseparable, both of them well and truly smitten. Just holding hands was thrilling. But late one night during fall semester, right before winter break, some thug grabbed Namaz in the stacks in the Grad Library. He wrestled her onto the floor but she forearmed him in the Adam's apple and just missed with a kick to the balls. The man fled, limping and gagging. She was her father's daughter all right. But the incident shook her badly, and she got it into her mind to transfer. Micah, his heart cracking, didn't protest or pout. Mr. Nouri made some calls to his government handlers and it was quickly arranged for Namaz to have a place at Harvard come January. It was a strange Christmas and New Year's.

Namaz relaxed right into Harvard, and because she was happy there, even if she was far away, Micah was happy too. She took rooms in Adams House, on Bow Street, one of the great B-entry suites with a balcony and a fireplace. Micah became a regular on weekend flights from Detroit Metro to Boston Logan and back. Their world, or most of it, simply pivoted from A-Squared to Cambridge: They drank slow-pulled pints of Guinness at the Plough and Stars, followed the Celtics, skated at the Frog Pond. They played squash at Dunster and got hooked on the red-pepper bisque at the Red House. At Harvest, over on Brattle Street, Namaz charmed the chef out of his vichyssoise recipe.

She made the Crimson swim team as a midseason walk-on and Micah went to her meets whenever he could. One of his favorite things, when they were spooning and drifting off to sleep on Bow Street, was to bury his face in her thick black curls and breathe deep, catching little bursts of leftover chlorine. He breathed her in. This usually woke her up, but she never let on. She liked it. Quietly, horizontally, she was feeling their future together.

She thought she might major in French, and she sneaked Micah into the language labs in Vanserg where he worked on his Arabic. (Once his Persian got better than Namaz's, he pretty much dropped it.) Up in the observation tower at Weld Hall, she taught him how to slow dance, which led to their learning how to make love standing up. They had a Farsi phrase they'd use whenever one of them wanted it. *"Dost beni beni,"* he would say, or she would say. "*Beni beni.* Come to me, to me."

One night in Weld, dancing close to some Al Green, Namaz whispered softly into his ear, *"Tu dis des choses qui font fermer les yeux.* You say the things that make me close my eyes. Micah, honey, we're growing up together. I love you."

Micah graduated double summa from Michigan in 1997 and went straight into doctoral programs in mathematics and computer science at Stanford. He was having to catch cross-country red-eyes to see Namaz now, yo-yoing from San Francisco to Boston and back. It wasn't easy, sleep-wise. His father never griped about the charges on the credit card. (Hank could see a bit of the future, too, with dots connecting.) Micah used the long flights to work on his courses, his thesis and his Arabic. He also tinkered with software programs and eventually sold a couple of them, DumbDown and Quicksand, for crazy VC money --- nearly $18 million after taxes.

DumbDown was essentially a filtering program that rewrote --- that is, plagiarized --- dense journal articles, academic papers or doctoral theses. The user set the filter anywhere from the seventh grade to the graduate-school level, uploaded the original text, and DumbDown produced a ready-made, grade-appropriate, fully footnoted term paper, double-spaced and bulletproof. The optional Feats of Clay application even inserted "smart errors" to throw off skeptical, CrossChecking professors. Thousand-dollar rebates were offered to any DumbDown user who was successfully busted for plagiarism. Nobody ever got caught. With 256-bit encryption, the hackers admired it. At $49.95, the slackers loved it.

A Pentagon front company, Finneyfrock Blacksmithing, of Olney, Maryland, bought another of Micah's programs, the stochastic malware package called Quicksand. The military planned to sic the program on computers belonging to the Chinese state shipbuilder, the Venezuelan Coast Guard and Robert Mugabe's personal PCs at his homes in Harare and Hong Kong. The final payment, $11 million, was laundered first in the Caymans and then through a Kremlin-controlled bank in Cyprus. Micah's total, once it reached his Wells Fargo checking account in Palo Alto, was $8.8 million. (The Defense Department went on to sell the Quicksand architecture at a handsome profit to the FBI for its Magic Lantern project. The CIA later hacked the DoD mainframe and just stole the Quicksand coding outright, and it became the go-to template for any number of the agency's international hacks.)

Micah still had a lot of undergrad code monkey in him, and at Stanford he did some freelance encryption projects for Bay Area start-ups. He was usually paid in shares of the companies, and he didn't particularly mind when the companies went bust.

Namaz made All-Ivy her senior year, 1999, and graduated with a degree in French and a minor in architecture. She had begun working nights as a prep cook (and then as sous-chef) at the Red House. She had joined the clandestine Harvard Munch Club and found that cooking was thrilling. She had become --- and she would confess this to friends with some embarrassment --- a foodie.

She and Micah talked about marriage in a casual, unhurried way. They knew. He gave her his mother's old diamond as an engagement ring. That was Hank's idea. Micah encouraged Namaz to leave her Red House job and take courses at a professional cooking school. If she didn't like it, she could join him in Palo Alto and plan a wedding. They had bales of money.

She was turned down for an internship with Alice Waters at Chez Panisse, which would have put her with Micah in the Bay Area. She enrolled instead at the Culinary Institute of America in Hyde Park, New York, just north of New York City, a nice train ride up the Hudson on the Water Route. Namaz teased her father that the Nouri family now had two members in the CIA.

Micah, for his part, became deeply immersed in his own work, venturing more profoundly into cryptography, brute force computer engineering and ever-more-ethereal realms of mathematics. There were maybe a couple dozen people worldwide who were working at his intersection of disciplines, and it could be solitary, brain-cramping work. But he kept to his zip-line flight schedule, doing the SFO/JFK/SFO turnaround every other weekend.

He would get to New York, Namaz would meet him at Grand Central and they'd catch a train north to Hyde Park, taking seats or stools in the bar car. Trip by trip they began working their way through the on-board drink menu, which at 37 pages, for unpracticed drinkers like themselves, amounted to a Britannica of booze. They started conventionally, alphabetically, with absinthe, Adios M.F., Afterbirth, agua de Valencia, various amarettos, americanos, Angel's Tit.

Serious drinking was new territory for these two, a wild country with its own fanciful language. Namaz went through a brief but *profonde* infatuation with French 75s, in part because she loved to order them, often a little too loudly, in her best Avenue Foch accent: *"Une Soixante-Quinze, s'il te plaît!"* On one trip they hit on a Latin theme: Tio Pepe and Tia Maria, cuba libres, el presidentes, bloody Aztecs, palomas, fruity drinks sugared with miel de agave. After a round of mojitos, they began a game of hearts. Namaz shot the moon on the first hand, then did it again.

She danced a happy little jig there in the lounge, took Micah's red-happy-boozy face in her hands, and said, *"Voy a dispararle a la luna del cielo por ti, bebé."*

Another time, Micah downed in quick succession a Moonwalk, an Oh Be Joyful, an Old Spanish, a One-Balled Dictator, a Perroquet, a Philips Screwdriver, a Pol Pot and a Prince of Wales. Oy. It was then that he first suggested that Namaz might take a couple million of his Quicksand money and start her own restaurant somewhere. Buy a building, build a kitchen. He'd follow her. Given enough bandwidth, he could finish his thesis anywhere.

He repeated the offer the next morning, still in bed, in the oh-be-woeful light of sobriety.

She smiled a big one, tilted her head at him and said, huskily, in her best Elvis, "Thank you very much. Now shut up, you, and beni beni."

• • • •

Investors were always coming by CIA, looking for the next hot chef to headline a new restaurant for them. They openly courted the stars of the school, and Namaz was certainly one of these --- bright, book-smart and poised, a French-speaker, a great-looking young woman with a good palate and developing skills. She could be the face of any hot, high-profile restaurant. By late spring she had three job offers.

The first was from a newly rich music producer who wanted her as executive chef for a new after-hours grill in Seattle. He was going to call it Cobain, and it would be open from midnight to dawn. He let it slip that Howie Schultz, the Starbucks guy, was going to be The Money. Another job offer came from a Taiwanese woman, Arlene Chu, who had made a fortune running (which of course meant *skimming*) the Taipei municipal lottery. She was starting a comfort-food place in Los Angeles called the

Hollywood Café. Namaz found the name unfortunately bland, but Arlene did hold an option on a gorgeous space at 742 Evergreen Terrace.

The job Namaz eventually took --- early in that mild summer of 2001 ---- was at Dora Maar, a new French bistro on Church Street in Lower Manhattan. She would create the menu, hire a kitchen staff and serve as executive chef. She liked that there was just one owner, a retired fountain designer of all things, with the preposterous name of Lillian Mountweazel. Lily was very widowed, very wealthy and more than a little wicked. She lived at 351 Riverside in New York, but during the Fifties she had exiled herself to Paris, to a hôtel particulier on the rue du Cherche Midi in the *sixième*, where she surrendered to a mad romance with Mlle. Maar.

Lily missed the bite of a zinc-bar cognac at breakfast. She longed for well-wined lunches and smoky late-nights at Montparnasse brasseries. That's what she wanted with her new restaurant, a whiff of the ancien régime. Namaz liked her instantly. They came to terms and set the opening for October 1.

Namaz and Micah set a date, too: Thanksgiving Day. It would be a simple ceremony --- in the lobby of the Flatiron Building, if they could get it, Namaz's favorite wedge of architecture in New York. The reception would be at Dora. In the meantime, Namaz moved into a couple of rooms at the back of Lily's mansion. She and Micah would look for their own apartment when they could.

• • • •

That morning, September 11, Namaz was excited that Hank was flying into New York to see her. She was eager to tell him about the wedding plans, to see how the role of daughter-in-law would fit her, and to show off what she was accomplishing at Dora. Lately she had been edgy and a bit weepy, which she ascribed to the restaurant's imminent opening and an extra few pounds on her tummy. Hank's request to visit made her feel special, like a new family was starting to take shape, with her and Micah at the center, their own family.

Hank reached the city early, 7-ish, and Namaz had some strong Vietnamese *cà phê sữa* waiting for him at the bistro. She set up a café table in the kitchen, and they talked as she cooked up some sweet-sausage hash and a chèvre omelette. She was wearing her favorite apron, a blue Bragard from Paris. Hank ate hungrily and mopped his plate clean with a husk of baguette. He clanked his coffee cup against hers and pronounced the meal "a total triumph." When her eyes started to brim at that, he reached across the table and held her hand for a long minute.

Then, rescuing them both, he grabbed his coat and satchel, and ordered her to walk him downtown a bit. They hit the sidewalk and hey, oh boy, what a beautiful morning, with a sky as blue as the waters off the Leelanau. Namaz took his arm as they walked. Hank was meeting an old U-M stockbroker buddy at the World Trade Center. With any luck, he said, he'd make his noon tee time at the Army-Navy Country Club with Cheney.

"Cheney?" Namaz said. "*Dick* Cheney? The vice president?"

"Yeah, but you can't tell anybody. Not that you would. But his whereabouts are always supposed to be a secret. That's kind of the way he is. A little paranoid. Actually, more than a little."

"OK, sure, I understand. But so, then, so Dick Cheney is a friend of yours, Hank? I never knew that."

"He's a friend. Yeah, sure he is. I've done some decent business with him over the years. And we've played a hell of a lot of golf." Hank didn't tell Namaz that he had once caught VPOTUS, during a hundred-dollar Nassau at Congressional, illegally toeing his ball out of a fairway divot.

"Here's a secret for you, Namaz: Under pressure, the man cannot make a putt. Our vice president. The No. 2 man in the free world. A heartbeat from the presidency. An eight-foot putt with five lousy bucks on the line and he gets the worst case of the yips you've ever seen."

"Yips? What are yips?"

"That means he chokes. A real choke artist."

"Choke artist. I like that. Artichoke, but backwards. So this afternoon during golfing, Hank, you're figuring on a total triumph?"

They both laughed hard at that. Hank got a little misty himself right then, and he stopped to give her a big hug. Then the plane hit the tower.

• • • •

The call was from some federal inspector of something something something in New York. Micah didn't catch many of the details. Searchers had finally found them in the Pile, Hank and Namaz: that was the nut graph of the call, the one-two solar plexus punch of it. Micah seemed not to care about what they had found. Didn't much matter. Not now. Although he tried to listen.

The federal guy said they had identified Namaz pretty quickly because they'd found a piece of a blue jacket with her name embroidered on it. That bit of her chef's jacket had held together somehow. It hadn't burned, and the name was still legible in its delicate silken cursive. The diggers also were surprised to find the shell of her cell phone, the little red StarTAC. It was still pretty much in one piece, protected under a helter-skelter of rebar, concrete, sternum and pelvis.

Micah did remember that particular word from the inspector's phone call --- surprised. The diggers had been surprised.

What could anyone, in these apocalyptic days, be surprised about any more? Nineteen men masturbate over dark-eyed virgins feeding them grapes in Paradise, Gabriel's song goes out of tune and angels' wings are woven into suicide vests. Scissors break rocks. Paper stops fire. Jets fly into buildings. How dare we be surprised any longer, by anything? It was now a Rashomon world. It was a "might be" world. And the words "might be" meant exactly the same thing as "might not be."

• • • •

Micah, sleep-groggy in California, was talking to Namaz after the second plane hit. She had called him from the sidewalk and said Hank was standing there with her and that there was shattered glass all over the place and people were running and screaming. She was gasping into the phone, not panicked exactly, but headed there. Sirens shouted in the background --- cop-car sirens, fire trucks and those hee-haw and whoop-whoop car alarms. She was trying to explain to Micah about the explosion above them and the chaos. She shouted something he couldn't make out. Then the phone went dead.

A positive ID on Hank came quickly, too, a shank of molar'd jawbone matched dental records churned up by the Veterans Affairs database. There had been no need for deeper forensics on Hank. It was him.

The crime-scene unit couldn't be sure, but it looked like Namaz had wrapped herself around Hank right at the end, as if she was trying to hug him or shield him or cover him. Maybe that was just a nice bit of story the FBI folks had come up with, something for grieving families to hang onto. Might be true, or maybe not, but it certainly sounded like Namaz. She could cover.

The federal guy on the phone told Micah there was evidence of another man being directly on top of Namaz and Hank, the three of them sandwiched together, fluids and organs and skeletons, before the jet-fuel cremation fires started. It was likely that this man had actually killed them, the federal guy said, and it probably happened a few minutes before the first tower collapsed onto itself.

Odds were that he was one of the jumpers, somebody from above the 109th floor, and he must have smashed down on top of them while they were on the sidewalk. Namaz had seen the hurtling man, shouted, and then grabbed for Hank. That must be it. But the falling man, the desperate diver down, it was the damnedest thing, the federal guy said, because they couldn't figure out who he was, even though they had collected plenty of DNA.

He might have been a newly hired janitor in the South Tower, or a guy selling gray-market copier toner. He could have been one of those foreign-currency sharpies, one of the transnationals who hit the office early to catch the overseas markets, trade some Swissy and short the yen. Talk about gray markets. The currency dealers called their universe C-World and they always had half a dozen passports and transit visas in play. Because the feds couldn't ID the falling man, they assumed he was illegal.

He was A-negative, they knew that much. And they were pretty sure he was a big man, 240 or more, a black guy with some diabetes ramping up. They got that from blood scrapings, a lipid analysis and an assay of some dried feces or something. Nigerian, maybe. (Or had the federal man said Liberian? Again, Micah missed a lot of what he said.)

They did know that the falling man wore Dolce & Gabbana boxers because of a bit of waistband they found in the Pile. Brains and hearts burn up, corneas and retinas disappear, clavicles, forearms and knees are pestled into powder, but a piece of waistband made in some Phnom Penh sweatshop, *that* is what survives?

Diamonds survived, although not many ever found their way home. Micah did inquire about Namaz's engagement ring, his mom's old ring. It never surfaced, or at least it was never returned to Micah or the Nouris. Only a few dozen rings --- out of a couple thousand buried in the Pile --- ever made it to the Recovered Property bins at the sifting sites. The stones were uncovered all right, but they were walked off the job by "reclamation technicians" who hid them in a lip-dip of Skoal, inside a Yankees cap or under a Band-Aid. Later, most of the gems would become available for good prices in Midtown jewelry stores and Hoboken pawnshops. The blood diamonds of 9/11.

3. AIN'T THAT AMERICA

It was well after the attacks, after Hank and Namaz had been found in the Pile, that the agency spooks and Pentagon cleaners arrived at the D Street townhouse. They copied Hank's hard drives and carted off some eyes-only stuff that was, technically, legally, well beyond Hank's clearance level.

His lawyer came over to watch the investigators, and there were plenty of papers for Micah to sign. There were investment portfolios to transfer and rebalance. He read out the will and gave Micah a key to a safe-deposit box that held various deeds, birth records, death certificates, Krugerrands.

They also opened up Hank's safe, a 6-foot-high Mosler Rock of Ages. The combination was Micah's birthday, 4-30-7-5. Inside was more family stuff, plus $800,000 in new, bank-wrapped hundreds. Some reels of Super-8 film. A Florsheim shoebox with fishing lures, Hank's Purple Heart and some other medals. A penknife. A rubber-banded stack of dog-eared 3x5 cards with words typed in red and black. An old Underwood typewriter. On the back wall of the safe, covered in plastic, hung a Boy Scout uniform, sashed and merit-badged, and a nurse's uniform, as white as white could be.

The lawyer told Micah he would handle the legalities, the probate, the mail, the upkeep on the houses. He'd pay Micah's credit cards each month. There was plenty of money. The Leelanau cabin had been winterized, but the Grosse Pointe house probably needed some attention. Micah said he'd go there first. He would drive up in Hank's old BMW, go to California to see his advisor about his dissertation, then back to Florida to stay with Jimmy B.

Micah should have gone by to see the Nouri family before he left Washington, and he thought about it, but he was in full retreat now. He telephoned instead and got the answering machine with Nava's voice. He left no message.

He packed light. Some books, the Underwood, one of his dad's old watches, his mom's uniform, the penknife. In Grosse Pointe he avoided most of the old friends and neighbors. He worked his way steadily through the house, his boyhood home, setting thermostats, draining pipes, covering furniture. Sleepwalking.

With the house buttoned up, he headed west to Ann Arbor and Kalamazoo, down to Kokomo, spent a night in Broad Ripple, then to Pawnee and onto the national backbone, U.S. 50, the loneliest road in America is what they called it. He cleared the 100th meridian into Bleeding Kansas, still bloody. Spent his second night, a restless one, at the Clutter House Inn. That was Holcomb, KS. Kansas, KS, Kaposi's Sarcoma. Then Sligo, Bachelor's Forest, Good Hope, Brown's Corner, Piping Rock. Teat. Greasy Grass. Wandering Rocks. Innisfree.

Across the Midwest it was Pine Valley, Salem, Springfield, Basin City, and on and on. A drumroll of American villages. Water-tower towns with Great War howitzers on courthouse lawns. Town after Main Streeted town. The Keeper of the Plains. It was terrible how near she was to his heart.

Micah drove into a bloodied sunset under a Comanche moon. Across the staked plains where the grass had once reached the stirrups of Coronado's men. This was Winnetou and Old Shatterhand territory, streams once spangled with the color, the land watered by the ancient creeks that fed the Platte River, an inch deep and a mile wide. Purple America. The mid-continent caliphate. 'Tis of thee. Quivira, Flowertown, Wormwood. The terrible magic of cholera and smallpox and dust pneumonia had come here once, laying low The People, strangling and coughing them to death, the ones who had made much meat on the Plains and had gleefully spit-roasted their enemies over their council fires.

Prairie --- it was such the perfect word. You could hear the wind in it, the breathing of the wheat, a creek's trickle, the dry summer lightning. Now the land held pipeline survey stakes, abortion billboards, Minuteman silos and empty farmsteads. Baptist churches beside baptismal creeks. People were still making book on the aquifer. Cuts-to-Pieces and Kicking Bird had lived here. So had the pale riders, Crazy Eye, the One Who Yawns, and Smells-Bad-When-Walking-Away. Now there were fracking crews, meth trailers, wind farms. The Pony Express had once been a going concern out here. That was before the suitcase farmers arrived to bust the sod with their one-way plows. That one little gadget had broken the topsoil and broken the heart of the Plains. Purple-hearted America. Huge tracts had been tractored out. Micah made a stop at Room 25 at the Dreamland Motel. He passed Moo University. The fruited plain. The Tooth of Time. He reached Zip codes beginning with 6s and 8s, like an iffy roll of the dice. New shooter comin' out. *A is for awful, which things are. Z is for zig-zag, which is each one's task.* There were new bridges over Kills-Himself Creek and the Acheron River.

Driving, driving, on into Colorado --- Walking Stick, Kiowa County, Sand Creek, Tomichi Dome. Bloody-handed America. Ranches cursed with snakes. Big Medicine above Hawikku and the Sun Corridor. Oscuro below Bird-Cloud and Jack Crick. Stars falling all night in tender arcs. The Black Canyon and Lava Falls. SuperMax prisons, slot canyons, ashrams, played-out uranium mines. Ten Wounds. When it stings, you know the medicine is working. This was the high chaparral. The land of The Misfits. The High Lonesome.

His cell phone didn't ring. Other than an occasional checking-in with Jimmy in Florida and the lawyer back in D.C., there was nobody left to call.

Late one afternoon, still headed west, moderately lost, moderately north of Salt Lake City --- could there really be a place called Bountiful? --- Micah's phone did ring. It startled him, the bumble-bee'ing of the thing, and he pulled into a small strip mall to take the call. It was another federal guy, different than before, different from the we-have-collected-some-relevant-Evidence-from-the-Pile guy. This man said he represented the something something Victims something fund. He said Micah was due to receive a one-time lump-sum payment of $3.7 million. From the fund.

"A payment? For what?"

"For your loss. As part of the healing of our collective national tragedy. It's the fund."

The man said "the fund" in a bright and earnest way, chipper as could be, a third-base coach calling down the line to his batter. He said "the fund" as if he were saying "attababy."

The shopping area was on some O-ring'd flange of exurban Bountiful. The strip had a Radio Shack, a Wells Fargo, a Starbucks and a Tanfastic. The names on the other storefronts he didn't recognize. Local owners. The International Institute of Hair Design. Blessed Assurance --- A Safe Place for Women. The BookSmith had a handmade sign in its front window: "Free New Testament w/ Any $10 Purchase." Next door was a restaurant called This Is The Place, and parked out front was a sign on a wheeled trailer. The red plastic letters said: "Todays Speciale Beef Tips. Dee-lish & Dee-vine."

Behind the shops, atop a small hill, was a squat brick windowless building --- a radio station, with a transmission tower carrying the call letters KUBL. (Later, with the Beemer's radio on Scan, he would find the station at 93.3 FM. *KUBL, the Bull. Today's Best Country. Home of the Moo Crew, with Shotgun Jackson and Coyote McCoy.*)

"I'm not sure about taking any money," Micah told the man from the fund. He said this in a weary and distracted way. He was looking dreamily at the red beacon-light on the radio tower. "I have enough money. Why would someone give us so much money?"

"Not *someone*! The *fund!*" said the federal man. He nearly shouted it, and he seemed aggrieved.

A beneficary hesitating? This was something that had not come up during the training sessions. A resistant grantee? He had been told that 89 percent of recipients would ask, in this order: 1) how much was their total payout, 2) when exactly would the check arrive, and 3) what about taxes? *How much? When? Taxes?* Those were the always-trending FAQs.

"It's for all the heroes of 9/11," the man said. "You're entitled to it. It's what you have coming to you. The lump sum. It's, you know, like, it's *the fund!*"

Micah gave him the attorney's name and number in Washington. That rebrightened the man's tone. "Excellent-super-awesome."

"From all of us at the fund" --- he was now reading a prepared text on his computer screen --- "we're terribly sorry for your loss. We know your son was a remarkable young man."

"My dad. You mean my dad. He was the one who died. I'm the son."

Not a beat was missed, and here was the training kicking in: "Oh, of course, my mistake, your father. I see that right here in my paperwork. I'm so very sorry. Your *father*. Yes. Well, yes. Well, all of us at the fund hope that there are happier days ahead for you and your surviving loved ones. We'll be in touch with your attorney forthwith. Goodbye now."

Forthwith.

• • • •

Micah drove south toward Salt Lake City, then west beneath the lower rim of the lake-bed. A great aridness.

He drove into hot winter winds, the stinging Santa Anas, across the Mojave's lava beds and alkali flats, through basin and range, through entire counties of the same sad sand --- basaltic, inert, pimpled with volcanic glass, sand that had no relationship to soil. This was the bomb-tested landscape. The dead land, the cactus land, the atomic desert. The bleached and broken jaw of a lost kingdom. A flattened sunburnt region, these Western lands, a place of forgotten roads, night-drilled with dry lightning, barely suitable for saltbush, just miles of cholla scrub and barranca, dogbane and rabbitbrush and greasewood and smoke trees. Dead and unkillable, both and simultaneous. Bring a thin sheet of rain and this whole country would *shout.* Call and response, history and death.

But there's no rain, hardly ever, just curlicues of old erosion and spent ordnance. Disordnance. The bones of test pilots. The Beemer could as well have been the Mars Rover. No-man's-land. No more men. Flyover Country, they called it back East. Between the sky and this earth Micah felt himself erased, blotted out, and yet comfortably numb, as if he was somehow bound to the dust in this estranged land. How to call it? There was no exact word for this exact kind of place, not really, not in his language, not in American. The Arabs, like the Inuit with their ice, had a dozen names for this kind of salted emptiness. *Falat. Sahra. Mahlakah. Hunalik.*

All the way across the desert, the call from the fund man nagged at Micah. It bothered him as he filled up with high-test at the Texaco in The Solitudes. (That's what his dad had always called it, "high-test." And "filling stations.") Farther along, crossing into Nevada, the fund-man's call troubled his sleep when he overnighted at a state-park lodge near the Charcoal Ovens. He just couldn't square it: What had Hank done to warrant such an amount of money being allocated in his name? What had he done, really, other than die? What had his father done except to be in a terrible place --- squarely on the X --- at a terrible moment? (The same with Namaz, for that matter. Presumably her family also would be getting a one-time lump-sum payment from the fund.) The 9/11 dead, how did they qualify as heroes? This is what he wondered, out there in the desert, in his practicality and his Hank-ness.

Deeper into Nevada now, way off the grid, no grid at all really, with no radio signals or telephone bars. The sun dropped away and the counterfeit stars began to set themselves into place. He rolled down a window and took in the cool, dry, rushing nighttime air. He wondered if the air was clean and cleansing, or was it forever isotoped with plutonium? Wouldn't surprise him either way. Half-lives, now there was a concept he was beginning to comprehend, like hopped-up biotite, muscovite, feldspar, nailhead, dogtooth. As he rolled up the window, he thought he caught just the slightest breath of chlorine.

Near Lovelock, deep in the pitchblende night, under the huge space of the winter sky, a chuckwalla suddenly appeared in the road, illuminated by the BMW's headlights. The animal was paddling hard across the sticky tarmac with its ancient comical gait, lizard-legged and loosely armored, scuttling across the floor of a dry and silent sea. The car's left front tire caught the thing nearly flush, then the back left got him too, with a quick thump-thump, the two hard syllables. Micah circled back to the still and oozing carcass. He pulled it off the road and gently eased it into the runoff ditch.

As he drove, he sometimes found himself talking to himself, or sometimes talking aloud to that fund fellow. Hank and Namaz hadn't been heroes, he might have said to the man. They hadn't rushed into blazing tenements to bring out burning babies. They didn't read the good book to blind pensioners. No rescuing of abused greyhounds or shampooing the fleas from the scabby scalps of the homeless. Here's what Hank and Namaz did that day: Ate a nice breakfast together, talked about the future, shared a hug and then got flattened on a New York sidewalk by a huge hurtling black man.

And now came this windfall. (*Windfall. Another word worth pondering. Windfalls and half-lives. Ugh.)*

He just couldn't make out how the 9/11 dead had become victims, or Victims, a title now apparently worthy of capitalization. Victims? Ain't we all? It's not like they had been targeted, not like they were Tutsis or Cherokees or a black American chained to a pickup and dragged down a farm-to-market road in East Texas.

The 9/11 folks had simply been unlucky. Bystanders. Pure collateral damage. They were boys on a beach in Gaza, polio vaccinators in Pakistan, shoppers on a bread line in Sarajevo. In one way, Micah thought, they'd been in the way. They no more "gave their lives for freedom" than had Johnny Cash, Rin Tin Tin or Liberace. They were dead, which was plenty tragedy enough, but they were accidentally dead. Accidentally, unlike martyrs. But maybe nobody believed in accidents any more. Victims, capital V, how we love 'em so.

• • • •

Micah had avoided reading the newspaper obits and instant biographies that began appearing soon after the attacks. Some of the pieces were too close-up: the Gracie Square father who kept calling his lost daughter's cell phone just to hear her leave-a-message voice. Or the Teterboro wife who choked to death while literally eating her missing husband's love letters. *Oh.*

He passed up the TV replays and the woe-is-us documentaries soundtracked with groaning cellos and bassoons. He turned away from the civilian mourners offering military salutes to heavily flagged coffins, the prurient drone of the cable-news loops, the tacky tyranny of the yellow-ribbon magnets, the lapel-pin patriots, the angry rants from fearful widows who now insisted on being called "survivors." (*That's rich. Survivors. As if they had lived through the Dust Bowl or emerged alive somehow from Sobibor.*) All of it had built into a collective national pornography, the euphoric HD godding-up of cops, firemen and lots of otherwise ordinary janes and joes. Everybody was trying to out-mourn everybody else. The country, so quickly, had fetishized the deaths, the day and the gloom. Fear and wonder --- it made for a powerful combination. Grief became adulterated with treacle.

In its role as The Official Hometown Newspaper of September 11, The New York Times undertook to write brief biographies of everyone killed that day in New York, in Pennsylvania and at the Pentagon. The series was called "Profiles in Courage and Tragedy," or some lite-syrup headline like that. Every death would be accounted for. It would be an ambitious and glorious project, a year-long commitment. The idea was quickly funded, vetted and blessed at the highest levels of the paper.

"We'll flood the fucking zone," said a bow-tied editor from National.

"Mortal lock for a Pulitzer," said somebody from the Foreign Desk.

The series started out in a poignant way, maybe a little too Hallmark, but each day's paper carried half a dozen well-crafted profiles accompanied by family-scrapbook photos. These Micah did read, on his drive, whenever he could find a national edition of The Times. There were Little League coaches, selfless foster mothers, seven different guys called "the fireman's fireman," Presbyterian deacons, upwardly mobile immigrants. Lots of grannies raising two generations of kids. Soup-kitchen saints. Scholarship underwriters. Retired cops who had raced, unbidden, to the scene of the 9/11 crime. Readers wept. Mortal lock.

The newspaper became a storybook. Reporters lobbied hard to be assigned to the Profiles, which were drawing admiring, worldwide attention. But the reporters soon began coming back to their assigning editors with troubling tales. Instead of coaches and deacons they were finding embezzlers and stalkers. They were turning up tax cheats, unindicted rapists, perfidious friends, convicted felons, brutalizing cops, heroin dealers. No fewer than 16 New York men had secret families stashed across the river in Jersey. One man had four. Scoutmasters and choir leaders were getting scarce.

Oh, there was some serious darkness in that Pile. Too many secrets. Too many brutish fingers (*etc., etc.*) in unwilling vaginas and unready bottoms. Corroded lungs, perforating colons, leaking implants, leaking backstories.

The newspaper editors hadn't expected *this.* All this new reporting was proving disruptive and injurious to The Narrative, their narrative, the national narrative that everyone was hooked on. The editors stared at their narrative, and it stared right back.

Truth was, in the real narrative, the people who died in the attacks had been splendid and flawed and damaged, just like everyone else in America. This was what the Times reporters actually found, and this was the bigger story, the untold one. Micah sensed, finally, that the Pile was nothing more or less than a cross-section, an ice core, a cemetery like any other. The paper had a lot to defend all of a sudden, a lot of mirrors to fog, a lot of Ambien to slip into the national bloodstream.

People saw in 9/11 what they wanted to see, so they welcomed the newspaper's fog. This was Micah's theory. He came to understand that no mention would be permitted in The Times of the IRS section chief from Murray Hill who had traveled to Chengdu and paid 8,000 cash American dollars to obtain the liver of a 23-year-old Tibetan monk sitting on Death Row. (A Chinese surgical team did the transplant right there in the prison hospital. Five weeks later, the tax man was back in New York, literally back in the pink, hoisting Boodles martinis in the Oak Room. *"Nothing cleaner than a monk's liver! My donor guy, God bless him, he never had a single drop of booze in his entire life! He took me from cirrhosis to ferocious! Here's to Buddhism!"*)

A little reality was going a long way in The New York Times. Impossible to bring up the practicing zoophile who in 1999 had been creamily besotted with his 3-year-old Dalmatian bitch. Shhhh. How about the Yemeni accountant from Enker+Tiv+Spak who on business trips always tore Genesis out of the Gideon Bible in his hotel room --- and then used those 58 tissuey pages as toilet paper?

The day before, they were clerks. Now they're the Honored Dead.

How about the commodities broker who had a 14-year-old Kentucky runaway shackled to the boiler in his Sunnyside basement? Now ain't that America? What of the Ponzi schemers, the colostomy-bagged, Ed Koch's secret boyfriend, the two NYU cinéastes who made snuff films on spring break in Cambodia? Something to see, baby.

The day before, they were pillars of their communities. Now they're landfill. This is what occurred to Micah Ford.

A dinner meeting for Times executives was called a week before Christmas, in the upstairs salon at Le Bernardin. Midway through the cheese course (when everyone agreed that a sublime Vallençay chèvre had stolen the show), the company A-shares announced they were pulling the plug on "this whole vignette thing you're doing." The Profiles had run their course, ahem, and the newsroom politburo was directed to scrub the series by December 31. (Besides, anything written after that was ineligible for Pulitzer consideration.) So they quietly unflooded the zone. Drained it dry, is what they did. Got themselves a Pulitzer anyway. Of course they did.

During one long stretch in Nevada, however, for several hours the empty wintry desert began to bring Micah back from his ulysses. Brought him at last into contact with some of his own anger, fears, sadness and loss. He began coming through to himself. Coming through in waves. He sensed, out there in that desert, the spectral presences of Namaz and his father. So much began to inflate inside his brain, pressing onto the mid-brain, in the karma collosum, between the computer-code logic of the left hemisphere and the sweet-song sonnets to starboard. For a hundred miles or more, he started to unblank.

The car radio, after cycling for the better part of an hour with no bites, finally hooked a song. A woman was singing: *There's no one to hear, you might as well scream, they'll never wake up from the American Dream.*

Micah took this as a kind of instruction. So scream he did. He slid open the moon roof of the Beemer and screamed upward through it. He waaah'd and hollered, going 120 across the dry basement of the Mojave in the clear planetarium midnight. He banged on the steering wheel in the middle of nowhere. No cars for 100 miles. He clicked on the hazard flashers and the fog lamps. He laid on the horn for a thousand yards. At one point, under the frothy river of the Milky Way, he pulled over in a screeching fishtail of a stop. He got out, knelt on the road, lay down on the warm asphalt, as if etherized upon a table, and pressed his cheek onto the roadway, as if to sleep. He already missed them both so much.

But then, without warning or farewell, Hank and Namaz left him again. He sensed they were gone. The blanking resumed. The silent night closed silently back around him, like an awful black ocean.

By the time Micah began to make out the High Sierra up ahead, the serrated breakwater of California, he had come to understand that the people who died on 9/11 deserved no more reverence than those who hadn't died --- and precisely no less. They didn't deserve monuments at Arlington or coffee-table books or lump-sum windfalls. If the planes hadn't hit the towers that day, well, for most people 9/12 was still going to pretty much suck. Everything forthwith, you know, it wasn't going to be just fine.

4. A PERFECT SECRECY

By the time Micah made it to Florida, his grandfather had a dozen tomato seedlings going, the sprouts already poking out of their little peat hassocks. Jimmy was going with Best Boys again this year. The Farmer's Almanac was predicting a mild summer for Apalachicola and the coast.

Katharine, the housekeeper, had already begun the spring cleaning, working as she always did, room by room, upstairs, downstairs, porches. She pulled a few of the cane-bottomed rockers out of storage and put them on the big front veranda. (It was Katharine who called it the veranda; Jimmy called it the porch.) People in town had started taking their evening walks again. Screens were being hung and front doors were being left open. It was March, and it was warm enough.

Micah moved into the little two-bedroom guest cottage out back. Jimmy had it renovated a few years ago in the coastal colonial style to match the large and stately main house --- plantation shutters, cedar shakes, a full-on kitchen, central air. Micah mostly kept to himself there. He didn't have cable or a land line. Just a few surge protectors. A house of splendid isolation. He and his grandfather started having coffee most mornings on the brick patio between their respective houses. The patio was shaded and cooled by a towering *ficus aurea*, what the locals called a strangler fig, this one 40 feet high and no telling how old. They would read the paper, examine the weather and avoid talking about the terrible events of the previous autumn. Jimmy let it lay.

As the weather warmed, Micah pulled an old three-speed Raleigh out of the back of the garage. A girl's bike. He put on new tires and brakes. Sanded off the salt-rust. Fixed the gears and the Sturmey-Archer shifter. Afternoons, he'd ride down to Forgotten Coast Beach and swim in the bay. Straight out toward Dry Bar, Cat Point or the Bob Sikes Cut. These outings eventually lengthened into longer swims of several miles. He wore cutoff jeans and a pair of Namaz's swim goggles from Harvard.

If he timed it right he could head out against the flow tide, then come back against the ebb. Made for a better workout that way. Sometimes he'd go out too far on the first leg, nearly all the way to the Cape San Blas Light, and his lungs would protest and his legs would cramp. But he didn't panic. That impulse --- panic --- was gone in him now. Panic was just anticipated loss, and he now had so little to lose. He wasn't afraid to be afraid.

His father had often told him, "Never worry about the swim back." That advice, in his father's voice, came to him quite often now.

Katherine had been with Jimmy for years, even before Adele passed away, and in addition to looking after the old man and the main house, she would clean the cottage every few days. She did Micah's laundry and changed the linens. Kept a bowl in the kitchen filled with local fruit. She got a nephew to hose down Micah's BMW every couple weeks to chase off the salt. She also taped handwritten Bible verses to the seat of his bike: 3x5 cards bearing her elegant and careful cursive. Psalm 91 was a favorite of hers, and Psalm 107. She knew.

Micah went most nights to the Roseate Spoonbill, an old brick saloon on a sandy alleyway between Paper Street and Water Street in what passed for downtown Apalachicola. An engineer named John Gorrie built the place in 1850 as an ice-making plant, the first such operation in the entire country. But Gorrie soon went bust: He lost his patent, his fortune and his mind.

For most of the past half-century the old ice house had been a bar, or rather a succession of bars, owned by a trot-line of commercial shrimpers and oystermen who had sold off their boats and gear, each one figuring they could run the saloon a far sight better than the previous guy. It was named (and renamed) the Windjammer, Cable Beach, Iggy's, the Tiki Bar, the Gold Hill Galley, the Windjammer (again), the Plank-Gate Tavern, the Half Shell, the Jerk House and O'Kelly's.

Voncille Sangaree was the latest owner of the bar, newly arrived back in town, an Apalach gal of considerable spunk and flair.

Voncy had gone to Chapman High School in town --- *Breeze up, Seahawks!* --- and she was a two-time Miss Teen Florida. A talent scout discovered her as a freshman cheerleader at Florida State, and the Ford Models agency moved her up to New York. She was 5-10, with white-blonde hair and aquamarine eyes flecked with shards of onyx. Art directors loved her changeable look --- cotillion deb, surfer chick, biker chick, naughty young MILF, naughty Tri-Delt, Olympic sprinter, Amazon, dominatrix, wraith, vampire, Chapin School legacy. One AD said that Voncille "puts the prêt in prêt-à-porter." Her book became the equal of Christy, Christie and Claudia. Talk about your bodies of work.

She liked the modeling business well enough. Travel, the money, the great clothes. Lee McQueen put her in his Highland Rape show and she was the girl in the glass box at his Voss event. Voncy was the fit model for Roland Mouret's famous Galaxy dress, and she always had runway work in Milan, Paris and Bryant Park. She blackened her hair and played the bass in the "Addicted to Love" video. Meanwhile, when she wasn't on the road, she took business classes at the New School.

Voncy didn't purge or puke or pill, and she never saw the appeal of heroin chic. (All those Soviet-diaspora girls with BMIs under 16. *Da nyet.* You could grate cheese on their rib cages.) Besides, as Voncy said, that whole bulimia thing was so overblown. Most models, the great ones anyway, they were built like borzois but they ate like Bulgarian shot putters. They had the good genes going for them, plus they smoked Gitanes around the clock and worked out like Channel swimmers. Kate Moss, she knocked back 5,800 calories a day --- Frosted Flakes drowned in half-and-half, steak frites, a nightly bottle of Malbec, the glory that is Cherry Garcia and three lumps in the café crème. Anorexia was for amateurs.

Voncy dated a Klitschko and bought a Rothko. No velvet rope in New York could hold her. Tiger Woods texted her. She started a bustiere line called Milkshake. Had an ownership stake in the Mudd Club and co-founded a juice bar called Liquiteria. She got rich. Took a meeting about being the next Bond Girl. She was the face of Almay cosmetics and, as she put it, "the bottom bitch" for Spanker jeans. She had friends named Busy, L'Wren and Capucine. Hanging out with Carla Bruni she eventually fell in with a French expat crowd in New York and married a low-rung Parisian aristocrat, Étienne de Vignolles. He went by Jacques, and he had very good hair. Jacques was in mergers and acquisitions at Elf Aquitaine, and he was handsome, rich, smart, titled, entitled --- all the most dangerous qualities. He and Voncy bought the trendiest art and the rarest stamps. Everything they owned had to have a pedigree or a provenance.

Jacques was married to Voncy, *oui oui,* and they did make for a stunning couple, but he was more fully and professionally in thrall to the French finance minister, Dominique Strauss-Kahn, his former econ professor at Paris X. Jacques became part of the DSK global entourage, one of the pilot fish always trailing the great man, a dashing accessory at Davos and Aspen. Voncy got worried when Jacques started referring to his testicles as Strauss and Kahn. He asked that she henceforth address his penis as Nique.

Voncy finally gave up on Jacques as the millennium began to turn. She went crying to Kate: "He called me 'a lovely zero,' which is not very fuckin' nice in the first place, but what really got me was him saying I acted vulgar when I'm drinking. Well, *fuck* vulgar. I never told a lie in my life. I'm authentic. But shit, Katie, I have one drink any more and I'm gonzo. Especially when I'm trying to drop a kilo and I'm sucking on those damn cotton balls soaked in vodka-and-lime juice. I used to be a happy drunk, but with him I'm just a mean sober."

When Voncy got the news that her mother was dying, she decided she had to move back to Apalachicola. Jacques was having none of it. Hell, he couldn't even pronounce it. She woke up one morning and told him, "We are not going to be married any more."

"That sent him freakin' loco," she told Kate. "His face, I swear, it went the color of liver pâté. After we talked about it some, when he realized I wasn't going to continue to be his glamorama arm-charm supermodel wife, he turned fucking *beige*. The creep."

She would not miss her vicomte and she wouldn't much miss the modeling. She had gotten too old, is partly what happened --- at 35 she was something of a dowager, an octogenarian under the cruel calculus of international modeling. She had gained some weight (11 pounds) and some amplitude (two cup sizes). Her scold of an agent called this her rounding error: "V, your tits, darling, you've got a cleavage I could *yodel* into."

Her editorial and runway work started drying up. Just to stay busy she started booking catalog shoots and commercial sessions for Valvoline calendars and Snap-On Tools. She even worked a series of Midwestern trade shows for Snap-On, leaning her breasts over gleaming trays of chrome socket wrenches for 9 hours at a stretch. That had made her back hurt.

Voncille's last job, the one that finally did her in, was a one-episode cameo on a reality show called "Orange County Choppers." She played Junior's big-city girlfriend who Senior clumsily gropes behind the Flowjet machine. After that she fired her agent, hired a realtor and sold the loft on West Street, *comme ça*, cue the finger snap, net-netting a tidy four-point-five. The deal closed on the 3rd of September and she beat it straight back to Apalach --- barely a week before 9/11 went down. Double-lucky for Voncille, she had already auctioned off her three Basquiats and a very nice middle-period Hockney. Her Frankenthaler went to MOMA as a tax deduction. She also sold Jacques' stamp collection, including the lovely TreSkilling yellow, the Blue Mauritius and the Inverted Jenny. The Ansel Adams "Moonrise" and the sweet little Giacometti, those she kept with her.

Jacques got the Rothko, the apartment in Paris, and pretty much all their friends.

So, Voncy was home. And happily so. "There's too much gorgeous in New York," she told her mother. "And besides, the photographers had sucked all the pretty out of me."

Her family was Old Florida. There had been Sangarees in Apalachicola since the time it was a Creek Indian settlement. "No place comes up to Apalachicola," her mama always said. St. Bart's, Cap Ferrat, El Bulli, Galle Fort, the Maldives, you could have them all. The sham-glam of the fashion world, at least for Voncille, was done. (She had once gushed a hello to Anna Wintour in an elevator at Condé Nast, and this was the great woman's entire reply, issued from behind her bug-eye sunglasses: "Lose the crease." It seems Voncille's pressed-linen pants had given immediate offense.) Anna, Heidi, Gisele, Naomi, André, that whole *uber*-luxe fashion crowd of boldface names --- it was over. *Uber* and out.

Voncy moved into her old bedroom upstairs in her mother's sprawling house, a lavender-colored Victorian on Bay Avenue. The Painted Lady, her mom called the house. Voncy variously called it Big Pink, the Labia Arms or The Old Gräfenberg Place. She drove her mother to various doctors, and she took over the running of the house, but she knew she would need something more to do. Within a week she had made an all-cash offer, with a 14-day close, for O'Kelly's. She figured she could run the place a far sight better than the shrimp-for-brains guy who was currently driving it into foreclosure. She had been away for years, but she knew that bar inside-out: She was swiping fifths of Tanqueray from Iggy's storeroom starting in the 10th grade. It was Voncy who renamed it the Spoonbill.

Micah drank himself blackout on most nights, or at least right up to the rim of the crater. He would drink steadily, unhurriedly, somewhere between a gulper and a sipper. He went with different drinks from night to night, like he and Namaz had done on their Amtrak rides in New York. He wasn't above a couple dozen Corona Lights or PBRs, but he tilted more than occasionally toward the brown liquors.

His pattern was that he would walk to the Spoonbill about 8, drink until closing, then walk home, about a mile and a half down Columbus Street, with a short left onto 12th. (He wasn't a stumbler, but he was always in flip-flops, so the inebriated walk back to Jimmy's could take a while.)

Some nights the police prowler would spot him on the road and pull up alongside. The deputies knew him, or knew about him. Most were about his own age.

"How's things, Micah?"

"Good."

"You been over to Voncille's? Want a lift home? Kinda hot tonight."

"OK."

"How's your grandfather?"

"Good, thanks."

In the back seat of the cop car, Micah would press his boozy-hot cheek against the window, which was cool from the air conditioning. That was nice. He'd close his eyes and wonder what Namaz was doing right then. He'd hum some Al Green. "*You oughta be with me.*" He'd sniff the briny air for chlorine.

"OK, Micah. Here we are. Home again home again. Y'all take 'er easy now."

"Good. OK. Thanks for the ride."

The Spoonbill occasionally reeled in a few of the pluckier tourists along Florida's Forgotten Coast, but the nightly regulars at the bar were mostly the Mile 13 and Joe Taranto oystermen, the shrimp-boat captains, the guys who worked the docks at Leavins and Lombardi's, the seafood buyers, marine mechanics and various other tradesmen. They all knew each other, and about each other --- who dated whom in high school, whose boat was going good now, which wives or girlfriends were cattin' around, which captains had the stink on them and were close to losing their vessels.

There was a lot of predictable nostalgia-yak in the bar about high school football games and monster storms. (Labor Day weekend, 1985, Elena had crushed the town, the fleet and the oyster reefs. Opal, in '95, now *she* was a bitch. Her secondary surge had done the real damage. Time and tide.) The Sports Illustrated people had come to town awhile back, and that was another enduring staple of Spoonbill conversation --- if only because one Voncille Sangaree appeared on the cover of the swimsuit issue that year. For years her bikin'd cover photo had hung in a frame directly over the men's urinal.

Micah almost always took a booth by himself near the door, far from the ancient, rabbit-eared television behind the bar. He was still very good at alone. It was his default setting. He didn't participate in the nightly debates with the regulars, which ever since the 9/11 attacks had become an angry and deeply alcoholic jawing about them Ay-rabs, Al Kedda and freedom fries. Night after night, alone in his booth, Micah seemed lost in thought --- even while drinking at a pretty good clip. People found this to be odd or pathetic or borderline autistic. "Hurricane drunk, looks like to me," one man said. "He's in the grip."

What floor? Which tower? That's what everybody really wanted to know about him. But Micah's look and manner, his darkness visible, it all seemed to say, "Keep clear, and don't ask." Everybody did, and nobody asked. This misery, his misery, it didn't love company.

Most people in town honestly seemed to care for him, knowing his basic story and all. It was a small town, so of course everyone knew. In one sense Micah was *their* 9/11 victim. Their very own. They claimed him. He singlehandedly linked Apalachicola to New York, to the attacks, to "America Under Attack!" With Micah's tragedy the locals had some real skin in the game. The anger game.

Micah, for his part, was largely unaware that anyone in town knew anything about him, except maybe that he was Jimmy Bloodworth's grandson. It simply never occurred to him that he might be the object of attention, talk or curiosity, and he was oblivious to the pitying glances and tender whispers. *(Did they know he was worth $40 million, give or take? Did they know that his fiancée had been Iranian, or that her father had been a Savak colonel and a jailer for the Shah? Did they know that Micah's granulated dad had been delivered to his doorstep in a plastic sack? No. Nobody. None of that.)*

Micah just went along day to day --- sleep, bike, swim, think, drink. He shut himself off from the daily commerce in gossip. People could see he was broken. It takes time to hit bottom. They figured he just needed a little more to regain his footing. "Find his sea legs," some folks said. "Get his bearings."

• • • •

It was a night for Bombay-and-tonic, rocks of course, and lime of course, and keep 'em coming. Mid-August 2002, and Apalachicola was as hot as Saigon.

"How many hours can a person physically fuckin' sweat?" griped a shrimper one evening, a bit loud, forearms pressed into the bar in the Spoonbill. It had been a long day on the river. "Consecutive, I mean. Consecutive fuckin' hours of sweating. Without fuckin' interruption. God *damn.* I feel like a fuckin' gecko."

Micah was in his usual booth, smelling of the gin and the lime and, vaguely, of saltwater. He was beginning the climb into his usual half-stupor, not hearing the jukebox. *"Just to make this dock my home."* It was then that Voncille Sangaree came over and sat down in the booth, facing him. They didn't know each other, not well anyway, not personally. That was fixin' to change.

"OK, it starts here and it starts tonight," Voncy said, shaking his hand across the table. "We're going to be friends. I've decided. I've kept my distance all this time, what is it, must be better than six months now, because I know you've been sad and you lost your dad in 9/11. I can't imagine. But enough is enough."

"You're Voncille, right? I've been meaning . . ."

"Wait, look, I've practiced this speech, so let me finish. You're one goddamned heap of misery as far as I can tell, and I think I can help you with that. You're going to tell me your story, I'm going to call you on your bullshit. People need that, of course. And I'll tell you about me, and we'll be friends, maybe even forever. It'll be worth it. I'm a girl who speaks her fucking mind. Ask anybody. Ask your grandpa. I love that man. He's one of the world's great fucking gentlemen."

"OK."

"OK? That's it? You mean it's OK that we'll talk and hang out a little? Or was the rant OK? It felt like I rushed it."

"OK to talk. Sure. Thank you. I guess I could use somebody to talk with. I know my grandpa is worried. I'm not very good at it. The talking. I'm out of practice, that's for sure."

"Look, advance notice, I'm a smart ass and a big mouth sometimes. OK, a *lot* of the time. A shrink I know --- OK, she's *my* shrink, all right? So I've got a shrink. Big deal. Who fuckin' cares, really? Anyway she says I'm overly empathic and pathologically truthful, which are traits that don't often work well in tandem. That's how she put it --- *in tandem*. I mean, who freakin' talks like that? Anyway I get away with shit because I'm reasonably smart and I can display very fine manners when necessary. I'm a woman of parts. I've got sand, as my daddy used to say."

"Sounds that way. Good. That's good."

"I don't 'collect' people, if you know what I mean. I'm serious. You should know that I don't make this offer lightly. And anyway, don't worry, I'm not hitting on you. I'm off men. Pretty much."

Her tone here went mildly ironic. "I'm quite the goddamn personality, in case you didn't know, like an astronaut, or the manager of the Yankees. People used to pay a good bit of money to have me show up at their clubs and gallery openings. This was in New York. People paid a lot to dress me up and walk me around."

"Walk you around?"

"I was a model. Fashion Week, runways, magazines, all that."

"But you're from here? Originally?"

"I grew up here, but I lived in New York for pretty much the last 15 years. Since high school, really. For a long time when I first got to New York I seemed to be in the 'too' category --- too tall, too athletic, too chinny. Peter Beard, this photographer, we were on a shoot one time in the Rift Valley --- that's in Africa --- and he told me, 'They should hang your tits in the Louvre, Voncy, but your smile is all wrong.' My friend Frankie Rayder was there, she's another model, maybe you've heard of her, and she told Peter he was full of shit because I had the filthiest little smile in the business. She meant it totally as a compliment. Anyway, who knows why, but suddenly my look got trendy, my body type, and I flared up for about five years. All the sexes were crazy for me. 'The Voncy Bubble' was one headline. French Vogue called it 'Voncisme' and some critic wrote that my lips were 'always poised somewhere between a pout and a slurp.' I actually liked that one. But if you're only good-looking, you know, that's not enough.

"So anyway I gave it all up. The modeling, New York, everything. It was just a goddamn impossible way to live. I dumped my shit-heel husband. The French jerk. I sold my apartment and came home. This was almost exactly a year ago now. Literally the week before 9/11. I've had the big life. I want to go small for awhile. Also my mama got cancer, and I realized I had never really gotten to know her, so that's the main reason I came back. I was a teenager, you know, when I left home. How don't you know all this --- my sordid history? Mama says I'm an 'unholy scandal.'

That's the way she talks: 'unholy scandal.' I thought everybody in town knew this stuff. A small town, as they say, is a vast hell."

"I don't hear much gossip. Around town. I guess I did know that you owned this bar. I like it here."

"So I gather, for as much as you're in here. But your grandfather, I've known him forever, my whole life pretty much, kind of like we've always been *in tandem*, in a way. He needs you to check back into the real world. He's afraid he's going to die or stroke out and you're going to be sitting in this fucking booth night after night like some Easter Island statue. Jesus, pardon my language. I've been contaminated by all these ignorant Panhandle fucknuts around here. Any more, I just can't seem to stop cussin'. Mother finds it highly unattractive. Anyway."

"Yeah, my granddad is getting on me for drinking too much. Not reaching my full potential. He's probably right. But I'm doing no harm. I don't bother anybody. I walk here and I walk home. I like it here. My dad would have liked it, too. He would have called it a gin mill."

"I see you on your bike sometimes. Down at the beach. It looks like a girl's bike."

"Yeah. I go swimming most days."

"What do you do? For work, I mean. For money. During the day."

"I'm getting my doctorate at Stanford. I'm ABD. At the thesis stage. I'm a little bit stalled on it."

"A doctorate in what?"

"Mathematics. Computer stuff."

" 'Computer stuff.' Jesus, Mary and Joseph. Condescend much? I'm in fucking Mensa, I'll have you know. And I got a B-plus in Algebra II in high school. So suck on *that*."

Micah actually grinned. He gulped some gin. "Sorry. It's just easier to. It's just. It's just not. My thesis is just not something that most people can understand. Even me, I can't understand it myself sometimes. Sometimes I lose the thread of it. My adviser won the Fields Medal and even he doesn't entirely get it."

"What's the topic, though? I mean, generally speaking. You know, for us gin-mill types."

"It's basically a new kind of number theory that extrapolates an unbreakable encryption program. Some people call it 'perfect secrecy.' It could be kind of a breakthrough." Another gin-gulp. "If I can ever get to a proof. The underlying math is pretty new, and kind of strange. My adviser calls it 'spooky-action math.' The whole idea is pretty much a joke in my area, like it's nuclear fusion or perpetual motion. Unbreakability is thought to be mathematically impossible. But sometimes I feel like I'm close."

"Is it huge? Like first-black-president huge? Like walk-on-the-moon huge?"

"Maybe. At least in the math world."

"Holy fuck."

"Yeah. Maybe."

Voices, suddenly, were being raised over at the bar, angry voices rearing above the general rumble of conversation. Fingers were pointed. Threats were grunted. A bottle of Hop Leaf IPA rocketed over the bar and crashed through the screen of the old television. The implosion was modest, almost tidy and cartoony. The tin-foiled rabbit ears stayed in place atop the set, and a small snort of grayish smoke issued from the back. The room went immediately quiet, and everybody turned to look at Voncille. She shot Micah a smiling wink and said primly, but so everyone could hear, "Doctor, would you excuse me, please?"

She sized things up, fined the combatants $200 each, in cash, which they paid on the spot without complaint.

Voncille shouted "good fucking riddance" at the TV, but when she turned back to Micah's booth, he was gone. Slipped out during the hubbub. There was a hundred under his empty glass. Exit ghost.

• • • •

Jimmy Bloodworth had seen his share of alkies in the big leagues, wonderful players undone by the booze, unmoored by it, unmanned by it, and he also had seen plenty of guys come back from two wars all turned around. *Did the war make them drink? Or were they born drinkers who got sucked into a war?* The years right after Korea were the worst. Certain ballplayers would be plastered almost all the time, even in the morning, even for day games, sneaking drinks, sometimes between innings. There was a bottle of rye in every bullpen in the majors.

Before the war they had been regular fellers, square Joes, but now they carried around short fuses that led to big explosions. Ballplayers had terrible and violent fights with wives, teammates, managers. These afflicted postwar men would scream at umpires, ball boys, traveling secretaries. They'd go right up into the stands after a beery heckler on a Sunday afternoon. They couldn't keep the signs straight during the games, so they'd be swinging away on 3-and-0 or trying to steal third with one out. It was like they'd been put to sleep at some vaudeville show --- stripping to their boxers on stage and belting out "Moonglow" in a girlish falsetto --- except the nitwit hypnotist hadn't been able to bring them all the way back. They got halfway home halfway intact. This was the hypnosis of gore. They became unknown even to themselves.

Jimmy had long been sensing this boozy undertow grabbing at his grandson, the only child of his only child, the computer genius, the tinkerer and chess prodigy and rock climber, this demolished, sweet-hearted boy. Micah wasn't explosive, violent or mean, but as the man had said, he was in the grip.

Voncy was always trying to get Micah to eat something at the Spoonbill, which meant she was always trying to get him to drink less. She wasn't a harpie about it, but she also wasn't shy about her druthers. From time to time she would pull up a chair and deliver a lecture. He would listen, nod, listen, and then ask about Voncy's mother or their weekend plans or the weather forecast. Now and then, maybe once a month, usually around closing time, Micah would lay his head on the table and drop off to sleep. Sleep, pass out, black out, however you wanted to say it, he did so in a polite and quiet fashion. Voncy, on her way out, would throw a shawl or a blanket over him and leave a set of keys on the table. Micah usually awoke to the growl of the motor-trawlers heading out to the fishing grounds. He'd let himself out, lock up the door and walk home through the cool salty darkness of the morning.

Micah and his grandfather would often sit on the veranda and eat a light dinner, and Jimmy would rattle on about any damned thing, trying to get Micah to engage. This was his version of the talking cure. The old man would tell baseball stories, or about how he had courted Adele, about working at the little post office in Apalach after he retired. About the polluted harbor and the dying river, about boats and oystering and Detroit and the melting glaciers and tomato blight. Everything but. For many months it was everything but.

Micah listened politely, as was his nature. He would talk some, too, even if this was not his nature. Grampa Sammy, his father's father, now *he* could talk. Hank, too. If he wanted to charm you, you didn't have a chance. He once sold a used diesel submarine to landlocked Laos to patrol an 8-mile stretch of the Mekong River. It was the same with Jimmy, when he got going. But their gifts were skipping this third generation. The patter gene, apparently, was recessive. Micah instead had found a comfort in his gloom, a real contentment, almost as if he had worked out a satisfactory algorithm to explain his silence and sadness. He seemed as calm as could be. He didn't weep privately in his room. Never drank in the daytime. He slept well and woke up early. Hank and Namaz did not come bloodily into his dreams. They stayed away.

It was true enough that Micah didn't smile very much. And he startled quite easily --- one night, when a Spoonbill waitress named Lavinia dropped two platters of fried calamari behind him, he was in a full-body sweat inside of 20 seconds. Plus there were the nightly binges and those long, chancy outbound swims. How to describe him? Encased. Sad. Private. Odd. When his hair had recently gotten long, nearly to his shoulders, he cut it himself, using Katharine's pinking shears. He hadn't bothered with a mirror. This ain't good, Jimmy thought, looking at the odd patch of fescue on his grandson's head.

This kind of thing with Micah --- boozing, drifting, the interminable thesis-pondering, ocean swimming, the Buckwheat haircut --- all this had been going on for three years now. Heart transplants heal faster. It was getting on to June, 2005, and the loggerhead turtles were arriving again to lay their eggs in the sea oats. Red snapper season was about to start. The Best Boys were already climbing their cages and another buggy summer was pushing hard at the window screens. Jimmy was getting tired of playing defense with Micah, which is how he put it to some of his poker buddies. Things had been put off for too long. He was actually becoming fearful for his grandson, even more so after he suggested that it might be good for Micah to talk to "somebody professional." Micah had waved him off.

"Micah, c'mon, you're in the bar every night. It seems like your thesis is on the shelf. This is not the man you want to be. It's not who. . . I've wanted to allow you some time. God knows, healing up, I can't imagine. Actually, I can. But I'm getting scared for you. I am. I am. The drinking and all. I cannot sit by and just watch you drop anchor. I will not. I'm way too old for this. To see you going down."

"I know, Grandpa. I'm sorry. I know you're worried. Sometimes I get a little worried myself. But I'm not you or my dad. I wish I was. Believe me. I wish I had more of that, what, resilience."

"It's not fair, Micah. What happened. Not by a long shot. But pain is assured in this life. You stand it like a man, and you push back."

"That's just what my dad would be saying. Talk about resilient. He'd be catching a plane somewhere and greasing some deals. Namaz, too. She'd have 20 balls in the air by now. Her New York restaurant would be some huge success. But I can't, for some reason. I just live more in my head. I've just been letting things happen to me. Riding things out, maybe. I must seem depressed to you. Probably I am. Probably."

"So what about maybe getting some help then?"

"You're helping me fine. Katharine leaves me her Bible verses. Voncy keeps an eye on me, and she's become a nice friend. And swimming, you know, I actually work on my thesis while I swim. The tides and the turbulence, I'm really onto something with that. I might even be close to finishing. Just in the last couple months I've been working on a new kind of math that is sending my thesis in a whole new direction. Toward a new kind of encryption. Using chaos theory."

"Chaos theory."

It was true. He had begun to discover these notions during his longer ocean swims. (Discover, or invent? He wasn't sure which.) He would see his hands pull through the water, the suck and lisp of his arms in the water. You could briefly see the swirls they caused, the little traces of their wake, and this was mostly visible when he was swimming on the surface. But the deeper he went the trickier it got. *The only vice of water is gravity.* Fully underwater you can't see a splash. Undertows grab. Tides roll. *I follow you deep sea, baby.* The invisible rapids and rivulets 30 feet down, they proceed unseen. Define "drenching" down deep. Rogue waves offer no warning or signature, they simply engulf. Blue nebulae in the blue room don't pulse; they exist only when they're exploding underneath you. *Blue is the warmest color.* Slipstreams slipping. All of this was invisible, like so many of the notions in Micah's mathematics. He reasoned that if he couldn't find a way to mathematically express the small chaos and huge turbulence of the water, then there must be an exploitable randomness inside them.

That was the eureka of his encryption models. The elegance of turbulence. Stream ciphering, inverse scatterings, Riccati's theorem, Bäcklund transformations. Vernam sequestering, Schrödinger's cat, quantum entanglement, you could really pickle your brain with this stuff. Sine, lambda, fractal, churn. The churn was it for Micah.

"The swimming puts me into a kind of relaxed state that makes the computations come more easily. I visualize the numbers and their connections much more clearly down there. Swirls, currents. I don't know, maybe none of this *actually* helps, but I think it does. I should tell you more about it, so you'll worry less.

"I've also started playing computer chess again. Replaying Bobby Fischer's big games. I don't know. Whenever I begin to reflect on things, which I admit isn't very often, I don't feel much of anything. There are worse things. I guess I think I feel pretty binary about it all."

"Binary."

"That sounds totally strange, I know, especially now that I hear myself saying it out loud. I do realize that."

"Binary, sure, like on and off. So you're feeling off? I get that. We all feel off from time to time. God knows. But we're talking about a long time now. A long time to be off."

"Well, for me I'd say it's not exactly *off.* It's more like on and not-on. It's more like I'm not-on."

"Well, I can't barely fathom what's happening inside that Deep Blue brain of yours. God knows. But *on* is what I want for you, kiddo. I want you switched on. Like you used to be. You were such a firecracker. You always had so much of your mom in you. Her same energy. I don't know. Maybe I'm just not helping you right."

"No, sir, no, no, no. Please don't feel that way." Micah reached across the porch table and took his grandfather's hand.

"I love you, Micah, and this is your home, you know that. That's two things you can always count on. Let's start with that, how about? Every day you count on that."

"I know that, Grandpa. I do count on it. You and this house are my entire world right now. There's no turbulence here. That's how I see it. I can see that clear as day."

They sat for a long minute like that, hand in hand, not talking.

"You know, now and then I have a hard time remembering Mom and Dad. My brain gets so tired from the math, maybe that's it. But I think, in a way, I was just getting to know my dad. He was always so capable and he took such good care of me after Mom died. I kind of idolized him, I guess, but I also realize there were parts of him I didn't know very much about, like when he was in the Army and when he and Mom were just starting out. He was crazy about Namaz, I know that. I'm just sad that I never got to show him what I'm really good at, my thesis and the new stuff I've been working on."

"He was proud of you, Micah, I can promise you that. He and I talked a lot. Whenever he took a trip overseas he would call beforehand and tell me where he was going. He was a great man, and that's not overstating it. He was a .400 hitter. Best thing of all, he loved your mom. He made her happy. That was plenty good enough for me."

Micah looked sad. The erratic memories of his mother, like the numbers deeper down in the sea. Seeing her in the hospital in those final days. So thin and groggy. And with his father, Micah had been too young at the time to know what fear looked like in adults.

"I don't think I can remember what Mom's voice sounded like," he said. "I think Voncille's voice is like hers. But I can't remember for sure. I wish I could. At Dad's funeral, you know, for some reason it didn't register with me that she was buried there, too. In the same grave as him, right in front of me. I was so out of it."

"I think Voncille's voice is like hers. But I can't remember for sure. I wish I could. At dad's funeral, you know, for some reason it didn't register with me that she was buried there, too. In the same grave as him, right in front of me. I was so out of it. Tired and sad and all."

"Oh, you knew that," Jimmy said. "You knew she was there. You did, Micah. They told me --- when you tried to dig into the grave with your hands. With the mud. You must have known she was there."

"What? No. I don't remember that. The mud? Who told you that? That's not, that's, no, that can't be right."

"Mr. Nouri called here a few days after the service. To check on you. They couldn't find you. He thought you might have come here. He told me about it."

"Jesus. I can't believe that. Jesus. I miss them so much."

After a minute the old man said, "I think you can lose everybody else and still maybe come out the other end OK. But not a child. Especially not your only child." He was near to crying. "I remember her voice from when she was 5 or 6. 'Little Lizzie's in a tizzy.' She used to sing that over and over about herself. While jumping rope. Drove us crazy and cracked us up. I used to have some Super-8 film of that. Somewhere. I don't know."

Jimmy was not used to pulling up the past like this. Especially about Lizzie. He talked a good game to Micah, but no.

He stood up and said it was getting late for him --- the sun's below the yardarm, that was his nightly phrase --- and he was heading off to bed at the back of the house. He gave Micah a long hug, more of a clutching, the two of them standing there on the porch in the gathering dusk and the heavy heat. The old man kissed his grandson's forehead and pushed a hand through that raggedy haircut. As he went into the house, he turned back and said, "That bike you fixed up, it was your mom's, you know. Way back when. She rode that thing all over town."

And with that, for the first time since September 11, after 44 desolate months, Micah Ford began to cry.

5. UNCLAIMED BAGGAGE

Strange how you get used to the give and take of an old porch, its creaks and complaints under the weight of a couple bent-willow rocking chairs. Twenty minutes go by, thirty, forty, barely a word being passed, the ice long gone in the drinks, thoughts gone woozy under the humid press of a summer evening. But if one of you falls out of rhythm, falls away from that tidal swoon, the other one might look up with a start, as if from sleep, and half-shout, "Huh? Wuzzat?"

"Nothing. Just rocking." This was Micah.

Later, his grandfather says this: "You know, you ought to take your car out. Air it out. Car like that, you gotta blow out the carbon from time to time. Get on the highway and let 'er rip."

"What, now?"

"Now, tomorrow, next week. Any time. Just an idea. Used to work for me, airing myself out."

Micah smiled at his grandfather, who was still slick enough after a couple fingers of bourbon or a fistful of gin. And even at 80, that Little League playground name, Jimmy B, it still seemed to fit him. Micah stood up, bent over, touched his toes, put his palms flat on the porch. It was coming on to dark.

A few days later, out on Florida 71, northbound from Apalachicola, the Beemer was pushing 90 and behaving just fine. His dad had always kept the car in good tune. Micah used the windshield squirter and the wipers, the radio and CD player, the power seats, all the lights and the moon roof, all the switches and toggles. Everything was a go, and Micah pretty soon had himself in that half-sleep that always made time pass so well. What finally roused him was the Teutonic bonging of the low-fuel alarm.

He was in northern Alabama, the real hookworm-and-rickets part of the state. *Sheesh, how long was I out? What the hell?* The road now was Interstate 59, and he was seeing signs for Pisgah, Paint Rock, Shiloh, Suttree, Macedonia, Scottsboro, Sylvania.

Shiloh: that was a Civil war battle, but he thought he remembered it being in Kentucky or Tennessee. His dad for sure would have known. Hank could have told you right off that Grant and Buell survived an ambush there and caught the Rebs in the Hornet's Nest. Pisgah: that was from the Bible, something about the Promised Land. Funny what you half-remembered from confirmation class. Scottsboro: that sounded familiar, too. The Scottsboro Boys --- an old R&B group, or something? Sylvania: he wondered if they made the lightbulbs there.

The sun was slipping behind a distant ridge of pines when he came to the Tennessee River. He rolled down the window to test the air, and there was a dead sour smell coming off the water. He turned onto State Route 35, and crossed an old WPA bridge with lots of black-iron fretwork. A plaque gave the completion date: "March 25, 1931." Fifty yards upriver was a parallel train trestle, painted on the side, painted long ago with "Southern Railway."

On the road into Scottsboro was the D&L Motel, a low-slung cinderblocked place, circa 1950, from back when they were called motor courts. The motel had about a dozen rooms grouped around a parking area and a kidney-bean swimming pool. The pool had a couple feet of black water in the bottom. Nearby were three folding chairs, a dead pindo palm and a tipped-over Coke machine. That was the roadside tableau presented by the D&L.

Micah thought he might keep driving, hold out for a Days Inn or a Super 8, but then across the road from the motel he noticed a stainless-steel diner, one of the old kind, one that might even pre-date the word "motel," and it was still in pretty good shape. A sign in one of the front windows said E-A-T. In red neon. That did it.

The evening desk clerk at the D&L was Lorraine, bored-to-tears Lorraine, gray-woeful Lorraine, 60-plus-plus, a plus-sized gal, about a decade overdue for an exfoliation, a hot-creme rinse and a vacation. She was the L. Owned the place with her husband, Dewey, and it's a wonder they hadn't gone for the obvious and named it the Dew Drop Inn or the Dixie Dew. Dewey worked the three-to-noon shift on the desk. Also kept him a turpentine still up on Jolly Six Creek. He was on the disability from Korea. KO-rea. A Commie gook had put a bullet through his left kneecap at Pork Chop Hill. "Dew's a cripple," is how Lorraine puts it.

"Single room, one night, that's 27 dollars American money, including the 4 bucks for Massa George Bush," she said. "You can pay cash, or you can pay cash." She had, of course, said this before, many times, in what passed for front-desk humor. She said any local phone calls could be direct-dialed but they'd be "extry." Phoning out-of-state, which Lorraine referred to as "foreign calls," was not possible.

Micah asked for a nonsmoking room, which caused Lorraine to give out a short barking laugh, like a barn owl. "That's a good one," she said. Lorraine herself was never very far from a lit Tareyton.

She handed Micah a single door key. A Schlage. Just the key. No plastic dangle-tag or even the room number stamped on it. "I got you in 306," she said. "It's a nass one. You can park ratt in front."

Micah would later be tempted to ask Lorraine about her numbering system, since Room 306 had Rooms 3, 8, 88 and 43 on one side and Room 237 on the other. The Fibonacci Sequence, he was thinking, had nothing on the D&L.

Three-oh-six had a low queen bed with a swaybacked mattress, four thin pillows and a maroon polyester bedspread that hit Micah with a bolt of static when he touched it. A boxy Admiral TV was padlocked to an old dresser. (Lorraine had mentioned that their cable package came with 748 channels, including 17 HBOs and 11 Showtimes. She said it sem-teen and lemm.) A bare fluorescent tube buzzed overhead. Masonite paneling. A water-stained watercolor of the Trevi Fountain. Room 306 had seen its share. In the bathroom: one towel, rust stains in the tub, nicotine burns on the rim of the sink, a communion wafer of soap, but no shampoo, times being what they was and all. A Coca-Cola ashtray on the toilet tank. Home sweet home Alabama.

The best thing about the D&L figured to be the diner across the road. Your classic meat-and-three place, from the looks of it. On the north side of the diner, angrily spray-painted on its metal skin, were the words FUCK AUBURN. Inside it was clean and bright, with a dozen chrome stools at a long Formica counter. This was a diner being a diner. Ten booths had been nicely tuck-and-rolled in red vinyl with black piping, like you were sliding into the back seat of a '68 Bonneville. There were those flip-card, push-button jukebox gizmos at each booth, like mini-aquariums holding songs instead of fish. Ruby and Victoria's, that was the official name of the diner. Folks called it the Vic.

It was nearly 9 o'clock and the place was empty. Hell, it was a Sunday. The dinner hour was long gone and everything had been wiped down. There was a pie case next to the cash register. A bowl of Thin Mints. A stack of unsold newspapers from Huntsville and Chattanooga. A small TV was mounted on the wall behind the register. Underneath was a rack of Bibles and a shirt-cardboard sign in blue ballpoint that said, "KJVs. Free." Another sign said, "No bad language. No credit. Don't ask."

On the counter, six ketchup bottles were dripping their dregs into six other bottles: a half-dozen red hourglasses: the nightly mouth-to-mouth. Ketchup, like sand, like time, was slipping away. Micah took a booth, and when a waitress came out of the back she looked startled for a moment. But she smiled across the room, grabbed a coffee mug and waggled it at him.

"Please," he said.

She brought the coffee, which had cooked down into a kind of road tar. The menu was a single sheet in a plastic sleeve, done in a Smith-Corona typeface and printed in mimeograph-blue. Retro. Nice touch. There was meatloaf, a slew of burgers, chicken salad, tuna salad, fries, rings, butter beans, collards, cobbler, the usual.

"Olen's already gone --- he's the cook," the waitress said. "Everybody's gone. But I can make you something."

"Whatever's good, or whatever's left. Whatever you guys do best. Anything'll be fine."

He looked up from the menu and gave her more of a double-take than she usually got. She looked mid-20's, Latina, black hair, faded jeans torn at the knees, a white guayabera, Puma sneakers, fingernails aflame in safflower red. Lovely, alarming. Salma, Salomé, Carmen, *a deep intake of breath here from Micah*, Movita, Battle, Callas. An opera goddess closing up a kitchen.

"OK, but with my cooking, you're asking for it," she said with a womanly half-smile and a girlie-girl half-giggle that she had actively been working to lose. "You're not from here, I am thinking."

"No. Uh-uh. Just driving through. I'm staying at the uh, the uh, the *motel.* Over there."

Her name tag had a piece of white surgical tape obscuring the last bit of her name, leaving only "BENI." Micah stared at the name, stared at it for a long while, 40 seconds or more, which is a very long time indeed to be staring directly --- and somewhat open-mouthed and barely breathing --- at a woman's breast. Waitress Beni went from her half-smile to a full smile to pissed off to fearful to somewhat worried, then finally settled on being quite pleased. Somewhere in there she might have even arched her back a little.

"That's your name. Your name. Your real name," Micah finally said. These had not come out as questions.

"Yeah, well, it's really Benita. Benita Madariaga. That's a little hard for the white people around here to say. Some friends call me Gaga, but I tell them Beni. I like Beni better."

"Nice."

"Vickie-my-manager, she won't get me a new name tag with just Beni. So I put this tape. She don't care."

"It's nice."

"I think Beni has more … *zest.* More than Benita. I've been reading this vocabulary book, you know, to try to elevate myself." She said it vo-kabbuh-larry. "I learned that one the other day: zest. Zesty."

Micah laughed, a little too long, until his eyes teared up. Which she noticed. Her threat posture returned to Somewhat Worried.

"I better get back there and elevate some food for you. I will make also some new coffee." She stopped at the swinging door that led back to the kitchen. "So what's your name again?"

"Micah Ford. Micah."

"OK. Cool."

Not possible. 'Beni.' What were the odds? He had never heard the word before he met Namaz. Benihana. Benny and the Jets. Those didn't count. Really, what were the odds? On a napkin he began to work out the astounding Boolean arithmetic of a certain Persian word being on a waitress' abbreviated name tag in northeastern Alabama on a Sunday night in August of 2005 --- and him being there to see it after having driven 400 miles, getting lost, running low on gas, and now being in this exact place. Of all the gin joints. But he stopped himself mid-algorithm: he put away his pen: he was acting too damn nutty again. *Get a grip, man.* Still, he hadn't thought once of *beni beni* since Namaz and Hank had been killed at the Trade Center, and that was now four weeks short of four years ago. He had had other thoughts, of course, grievous ones, lots of them, on and on and on, but not about *beni beni.* That had been theirs. Their open sesame. *Beni beni. To me, to me.* A small unbidden anger began rising in him, as if this random girl in this outlandish outland had somehow crossed onto his private gated property and was trespassing. But he was being absurd.

By the time she came back to the table, carrying a soup bowl and an oblong platter, the resentment had washed out of him. *It's not her fault*, he heard his father saying. *So what? Put a sock in it, son. Namaz and I, we're dead and gone. Buck up.* And he was right. Hank was right.

"So, we have tomato soup, meatloaf, succotash. This cornbread has bourbon butter. It's about all I could find back there. But today it was everything fresh made. We have Coca-Cola cake for dessert, if you want. Ruby makes it special."

"Looks great. Wow. Thanks a lot. I'm sorry to bother you. I'm sure it's a pain, keeping you late and all, you know, 'cause I just kinda jumped in the car this morning on an impulse and just sort of found myself here and then I got pretty lost and I was just now running out of gas." He was babbling, yes.

"I haven't eaten anything since breakfast. So this is great. Have a seat." This was a very un-Micah move. "If you want."

She brought two fresh coffees and sat across from him in the booth. She told him about moving up from Chiapas as a little kid, weeding onions and picking kale with her family, working seasonal at first. The struggle to get a green card without marrying one of the locals. Taking culinary-arts classes at Drake State up in Huntsville. Keeping her little Datsun 720 on the road. Playing online Scrabble. Working weekends at the diner and all the characters who came in, most of them real nice, but you also had, you know, plenty of your haters and your grabbers. Working days, for just above minimum, at UBC.

"UBC? What's that, a hospital?"

"You don't know the UBC? The Unclaimed Baggage Center. Really you don't know? Everybody who don't pick up their luggages at the airport, it comes here. From all over the country it is coming. The UBC, we are buying it from the airlines after, like, 90 days or something, I dunno the exact rules, and then we are selling the stuff. Sometimes I'm on Checkout or Cleaning Crew, but usually I work Sort. I go through the luggages and pick out the good stuff and we sell it. Employees get first pick. And we got our 20 percent discount."

"So let me get this straight: If I don't pick up my suitcase in San Francisco or Boston, the airline gets to sell it? My stuff comes here and gets sold? Here. In Scottsdale."

"Scotts*boro*," she said, fake-astonished.

"My underwear and my pants and my portable chess set, they come *here*. My socks. Somebody would actually buy my socks."

"Of course they will buy it," she said, and laughed. She felt like she was explaining gravity to a third-grader. "I'm telling you. People come from all over. From all the states they are coming here. And people will buy *anything*. Seriously. They bring trucks with them. People are spending their *vacations* here."

"The world of unclaimed baggage. The unclaimed underworld. Amazing."

He ate slowly and told her about staying down in Apalachicola at his grandfather Jimmy's house. Told her about Jimmy being a major league baseball player when he was young, about Jimmy's theories on oysters, steroids, relief pitchers and the airing-out of cars. About how he, Micah, didn't have a change of clothes or shampoo with him, not even a toothbrush. How he has been in "kind of a daze" since 9/11, losing his father, and his mother before that. It was all coming out in a rush. He didn't know how or why. He told her about the road trips in the BMW with his father when he was a kid and their rule about stopping at places with E-A-T signs. He told her he had "a college degree in computers." He didn't mention the call from the man from the fund or how big a deal he was in the math world or the millions he had made from his software ideas. He didn't mention Namaz, or how she had been from Iran, or how they were engaged and had big plans, or how she and Hank had died together on the sidewalk.

As he talked, he also stared. Not at Beni's breasts or her black eyes or her name tag. At nothing in particular, really. It was more a *sensation* of staring, a middle-distance stupor, of being so close to this woman, two feet away from her vigor and smile, of being aroused by her face and her innocent questions and her sweet plans for her future. And now he was getting his first natural erection in so so so long, right here, sitting on this red-vinyl Pontiac upholstery. Was he imagining all this? The motor court and the stank of the river and E-A-T? What were the odds? Was he going to wake up, covered in Florida-morning dew, hung over, on the floor of Jimmy's porch? What *was* this? How? He had pretty much given up on his endocrine system and all that.

"Blah, blah, blah," Micah said, finally interrupting himself, shifting in the booth, and she laughed. "Pretty banal stuff, I know."

"Banal? What's that? What's that mean? How you spell it?"

"Banal. B-a-n-a-l. Well, let's see, I guess it's an adjective that means, like, ordinary, ho-hum, boring."

"You're not boring. Are you being serious right now? As if. This whole *town* is what's banal. B-a-n-a-l. You got that right. I'm gonna remember that one --- banal. Use it on some of these guys coming in here acting so conceited and all. Saying nasty things to me. They are troglodytes."

"Wow, that's a good one," Micah said. "Troglodytes."

That one hadn't been in her vocabulary book. She had gone looking for that one. She searched in the big thesaurus down at the library, looking for something to use on the men who pestered her at the diner. *If you give me a massage does that make it a wetback-rub? How 'bout havin' a few poco cervezas with me, senorita? I got me cinco Bud Lights right out there in my truck. I'll show you my pistola and you can show me your green card.* Sometimes it felt like every gabacho asshole in Jackson County had brushed past her tits or palmed her ass. Embarrassing them with a nice big word seemed like the only way to really shut 'em up --- the only way short of a real pistola. They even seemed to like it when she smacked their hands away. Troglodytes. The elderly librarian, Miss Lacks, had suggested that one, and she told Beni how to pronounce it just right.

Now Beni was thinking about banal, running over the possible sentences in her mind, testing the sound of the word against its practical applications. Short, and no bullshit. She liked it.

"Give me another word. Just one, OK? Oh, man, I'd love to play you in Scrabble."

There was a lot of Namaz Nouri in Benita Madariaga. Her dark glow, an internal resolve, the eager and insistent (but careful) manner, a lot of churn and burn inside, needs and wants, a quickness, a woman convinced of her own enthusiasms. *Zest* --- that was the word all right.

And plainly, now that he noticed it, she was quite beautiful. This girl, Benita, que bonita, except she somehow didn't seem to know this about herself. Maybe she just didn't pay heed to it. The cornpone lust she fought off every day, she didn't let it diminish her by a single lumen. They had no idea what they had in their midst, these yayhoos. She defied the kind of grab-ass aggression that would make the anger flare or the shoulders slump in fancier, lesser women. The huckleberries tried to touch her, but they could not. Not in any important way. She would not act like they expected. That's what the elevated vocabulary was for.

No passive Zen posture for Beni, no downward dog or bound-angle poses. She belonged to herself. She cut her own hair and did her own nails and was always wearing clothes that she had Sorted out of other women's wayward American Touristers. She used their makeup, their facial masks, their body scrubs. Scrub as she might, though, she couldn't get the smell of the diner off her, the onions and the fatback, the pore-seep of the Fryolator. She sometimes thought people --- in her hair, through her clothes --- could sniff out the burgers and the Pan-Fry.

In truth, Benita Madariaga was nearly regal, even being so young, even in her Vic diner apron or the UBC smock. She was an apocalypta, a daughter of Jaguar Paw, coolly walking out of a rainforest under dripping leaves, beneath the smoking cone of a volcano, glistening, brown, beaded and pierced and feathered, deserving of worship, her DNA stranding her to fierce Toltec warrior-queens and the almond-eyed princesses of Chichén Itzá. She was a woman for whom you named tequilas, rivers, comets, zócalos. A people might build cenotaphs, cities or religions around her. Micah had been struck by heat lightning. Beni might have climbed directly down from the east wall of Rivera's murals in Detroit, a *campesina*, fertile and glowering, or the leader of a Shining Path women's brigade, a *campanera en armas*, a woman for Soledad Bravo to sing ballads about. She might have been a Miss Mazatlán, or Miss Ground Zero, or the Empress of Far-and-Away Zanzibar. Reverse the negative, and she's Lana Turner at Schwab's in that angora sweater. She should have orchids and waterfalls named after her. She deserved her own constellation, in your deepest space, the stars winking the outlines of her hips and secrets and biceps. A woman like this, you brought her frankincense and myrrh. This girl, Micah was thinking, this girl could stop a heart. Or restart one.

"How about, how about intrepid?" Micah said.

"What's that? It *sounds* good."

"You seem really determined to me, Beni." *There, he'd said it. Said it out loud. That word. Beni. It was out there, in his own voice. The word that dared not be spoken. Embargo lifted.* "I bet you tough things out. You stick. You don't whine or complain much, am I right? You're not afraid. Something breaks, you fix it. You're a fixer, right? So you're *intrepid*. It means bold. Persistent."

"Hey, that's so *nice* of you. Not to sound conceited and all, but yeah, that's sometimes how I am thinking I am. Intrepid. Yeah. *Cool.*" She printed the word on the back of Micah's algorithm napkin. "Like this?"

"Exactly."

"OK, the check is on me. For the vocabulary lessons. If you came in every day I would be a full genius in no time. I would not be so … banal." She slid out of the booth and collected his dishes.

"Hey, listen, is there a bar or a liquor store in town?" Micah said. "After all this coffee I might need a gin-and-tonic to put me to sleep."

"It's Sunday night. Everything must be closed."

"Oh, right, Sunday, of course. I knew that. Damn. Well, anyway, thanks a lot for the food. But hey, I'm leaving you a tip at least." He folded a five over a hundred, which she didn't notice, and he slid it under his mug. "I'm sorry I ruined your night. You could have been home watching 'American Idol' or something."

"That's OK. It was fun. I am happy to know intrepid." She walked him to the door, said good night, and double-locked herself in.

Crossing the two-lane back to the motel, Micah remembered the flask that his father had always kept in the glove compartment. It was still there, and full. Been in there four years now. He took a sniff, a sip, then a long pull. Bourbon, of course, the good stuff, it being Hank. He sat in one of the folding chairs next to the fallen Coke machine, beside a shank of broken-off diving board. He drank slowly, but steadily. A big J.B. Hunt trailer churned past, gearing down, looking for cops, then another big one, a Red Ball reefer, then a converted-Greyhound tour bus hauling Skeeter Bob and his Country Pals. The smell of diesel in the muggy night.

A bug-zapper fizzed and popped above the screen door of the motel office.

From across the road he saw the lights go off inside the diner, although Beni left the E-A-T sign on. He watched her get into her little pickup and pull away. The mosquitoes had begun to zero in on him, so he glug-glugged the rest of the bourbon and went inside. He was fizzing and popping a little himself.

• • • •

A soft knock like that, it shouldn't have roused him. But ever since That Day he had become twitchier, quicker to startle, a fitful sleeper. He opened the door, and there was Beni. She had a plum-colored Coach-brand Maggie bag slung over one shoulder. There was an Ultra-Massive Totally-Super-Huge Big Gulp cup in her right hand, and a plastic Boy Scout canteen in her left.

"Wow," she said, no exclamation point, looking at him there in the doorway. "Joe Boxers. Nice ensemble."

"Was that in your vocab book --- ensemble?" he croaked, and it came out meaner than he intended. She let it go.

"Nope. I learned that one at the UBC. Everybody in retail knows certain words."

"What time is it? Is it morning already?" He was sleep-squinting at her. The bug-zapper zapped.

"It's only 11:30. At night," she said. "Sorry if I waked you up. But I went home and got you some shampoo and toothpaste and stuff. You said you didn't bring nothing with you. I figured this was your room. That's your car, right?"

"Yes."

"So, look, I brought tonic." She raised the Big Gulp. "And I got some gin." Up went the canteen.

"After I left the diner," Micah said, "I found some of my dad's whiskey in the car and I think I killed it in about 7 minutes. So I'm about a hundred drinks ahead of you."

He hadn't meant it as an invitation, or maybe he had, but that's how she took it. She slid past him, into the room. He thought he smelled Ivory soap on her, with top notes of cocoa butter and hints of the Fryolator and the Sunday meatloaf. She had on blue digital-camouflage gym shorts, a white T-shirt that said "Hard Rock Tulum," and a pair of Crocs --- one green, one yellow. Quite the ensemble herself. Her hair was French-braided in back and fastened with a clip. She had gone to *some* trouble, but not much.

She pulled a small vinyl pouch from the Coach bag and put it on the dresser. It was navy-blue and said "Delta Airlines."

Two Styrofoam cups also emerged from the big tote, along with a Ziploc bag of ice cubes. There was a lime-green container of lime juice that was shaped like a lime. And a Scrabble game.

"Let's play," Beni said. "Come on. Just one game. Is it OK?"

"This is great of you, but I'm really. I'm pretty much totally half-shit-faced."

"Oh, I'm sorry. No, I can go. *Mierda*, you have a girlfriend or something. Or a wife. God. I never even thought. You just seemed alone-like. Oh shit. My bad. I'm really sorry. I am going."

She grabbed her bag, but he said no, wait, no, there was no wife or anything at all like that, and one game of Scrabble would be cool, and they could have a gin-and-tonic.

"It can just be a gin-and-platonic," she said.

"Hey, that's pretty good," Micah said. "I'm gonna use that one. Where did you hear that?"

"Nowhere. I was thinking up something to say to you. Something not *banal.* Platonic --- that was in my book."

Sitting cross-legged opposite each other on the sparking bedspread, they played Scrabble. They drank. Micah pulled on his shirt but stayed in his boxers, they drank more, they talked vaguely and boozily. She told him about not having a boyfriend in a long time and being a strong Catholic and wanting to become a chef in a hotel some day. It didn't seem impossible-dreamy or delusional, her plans and striving, her self-improvement. She didn't sound like the hooker or the cabbie or the reporter: *I'm not gonna be doing this forever, you know. This is just a temporary thing, man. I'm in transition. I've got me an exit strategy.* They drank more. The score was close. She knew the game and how to manage her tiles. At one point Micah had the word "syzygy" ready to put down for a triple word score and 159 points --- pretty much game over. But he didn't play it.

The gin was nearly gone by the time he played the word "inane."

"Challenge!" Beni squealed. "You left out the s. You are peen, penal, penalized!"

"And you, you're insane!"

Both of them were fully drunk now, and laughing for real. Micah was barely able to sit up, but somehow he knew enough --- his heart was still good enough --- not to correct her about inane.

"You win. Shit. I'm totally totaled," he said suddenly and a little seriously. His switch had flipped: He was binary-drunk. On/not-on. "Sorry. I gotta turn in."

And with that he was between the sheets, facing away from her, hugging one of the pillows to his chest and fading fast.

Beni packed up the game, took a packet of BC powder from her bag and mixed it with the last of the tonic. She turned up the A/C unit, turned off the lights and got down to her undies. She felt warm, flushed-warm, jungle-warm, and it was only partly from the gin. She crawled in next to Micah, spoon-hugging him from behind. Pillow-Micah-Beni, west to east, left to right, in that order, Moon-Sun-Earth. They were in syzygy.

"Good night, Micah Ford." A whisper.

"Beni beni," he said, sleep-sobbing.

"Yes, Beni Beni. It'll be OK. I've got you. *Pobrecito.*"

She kissed his neck, and then they were both asleep.

• • • •

Kaboom. Blood braying in the ears. Mystery bruises. The Alabammy heat was banging at the drawn vinyl drapes. Was it 6 in the morning or 4 in the afternoon? The goddamned trucks roaring outside. A mouthful of vomit. No, not vomit. Dead air, but plenty foul. He was a snail on a hot sidewalk being covered with salt. He was getting what he deserved. The revenge of the juniper. Gin on whiskey, mighty risky.

No Beni. No note. The Delta toiletries bag was on the dresser. Pantene, toothbrush, Scope, a plastic razor and tiny tubes of toothpaste and shave cream. He cupped his hands at the sink and drank as much as he could. The water smelled of Tareytons. He showered and shaved, but while brushing his teeth he came to realize that he had shaved with the toothpaste. He went vigorously at the Scope.

Outside, it felt high-noonish. On the hood of the Beemer was a tidy row of Scrabble tiles: XO BENI. If men swooned, he would have. He scooped up the tiles, then walked to the motel office to return the room key. There was no sign of Lorraine. It was Dewey behind the counter. He had an Old Gold going. Micah asked him for an envelope.

"OK, but that'll be forty cent," Dewey said.

"You're kidding," Micah said, and he wondered if this was some lame bit of extortion for Beni's overnighter. They must have seen her pickup in front of his room.

"Sorry," said the Dew-Man, "but you know how it is, times being what they is and all." He shifted his weight on his cane, winced, and gave out a small whimper. He had done this, of course, many times before.

Micah offered up his American Express Depleted Uranium card, which weighed about as much as the Dale Junior ceramic ashtray that Lorraine kept on the front desk. Seeing the card, Dewey went all dewy, all sunflower-honey-on-warm-grits, and said aww shucks forget it, that's OK, son, have a nice day, dravv safe, God bless you and God bless Amurrca. (The Amex handling charge, as Dewey well knew, would have cost him about 10 times the measly forty cent.)

Micah printed BENITA on the front of the envelope. He thought about adding a note about Southern comfort or something. Instead he wrote his name, phone number and the word INTREPID, in caps, on the inside of the flap. He put the Scrabble tiles inside but pocketed the B and the X. The envelope was one of those international ones, flimsy-thin, with an airplane silhouette and "Par Avion" on the front.

There was no glue on the flap for licking and sealing, so Micah got Hank's emergency kit out of the trunk and sealed the envelope with two flesh-colored Band-Aids. He crossed the road to the diner, which was starting to get busy for the Monday lunch special: hamburg steak, stewed okra, sweet corn. He asked a woman pouring coffee behind the counter if Benita was around.

"Beni? Nope, sorry, hon. She's off today. You might could catch her down to the UBC."

"I'm kinda on the run. I mean, you know, on the go. Could I leave this envelope for her?"

"Sure, darlin', just leave it by the register. I'll make sure she gets it. I'm kinda on the run myownself right now."

Micah stopped at the register and watched an orange-red-purple weather map on the TV. The sound was off, but a conga line of twitchy pixels was spinning ominously across the blue-blue Gulf, heading toward the green coastline. The time-lapse animation showed the storm's likely landfall with a pulsing line of yellow, cartoony time-bombs that exploded all along the panhandle.

At the door Micah found a tool-belted man fiddling with the E-A-T sign in the front window. "What's up?" Micah said. "Problem with the neon?"

"Nah. It's almost never the neon with these things. Good old neon. But the dang A keeps going out. Lookit here." The man touched a naked wire with his screwdriver and sure enough, the A went dark.

"Some fool --- *and I ain't sayin' who!* --- wired the E and the T in parallel, but they done put the A on a separate circuit. Makes *no* kinda damn sense."

"Should be an easy fix, though, right?"

"Oh yeah. Simple job. Best thing is, I'm gettin' me a lunch steak out of it."

"Fuckin' A," Micah said.

In the parking lot, ready to gas up and head back to Florida, he felt not quite up to seeing Beni again, at the UBC. He wasn't sure why. Anyway, he probably needed to get back to help Jimmy with any hatches that needed battening.

He hung a U-turn for a last look at the diner, with the sign winking and blinking from EAT to ET --- imperative present to hillbilly past.

E-A-T. Not much as a Scrabble word on its own, but three good tiles to have at the ready in your rack. Meat, treason, heat, defeat, betray. Necessary for retreat, necessary for weather, and right there at the very center of death.

PART II

6. A TENDER GRAVITY

He was halfway up the wall now, 200 feet above the river, really an exceptional day for climbing, good sun and a cool breeze, although for the last 20 minutes he had been unable to move.

Micah was stuck, for lack of a better word, spread-eagled on the granite wall with his feet splayed out and his arms raised overhead, as if he was surrendering during a bank heist. There was a good 2-inch nipple of rock for the ball of his left foot, a smear of frictiony granite for his right shoe, and two shallow holds overhead for his hands.

The wall overhung the great gouge of the Connecticut River, a few miles west of Dartmouth College. Just a mile upstream were the storied Reichenbach Falls, and the spray often drifted down the valley and bumped into the wall, licking it like a cat's paw and making for some slick and tricky passages for a climber. But the wind today was sending the mist upriver, away from the wall, so the rock was unusually dry and speedy.

Micah had angry scrapes on both wrists, no worries about those, and besides, that was part of the bargain you always struck with granite. But he had dinged his left eyebrow and banged the knuckle of his left ring finger while making a jump to his current (and most unfortunate) position on the rockface. The swollen knuckle was the size and complexion of a cherry tomato. Also, his right pinkie was fully cramped now --- another finger out of operation. And the lactic acid pooling in his forearms would keep him from pulling himself up the wall with his fingers.

Micah had been in similar predicaments before, immobilized on some expanse of rock with no apparent way to move up, down or sideways. (He had even fallen once, and badly, a 30-foot drop from Pol Pot in the Verdon Gorge in France. It had taken 23 stitches to close up the gash on his right thigh, an injury that was rock language for "get the fuck off me.") Usually, though, in a difficult spot, with a few minutes of patient probing he would feel out a small crack or crevice in a wall, something even as slight and shallow as cuneiform --- and he'd have his escape hatch. Or he'd drag a toe and find a scratchy patch of stubble, good enough for a new foothold. In rock language: "You're welcome."

But not today. Not so far.

The lower sections at the base of the Reichenbach wall were anything but difficult. The kids from the Dartmouth Outdoors Club used them for training --- especially the gentle bottom pieces called AmLit 101, Office Hours and Event Horizon. Those first 30 feet of the wall above the river were studded with plenty of bolts and anchors for heavily roped beginners to clip onto.

Micah had sprinted through these lower portions earlier in the day. He bridged easily across Frying Pan, Special Treatment and Yellowstain Blues. He figured to make the summit in another 90 minutes, then he'd jog down the Forest Service road to his car at the trailhead. He'd be back in Hanover for afternoon cocktails.

The hard sections of the wall were higher up. It was pure face climbing above 150 feet, and it could be especially tricky for the free solo guys like Micah who didn't use ropes, pitons, partners or cellphones. You fall, you die. That was the entire syllogism of their type of climbing. If x, then y. Plenty of wall rats thought this was reckless, bordering on suicidal. Bad karma, they'd say. Disrespectful of the rock, they'd say. "Sport climbing" is neither, they'd say.

Micah thought just the opposite. He had seen weak climbers with meager experience now taking on some of the hardest technical routes in the world. If you had high-end equipment and enough time, hell, you could climb anything. Newbies were going up Crack House and Intifada at Moab. Wings of Steel and Dawn Wall at El Cap, same thing. The climbers moved like parrots --- beak, claw, beak, claw --- and if they got tired they just overnighted in a portaledge. Total rookies were going up Jimmy Cliff, Al Buraq, Union Jack, Ya Kus, Social Outcast, The Taint. On the topos now, these routes looked like bolt ladders. You fall, you don't die. You dangle.

At a bumpy traverse today called Knuckle Sandwich, about 170 feet above the river, Micah had pushed himself out and away from the rockface, swinging perpendicular to the wall, balancing on one foot and using a single handhold overhead. A barn door, that was the climbing term. He even let out a whoop, which was not like him. After that, onward and upward, he had no trouble with the overhangs of Caerus, Harelip, Kuss Ummak, Cyranose, Make It So and Jacob's Ladder. Likewise, no issues with the adjoining switchbacks called Tenth Avenue and Freeze Out.

Final Problem was a difficult chimney a hundred feet below the summit, but he climbed through it easily. He was feeling strong and confident --- he was having what he called a low-gravity day --- and the weather was holding. After exiting Final Problem he always took the same route to the top ---- a left turn into a series of short, connected, well-traveled stretches called Route Irish, All the Way, Moriarty and Baker Street. This time, however, he had jumped to his right to reach a small bulge in the wall. This downward sidelong sproing had put him momentarily airborne along the rockface. After landing the jump, despite the head-bang landing that cut open his brow, he assumed there would be foot cracks and handholds farther along. That's what big granite always gave you --- just enough.

Not this time. In this vertical stance he couldn't lean back more than a few degrees. He was on the wall, but only just, attached as much to the air as to the rock. A fly on a windshield. He had seen no other climbers working any of the regular routes today, so help would not be on the way. Frying Pan had led to fire, and there seemed to be no solving for X. A pair of peregrine falcons buzzed him, flaring downward along the wall. They came like swallows from the bright center of heaven.

Micah traveled his hands over the rockface as best he could, first one hand reaching, then the other, hedging his adhesiveness, making a close reading of the wall, a Braille-ing of the rock. Insight and blindness both, exploring the insistent planarity of the wall. Every square inch was equally important. This sideways jump had been a bad move, a real fuckin' spastic Spassky. Check, and mate, in four. Still, he wasn't panicked. Not yet. So far, he was calm as marble. But he knew, sure he knew, he knew he was in trouble.

This was going to be, Micah figured, a fair enough way to die, even if he was only 37. In a sense this was merely the playing-out of the actuarial math: Any reasonable algorithm would have predicted he'd be killed during a free solo climb. He had never thought much about how he'd die, or when, or where. Truth was, after losing his parents and Namaz so early, and then after Jimmy died, and then after he learned about Beni's murder, most of the fight had gone out of him.

• • • •

Micah hadn't beaten the storm to Apalachicola that Monday, the day after he first met Beni in the diner. Hurricane Katrina began slamming the coast around daybreak, and by the time Micah got away from Scottsboro, many of the highways in Panhandle Florida and southern Alabama were closed. He had to county-road it most of the way back home.

The whole geography of the Gulf coast was going horizontal. Trees, stores and houses uprooted. He saw the roof blow off the Nehi plant in Opelika. The livestock pavilion collapsed at the Chilton County fair. Double-wides spun on their slabs like pinwheels. Travel trailers traveled. Septic tanks bobbed up out of the ground. So did coffins.

Katherine kept shouting into the phone when Micah reached her on Jimmy's land line: "The whole county be in a shout --- everybody but your grandfather --- *that man* --- Lord have mercy --- all this hellzapoppin and he still be sleepin'." This was Monday just before noon, when the storm was flat-out and full-on. "Everything all turnt around here. Worst part still comin' --- that's what the TV says. You watch out now, sugar. Whatever's south now gonna be goin' north."

Boats were going to be flung a hundred miles. Cars, too. Culverts and bridges were already disappearing under the floodwaters. People, too. The out-tide was flinging up wonders: rivers, beercans, mussels, bicycles, bloodstreams.

Early afternoon and Micah was still sidewinding his way through Alabama. Missile Gap, Threestep, Robertlee, Monroeville, Slapout, Frog Eye, Scratch Ankle. He stopped at one point to help some men clear off Hobdy's Bridge. The Pea River wasn't exactly minding its manners, and the bridge was blocked by a backwashed half-acre of foul green mud, dead shellcrackers, and the usual sort of sad debris that comes with big blows --- small trees, a roll of chicken wire, an old Fedders window unit, a busted-up chifferobe, many sheets of corrugated roofing, two drowned dogs, a peach-colored toilet, and a plastic Roll Tide ice chest. Micah kicked at the cooler to get it off the bridge but the thing had some weight to it. Holes had been gouged into the clamshell top and it was all bound up with duct tape. Inside was a baby. Almost a newborn, looked like, as small as she was, wearing a diaper soggy with seawater. There was a note baby-pinned to her shirt, but the ink had bled off the page.

He tried to get the local men to take the baby, but they saw the child and scattered like minnows. Micah looked in the trunk of the BMW for a blanket or a towel, but all he had was his mother's old nurse's uniform, folded up and still in its dry-cleaner's plastic. He got the baby out of her wet diaper and swaddled her in the uniform.

Two hours later, down a drowning and storm-littered Highway 130, a sheriff at a checkpoint turned him back. There was no reaching Apalach just now. "You gotta find a new way home," said the officer. "This way won't get you there no more."

The officer placed the child in the front seat of his cruiser. Through it all, through the river-heave and river-wrack, even wearing a wet diaper inside the bobbing Bama bassinet, the child had not cried once. The sheriff asked Micah a few questions, made some notes, then handed him his card, in case he wanted to follow up later about the child. "Cpl. John W. Skinner," the card said. "Protect and Serve. Geneva County, Alabama."

He slept in the BMW that night, that stormy Monday night. Pulled into a rest area in Tate's Hell while the bridge from Eastpoint to Apalachicola was being checked for damage. It was noon the next day before the state police began letting people go across. He drove slowly into town past Voncy's bar --- mud clear up to the windows, nobody around. At her mother's house on Bay Avenue, the doors were wide open, and the cupola and the wraparound porch were gone. Rhonat's Barber Shop, gone, swirly pole and all. Robin's Drug Store, mostly gone, caved in on itself. The streets were quiet, sandy-muddy, clotted with leaves, oyster shells, roof shingles and dead fish. No power in the downtown. At the port, only one dock remained out of the original sixteen, and not a vessel in sight. Two of the boats normally berthed there, a 32-foot Grady White and a center-console Bayliner, had come to rest in front of Jimmy's house on 12th Street, both boats intact and upright and neat as you please. The blacktop hissed and steamed.

The house appeared untouched, at least from the front. A baby nurse shark was thrashing around, frenzied and stranded, in the flooded drainage ditch by the street. Micah walked up the driveway toward the guest house, which looked OK, too. The Raleigh was still there, just as he had left it, leaning against the garage. A phone kept ringing in a house down the street. Then he saw the huge fig tree laying over on its side in the backyard. The storm had wrenched it from its moorings and nudged it over, as easily as a person might push through a turnstile at a ballpark. The tree's heavy upper half had crashed through the roof of the main house, demolishing the attic and taking out the second floor. The whole back half of the house was now pretty much gone. Late coffee and oranges in a sunny chair --- never again.

For all this violence, the backyard was especially quiet just now, peaceful even, and the sky was a deep calm cobalt. Dead weather, humid-warm, and just the smallest breeze. The day was like wide water.

Micah called loudly for Katherine and Jimmy as he climbed into the wreckage of the house. No reply. No one. He clambered through three rooms of wet books, smashed furniture and splintered tree limbs. His grandfather's room was now just tree and sky and broken glass. A room without a roof. The room no longer felt like a room at all; it was part of the outside; everything was changed around; the outside had come inside.

A Mason jar of spare change was smashed on the floor, the coins all scattered.

The great main trunk occupied the room almost entirely, and it had just missed scoring a direct hit on Jimmy's bed. But a small secondary branch, stiff and solid, but only as big around as a ballpark souvenir on Bat Day, it was this branch had caught the old man through his right side.

Micah understood things were exactly what they were. It seemed more than he could bear. His grandfather was wearing his blue seersucker pajamas, and that wouldn't be all that Micah would remember. He lay in bed with the old man, holding him and crying and kissing his salty-dirty face, when a police car and the mortuary van pulled up.

• • • •

Shadows were falling, he'd been there all day. Not dark yet, but it was heading that way. His calves were in fair shape, and so were his shoulders, but the lactic acid was surging now and his forearms were cramping. He kept feeling for an opening in the granite, but the slab still felt smooth and featureless. The obvious was becoming more obvious.

Obvious. His decision to join the military had seemed obvious, too, a plausible path through the gloom of his being alone in the world. The aftermath of Katrina had been its own kind of rockface. The military would perhaps provide an escape route. Get him off the X.

For several years after Jimmy's death and after he had completed his celebrated thesis, Micah did contract work as a civilian for various spy agencies. He was the sole architect of the data-mining system Topcat, and he designed Cain Enable, which blacked out North Korea with a vengeance after somebody in Pyongyang had hacked into Sony. He worked on the Blarney Team at NSA, plus Bullrun, Stateroom, Finkspy, Thieving Magpie and the whole Stuxnet family of weevils. He had

SuperUser clearance at every intel branch and spy shop in the government. He had what they called the God View.

The Pentagon kept trying to hire him, too, and an old friend of his father's, a three-star general in Cyber Command, eventually persuaded him to join up as a uniformed soldier. Micah partly bought into the idea of the Army being a kind of replacement family, and he felt a little bit like he was following his father's path. They made him a chief warrant officer straightaway, but he had insisted on first going through Basic Training. His dad would have liked that idea, and Micah wanted the uniform to feel right to him when he put it on. So, late in the autumn of 2012, at the improbable age of 37, Micah Ford became just another Army grunt, grunting his way through Basic at Fort Jackson.

They had crypto projects lined up and waiting for him, and the Army would soon be loaning him out for cyberwarfare projects at CIA.

But then came this latest mission, headed by an Army colonel in harness with CIA and some other spooky, acronym'd agencies. Micah knew more than a little about secrecy protocols, but this new op carried an added tincture of paranoia. And so far it had had nothing to do with ones and zeroes, his specialties. Instead, they were tasking him with renewing his fluency in Arabic, specifically Iraqi Arabic, with classes and tutors at Dartmouth and Bennington. It was good temporary duty and he got the chance to do some serious climbing again. He had recently begun dreaming in Arabic, always a good sign. The lessons were embedding.

Even so, here he was, stuck on this granite wall, about to die.

Would he slide off the rock and scream as he fell? Would he be frightened? Maybe relieved? He tried to imagine the panic he expected. He was at the still point in a turning world, as if he was alone on the planet. Would his concentration lapse and he'd slip off by accident? Should he push off from the wall and make it more of a choice? He hoped he wouldn't cry out as he fell.

Fear had not yet settled onto him. Not fully. He had had an unnamable conversation with himself at these still points on other climbs: "You must go on. I can't go on. I'll go on." This to-and-fro was underwritten by doubt, not fear. He had once heard a veteran climber talking about making a risky move on a dangerous section of rock, like the decision a hang glider faces at the very edge of a cliff. Go, no go. At such moments, the man said, he heard three distinct voices in his head --- Yes, Fear and No. The tough part was distinguishing between Fear and No, because they're both telling you the same thing. "No" is that sixth sense that's trying to save your life.

A god of rescue is really what was needed. That's what Micah was somehow counting on, as in "Dear Jesus, do something." His mom's priest had talked a lot about that version of God, a kind of ad hoc deity who came to you when He was needed, to rescue, to confront, punish, pardon, comfort, redeem. This was not exactly Big Church doctrine, but the notion had given some relief to his mom. "Your God will come for you, Elizabeth," the priest had said, cutting some corners on Isaiah 35. "He will come to succor you. He will rescue you, and He will save you."

"He'll save you, Dimey," his mother was saying to her son now, her voice coming from inside the granite, from the other side of things. Dimey was what she had called him when he was little. "Bright and shiny as a brand new dime." It was her, her voice, warm and low and unmistakable to him now, issuing from some chamber deep in the rock. "God is here for you. He gives justice to the fatherless. He rescues the needy. I'm with you, Dimey, my shining boy. We've got you now."

Micah began to cry and he pressed the side of his face against the cool rock. Cleft for me. He wasn't sure if he was hallucinating or not. *"We've got you now?"* This was the fatigue talking now, that must be it. He had been stuck on the wall for nearly seven hours and he was far gone in weariness, in oblivion, and all this had set the twilight reeling. I just can't face myself alone again --- this was another thought that kept coming to him.

"Mom, mom, mom," was what Micah was saying now, calling down into the granite.

They had gone climbing together just once, Hank and Micah, an ascent of Mount Kilimanjaro in September of 2000. Hank and four execs from General Dynamics had signed a sweet little deal with the Tanzanian Ministry of Defense --- a radar installation and some Kiowa helicopters --- and Micah took a week off to join Hank and his colleagues afterward for the expedition. They hired an experienced outfitter in Dar and were met at their mustering point in Arusha by 50 porters and a dozen Land-Rovers. "We chased Saddam out of Kuwait with less gear than this," said one of the men from Dynamics.

Going up Kilimanjaro did not exactly qualify as an "ascent." It was more like a damned hard walk. There was no technical climbing, no roping or belaying. Still, the summit was 19,000 feet and change, so it was good that the men had done a little cardio training beforehand. Not a bad idea to have rinsed some of the Bombay and béarnaise out of those bloodstreams.

They went poli-poli at first, slowly-slowly, up through the initial zones of forest and heather. Lovely trekking. Then at 10,000 feet the breathing became more labored. They overnighted at 15. The older men complained of headaches, no surprise in that, and the expedition medic checked their vitals and handed out aspirin. They set out well before dawn to make Stella Point by sun-up, after which they'd press on to the summit at the rim of the old volcano. They walked slowly and quietly in the dark, their headlamps bobbing along the trail. Micah was in the lead.

Just below the crater, when they stopped to take pictures, the older men appeared blank-eyed, unsmiling, wrung out. A wooden sign pointed to the final stretch to Uhuru Peak. "Twenty minutes more," said their guide.

Micah was eager to go, and he was feeling good, but his father and the others were struggling. Hank was 55, and the other men were at least another decade older. They couldn't seem to gulp down enough oxygen. It was like drowning in mid-air. "I'm taking three deep breaths for every step," wheezed one of the men. It was simply proving too much for them. No shame in that, and although they hated the idea of not summiting, the threshold of the crater was its own kind of summit. They decided they'd wait for Micah to reach the top, then they'd all go back down together.

Micah pulled his father aside, held both his hands, and brought their faces close together.

"We're going up, Dad, you and me," he whispered. "That's the deal. The other men can stay, that's fine, that's on them. But we are. going. up." His tone was serious and challenging, no pleading, no rah-rah. This was a man talking now. The things he was saying were short, sharp and full-stopped, like lines from a telegram. He had never spoken to his father this way. Maybe no one ever had. But this face-off, this moment, this was what Hank had raised Micah for. This was Micah going all in. The whole pot. The real payoff.

"We can do it, Dad. Poli-poli, that's fine. Slow is fine. But we're going. You're gonna dig down and do it. Eat some peanut butter and get some water. Then we go. You set the pace. You take the point."

They were doubled over, gasping, both of them, and crying and smiling like idiots, when they reached the summit.

"I wish Mom could see us now," Micah said.

"She can see us," Hank said. He put his forehead on his son's chest. "She's right here."

• • • •

On these days of brightness, why should the dead intrude?

Micah was still stuck on the rock, but he also was rappelling down Burton Tower with Namaz on one of their first dates. Now he was a kid again, burning off the poison sumac behind the Leelanau cabin, and it was getting into his eyes and throat. He was on the erg at Argo Boathouse, on a 2 a.m. sprint for burritos, splayed on the front lawn of the DG house. Cheering Namaz in the 400 IM, away, against Yale. Playing chess with RastaMan outside the Coop in Harvard Square. The letter from NASA Space Flight Center had said he was an official astronaut trainee, even though he was only 9 years old. He had won a Westinghouse prize for making a remote-controlled telescope --- used the new garage-door opener and a junked Garrard turntable for that one. He was seeing that his father's flight suit was soaked and dark, stained around the seat as if he had shit himself but no, it was sopping with blood from getting shot. A VC bullet went through the belly of the chopper and nicked Captain Ford in the groin. Just missed the old block and tackle, was a line Hank often used when telling that story. Blood and more blood. Sammy and Frances, Hank's parents, there they were, up on the granite wall with Micah now and trapped in the wreckage under that semi on I-94, outside Ypsi, Sammy's new convertible flattened by the huge truck loaded with frozen chicken parts. Their Jack Russell terriers, Good Friday and Jackpot, the little guys were dead in there, too. The things you remember. The way you unspool, with each blind lurch of the world. In his mind, a whitetail ran past him. Micah was walking among the tombstones at Arlington again, with Spot Poles and the rest. Cold mud in his mouth. Now he was being pushed around by the tidal ebb of the bay, mid-swim, a mile offshore, more like floating face down, riding the swells, and the solution to the P vs. NP problem had just come to him, loomed up to him out of the dark throat of the water, the proof so sudden and clear. In the deep limbus of the water, a moderate chop, breathing slowly, swimming in numbers was how he saw himself out there, and the turbulence had cracked the code for him. A regular prince of tides. His thinking until then about P/NP had been so uptight. One of the great remaining problems in mathematics --- resolved through churn, swirl and swell. This brought him the Fields Medal, the Abel Prize, a MacArthur, a Wolf, a Wozniak. Salacia had spoken to him: *This is water, Micah.* After that swim, he woke up on an empty beach, face down in the cold sand, and it was beginning to rain out of a violet sky. The tide was way out. Where is the mother who buttoned his coat? The smell of the hospital, his Mom's room, ick, that bleach-and-sickness smell. She was in bed under her plastic tent. And they wouldn't let him touch her. They could only touch fingers through the plastic, and it reminded Micah of how they had folded sheets together in the backyard at Grosse Pointe, walking their pieces toward each other, his corners meeting hers. "GRID, they call it, it's that new cancer," some nurse had said, almost out of earshot. He wasn't sure what cancer was. Mom had looked so tiny in that plastic house. Can't you smell that smell? "When your mother dies, that's you," he heard a nurse say to a doctor. Now the certified check was arriving at Jimmy's house via FedEx, only it was a much bigger check than Elon and Peter had said --- $44 million, made out to Micah Bloodworth Ford. So much money. He felt like an orphan. Things got broken. Things got lost. Now he's 15, an Eagle Scout jumping into the river at Philmont, saving a scared little Webelos who was about to drown. More water. Voncille came to Micah on the wall, her voice whispering from inside the granite. He had visited her in the Ruby McCollum wing of the State Hospital after Big Pink burned down, after all her paintings were destroyed and the insurance refused to pay, and the BP spill ruined the Spoonbill, the town and the oystering once and for all. "Here's the bullet point: I've gone fuckin' haywire," she told Micah. She said this quietly when he visited, and she seemed sad about it, like she knew there was no way back. No way off her own rockface. Long is the way, and hard. Voncy's mother was in there with her, too. She beat the cancer but couldn't dodge the crazy. The nervous hospital is what the Sangaree women called it, and they often laughed together very loudly now, whooping like contestants on a game show. "I make schizophrenia look fuckin' *good*," Voncy said over and over and over. "I'm as nimble as a forest creature," said her crazy spindly mother. They both smoked all the time now, too, one Merit filter after the other, end to end. Micah paid for their nursing. Then two weeks after Basic Training he's sitting in Room 2E687 at the Pentagon. Now Micah is hanging off the St. George Light buoy in Apalachicola Bay, chest heaving, and this is the first time he has reached the buoy. Don't worry about the swim back: That old saying of his dad's came to him now on the rock, and it never had very much to do with swimming. Micah had said it once to Beni, making like it was something he had come up with himself, and she wrote it into her school notebook, but then, Jesus, when Micah called her at the Unclaimed Baggage Center --- this was a month after Jimmy died --- the manager told him the cops had found Benita a week earlier, dead in the woods at King Caldwell Park, under a stand of cedar and persimmon trees. They called in two local men who confessed right off. Names of Forrest and Sherwood.

No, no, the second one was *Sherman*. That's what it was, Sherman. Sounded like they was happy to admit to what they done, the manager said. Beni had disrespected them when they was in the diner. Called them "banal." Not sure what that means exactly, but it don't sound so bad to me. Surely nothin' to get killt over. They waited a few days afore they grabbed her up out of her trailer. They must've had to go look up what banal meant. Got us some beers and showed that señorita a right good time, is what they said to the po-lice. All this was in the newspaper, word for word. Them old boys took her all kindsa whichaways, and them talkin' about it all open-like, like it was nothin', nothin' wrong with it at all. This world. "Played us a quick nine holes," Forrest had told the cops. They cut open her navel and raped here there, too. And them *laughin'* about it on the interrogation tapes that was played on Channel 8. Can you imagine? What kind of raising-up could those boys have had? Lord Lord. The coroner's autopsy would show that the killers had torn a page from the little pocket dictionary that Beni always carried with her. Page 19, Baleful to Barbed, and they had worked it up into her bottom. There was DNA everywhere. Beni was a good girl, the UBC manager said. Them boys, they need 'em a come-to-Jesus session with Yellow Mama, the 'lectric chair. FBI callin' it a hate crime. I guess *so*. Chicken farmers from Sand Mountain, both of them boys, I believe is what the paper said. When they was done with her, I forget which one, one of them boys, he defecated onto her vagina. Sacred harp of Jesus! Told the detectives he give her a "Alabama hot pocket." Lordamercy. This world. Rape and murder, just a shout away, just a word away. Beni's killing, that erased everything for Micah. Erased everything that was left. He was alive, but it was a strange sort of alive.

• • • •

He shut his eyes. It was nearly dark, and it was time. The overdose was in the bloodstream. His hands were cold. The voices had receded. He just leaned backward, a scuba diver going over a gunwale into the water. A man on a castaway raft slipping quietly overboard, no life jacket, just waiting now for the lungs to quit or the sharks to come. There goes gravity. He gave no shout or cry as he separated from the rock. Maybe there was a brief fillip of fear, down in the gristle. Heart racing. He didn't want to die. There was a brief silence, like an indrawn breath. Then something bent down and took hold of him and shook him like the end of the world. A crackling blue light, a great jolt, and he felt as if his bones would break. As if the sap would fly out of him like a split plant. He wondered what terrible thing he had done.

The rocky gorge was down there waiting for him.

He stepped free from the cold magnetism of the wall but instead of an immediate north-south plummet he was somehow pushed directly away from the rockface, swept out into the ocean of air that was the river valley, pushed out far enough to clear the talus slope at the base of the wall and the trees on the riverbank. It must have been 200 feet that he was flung sideways. But flung by what? A chance column of air? A jet of air, a chute, a wave? Was it meteorology, or theology? A great wind carried him across the sky. The tender gravity beneath a kite. The unseen hand of a Rescuing God. A full-force gale, lifting a dweller off the threshold.

Micah was unaware as he was hurtling downward that he was also traveling outward, away from the rock. He sensed only that he was tumbling --- a fly swatted in mid-air or a bird that had flown into the polished window of a skyscraper. He was going down, yes, but sideways too. He was thinking *9.8 meters per second per second.* That's what was in his head.

He had not thought once about the possibility of falling into the river. The *river?* A solution to P vs. NP was possible. At least it was *thinkable upon.* But plunging from the wall and reaching the river was not. Some dots do not connect, and could not.

The whole fall took 6.9 seconds.

The river, by any reckoning, was an odd stretch of water, especially the 8-mile loop above Reichenbach Falls where it was ho-hum, shallow, insipid. Long pieces of the river there were ankle high, sand-barred, even creek-like. Other parts, though, were pure torment, a limpopo of chutes and ladders and wells and scours and trenches and dervish-pools. Oh, this river had its dramas and turmoils. Deep passages of boil and churn suggested foundries, turbines and razor blades were at work below. The river, yes, it kept some secrets. Deep Six was one of them.

If falling into the river from the cliff-face was unthinkable, it would require a fancy algorithm indeed --- some preposterous number to the power of ***x*** --- to describe Micah nailing a back dive into Deep Six. It was the algebraic equivalent of cold fusion.

Deep Six was a vertical column of rips and currents that was said to have sucked boats right off the surface of the river, gulping them down like a brownie hitting a Woolly Bugger on the Battenkill. It was said that Deep Six could hold a canoe under the water, 40 feet down, hold it there while calmly spinning it on plane, a lathe turning a table leg, a relish dish on a lazy Susan. This, anyway, is what some survivors had reported. Six fathoms down. Let the great world spin. Any number of canoes and kayaks are said to be down there still.

Deep Six swallowed Micah Ford when he hit the water, gulped him down deep, the full 40, but it also spouted him right back up, shaken, coughing in disbelief, with a cracked rib and that busted knuckle and one hell of a headache, but otherwise unhurt. His testicles had not jammed up into his nostrils in the fall. His toes did not break, his shoulders did not dislocate, and he had missed every rock and outcrop.

All this was impossible, of course --- all of it, each piece of the whole day. The mathematician in Micah resisted it, but in later years the word "miracle" would occur to him more than once as the most reasonable explanation for all manner of things.

PART III

7. 'WE SEE YOUR MOTIVES'

The extraction team found him in the corner of the yard. Heard him before they saw him. That wet gurgling moan.

The corporal they called Rascal, he was on point as the squad moved slowly through the empty house, mindful of booby traps, their big weapons twitching back and forth like insect feelers. When Rascal spotted Zimmy through a side door at the back of the house, he stopped short and gave a quick two-toned whistle, the high-low that signaled uh-oh. The big first sergeant came up, the team leader, Marchand.

"Holy Christ," Marchand says softly, and he swallows back the acid-sick coming up in his throat.

"Get Romo up here. And tell everybody I want a good perimeter. Noses open. Quiet-quiet, and no radios. We don't wanna be triggering anything in here."

The yard stretches along one side of the low-slung house, which is your basic concrete Iraqi shit-box. A high stucco wall fully encloses the yard, which at some point might have been a kind of pleasant interior garden. Now it's more like an empty lot, like all the other empty lots in every other ruined Iraqi town. Some thin weeds and dead grass, plastic bags, an old newspaper. The usual litter. An empty paint can, a torn innertube, a pair of broken scissors, the smell of cat piss, a rusted shovel blade with no handle, one flip-flop, a cinderblock cracked into three pieces.

Zimmy is wearing a ragged purple abaya. A woman's long cloak. No trace of his uniform. The cross they've nailed him to, it's made of two big wooden posts, rough-cut and heavy. The thing stands about 10 feet high, and it's leaning backward into a far corner of the garden wall. It's just propped there, in the corner, with Zimmy pinned to it.

The bomb tech comes up, the ordnance guy they call Romo. Marchand asks about Botulism. The bomb-disposal robot.

"He's broken," Romo says. "It's back at the base. We didn't bring it."

Romo shoots a quick nervous glance across the yard at Zimmy, then sets to work, hand-clearing a path across the yard, 50 feet give or take. He works doggie-style in the full sun, inching along on his kneepads, head down, sweat dropping onto the inside of his face-shield. He moves a small electronic wand slowly over the cracked dirt, straining at his earphones, listening for red beeps underneath the gray static.

Every few feet he'll flip up his mask and put his face close to the ground, to get a sniff. In ordnance school Romo became convinced he could *smell* a bomb, the meld of plastique and magnesium and copper and powder. Thinks he can actually smell the stuff under the dirt, like a bomb dog. It's an almondy scent, he says, like the dryer sheets his mom uses back home.

He places tiny plastic flags on either side of him as he goes, marking out a safe lane to Zimmy.

Marchand and Rascal can only stand and wait and sweat and hydrate and fidget and watch Romo working.

Zimmy, the poor fuck, he's still alive, in a way, and Marchand keeps calling to him to hang on, we're coming, hang in there dude, you're OK, stay strong Private. One of the squad quietly whistles to Marchand from inside the house and hands him a plastic bag: stuff they found while searching the house: wire cutters, an aerosol can, some bloody rags and a DVD with a typewritten label: "Zimmerman."

• • • •

Marchand's family was spirit-filled Church of Christ from a one-Sunoco town in central Nebraska, a little place called, get this, Smackdab. Those

Husker hayseeds had got that right. Smack fuckin' dab in the middle of fuckin' nowhere.

The Marchands were the only black family in all of Franklin County, so William never had many friends. Never went to a May Dance, a Sadie Hawkins or even had a regular date. He mostly just worked, doing chores, cuttin' hay and buckin' bales. Ate, slept, worked, read history books and car magazines, watched a lot of SportsCenter, jerked off a *whole* lot. When you live a long way out, 55 miles to the gas pump, you make your own fun. He never even kissed a girl until he was 16, and even then it was a third cousin, Octavia Hill, at a family reunion up to Kansas City, so that didn't count, not really. He had to drive the pickup three hours to Lincoln just to sneak a few beers and try to chat up the college girls.

His mother had passed young. His father, what they used to call a hired man, worked every day from cain't to cain't. Then one afternoon he got chewed up under a combine. Died right there in a soybean field, his legs all churned up in the blades. Just bled out. If he was screaming, which he must have been, nobody heard. Nobody could have. Soon after that, William got the hell out of Smackdab. Joined the Army and found a home. As they say.

• • • •

Marchand walks back through the house and checks on the positioning of the vehicles in the street --- the platoon's big Stryker and the five Humvees. There was his own gun truck, called Death Cab, plus Hum Job, Heavy Chevy, Canned Heat and Laughing Clown.

He briefs Sergeant Major Tran about the situation --- she's the new Whiskey in their unit, the new medic --- and she goes through the house to check out Zimmy for herself. Marchand uses his sat phone to call Colonel Magazine back at the base, and he gives the old man a quick sit-rep: Zimmy's in deep shock for sure, exposure, obvious torture, the gurgling, basically that the boy is fucked to a fare-thee-well. Magazine tells him to have Tran get Zimmy stabilized ay-sap. They'll get the base clinic ready for him. He also says to get Spielberg involved. He wants good video on this.

Romo has cleared his way to the base of the cross, but he can't bring himself to look up at Zimmy. The sputtering and choking are bad enough. But there's also a million shiny green flies all over the poor guy, spangled whirring zuzzing clouds of them, swarming his face, working at his blood-black eyes, getting at his ears, getting up his nose and into his mouth, and all kinds of flies and bees are flying up into the wide sleeves of the purple cloak. Romo walks back to Marchand and says he can't do it. He can't check Zimmy's body. He can't bear to work on the bloody, glugging, vaguely human mess that used to be Robert Moses Zimmerman.

Romo, it's clear enough to First Sergeant Marchand, is just plain scared. (He saw lots of this in Fallujah. Same kind of freak-out.) Normally, Romo has the hands of a safecracker and the balls of a matador. But Zimmy hanging up there on that cross, that's anything *but* fucking normal, and the whole shitty scene has started to unravel him. Feels like somebody's about to drop a Satan bus on his head. They had used Zimmerman like a voodoo doll.

"What do you mean you can't check him? Romo, are you shittin' me right now? Get the fuck back over there and do your job."

"Sarge, I don't know, I don't know, but I think I'm going into shock or something. Look at me, what the fuck, I've stopped sweating, but my heart's still beatin' like a bastidd. I'm wicked pale, right? I'm pale? And I got no spit. And my fingers, my fuckin' fingers are fuckin' *cold*. Hot as hell out here and my hands are *cold*? That can't be right. I got a bad feeling about this one, Sarge. Oh man, I got *no* fuckin' spit."

• • • •

Romo was solid. Short, dark, good-looking Italian kid from the North End of Boston. A cradle Catholic and a former altar boy --- ungroped, *mirabile dictu* --- and he was still smitten with the Big Church. He wears a Saint Christopher and a Pope Francis with his dog tags. Comes from a working-class Sicilian family, old school, nine children, where all the kids have these hyper-Italian names better suited to Vatican cardinals or 18th-century opera singers. Romo's real name is Carlo Dante Senesino Farinelli. Like some brand of imported pasta or fancy olive oil. The older kids on the playground at St. Catherine Labouré called him Carla. Plenty of scraps and bloody noses behind that.

His old man is a pressman at the Globe, works the lobster shift, and his mother, the one with the real *coglioni* in the family, she's a union firefighter. Romo was a bright enough guy, but he tied on a pretty good package one night at Fenway and got a little too operatic with a couple of security guards after a Yankee game. Some Staties happened along and Romo threw a right hook at one of them, which caught him an assault charge and a 50-day bit at Deer Island. That bit of coloratura also got him booted out of Boston Latin --- his sweet Jesuit scholarship and three years of *Omnia Gallia* and *sumus primi*, all of it was gonzo. His parish priest had to intervene just so he could finish up at Verbum Dei. Signora Farinelli was not fuckin' amused.

Good SAT scores got him into Notre Dame, but when Romo was home on Christmas break during his sophomore year he won 800-grand on a Mass Cash lottery ticket that one of his sisters slipped into his stocking on Christmas Eve. He took the lump-sum payout. Paid off the mortgage on the family house, paid off his mom's car note, got his father a Boston Whaler and a 50-inch plasma, gave his sister 10-grand. He said goodbye to Touchdown Jesus, moved back to Boston, leased an apartment in the Fens, bought season tickets to the Sox and the C's, and got himself into day trading.

He was up 100-grand at the All-Star break that July, but he started hedging euros against the dollar, then went long on gold and shorted Exxon. It was all gone, all the money, by the time the World Series started.

He applied for broker-training classes at Lehman, Merrill, Vanguard, all over, but nobody was interested, not with that assault beef on his record. He carried rebar and mixed mud for a couple months on the Big Dig, just to make rent. But one Saturday evening after a heroic stint at JJ Foley's --- he outlasted three bartenders that day, drinking balls and beers through two shift changes --- he found himself at the Army recruiting station on Dot Ave. He was trading one Combat Zone for another.

The gung-ho, all-go, no-quit, Army-of-One hoo-ah bullshit, all that was kind of a smile for Romo. He was the most educated guy in his platoon, by far, and also one of the fittest. The drill instructors spotted the kid right off, so they laid off him some. With all the retards, criminals, morons, pervs, alkies, fatsos, dope fiends and whack jobs enlisting these days, the United States Army needed all the Carlo Farinellis it could get.

All through Basic and then at EOD school at Aberdeen he kept up with the stock market. He read the Jim Cramer books as soon as they came out, and he subscribed to a bunch of private investment newsletters. Even after deploying to Iraq that first time he kept watching the financial TV shows on satellite. He could usually catch the final Wall Street numbers right before lights out. When the Sox and the market both tanked in '08, Romo claimed he had seen both tragedies coming.

Romo's original Army nicknames were entirely unoriginal --- Banger, Bam-Bam, Boomer, Little Dynamite, the same obvious names that a lot of bomb techs got. They called him Guido for a few weeks, but that was too "Jersey Shore" and too predictable. When the guys in the squad heard about his fuck-up with all that lottery money, there was no end to the shit he took about that. He was Lotto for awhile, then Wall Street, Streeter, Dowjones, Jonesey, Hedgefund, Gekko. Nothing really stuck, not until they caught him jerking off one night under his blanket while watching

Maria Bartiromo, the Money Honey herself, on the Closing Bell stock market show. After that, now and forever amen, he was Romo.

• • • •

But now Marchand is legit pissed. He doesn't like having his squad out there in the open for so long. He needs to get them off the X and out of danger. He isn't having any of Romo's no-spit bullshit.

The sergeant leans in toward him, close by Romo's ear, and speaks in a hard whisper: "Look, he could be booby-trapped. That's something these hajji motherfuckers would do, right? Rig him up, lookin' to get the rest of us? But goddamnit, Romo, you're jeopardizin' all of us here. We're fuckin' *exposed* right now, and Zimmy is up there bleeding out. Now I want you to wash the sand out your clit and get busy. Do you hear me, Staffsarnt? You need to man the fuck *up*. I know you got the fuckin' ingredients, son. So you're gonna seriously unfuck yourself, right fuckin' *now*, do you understand me, and regain your fuckin' focus."

Romo is calming down, listening to his senior sergeant's hard language. He's searching for his ingredients. But he isn't there yet. It's like the dream he's always having about being in the tunnels under Boston Garden, running and running, after a night game. He can hear the metal gates clanking shut and closing him in, but he can't find an exit.

Marchand eases off on his tone.

"Look, Romo, this shit ain't no movie. It ain't no fuckin' 'Hurt Locker.' You got one job here, Staff Sergeant, and that's makin' sure that that poor bastard over there ain't wired up. We gotta get him back to Freehold, you *know* this. Tran's gotta get him stabilized. And we can't do it without you. So man the fuck up. Let's fuckin' *go*."

Romo, a little calmer now, takes a slug of water, two, three, then Catholic-crosses himself and adds the little kiss on the thumb and the skyward glance at the end --- Big Papi getting ready to hit. When he gets back to Zimmy, he works as if he's in slow motion, like he's underwater, moving with care, remembering the drill, just like they taught him, thinking like the predator and not like the prey.

Most of what he does is look. Bomb situations are almost never about your nerves or the steadiness of your hands. It's about knowing what to look for, holding onto the patience to work the problem, even while the snakes in your rectum are waking up and slithering around. Snipping a wire isn't hard. The bitch is figuring out *which* wire to snip ---- *the red one, no the green, no wait the white, maybe the black one, no it's the purple one, yes yes yes yes yes the striped one.* Knocking back the fear, stop-cocking the cortisol, he *did* feel like he was in a movie sometimes. It was kind of like trading commodities. Minus the possibility of actual gore.

• • • •

Romo, having mostly unfucked himself, finishes his protocols with Zimmy and signals to Marchand that it's OK for him and Tran to come across.

Tran has only been at Freehold for a week now, and she isn't technically a Whiskey --- no, she's way beyond a 68-W, your regular Army medic. She's a sergeant major, second only to Colonel Magazine in rank at Freehold, and these days you didn't make SGM without serious combat experience. Her MOS at Freehold is 18-D, a Special Forces medical sergeant, a licensed nurse practitioner with psych-nursing and combat stress qualifications. She's damn near a doctor, with prescription privileges, and she's surgery-certified for ERs, ORs and downrange field hospitals. She's also a weapons sergeant and a close-combat instructor. Hoo-ah that.

The triple canopy on her sleeve got the immediate attention of everyone on base when she arrived --- the stacked patches for Special Forces, Ranger and Airborne. Maggie hasn't said much of anything about her. Hasn't even introduced her to the sergeants. He wants some mystique to build around her. Word on base is, Tran was in the first class of women Green Beret candidates that President Obama approved. Word on base is, she's the only one who finished the course on her first try.

Sergeant Major Sistine Tran, personally, she didn't care about any of that junior-high gossipy shit, the name-calling about Mickeys or Me-She's or Obama's Mamas or whatever. She was raised military. She had earned those patches and she had earned her place. She had gone through RAP, the Qualification Course, SERE, Robin Sage and the Hundred Hours of Hell, just like the rest of the Rangers, 61 days wall to wall, and no re-starts. She had damn near drowned saving another trooper in the Yellow River swamp at Eglin. Earned a 140 technical score and a near-perfect 295 on the physical. Sistine Tran had skills, both brute and nuanced, the skills that marked her out as a professional soldier. She spoke good Urdu and a passable Pashto. She had been in any number of firefights and rescue ops with the 75th Ranger Regiment, even if the brass wouldn't let her be a full member of the unit. Not yet, anyway. She had been in the alleyways of Ramadi, Indian country in Zabul and Sanur, and the torture rooms at Bagram. She had paid her rent every day in the field, and if any of her fellow troops wanted to throw down and test her, well hey, let's get in the ring. She could fuck a man up. Roger that.

Magazine had signed her up after looking at her personnel jacket for all of three minutes. He wanted a no-bullshit sergeant major as his ramrod and chief medical officer, a career soldier, and Tran was it. Still, her CIA vetting took 15 days, instead of the usual five, while the programmaticians and civilian nimrods at Langley spun out a blizzard of whaddafuck memos.

Tran was a first-generation Vietnamese-American, the daughter of an ARVN surgeon-dad and a nurse-mom who had landed at Fort Sam, in San Antonio, after things went all pear-shaped in Saigon. They were Catholics through and through. The family had swum out of the undertow of three separate diasporas: down from North Vietnam at first, then out of Saigon to a refugee camp in Hong Kong, and finally into the setting sun of the West. There was no feather-edged, banjo-music'd Ken Burns Effect to any of it. It had been humiliating and desperate and awful.

Sistine had been called Teeny by her family since she was a baby. Her toddler's lisp made her baptized name impossible for her to pronounce. Thithtine. She said Teeny, and so did they.

But in the Army she's just Tran, or Sergeant Major, or Ma'am. Never Sarge and never Miss. And no nicknames, not even "Doc." At least not to her face.

She is short, strong, striking, very nearly beautiful, with that blue-black Asian hair. Obsidian eyes. The body-confidence of an all-grown-up Olympic gymnast. The arms and lats of a union-card stevedore. Able-bodied, you might say. Sistine Tran seemed born to soldiering. It was native to her. Putting her through Basic Training was like sending a tiger to jungle school.

How she moves is like a cautious, compact athlete, feet just the slightest bit pigeon-toed, with a slight forward lean. It suggests a feline aspect, if by feline you meant a mother leopard on the scent in the savannah. Cornerback-tough, octagon-tough. In jump school, on the first try from 11,000 feet, she instinctively knew to run toward the ramp. The Ranger instructor had barked something at her during her first live-fire exercise, and it had stayed with her: Run toward the fire, run to the noise. It had made complete and immediate sense to Tran: the fire, the guns, the gunfire, the noise, the noise, the louder the better, that's where the battle would be. That's where the fight was. That's where she was going.

• • • •

Tran and Marchand come across the yard, him trailing her, both of them carefully single-filing between Romo's little yellow flags. Tran carefully lifts up the bottom edge of Zimmy's long robe and sees that his calves have been nailed to the vertical piece of the cross. There are several large spikes in each leg, right through the meaty parts. In his thighs, too. *The fuckers had to break his knees to get the legs to lay sideways like that, flat against the wood. Broke his knees and then nailed down his legs. God, the pain in that.* This is what Tran is thinking.

They had cut into the back of both of Zimmy's ankles, slicing through the Achilles, then roughly sewing up the cuts with what looks like nylon fishing line. "They probably did that first," Tran says to Marchand, fingering the rough sutures. "Probably so he wouldn't escape. *Couldn't* escape. But they also didn't want him to bleed out too fast. So they sewed him up. Smart."

The three soldiers now in the yard --- Tran, Marchand and Romo --- ease the cross down from the corner of the wall and lay it there in the dirt with Zimmerman still attached. Tran pushes 10 quick mills of morphine into him. Not your standard field protocol, but he was going to die anyway. Some naloxone for his breathing, and she rigs up a saline drip that Romo holds. She has to make it look like she's trying to save his life, as if he's got a fighting chance.

"Wire snips. And a hammer. And more water," Tran says to no one in particular, clear, firm, without looking up, and with no trace of hurry or panic. It's not an order, but it is. Rascal, the vigilant corporal, he's standing in the doorway of the house, and he says, "I got it."

• • • •

Colonel Magazine found Rascal while recruiting military prison guards to work in Jungleland, which is the underground prison wing at Combat Outpost Freehold. Magazine wanted people with maturity, patience and presence, guards who knew how to stick to procedures in "difficult incarceration environments." What he did not want were the bully-sadists, the white-trash mouth-breathers and the untrained gun-nut Reservists who had fucked things up at Abu G.

One of Maggie's prospective hires was a deputy warden in California, a decorated former Army lieutenant. The man turned the colonel down, but he recommended a former prisoner of his, an immigrant kid with a gang-banger past and lots of free-world potential. This was Rascal. The kid had once saved the lieutenant from being stabbed by another con armed with an HIV-dirty shiv.

Magazine tracked down Rascal in San Jose. He was on parole, laying asphalt during the day and striping parking lots at night. They did the enlistment interview over spring rolls and shrimp curry at Thai One On, a fried-noodle joint in Sunnyvale. The colonel liked him right off. He got Rascal sprung from his ankle monitor and pulled some strings at Justice to get his record expunged. In return, Rascal enlisted. After boot camp and MP school in Missouri, he was assigned to Maggie's unit.

Rascal, who maybe went 5-foot-5, had a dozen TRG tattoos on his chest and his back. These were florid souvenirs from his old set, the Tiny Rascal Gangsters --- meth-cookers and car-jackers and dead-enders, second-generation Cambodians and Laotians with the stink of the Mekong still on them. Word was, Rascal had a boldface Olde English tatt on his dick, too, but nobody in Maggie's new unit had actually seen it. When he was just walking around, flaccid, the tattoo said TRG. But when he got a full hard-on you supposedly could read the expanded, full-length version: TRG-Boyz-4-Evah-Yo. Seven inches, or so they said, which would make for an impressive dick-to-height ratio.

Rascal's real name is Sok Sin, which is already pretty damn good as a war-fighter name. But when he first arrived at Freehold, the guys right off started calling him Tiny. He had put up with that mocking mini-me shit his whole shitty life: Pee-Wee, Squirt, Short Round, Tater Tot, Danger Mouse. For awhile the Freehold guys called him Nuprin --- little, yellow, different.

When they switched to calling him Rascal, he let it be known that he could live with that. Most everybody else had a nickname, so fuck it.

Many of the soldiers now signing up, especially the young ones, most of what they wanted was a shot at becoming someone else. Nicknames were crucial to this. The military was a chance for them to rewrite their own personal histories, a way to leave behind their crap circumstances --- the pregnant girlfriend, the repo'd pickup, the parents' basement full of mold and radon, whatever. They were happy to shed the joyless dread of the nine-dollar job at Pep Boys or the wrangling of shopping carts at Target. Joining the military was a reboot, a sloughing-off, snakes shedding skins, a reinvention. Nicknames were essential to the rebranding. Everybody in the Army was called something else.

Rascal had been quite the violent fuck-up as a kid, and he still had something of a dangerous air about him, moving in his own unpredictable weather, capable of upgrading to a Category 4 just like that. But he found religion in boot camp, that old-time olive-drab religion. He was good at soldiering, and he liked it. Even the ruck-marching in the dark. He liked folding his uniform just so, keeping his weapon clean, his fingernails trimmed and his gear squared away. He was now one of Maggie's most reliable guys. He was prepping for the sergeant's exam.

The bloody shit they were seeing now with Zimmy, it honestly didn't bother Rascal so much. He had seen worse on K Block at Vacaville and in the Shoe at Pelican Bay. Still, he was thinking to himself that the fuckers who did this to Zimmy, they'd been nasty and they'd been patient. They had definitely got medieval on his ass. Yeah, this was going to be a pretty fucked-up way to die.

• • • •

Tran uses her Yarborough knife to start cutting away the top half of Zimmy's robe while Marchand keeps talking quietly to him, brushing away the flies as best he can and telling him it's going to be OK. Marchand knows full well that this is not true.

He's not even sure that Zimmy can hear him. A pinkish ooze has started to come up out of the young soldier's mouth, and you could hear the storm clouds raining in his chest. The lungs are corrupted now, filling with foam and froth, and he could well be drowning internally. A yellowish fluid, a kind of yolky mayonnaise, issues from his nostrils.

A National Guard softie from Phoenix has come into the yard with a video camera --- this is Posner, a Fuckin' New Guy, an E-4 they've already nicknamed Spielberg. After seeing Zimmy he soon has tears streaming down his face and his nose is dripping snot. Gag Factor 15. He vomits into the dirt when Tran pulls back the sleeves of the robe and they see the stump.

Damn, somebody says. They cut off his fuckin' hand.

• • • •

Zimmy, the vic, he's your basic 11-B, 11-Bravo, pure infantry, just another ground-pounder with limited oomph. He looks like that guy Kramer, on Seinfeld. Tall, thin, goofy. Ichabod Crane. Red-brown chia-pet hair. You could scour pots with that hair. Except he had these laser eyes, blue-over-blue, blue as billiard chalk.

He's from Minnesota, way up the Iron Range. Had to enlist in the Army after he got in a little hometown jam. Some socialist homo tree-hugging judge in Koochiching County, name of Poe, found Zimmerman guilty of killing a female American bald eagle with his AR-15. When Zimmy took the bird to get mounted the taxidermist called the DNR on him. Jail or the military, that was the final offer from the judge, who told the newspaper his ruling was Poetic Justice.

For Zimmy, it wasn't a tough call: If he chose jail he would certainly get ass-raped at Stillwater by some Large Martti or Big Sven. And there was no compelling reason to hang onto his day job bussing tables at the Red Apple Café or the night gig delivering "French baguettes" to the area Walmarts. (Zimmy called it Y'all-Mart. He found this to be hilarious, every single time he said it, which was often.)

He was like that. Sometimes, in a group, he would inexplicably grab his crotch and shout, "Say hello to my little friend!" He ended many of his sentences with "f'shizzle." He used these jackass phrases that were long out of date, saying them as if they were completely new and highly original.

"Just shows to go ya!" "Hey, girlie-mon." "Who's your daddy?" "I could tell you, but then I'd have to kill you."

"Smokin'!" "Hey, you two! Get a room!" And the wholly moronic, "It is what it is."

The ass-rape option eventually won the day with Zimmy, so he joined up. As a soldier, he seemed incapable of doing any serious harm to anyone, except maybe himself. He had shot off his right earlobe a few months earlier while imitating that Riverdance guy: He was gettin' Irish-jiggy with it in the squad room at Freehold when he dropped his rifle and it discharged. The bullet clipped his ear and tore into an air-conditioning duct overhead in the Quonset hut. The dumb fuck had the safety off and no T-block in place. That little stunt got him an outdoor billet, a week of PT in full MOPP gear, and bread and water for 10 days. Zimmy didn't see what the big deal was, and he did a lot of gee-whizzing about always being what he called the "escapegoat" for things that went wrong in the platoon.

Before a junior high dance he once ate 3 pounds of Beer Nuts, thinking it would get him drunk, a necessary prelude to putting "a sex move" on his date. In his wallet, starting in 9th grade, he kept a condom carefully positioned so it would emboss a telltale circle through the leather. At Freehold he would walk around humming to himself, a kind of mumble-singing, "I got a feelin', boom boom pow." He thought he might have some tiger blood in him, like that TV actor-lunatic. He could relate. He often said, for no apparent reason, "Winning!"

Who the fuck knew with Zimmy? Even in 2015 his default put-down was calling somebody a "homo" or "queer bait."

He referred to himself as Z-Man, or The Z. He often called the other soldiers "homes," or "gangsta," or "playuh." He spoke a strange hooplehead minstrel-show ebonics. Coming into the chow hall for breakfast he'd usually be singing that Sopranos song: "Woke up this mornin', got myself a gun." Idiot.

Leaving the table after a meal he'd bend his fingers together to make the letter Z, or what he thought looked like a Z, and he'd flash this "gang sign" at the other men. Then he'd say, "OK, my brothers, The Z be on the bounce. Heltah skeltah. Hollah. Peace out. F'shizzle."

Yep. Idiot.

• • • •

Zimmerman had been grabbed by an ISIS splinter franchise during an ambush three weeks earlier. It was Palm Sunday and they were pulling a routine patrol, paying a courtesy call on Wasfi al-Aasi and Sheikh Zuber, a couple of important Obeidi tribal leaders up in Ar Rutbah.

This kind of operation was way outside Freehold's mission and its AO, but Military Intelligence said the area was clean --- "spic and span," the cable from Centcom had actually said --- and an Iraqi SF team had gone ahead and performed a Route Clearance Package. The request for the op had come down from division, so Maggie agreed. Refusing a patrol ran the risk of pissing off some three-star back in Tampa, and dollars to doughnuts the guy would be sitting on his promotion-review board in a few months. That would sink his chance of ever making general. Still, fuck, it was a lot of trouble just to deliver a little tea and sympathy.

So they made the trip, keeping it low-viz and pretending they had come all the way out from Baghdad. Magazine bought a couple goats and they had quite the little feast. The sheikhs seemed happy, which was the point. The squad only stayed a couple hours but taking a roundabout route back to Freehold the moozh shit-bags were waiting for them with small arms and

RPGs. Really lit 'em up in a nasty crossfire just outside the city, in a village neighborhood called Al-Malmedi. Just another brown spot in the road. An almond grove on one side and a string of low houses on the other. Bullets were in the air like hornets.

The squad dismounted, returned fire and gave chase for awhile, then gave up --- which is how most of these bump-and-run gunfights played out. They took no casualties, but then Zimmy didn't report back. He had last been seen moving by himself down an alleyway; his teammate, Posner, had tripped and fallen and lost eyes on Zimmy. The 12th General Order had been violated: Don't get caught.

Maggie called in a slew of backup. He sent a full Kinetic Strike Request up the line, and Special Operations and MI teams swooped in from Baghdad. They set up a cordon and swept the whole damn ville. Stayed there for three days, searching cars, banging down doors, heavy-petting anybody suspicious, bayoneting haystacks and woodpiles and heaps of blankets. They basically went around scaring the bejeezus out of everybody. They rolled up a couple dozen of the younger Malmedi men, dispensing some tough love to those with the bushiest beards. *The longer your hair, the shorter my fuse.* They even hauled in the two sheikhs, the mayor and the chief mullah for a come-to-Jesus session, so to speak, but they got no actionable intel. *No ISIS here, mister, never, no, no, no liking Daesh, no sir mister.* Spic and fuckin' span.

Colonel Magazine called in some of the bosses of the local Committee of Public Safety, threatening them at first, then damn near begging them for information on Zimmy. Maggie was bad-copping and good-copping them all by himself: One minute he promised to blow the minarets off their mosques. Next he would offer to build a school and dig some wells. But the capos gave up nothing. *No ISIS, no Daesh.* They sat there and drank their shitty tea, stroked their Crayola-orange beards, smoked their nasty Turkish smokes. They nodded glumly, took more tea, didn't say shit.

Finally, two weeks later, through the arrest of a rookie jihadi way downrange, some junior J-man, the message came into Green Zone headquarters that the infidel American soldier might be found in an empty house at the end of Dyer al-Jannah Street in a desert waystation called Wadi Ad-Dhari.

• • • •

The Wadi was a dry scab of a hamlet, and getting there was pretty much like driving through the most barren chapters of the Old Testament. Abraham and Isaac might have lived there, as recently as last week.

Desert legend held that the town was haunted, but now it felt like even the ghosts had gone. It was a desolate place, maybe 20 houses in all, stacked-stone sheds and thorn-railed goat corrals surrounded by alkali flats and fruitless orchards. It hadn't rained there in years. The wells were old and the water was sour --- a poisoned oasis. The soil was shot, with a crumbled, asbestos feel to it.

In the local dialect there were no longer any words for tides, drowning, songbird, earthworms. These words had simply fallen out of use and relevance. No historians would ever write about the Wadi, nor would any poets. No songs would be sung. It was a scorched and granulated place, and the unplowed fields seemed salted. The locusts no longer bothered. The sky held a sickly pallor year-round, the color of cement, the color of old-man saliva. Some years ago, it was said, the few remaining goats in the village committed suicide from the desolation. The wide-angled palette of the place in the spring was a combination of ocher and a thin green, saddened with gray. A few things somehow turned green, but in vain. Blackened zinc trees lined the vacant horizon. All this gave rise to a feeling of anxiety and woe.

And that's where the Freehold squad found Private Zimmerman --- nailed to a cross in the dismal yard of a decayed house in this anxious, woeful place.

• • • •

Zimmy has been nailed through his wrists and forearms, with the same spikes they used on his legs. Apparently the spikes wouldn't hold him when they had raised up the cross the first time, so they also tied him across the chest and then under the armpits with bicycle innertubes and with lengths of the thick baling twine used locally for tethering mules.

They've lashed both of his upper arms to the cross-beam with braided copper wire. Romo notices that it's the same type of wire that many of the Iraqi suicide bombers use in their martyrdom vests. His arms are tied so tight --- or Zimmy had struggled so much --- that the strands have cut deep into the flesh of his biceps.

Around his head they've looped razor wire, six or seven turns of it, an angry crown of the stuff, which is new and steel-bright and scalpel-sharp. The barbs have bitten into his skin, seating themselves in his forehead and ears. His eyelids have been sewn open with a waxed yellow thread. The eyes, well, the eyes are gone. Scooped out, or plucked out somehow. They're now just shallow cups of goo rimmed all around with dried blood.

A final loop of the razor wire cuts across Zimmy's open mouth, like the bit on a bridle.

His mouth is filled with blood and bile and that pink foam and drowned flies and gravel. *Gravel, damn.* When Tran snips away the mouth-wire and flushes out the gunk she sees that his tongue has been sliced clean through. Lengthwise. It's a thin, straight cut, which suggests a shaving razor. The exposed meat of the tongue, this forked tongue, has turned blue-back, the color of eggplant, all rancid and clotted. When she pokes at it, Zimmy gags, and wet bits of mouth-muck fly onto her chin and her lower lip. She doesn't flinch. Just wipes it away with her sleeve, spits once into the dust and keeps working. She gets a fentanyl lollipop from her Molle bag, snaps off the stick and wedges the lozenge in front of Zimmy's Number 7 molar.

It looks to her like Zimmy's face and skull have been shaved. Scraped is more like it, maybe with a knife, or god forbid it was some kind of acid. His neck under the jawline is mostly scabbed-over welts.

All the way around his neck, using some kind of black marker, the kidnappers have drawn a thick dotted line. Like a cutting line from a sewing pattern. The line traces right over the Adam's apple.

Tran fingers Zimmy's right ear and notices the missing lobe --- unaware that it's from the Riverdance episode. She locates a round puncture wound on his right torso, between two ribs, and the cut is weeping pus. The cloth of the abaya sticks there a moment as she pulls at it. She swabs the cut, pours some QuickClot beads into the puncture hole, presses in some Kerflix gauze behind it, and tapes it all down. *None of this will help. It's like taking one Advil.*

On the opposite side, under his left rib cage, there are more stab holes, but Zimmy's meat tag is still there, his identifying tattoo. Rascal had done the tattoo for him a month earlier: The big initials R.M.Z., his Social Security number 175-77-0093, his blood type O-Neg, and NKA. No known allergies.

Tran begins to cut away the rest of the robe at Zimmy's waist. Marchand, fearing the worst about the condition of Zimmerman's genitals, says, "OK, shit, here we go, here we go, this shit is about to get fuckin' real."

Robert Zimmerman is naked underneath, sure enough, but his stuff is intact. The private's privates. As if that would even matter any more.

• • • •

Tran gets all the wires and ropes and shit off him, then takes the hammer and gently taps sideways at one of the spikes that has been driven through Zimmerman's left foot. There is a solid, deep, pig-iron sound to it, but the spike also gives a little. From Zimmy, there's no reaction. He's going in and out of consciousness now. The rest of the spikes come out less easily.

"He's gonna make it, right?" Marchand asks her.

"Not sure. Tell you one thing. He's not gonna win the Heisman. Playing the cello is probably out, too."

Damn that's cold, is what Marchand thinks. He thought the same thing earlier when Tran said the hajjis had been smart to slice into Zimmy's heels. *The girl could be knitting a scarf or cleaning her weapon. Doing a fucking crossword.* Now Marchand is imagining his father in the soybean field, bleeding and scared and caught in the blades of the combine.

"Corporal, bring a stretcher," Tran says to Rascal, without looking up.

"And you bring it yourself," says Marchand. "Nobody else comes out here." He looks at Romo and Spielberg. "And you guys --- not a word of this gets out. You can consider that a direct fuckin' order. Got it? No details. To nobody." He says it harder than he means to, but he's on edge, and at this point in the proceedings, fuck it.

Rascal arrives with a backboard and a mylar blanket, and Tran tells him, "You. Corporal Sin. Take his head. Cradle it from underneath. Careful." Rascal squats down and reaches under the back of Zimmy's head, but he quickly jerks away. A bloody-hairy piece of skin has come off in his hands, a thick round flap, about the size of a drink coaster.

"Jesus fucking Christ they scalped him!" says Marchand. "What the fuck is that about?"

Tran takes the fuzzy sopping yarmulke and puts it in a Ziploc bag. Herniated brain, she notices, but keeps it to herself. She hands Rascal a fresh square of HemCon bandage, and he lays it onto the wound. She and Marchand squat down on either side of the cross and work their hands under Zimmerman's back. It's all gooey-slippery with blood there, too, and when Marchand feels the wet he yelps and falls backward onto his butt in the dirt. It's a slapstick move, *oof-boink-owww*.

"Oh man, sorry, God-damn," he says, then gets up and manages a better grip. "This is sure enough some bizarre shit up in here."

"They must have worked on his back before they nailed him up," Tran says, her tone flat, as if she's dealt with dozens of cases like this, rather than just this one. "Maybe tied him to a whipping post or something. OK, here we go. On me, on three."

They ease Zimmy onto the board. Tran puts the blanket over his body, right up to his chin, and they secure him with bungees and duct tape. She cuts a mesh mask out of some white burn gauze and lays it over his face. No eye holes. Medically, she knows, this will be no help. But she doesn't want the other troopers seeing his missing eyes and the foamy mouth and all the cuts. Romo and Rascal carry the stretcher out of the yard, back through the cool interior of the house, and then up the rear ramp of the Stryker.

In the front seat of Death Cab, Marchand radios ahead to Colonel Magazine, saying they're ready to move. He listens for a long minute, then says, "Roger that, sir. Golf tango golf. Inbound five mikes. Bravo out."

Marchand gets out of the jeep, unlatches two jerry cans of diesel and heads back into the house.

"Light' em up, First Sergeant!" shouts one of the soldiers. "Burn, baby, burn!"

"Shut the fuck up," Marchand says.

He drags the big cross from the back yard into the front room of the house, pours out all the fuel, sets everything alight and gets back in his truck.

"Oscar mike," he tells the wheelman, a scrawny, pimply private named Arnie Bragg. "Move the fuck out."

• • • •

For all of Marchand's precautions about keeping a lid on Zimmy's injuries, one of the soldiers in the squad outside has seen everything --- the crucifixion, the razor wire, Romo, the green flags, the purple robe and the pink foam, Tran hammering at those spikes, the whole deal. The .50-caliber gunner on Death Cab has been on overwatch the whole time, high up in his gun-turret, scanning his sector and checking his corners, sure, doing his job. But from his perch he also has been able to see over the garden wall and down into the yard.

This is the gunner they call Fitty, real name Jimmy Thurber, a stringy-wiry, over-amped, over-deployed staff sergeant from Mingus, Texas. Jumpy as a parakeet, he always seems to have something in his mouth --- Boom Boom, prune candy, Jolly Ranchers, Red Bull, Skoal, Black & Milds, a wide variety of tonics and sodas and ballpoints. The toothpicks he marinates himself in cinnamon. Ripped Fuel, Fiddle Faddle, chewable C, SmartWater, Pez, 5 Hours, pretty much anything you might find on the middle racks of a 7-Eleven. Hydroxycut gummies, Lunchables, purple drank. Fitty even sucks on the Lucky Charms from the MREs. No other solider would dare touch a Lucky Charm. They're bad luck, even the greenest bootest grunt knows that. Doesn't faze Fitty one bit.

Back home in Texas, his parents have a half-dozen acres of half-assed desert full of thistles and johnsongrass, with a single pump-jack working a stripper well. Fitty calls it his "spread," or his "ranch," even though it has no cattle and produces all of about 40 barrels of crude a month. All hat and no cattle, as they say. The ranch is called 10 Shy, a broke-dick operation, for sure, but it helps Fitty with the line that he uses on girls and bartenders when he's on leave: He says he's one sure-enough-crazy sumbitch Texas oilman-soldier lookin' for some glory-hole. He's always fixin' to lasso a string of fillies some night and put his brand on a stray.

He actually talks that way, cowpokey, and frequently allows that his bedroom techniques are just like the oil he's pumping back home: light, sweet and crude. Latt, is how he pronounces it.

In Iraq, out on patrol, and even sometimes back at base, Fitty smears eye-black across his cheeks, he says it's to cut the glare, like a quarterback or a wide receiver, even though he never played a single down of varsity football at Mingus High. *Get em, Jackrabbits!* He talks mostly in oil, rodeo and sports metaphors, and still uses adjectives like sure-fire, no-account and whiz-bang. Wants to name his first two kids Troy Aikman Thurber and Roger Staubach Thurber. He's pretty much a hick.

He calls his big machine gun "No Vaseline," and the name is stenciled along the barrel. He's a crack shot, maybe the best in the battalion, and has taken to naming his bursts of gunfire. A warning spray over a crowd of burqa-wearing women, he calls that one a "Ho-Down." Shooting stray dogs is "Kibbles and Bits." With cats it's "Pussy Riot." Sometimes he'll fire on an aggravating loudspeaker in a minaret over a mosque, which is "Shut the Fuck Up." Once in a fight in Ramadi, he spotted a moozh who was aiming an RPG at Marchand's Humvee. Fitty blew off the man's left arm at the elbow. He called that one his "Bob Dole." "Turned that fuckin' arm to peanut butter," he said.

This is Fitty's fourth tour in Iraq, plus he did 11 months with the 2/4 Cav in southern Afghanistan. All along he has been a Bush guy, a McCain guy, a Petraeus guy. Liked Stan McChrystal, too, surge and all. But now he's pissed that Obama has sent him and the others back in. Back into *this.* He has blackened too many years in this brown, impossible place.

Truth is, Fitty never cared too much for Zimmy. Thinks he's pretty much a pussy and a retard. *But he's one of our guys, by God, and this crucifying shit is just too damn much, man. These murderin' Ay-rabs, they're like vampires, these hajji-moozh motherfuckers. They knew damn well what they were doing. They just butchered this poor sumbitch. Might as well send him straight to Section 60. And you know they planned this shit. Old man Bush was right: This is evil, man. This shit cannot stand, man.*

• • • •

With Zimmy loaded in, the little convoy starts back to base, heading out toward Route Bluebird. The town appears empty.

Wadi Ad-Dhari is never a busy place, not even around Friday prayers. There's only about 50 people who live here total. It's too poor and too remote to be an ISIS target or a Qaeda haven. But it's odd how there are no kids on the streets just now, no donkey carts moving, no waddling women, no old men in pajamas shuffling around, pulling at their beards with one hand and scratching their nuts with the other. Things have gone all weird and creepy, pre-hurricane-creepy, and everyone in the squad can feel it. The locals clearly know what the dirt-worshippers did to Zimmy in that house --- and now they have moved the fuck out. If there's going to be blowback, they want to be well upwind of it.

A hot grating breeze has started to pick up, ominous coughs and whorls and gusts that is putting plenty of dust and grit in the air. The shamal was starting early this year, the blasting microwave wind that the Iraqis call Al-Haffar, the Driller. One did not argue with Mister Shamal.

Saddam called this wedge of Anbar his well-tempered sword, and it's damn sure hot as a forge right now. It's widely known in the region that the western Anbar heat can cause women to ovulate out of cycle. (Back when it was a viable village, the Wadi girls always menstruated early.) Donkey droppings were known to suddenly burst into flame here, along with straw bales, baskets and paperback Korans left out in the sun. Uncovered hair could ignite, and sometimes kittens. The cashew and pistachio trees gave up decades ago. A few years ago, in the next town over, a grim hamlet called Aswad Haleeb, the last surviving cow gave 2 liters of black milk one morning, then fell over dead. The dairyman shrugged and said, "God is great," then ushered himself into Paradise with a bullet from his Enfield rifle. In the worst summers, the local men say, the hot wind forces the constellations to blink out. The bear, the belt, the two spoons, they flee the sky.

The heat has certainly addled the Americans. Out here sometimes you couldn't even remember your own name. You'd forget how the furniture was arranged in your parents' rec room back home. The foil shimmer on the horizon, plus the way the sun boinks off the dunes, even the surfer guys from California and Florida were sure there must be a beach up ahead, just over the next rise. Sun and sand *could* mean ocean. *There must be a Zuma or South Padre or Kill Devil Hills around here somewhere.* There never was, of course, but that was the suck, wasn't it? A big fucking tease. The smoke and the mirrors.

The convoy hadn't yet cleared the village when Romo, on the binoculars in the lead truck and back on his A-game, he calls back to Marchand to say he wants to check a piece of the road that looks weird to him. *Anomaly in the road, Firsarnt, my 2 o'clock.* He thinks it could be a newly placed IED or maybe a buried pressure plate. Marchand radios for the convoy to stop, and says, "Bravo Actual, noses open. Keep your op-sec." The guys in the turrets go to safeties off on their .50s. The others click their M-16s from Safe to Fire.

Just as Romo is climbing out of Heavy Chevy, the PA speakers from the local mosque start up, extra loud it seems, blasting out the muezzin's call to late-afternoon prayer. The recording crackles, feedbacks and ricochets through the empty streets, banging off the stucco buildings. This is somebody watching and fucking with the Americans. *Allahu akbar, Allahu akbar, Allahblah akblah, blah blah blah*, over and over, loud as hell. Still, none of the locals are coming into the street. They know the Americans are here, and nobody's coming out, not even to pray away the infidels.

Three dogs appear from an alley. Scabby, dun-colored, stubbed-out tails. Your basic Iraqi mongrels, slim slow sliders, with twitchy eyes and that uneasy sidewinder way of walking. They come out of an alley, slow as scorpions, their bodies shuddering with a combination of rage, fear and starvation.

They have picked up Romo's scent --- he's 50 feet away, head down, his own version of doggie, sniffing at his piece of chewed-up road. Odd that the dogs would be moving at all, at this hour, in this heat. But they sense that something's up, and they intend to be in on it. There's some deep growling, some flarings of incisors. Romo, head now up, chambers a round into his Glock.

He calls up to Fitty to throw down some food to keep the dogs occupied while he finishes checking the road. Fitty grabs some cherry Pop-Tarts from his stash in the turret and tosses them down, right in front of the dogs. The dogs jump back a bit, take a smell at the food but quickly ignore it: The pastries are still sealed in their foil wrappers. The dogs are more agitated now, growl-barking, and they're first-and-goal on Romo.

With the havoc of the dogs getting vocal, and the blaring of the Allahus and akbars, and with Romo down there in the street alone, and with this fucking wind and heat and scorch, all this is now pounding mightily on Fitty. It's bringing up the beast from the belly. It's ricochet to the infinity power. It's the grind and ratchet and clank of the gears of war. *But this. This isn't war. It couldn't be. If it is, it's war shitting all over itself.*

Fitty had actually awakened last night --- his sleeping had been all fucked up lately, even with all the pills they were giving him --- and he couldn't remember his own damn Zip code back home. And now this fucking situation with Zimmerman the poor bastard and that razor wire on his head and all the sand and shit. Those scooped-out eyes, like they'd used a fucking melon baller on him. Plus this morning he probably had swigged too much purple drank, or maybe not enough, and besides that he suspected that Kimber, Randye, Misti and Joetta were sleeping around on him back home and he had all these leftover hot memories about Ramadi and Wanat and that Bob Dole episode always nagging at his dreams, and his eyes were always sun-burning with black-tar fever from staring at the fuckin' road all the fuckin' time looking for fuckin' IEDs. And he still could be looking at another seven months of this shit before he could get home.

This is how it happens, the going haywire --- gradually, then suddenly. All of it has crashed down on Jimmy Thurber now, and his other safety, not the one on his weapon but the one on his soldierly patience, it switches right the fuck off. He fires a quick pinpoint burst at the dogs, who separate into a spray of meat and fur and a fine pink mist. It's like manga, or a slasher flick. The dogs hadn't even had time to yelp before Fitty had pump-jacked some massive fuckin' glory-holes in them. He just yelled, "Pardon the interruption, you motherfuckers!" and he let fly with a dozen rounds of crunchy .50-caliber goodness. Kibbles and bits.

The radios in all five trucks come alive now, everybody shouting. *"Contact! We got contact!"* Thirteen goggle-eyed soldiers roll heavy out of the Humvees, every gun on Burst, everything at full battle-rattle, the men crouched low, heads on the swivel. They're all scanning for targets, which, at the squad's current level of adrenalized freak-out, is basically anything that has the bad luck to be alive or moving.

One of the other .50-cal gunners pours a burst into the mosque. It's a real death-blossoming. Things have gone kinetic in a hurry, and it's a red-hot-chili-pepper minute before Marchand figures out what's what. He shouts for everybody to hold their fire. Later, back at the base, they will do an ammo count: Four guys in the squad got off a total of 41 shots. They had taken no incoming fire.

• • • •

The rest of the route back to Combat Outpost Freehold takes them through a wide, dry valley of ashes and rising smoke, and the few people in the few desert villages move slowly through the powdery air. Everything seems ravaged, everything seems burned. The countryside is whited and dirty-yellowed, all bleached and bled out. Squint hard, you can see the 7th century.

The team finally rolls into the base through the main gate, the one they call the E Street Gate, one of just two entrances into Freehold's huge walled compound. Colonel Magazine is there, waiting for them as the trucks pull in, and right away he ducks into the back of the Stryker for a look at Zimmy.

Tran gives the colonel a quick nod and a half-salute, then pulls back the blanket and peels away the face-mask. Without the spikes and the cross and womanly robe and the razor wire, without the context, Zimmy looks pretty much like any other trooper who got into a bad IED situation or got fucked up in a firefight. Except those eyes, of course, which had once been as blue as Biwabik skies. Israeli blue. Y'all-Mart blue. Empty eye sockets, you didn't see *that* shit every day. All Maggie says is a grim "OK," and he jerks his head toward the clinic.

Marchand hands Magazine the SIM card from Spielberg's camera and the hajjis' DVD, and they walk together across the compound, heads down against the blowing grit.

Colonel Magazine runs Freehold out of two Airstream Flying Clouds, identical 28-footers placed side by side, movie-star trailers, stainless and gleaming, their New Jersey temporary tags still on them. He got the idea from Dick Cheney, who had an Airstream installed in the belly-pooch of Air Force Two. Cheney's trailer, known as the Silver Bullet, sat on rails for fast load-ins and quick getaways.

The Freehold trailer known as Safeway is the operations office. The other one, Piggly Wiggly, or just the Pig, has Magazine's living quarters. Exactly why the supermarket names, nobody seems to know.

Safeway is cabled to half a dozen satellite dishes and some strange, black, spiky antennas. The trailers have their own generators, plus backups for the backups. The whole damn COP is laced with redundancies. Maggie holds mission briefings in Safeway but nobody gets into the Pig. Both Airstreams are kept shiny and polished, as bright as diamonds, and it's part of the Magazine legend that the glinting trailers, in just the right light, can be seen from the International Space Station.

Inside the Safeway office, First Sergeant Marchand gives his account of the Zimmy event, and he is specific, linear, thorough and brief. He has given the old man a number of these after-action reports, although certainly none this grisly. He knows the level of detail the colonel likes. Magazine, working at an unlit cigar, mostly just nods. *Uh-huh. Uh-huh. What next? Uh-huh. Hmm. No shit? Yeah, right. OK, good.*

Marchand finishes, and Magazine says: "OK, William, three things. One, I need a written report from you, tonight, before chow, while it's still fresh in your head. Do it on this computer here. Make the file name, uh, let's call it Calvary."

"Cavalry?"

"No, Cal-va-ry. As in Jesus-Christ-on-the-cross Calvary."

"Hoo-ah that, sir. Sorry, sir. I mis-heard you."

"Second, don't mention the cross in the report. Just say you found Private Zimmerman in the yard, lying in the yard all fucked up, wounded, whatever. Just the basics. No need to be as detailed as you were just now.

"Three, get your squad together and tell them not to talk about this. Tell the entire squad as a group. Then later, and I mean quietly, reinforce it with the more talkative ones, man-to-man. Maybe it's too late and the story has already gotten around, and I guess we can't help that. But there's gonna be zero-tolerance on this leaking out. Tell 'em all that the entire incident is now considered highly secured information. Anybody who talks about it, they'll get the brig here, that's absolutely automatic, and I'll guarantee them a court-martial ASAP back at Bragg. Firsarnt? You got me? You make sure they know that this is both a promise and a threat. From me personally."

"Hoo-ah that, sir. Understood." Marchand got up to leave.

"Wait, William, a fourth thing. Everybody in the squad, tell them nice job, under what I know were tough conditions, and they all get the day off tomorrow. Go to Force Protection White. But Tran will need to watch Zimmerman. I hope she can staple the poor kid back together. But tell 'em they did a nice job. I'll get with Tran myself. And I'll definitely talk to Thurber about his bullshit little stunt on the .50. Maybe I'll have him wash and wax the Airstreams --- after The Driller gets through grinding on us.

"I'll order up a couple cold cases of O'Doul's for the guys for dinner tonight. And listen, we're going to start keeping things more buttoned-up around here. We've got new teams and a new chief warrant officer coming in. He's gonna be my XO. It's going to be a big turnover. Only a few of you current guys will be staying on. I'll keep you in the loop as much as I can. All the new guys are in Amman now, waiting for the weather to clear. We'll put Zimmerman on the same Chinook going out."

Magazine is working his cigar, and pacing. "Poor guy. Zimmerman. They really did a number on him. Was he any good? Seemed like a fuck-up, what with discharging his weapon and all. I knew he was a bad fit for a group like ours, but I had to take him as a favor to my boss."

Marchand hears the past tense, and he winces without wincing. "He's 11-Bravo all the way, sir, but a pretty weak skill set, yes sir. One thing, though, he's kinda good for morale. He's a mess-up, but he's one of those guys you can make fun of and he doesn't get too pissed off. Comic relief, in a way."

"Yeah, I hear you," the colonel said. "I know plenty of officers like that, believe me. But that's a story for another time. OK, thanks, William. And great work yourself today. You showed some outstanding leadership out there, and it'll be duly noted up the line to division. That was a tough one, I know. Anyway, see you at dinner. Crab legs tonight."

Salute, salute, exit Marchand.

• • • •

Later that night, The Driller definitely got dental on them --- and the wind didn't let up for the next two days. It stormed like the hard parts of the Bible, as if every inch of desert in Jordan and Syria had been scraped loose, tossed airborne, blown west, and was now crashing down on top of them. Even ISIS would be taking cover.

At night, the hot wind would slacken and it would rain like a bastard. It first came almost sideways, then went vertical. Heavy and magnificent torrents of warmed-up mud is what it was. Volcanic archives of the stuff, plopping down, thudding down. All that swirling desert, aerated during the day, got mixed with the rain at night. *Mud storms, damn.*

The Americans mostly stayed in their barracks during the Drilling, only venturing out for chow, changes of the guard, or to hose off the snorkels on the air cons. On the third day, the skies cleared to cerulean, then to cobalt, a blue deep and perfect enough to make anybody believe in a higher power. That's when Zimmy died.

Tran had done her best, not just in sewing him back together and keeping vigil, but also keeping him out of pain. She stroked his hand and talked to him quiet-sweet when nobody else was around. He had suffered too much. He had suffered enough. He was 23 and never had a chance.

A Mortuary Affairs team from Baghdad arrived on a Chinook later that afternoon, along with the new chief and the new troops. Magazine gathered all the men inside Freehold for a sendoff for Zimmy. It was 5 in the afternoon. It was exactly 5 in the afternoon when the two platoons got fully assembled, 40 troopers arriving, another 30-some going home. It was quiet, no wind, and it felt almost cool now, after the heat and torment of the previous days. There was an evening redness in the west.

An MA captain brought out a flag and tied it over Zimmy's aluminum transfer case, which was bungee'd onto the back of one of the Gators they used for chores around the base. The men bunched up around the coffin and the colonel. They hadn't rehearsed a funeral or a homegoing service; some had never even seen one. They didn't know how to act. They were just standing there, pressed in together, waiting together.

Maggie returned the captain's salute, and the MA bugler stepped forward and played Taps.

"He was one of us, and we are part of each other, hoo-ah?" Magazine said after the bugler finished. He had said it quietly enough that some of the soldiers pressed in closer to hear better. There were some hoo-ahs in response, soft and spluttered.

"Private Zimmerman was an uncomplaining man," Magazine said, louder now, "a man without pretense or authority who was done in by the bludgeonings of chance. A terrible cruelty happened to him. And cruelty, as we all know, and as we are reminded in the military every day, cruelty has a huge following. It was this cruelty that overtook Private Zimmerman.

"Many of you in recent days may have asked, how does God have the heart to allow this? It is impossible, sometimes, to even believe that God actually exists out here. But we also know, *we know*, that it's impossible to believe that God *doesn't* exist. Right now, right here, being so mindful of the world's persistent cruelty, we damn sure want our God back.

"We should remember that God uses broken things. Broken soil to produce a crop. Broken clouds to give rain. Peter, weeping and bitter, who returned to a greater power than before, Peter had been broken, like Zimmerman. There is a lesson here for us about mending. When broken bones heal up, they become stronger at the point of the break."

Magazine walked around to the back of the cart, put his hand on the coffin, and without realizing it he clenched a corner of the flag into his fist. His thoughts drifted to the video that the moozh had made of Zimmerman being tortured. He had watched it with Sergeant Major Tran, while the storm was blowing, and now, being physically close to that poor kid again, it made his color rise and the sweat start to come.

The fuckers in the video had the kid's body strapped to a metal table, and they had moved around him, drunken quasimodo-surgeons, just like those shiny green flies, almost calm in their choreography, but busy, too, a tempest of fucking calibans attacking him, shouting *Allahu akbar!* at every cut and stab and assault. The ceiling of the room was low, and the lighting in the video was jerky and shadowy. The men moved like black smoke, like demented giants, pulling Zimmy apart almost nerve by nerve, pulling him apart like warm bread. They were wearing black hood-masks and listened to someone off-camera who whispered instructions about what to do next. Often, in the middle of some gruesome act, they would stop and look directly at the unseen director, waiting for the go-ahead. It was like amateur porn, except it was passionate.

When a fresh cut would start to spew or spurt, like with the gashes in Zimmy's legs and biceps and head, one of the torturers would move in and spray it with a squat white aerosol can marked "AC-Super." When she saw it, Tran guessed it was automotive freon. At one point they also injected him with something from a red syringe. "Could be clotting factor," she had said. "So he wouldn't bleed out." They knew how to kill him, which was easy, and they also knew the blacker art of keeping him barely alive.

They had tied off his upper arm with a tourniquet, and Zimmy was shouting at them when they cut the yellow WWJD bracelet off his wrist. He finally passed out when they sawed off his hand. There wasn't much blood, and one of them sealed the wet dribbling stub with a laundry iron. Several of the torturers fell back horrified at the small puffy explosion of black steam when the hot iron hit home.

They daubed honey into his ears and up his nose, presumably to draw flies, fire ants and scorpions. No Prophet watching this could be pleased with his followers. Zimmerman was pretty much comatose when they went to work with the hammers and spikes. Then four of them, the most eager of the fucking pallbearers, these believers in a merciful God and a peaceful religion, they carried the cross into the yard and propped it up in the corner, the camera jerking along behind them.

One of the moozh then sat in a chair and read a rambling message into the camera. He had a stutter, and the rant took a long time.

• • • •

Magazine looked out at his young troopers gathered around the Gator, but when he began again to speak he was no longer dazed or confused. He didn't search for the words. They came to him.

"The evil that men do, it lives after them. And the evil that has been done to Private Zimmerman has hardened our hearts and darkened our souls. We all have bloody thoughts. Of course we do. There is so much resentment in us now that if any Iraqi might offer us apology, or fruit, or bread, we would be right to think it was poisoned.

"They have snuffed out our brother's brief candle, and now, I promise you, our fury will follow them down. We will track them down, into their caves, into their bedrooms and their outhouses. There isn't a place in this world that doesn't sooner or later drown in the indigos of darkness. And we will find these men within that darkness. Private Zimmerman, we will not forsake you. We will follow your tormentors into the dark places where they live and hide. We will pull a thick blanket of blue night over their bodies, and we will leave them where we kill them. We will not dig them graves. They think they have blunted the tip of our spear. Not even close. They have sharpened it. They have sharpened it.

"Somebody once said to beware the fury of a patient man. And we will be as patient as death, as patient as the planets in their orbits. We will turn sparks into ice. We will grind their mountains into gravel. Into sand. We will not be meek with these butchers. We will not be gentle. They've choked all the pity right out of us. They are not worthy of our pity. We will have no sympathy for these backward devils. I will see them in their graves. Nothing emboldens evil and cruelty so much as mercy, and God, if you should come back to us, *when* you come back to us, you will need to restrain us. You will need to hold back our fury and our vengeance. We will waste no more mercy on this land.

"So, Lord, please now spend your mercy on Private Zimmerman and welcome him into your house of angels. We swore to travel side by side, and to help each other stay in stride. But now our brother's hand has slipped free, and he flies toward grace. He flies to thee. He flies to thee."

8. 'DO OUR CHAINS OFFEND YOU?'

He had really worked on this. It's not the usual great-guy, fallen-hero crap. It doesn't even sound phony. It's like he actually means it. It's literary, historical, almost elegant. Evangelical, and heavy on the brimstone. Wonder how many of his fancy references these guys are picking up on.

This is what Chief Warrant Officer Micah Ford was thinking.

Colonel Magazine *had* worked on his speech, which he needed to do three things --- to give Private Zimmerman a decent sendoff, to applaud the 36 troops who were now leaving on the same Chinook back to Amman, and to welcome a new group of hand-picked soldiers who would be running his base for the next year or so.

Magazine expected the new troops would get up to speed quickly at Freehold. They were experienced soldiers --- all of them sergeants of various stripes and specialties --- but Maggie had wanted no SEALs or Delta among them. He did this on purpose. The Noise Boys from Delta were too much in thrall to the bang-bang. They *needed* the bang-bang. Their endocrine systems ran about 20 degrees hot, and the daily monotony of handling prisoners at an isolated desert compound would drive them batty inside of a week. Those guys, they liked hunting things that could hunt you back. Magazine called them ammosexuals.

Instead, his final Freehold team had been assembled through months of hard physical training and simulations at a full-scale Freehold mockup in the Arizona desert, out near Fort Huachuca. From an original group of 209 volunteers, just 40 soldiers remained.

From the original group at Freehold, Marchand, Romo, Rascal and Spielberg would be staying on. Tran would be staying, too, although she had only just arrived and still counted as new. The holdovers knew the base and could help the new bunch with the transition to optempo. The rest of the guys flying out --- engineers, wrench-turners, Seabees, supply sergeants, a few Force Protection teams --- they were the ones who had gotten the base up and running. "Outstanding work in hellish conditions," Magazine told them. "I salute you."

Freehold hadn't exactly been plug-and-play like its planners and architects had promised. There were kinks in the ventilation systems and the water supply. Glitches with the comms and the generators. E Street Gate, which weighed 4 tons, would sometimes jam open, or sometimes wouldn't open at all. Sand kept sifting into the Tunnel of Love. The departing team had eventually fixed all this stuff, and now Maggie's new group was taking over a fully functioning battle platform, a TOMBS total-war module, and probably the blackest damn hole this side of the Spanish Inquisition.

Magazine spotted his new executive officer among the incoming troopers gathered at the gate. "Chief Ford, Micah, welcome to Freehold," he said. "Good to see you, finally."

"Thank you, sir. Happy to be here, finally. Sorry about Private Zimmerman."

"Yeah, a bad way to start this thing. A bad deal like you can't believe, but we'll get to that later." He turned and raised his voice to include the other soldiers. "Gentlemen, welcome to Combat Outpost Freehold. First Sergeant Marchand and Corporal Sin will take you over to the barracks to get you settled in. We'll brief tomorrow morning after breakfast. More importantly right now, chow is at 1900, which is, what, First Sergeant, an hour from now? Steak and crab legs tonight." Then quietly again to Micah: "Why don't we meet in Safeway at 2100. State of the union. You, me and Tran."

The colonel pointed toward the two Airstreams at the far end of the compound and said, "Safeway's the one on the left."

The interior of Safeway, the Freehold operations trailer, had an aquarium aspect to it. Luminous flat panels and computer monitors were hung on every wall, and there were several desks and laptops and map tables. A full bath and a small kitchenette in the back. A Kitnerboy Redoubt standing safe. An acid-bath document shredder. Recessed can lights overhead created pools of white throughout the stubbornly illuminated trailer.

Tran was already there when Micah arrived. They sat in two camp chairs. The colonel was a pacer, so he paced. With the approximate demeanor of a caged eagle.

"Well, our little oasis here, it ain't exactly Wayne Manor," Magazine said. "You know, in 1945 the OSS took over a Champagne warehouse for their headquarters in Berlin. What did we get? A freakin' aspirin factory.

"What Saddam was doing making aspirin way the fuck out here, I have no idea. When the MET-Alpha team came across this place in oh-three, oh man, they thought they'd found the treasure of the Sierra Madre. Gated compound in the middle of nowhere. High walls. Deep wells. There was modern machinery, stainless tubing, hundreds of old gas masks laying around. And drums of white powder stacked 15 feet high. They quarantined the place for two months. Tested every fucking barrel, but it was all corn starch, cellulose and acetylsalicylic acid. They were hoping for anthrax and came up with Bufferin.

"Right now we're either in Iraq or Jordan, depending on whose map you believe. In six months or a year, Iraq itself might not even exist. Not as we've known it. Anyway, where we are now, we say it's Jordan. King Abdullah granted us a kind of easement to use the place. They call this area Al-Sin, or The Notch, which is about how it looks on the map. The Iraqi Sunnis call it Madeena Wardiyah. The Shiite leadership calls it Jazeera Ramliyah. I hope you're duly impressed, Chief. It took me a good little while to get those pronunciations down." Micah smiled and thumbed him up.

Some three-way chat followed about the Freehold barracks, the recent storm, the quality of the crab at dinner, Micah's flight from Amman. Tran said she liked how Marchand had helped get the new guys squared away in their quarters.

"You know, he's from a town in Nebraska called Smackdab," Magazine said. "What do you imagine that place is like?"

"I bet it ain't exactly Wayne Manor," Micah said, and they all laughed.

Magazine ran his hand over his crewcut and said, "OK, look, there's no way around it, so I'll tell you straight out, we're here to clean up a lot of other people's shit. Bush, Cheney, Obama, Panetta, MI, CIA. And plenty more. FBI, Yoo, Hadley, Feith, Tenet. Feith and Tenet most of all. Christ, the honor roll goes on and on. Addington. Lots of dirty hands. And bloody hands, too, to be frank. We're on deep background here, as you've been told in your ROE briefings, so you know the ground rules, and I'm going to lay it all out. We need to be clear and direct with each other, the three of us. Because we're the ones who are going to make this operation go. Our decision tree here has three branches, that's it. It's a dirty fucking mission and it might feel a little janitorial at times, but it's a critically important mission nonetheless. Chief Ford? Sergeant Major?"

"Sir," with a solid nod from Micah.

"Yes, sir," said Tran. "What's the drill?"

"Thank you, Sarnmajor --- getting me down to cases. To be a bit crude about it, the president is having premenstrual cramps about his legacy. His time is getting short, and legacy is all these people can talk about at the White House. It's like a honeyed potion or some Masonic handshake.

"The trouble is, Guantánamo, in a word, is fucked. It's a dead stick. The president's people finally realized that. Denis McDonough and them. Congress won't let them transfer any of the significant hard-case prisoners out of Gitmo, which means de facto that it can't be closed. The Dirty 30 will always be there. Obviously, the Republicans want to keep the president from scoring any touchdowns so late in the game. They *love* the idea of him not reaching one of his original policy promises. But even his own lawyers won't sign off on the big Gitmo transfers.

"Meanwhile, of course, the detainees there are so lawyered up, Christ, they've probably applied for Obamacare and Pell grants by now. Those fuckers have a better cable package at Gitmo than I do at home in Cloverlyfreakingmaryland. Even before Ash Carter got confirmed they sent some elderly Afghans to Kabul and some ancient Yemenis back to Yemen. 'Terrorists.' My ass. I guarantee those old fucks were way more concerned about their prostates than about any caliphate."

Magazine worked some sanitizer gel into his hands. As he paced.

"This is a long way of getting around to our own little slice of heaven. Freehold was originally conceived as a kind of halfway house for the Gitmo detainees, pending their eventual transfers. But now, in a textbook case of mission creep, instead of processing people from Gitmo, we're going to be handling leftover Iraqi prisoners. We're going to bring them here and let them go. It's as simple as that. It really is. We'll be dropping them right back into Iraq. That's why we've had you drilling so hard on the Iraqi Arabic, Chief."

"These prisoners are left over from what, sir? From where?"

"From the war. The big war. 2003, four, five. Some of them were in the deck of cards. Remember that gimmick? Fucking Jerry Bremer. Don't get me going on *that* guy."

"So these detainees have been at Gitmo all this time?"

"No. They've never been to Gitmo. Way too many lawyers there. And too much Red Cross. These guys, well. Hmmm. They're sort of. They're like non-persons. They barely exist."

"But we still have them in custody? That's going on 10 or 12 years now."

"Uh-huh." Magazine shot a brief look at Tran.

"Sir, I apologize if it sounds like I'm interviewing you," Micah said. "I don't mean to. I'm just not very clear about what you're saying."

"No apologies, Chief. I was the one who was just running his mouth about being clear and direct. Look, these guys were some of the nastiest actors in the old Iraq. Baath Party goons, Saddam-family flunkies, Mukhabarat, arms dealers. Interior Ministry agents. You'll see their dossiers. Atrocity generals. Assassins. A real fucking nest of vipers. We grabbed them up, a lot of them, during the first few months of the war. We just didn't always announce that we had arrested them. We pretty much *ghosted* them, is what we did. We could have disappeared them" --- Magazine slit his throat with his index finger --- "but instead we've had them all this time."

"Had them where?"

"In lots of places. Hard sites. All over. At first they made the usual rounds --- Camp Bucca, the Vault at Abu G, the Salt Pit, Bagram. Several places in Syria and Saudi. Diego Garcia, most recently. Samois. Nineveh Wall. Some place called Alta'ash Alsafra. Some private prisons. Round and round the mulberry bush. Military Intelligence considered them certifiably toxic and kept transferring them from one Love Canal to another. MI didn't want to let *any* of them go, even after we'd wrung all the intel out of them. None of these guys was ever registered at any of the sites, not officially, so the ICRC never got a good fix on them. Never got *any* fix on them."

"Alta'ash Alsafra?" said Micah. "In Iraqi Arabic that means 'Yellow Misery.' "

"Izzat so?" Magazine said. "Huh. I never knew that."

"It's a prison?"

"It *was* a prison. It was one of Saddam's smaller palaces on the Euphrates and it had a jail in the basement. Uday threw the Iraqi national soccer team in there after they lost some big tournament back in the '90s.

Apparently he kneecapped the captain and the goalie so they'd never play again. Sweet guy."

"Yellow Misery --- I think that's going to be my new nickname," said Tran. A bit of a smile. The two men laughed.

"And now these guys, these detainees, they're coming here to be released?" Micah said. "Where are they now?"

More hand sanitizer.

"Look, there's no way to finesse this. And again, we're on deep background and need-to-know, so." Magazine walked over to a side table and turned on a small fan.

"So the prisoners coming here are currently at our black sites. That's Big Secret No. 2. They've been in the farm system for the last 10 years or so. There's 151 of them, prisoners I mean, all told. They're in Poland, Morocco, Brazil. Shit, they're all over, really. Russia has a bunch of them. Putin agreed to take them if we didn't squawk about what he was doing in Georgia and Chechnya way back when. The Chinese, same deal. Beijing took 67 of them after Bush agreed not to meet with the Dalai Lama at the White House. In the end, CIA outsourced them to, what, something like 30 countries in all."

Micah: "The rendition program is dead, though. That was announced a few years ago."

"They did announce that, yes. 'The CIA no longer operates black sites.' That was Panetta himself, 2009, when he was DCI. Those might have been his exact words. Technically, he wasn't lying --- the CIA *was* out of the black-site business. But it was a con. CIA accountants were told to switch the agency's sites to Pentagon control and Pentagon funding. So just like that, the CIA, bang, was legally in the clear. The prisons were still there, they just had a new landlord --- Ye Olde Department of Defense. It was all black-boxed, of course, so nobody saw the budget lines and nobody followed up. Nobody *could* follow up.

"Meanwhile, the Renditions and Detentions Group is busier than ever. It kills me that the big shots go up to Congress to testify and they always call it 'extraordinary rendition,' as if it was 1 or 2 parts per billion. There was never anything 'extra-ordinary' about it. In fact it was *completely* ordinary. Always was. If anything it was rote. Rote rendition. Ho-hum rendition."

The table fan turned and whirred and turned back.

"So now, to further complicate things, here come the Russians, who are more than a little pissed at Mr. Obama's sanctions over Ukraine and their own suck-ass economy with the ruble being in the toilet and all. Sergei Lavrov has been threatening to reveal that our black sites are still operational. Talk about pulling a Crazy Ivan. You can imagine what this would do to The Obama Legacy, capital T, capital O, capital L.

"So Lavrov gets deep into the J.T.S. Brown one night at a U.N. party and he starts groping Sam Power. She gives him a pretty nasty titty-twister to get him off her --- that's the version I heard, anyway --- and he gets pissed off. I guess he threw down one bolshoi tantrum. Later, more whiskey, same party, he privately told [redacted] they were thinking about releasing the detainees they've been keeping for us. He said they were going to aeroflot them to Cuba, put them on a tugboat at Mariel and set the autopilot for South Beach in Miami.

" [redacted] panicked and persuaded Samantha to apologize. She hated doing it, but she did."

Ah, diplomacy. This was the kind of stuff that Micah's dad had always known about. The deals and the dealing and the double-crossing.

"Hey, how about something to drink?" Magazine said. "I could use a Coke, all this talking. Chief?"

"A Coke, sure, thank you, sir."

"Sarnmajor?"

"Red Bull for me, sir, thank you."

A fly landed just then on the back of Tran's wrist. She flipped her hand over and caught the fly in mid-air. She went to the door of the trailer, opened it, and let the fly go. Micah and Magazine just looked at each other, a little wide-eyed and holy-shit.

Micah tried some small talk with Tran as the colonel got their drinks and fiddled with a big video monitor. She had barely said a thing so far. He asked her about people they knew in common at Fort Huachuca, what had been the toughest part of the Ranger course, whether Zimmerman had been in much pain at the end. She answered briefly, politely, as if being careful. Or evasive. He sensed that she already knew (and understood) a good bit more about the Freehold situation than he did, but she wasn't giving anything away. The mark of a good security officer, Micah was thinking. She had been this way at Huachuca, too --- private, aloof, occasionally friendly, but pretty much all business. But weren't they all on the same team now, the three of them?

"Sergeant Major, how about you tell us your life story?" Micah said. "Start at the beginning, don't leave anything out and make it interesting."

Head shake and eye roll from Tran.

"OK, no, seriously, how long have you been a sergeant major?"

"Two years, 264 days and this morning," she said evenly.

" 'Gladiator'," Micah said. "Nice." That drew thin smiles from both of them. So there *was* something in her.

Magazine: "Chief, I've seen this goddamn video a few times now since we retrieved Private Zimmerman, and the sergeant major has watched it with me once. I haven't uploaded it to Langley or Washington yet because there's some Arabic in here that I want translated first. Some stuff I want to understand before I send it up to the Big Brains. I want us to look at it forensically. You good with that?"

"Absolutely, sir." Micah pulled out a small leather Moleskine and a pen.

"Now, this is pretty rough stuff, I just want you to know. This videotape. Another Coke before we start? I wish I had some Jack to liven it up for you."

"I'm good, sir. I'm off the Jack."

"I know you are, Chief. I know you are. I can be a dumb-ass sometimes. Sorry."

"No worries, sir. I'm all set."

The young man's long body was on the table. The purple cloak. The hooded men moved around him so slowly, so carefully. They hooked his toes to wires from a car battery and something sizzled. Then his testicles. Zimmy shouted madly, straining at the straps on his legs, then his body tried to go rigid and fetal. *"Ba kellim Suzan! Ba kellim Suzan! Allahu akbar!"*

Magazine paused the video and looked at Micah. "What the fuck is that?"

"*Ba kellim Suzan* --- it literally means 'talking with Susan.' I've never heard that before. It must be Iraqi slang for this particular act of torture."

When the video resumed, a man sprayed a large cut with an aerosol can.

"That's automotive freon they're using to seal the wound," Tran said to Micah. "To freeze it. Like cauterizing it."

They got to the point in the video where the hot iron steamed against Zimmerman's severed wrist. Someone off-camera shouted at the startled torturers.

" 'You're showing weakness,' that's what he's saying to them," Micah said, intent on the voice and not looking away from the screen. "Now he's telling them to calm themselves or leave the room. 'You are soldiers of Allah. You are the instruments of God. Now act like it.' "

"These motherfuckers," the colonel said.

Zimmerman was revived, and an older Muslim man, unmasked, brought in clamps to keep Zimmy's eyes open as he pulled up the eyelids and sewed them to the brows. He then used a scalpel to take the eyeballs out of the head. *Takbir! Allahu akbar! Allahu akbar!* The room was riotous with shouting and blood. Zimmy thrashed wildly on the table, he made terrifying animal sounds, then passed out. More freon. And gauzy bandages, packed right into the empty sockets.

"Jesus Christ," Micah said.

"Why do men do this?" Tran said, almost to herself. "I know women kill, too, but not like this. Only men do this."

"There's nothing one man will not do to another man, especially when religion's involved. The religion uncages the cruelty," the colonel said. "It's what somebody wrote about Northern Ireland: 'Trust had gone out of the land, and brother no longer gasped at the bloodshed of brother.' "

The torturers in the video were now going to work with the hammers and spikes.

Later, out in the backyard, when Zimmy's body started to slide off the cross, several men came out with a coil of wire and loops of innertube.

"Look. The cross won't support his weight but they're not panicking," Micah said. "They have the supplies they need right there, like they've done this before or they know what they're doing."

The camera went back inside. The head torturer sat in a chair and read a message into the camera --- speaking in vaguely excited, heavily accented

English. Was that a British accent? He was a young guy, no mask, with a patchy black beard. Had a bit of a stutter, going open-mouthed and panicky-tense on the M's and W's. It was a formal and unoriginal rant, the usual claptrap about the Prophet's wisdom and the filth of the infidels: the standard jihadi nonsense that had been twisted from some of the Koran's loveliest verses.

"We see your muh, muh, muh mo-tives. You are wrong. You do not belong here. Two of our lions terrified all of P-P-Paris and avenged the Prophet. Just as the filthy French people paid in b-b-blood, so will you. This unbeliever wuh, wuh, was a wuh, wuh, wuh, wonderful gift to us from Allah. You have orphaned our children, n-n-now this one is left for *you*, as gift for your President Obama whose crimes are muh, muh, more evil than the Bush. We will break Am, Am, America in two, and the caliphate wuuuhh, wuh, will last until the end of the world."

He then switched from English to Arabic --- Iraqi or Syrian Arabic, Micah couldn't be sure right off. The stutter disappeared. But it was the same sort of terrible holy gibberish. The jargony parts sounded Iraqi. Instead of saying "leaders," the young man would use the term *al mudbakh*, literally "the kitchen," which in casual conversation meant "the decision-makers." He also referred to Zimmerman a few times as a sheep, *al-tali*, which Micah knew was widely-used jihadi slang for kidnap victim.

"What's he saying now, Chief?"

"He's explaining that they cut off the back of Zimmerman's head so the birds could eat from his brains, as the Holy Koran instructs. They cut off the right hand so he could never salute his officers again, or shake another man's hand, or properly caress his wife. Caress or massage, I'm not sure, I'll have to listen to that again. He's saying the black line on Zimmerman's throat was personally ordered by the Caliph al-Baghdadi with this message: 'We could have beheaded this infidel invader like we did the others, like John the Baptist, but we have spared his throat in order to show the beauty and completeness of our mercy. We have a code of honor in Islam. We've had our revenge.' The rest of you infidels should prepare your throats. Malahim awaits you. We mean to martyr you all, and we'll grind your bones to dust."

"All they're missing are the fava beans and a nice Chianti," Tran said, the anger rising.

Micah, translating: " 'The Caliph has quenched our thirst and restored our souls.' That sounds like the 23rd Psalm. 'He is a *river* to our people!' "

The rant in Arabic went on and on, the young man veering from a calm anger to finger-wagging shouts.

Micah: "He's talking a lot about *jihad bil saif* --- jihad by the sword. He's denouncing 'those who tear the skin off my people.' That's weird. I think that's actually from the Bible, too, but it's the Old Testament. He says the Islamic State fighters will break our bones into pieces and quote 'chop your bodies like meat going into a kettle.' Or a pot. A stew pot. 'We will eat these bits of meat like they are sweetmeats of vengeance. We will eat them at your graves. We will eat them in the rain and in the dark."

"That sounds like fuckin' Dr. Seuss," said Tran.

Micah made notes as the jihadi talked more quickly. The guy had a kind of diabolical charisma to him. Micah quickly let go of that thought. He pointed out to Magazine the black ISIS flag in the video, which hung as a backdrop.

"We need to *spray* these fuckers with Black Flag," Magazine said. "Fucking termites. D-Con their ass. Call in the fucking Orkin Man with some B-52 fumigation."

Micah translated: " 'Do our chains offend you? Do you know our sins? You have colluded with our enemies. You will descend into Hell through three folds of smoke, as the Prophet has told us, and you will find no shelter from the flames. Sparks as high as mountains will issue forth. The Day of Sorting Out is coming. You are rejecting the truth and you cannot trick Allah. We will burn your chariots' --- I guess he means vehicles ---

'we will burn your chariots in the smoke and our swords shall devour your baby lions. Your soldiers are weaklings. They already feel the crack of our whips. American soldiers, we are coming, watch your back. Because your names stick in the throat of God. Leave our land, our wheat, our salt, our wound. The entire world is applauding your downfall, for who has not felt your cruelty? For five hundred years you have treated us like dogs. But now we have become wolves.' "

It was a lot to take in. The razor wire, the spikes, the ranting, the squirts of freon, the scalding iron on the bloody hand, the astonished giddiness of the torturers. They took his *eyes*. These ISIS guys were putting the war back into warfare. If Americans back home ever got a look at this video, it'd be so much for Geneva. This was wet work worthy of the Janjaweed. Hutus. South Carolina slavemasters. This wasn't any version of war imagined by Patton or the Iliad. It was psychotic and grotesque. It was serial, industrial murder. Heads on pikes, sewing up vaginas, mass graves, murdering cartoonists, blowing up nursery schools. This was a whole new branch of mathematics.

"Chief?" the colonel said. "You OK there?"

Micah twitched, startled to hear Magazine's voice. His concentration had wandered after the video ended. His mind, oddly, began scrolling through prime-number distributions and the Riemann hypothesis. Divisible by 1 and itself. By 1 and himself. A God of rescue. Just a shout away. Just a shot away. The violence of the torture session was working on him. He thought he had put all these tremors away. He thought he was better. He *had* felt better. Now this.

"Yes, sir, I'm OK. Sorry. That was really something. You warned me. But that. That was something else."

"Some terrible shit," Magazine said. "Worst I've ever seen, and I had a first-hand look at what the Srpska Scorpions did in Bosnia. They stopped just short of turning all the Muslims into soap and lampshades. Look, I'm sorry to keep you guys so late, but I want to get in the full brief. You can hit me with any questions tomorrow. Or any time. A lot of this logistics stuff will work itself out in the drills."

The colonel resumed his pacing. His throat hurt. He ran through the basic intake procedures for the detainees. Some would arrive by truck through Jordan, most would come by helo from Amman or Baghdad. They'd be wearing the full blackout package --- hoods, goggles, gags and earmuffs. Five-point shackles. The orange jumpsuits. No food en route, only sips of water. Prochlorperazine suppositories and Depends. No talking whatsoever by the guards, everybody gloved up, no skin-to-skin contact. Just like the run-throughs in Arizona.

"We'll do our work in the dark, we'll do what we can, we'll give what we have," Magazine said quietly, as if to himself. "The best important work isn't done by limelight. Here is the truth --- actual heroism has no audience and receives no ovation. No one queues up to see it. End of the day, this mission is our least bad choice."

He stopped and faced his XO directly.

"This is where we're calling an audible on you, Micah. We're not going to interrogate these guys --- they truly have nothing left to say --- but we do want them to sign a release form before we let them go. It's not a confession, and we have to drive that idea home to them. Not a confession. They aren't pleading guilty to anything. [redacted] at the White House came up with the legal language and we have the forms already translated and printed out in Arabic. You can look at them tomorrow. For the prisoners it's the friggin' emancipation proclamation. Basically it says they agree not to fight against the United States or our allies once they're released, and they also won't associate with anyone who intends to harm us. If they do resume the fight or fraternize with any bad guys, they acknowledge that we can go after them. It's pretty simple. They sign the form and they can check right out of our little roach motel. They'll be home --- or at least back in Iraq --- inside of 72 hours."

"I would think these guys are pretty hard cases after all these years," Micah said. "What if they won't sign? We didn't game any of this at Huachuca."

"My boss says everybody should sign. We've only got 24 cells and we'll have 150 guys to crank through here. Deptempo is going to be high.

"Most of this is going to be on you, Micah --- you talking to them in Arabic and getting them to sign. They need to believe that it'll be horrifying here if they refuse to sign. No instigated physical brutality, absolutely none, just like we drilled at Huachuca. But they also have to think this is the end of the line, the last station. They have to be convinced that we've *finally* thrown out the rule book. 'Fuck Geneva.' That's the mantra. Convince them they're going to be living in a mayonnaise jar --- forever.

"They also have to be made to understand that we are now completely expert in this kind of deep imprisonment. Which we are. We've been learning it, refining it. The shrinks say this kind of incarceration --- in every single case --- results in something called acute induced dysphrenia. A.I.D., an unfortunate acronym, I know. But every deet must understand that he will very rapidly lose his mind in here --- and that we won't care if he does. It's an entirely new game, and they have no idea of the new rules."

Micah: "Sir, if they can go free after signing the release form, what's the downside? Why *wouldn't* they sign?"

Magazine: "There *is* no downside, Chief, and that's the other point you'll make to them. Look, we're not going to negotiate with these fuckers. They're still the freakin' enemy. They're all as guilty as hell and I'm convinced they mean to do us harm, given the chance. We make the offer, then lock 'em down and let 'em chew on things. We know from their Penske files that several of them won't sign no matter what, either because they're authority-adverse or they've already gone mental or whatever.

"They won't know this, but we're going to release them anyway. Nobody overstays. But we still want those signatures, principally for legal cover. I'm probably going to be on your ass, Micah, if any one guy is here longer than three or four weeks."

"Understood."

Colonel Magazine was still burying the lede on the Freehold mission, and Tran knew this operation wasn't going to be the simple phantom toll-booth that he was describing.

"For all the political water we're carrying here," Magazine said, "the mission isn't just an escape hatch for the agency guys and the politicians. It's not *completely* janitorial. We have a significant tactical component, too, which might even be the key to the whole deal. If we get this thing right it could go a long way to stopping these ISIS bastards."

He was back on the hand sanitizer.

"Even though we won't be keeping them long-term, when they leave here we want them angry, hateful and foaming at the friggin' mouth."

"What's the strategy to that, sir?" Tran asked, lobbing the colonel a softball. She knew very well what the strategy was. This was a prod to the old man to close the damn circle. *Get your foot in the door, sir, then drop the hammer.*

"Chief, a bunch of DARPA medical engineers from Lab 257 at Plum Island have come up with a miniature tracking device that can be easily implanted. They call them nano-tags. They're about half the size of a pencil eraser."

"Implanted? Into a person?"

"Uh-huh. Yep. They draw their power from the body's own warmth. It's incredible. They never run down or turn off. I'm correct on this, right, Sarnmajor?"

"That's correct, sir."

"These babies apparently put out one hell of a signal, and they're *unique* signals, so we can track each guy individually. Anywhere. They're micro-transponders is what they are. Like the black box on an airplane, except they're the size of teenager's zit.

"We can track anydamnthing now --- cars, donkeys, weapons. And released prisoners. Track them from drones, helicopters, Humvees, AWACS. Even an F-16 can draw a bead on these fuckers. It's just an astounding breakthrough. So many applications. We're going to be sciencing the hell out of these things. Anyway, we've been legally cleared to use them on the detainees, and we'll be tagging everyone who comes through here. That's the principal part of Tran's tasking. She has actually seen the tags in action. Even I haven't done that."

Micah turned to look at Tran. She looked to Maggie, who nodded.

"I've seen them in action three times, Chief," she said. "The first time was at MacDill, on a drone pilot's scope. There's incredible clarity to the signal blooms. They just *sparkle.* It's like I was watching HBO on my Samsung plasma. The Air Force tagged seven sheep in New Mexico and turned them loose in the desert at the White Sands Missile Range. A Predator drone was launched out of Holloman and acquired the signals. Predator 3034 was the call sign. We actually ran things from MacDill, even though the pilot was physically at Creech Air Force Base, a female pilot, and she took out six of the sheep with Hellfires.

"The second time was just a surveillance and training op out of Carlisle Barracks, and then, uh, yeah, well, the third time was Columbia. Three weeks ago."

"Colombia? What, against the FARC?"

"Not that Colombia. Columbia. Maryland. NSA."

"Oh, uh-huh. I got it. Of course."

"Stryker, Medtronic and the Office of Technical Service also engineered us a nifty injector gun," she said. "The sheep barely flinched when it hit them. In human trials, though, it can sometimes take a couple of stitches to close up the site. I've been trying butterfly bandages and liquid stitches, too. And I've been practicing with the gun."

"Practicing on who?"

"Not on *who*, Chief. Jeez, it's not so sinister as all that. On cadavers, back in the States. And on potatoes."

"Chief, look, now don't be pissed, you're fully in the loop here," said Magazine. "I understand if you're maybe feeling a little excluded, but that wasn't my call. From here on, you're going to be pretty much running the whole mission above ground. You'll be reading all the traffic with Langley, all the outgoing mail. Hell, even my mail. Nurse Ratched here will be the queen of the underworld. The underboss."

"No worries, sir," Micah said. Dead calm. He could hear his father telling him to breathe. "I understand. This was highly secured information and we were in a need-to-know posture. I get that. I didn't need to know before. And now I do. But can I ask? Obviously the prisoners won't agree to these injections. So how will we tag them? I'm guessing that's the operative verb --- tag?"

"Tag, chip, mark, paint --- those are the ones I've heard," said Tran. "An earlier generation of the tags were called microdots, and before that they tried using super-thin filaments of copper that were stranded and braided together. Those were too hard to inject. 'Poor functionality,' they called it.

"But we have lots of ideas about implant strategies. They've been gaming it at the War College. They call it 'slipping in the medicine.' During routine dental work is one obvious way. We can put a camel spider in their cell and wait for a bite that needs treatment. I can 'inadvertently' scratch a guy with a blistering agent that will require 'treatment.' We can say we're giving them flu shots. That may prove to be the easiest way. Treating a bite from a dog on a K-9 team. Take off a pre-cancerous mole. A hepatitis vaccination, or a tetanus shot, or a vitamin shot. I could also just zap them in their cell with a fentanyl aerosol and they'd be out for an hour or so. They'll wake up with a little cut or a butterfly bandage under their butt or in their tricep. We can tell them they fainted and fell into a table or something, so we stitched up the cut while they were out. Flunitrazepam will work, too. They won't remember a damn thing. GHB. Ketamine. Adropan. Lethedrine. Rohypnol."

"The date-rape drug?"

"Yeah. Roofies. That shit *works.*"

Magazine could see that Micah, even with that big brain of his, was now approaching some level of overload. (He wouldn't mention for now that Corporal Sin had been secretly training as the mission's spider wrangler, should they need to go that way.)

"OK, guys, let's start wrapping this up. It's already past 1. Micah, I know I've dumped a lot on you tonight, but you're going to make an outstanding XO and we're going to accomplish good things here. Believe me. It's great to have you on board.

"And really, when you think about it, imagine, down the road, these nano-tags could very well change the nature of warfare. At the very least in the short term they'll help with the fight against these Islamic State cocksuckers. We've got to start thinking beyond our guns. Those days are closing fast. I think we're moving away, finally, from the Rumsfeld doctrine of 'Fix' to the Cheney doctrine of 'Punish.' Although to tell you the truth, we've got no codified strategy over the horizon because this ISIS bunch is so asymmetric. We might just end up having to bleed them. It could take a decade or more, but all the smart guys already know it'll be a long game. And maybe there'll be no 'winning' at all, at least not winning as we've always defined it. Maybe one side just loses more slowly than the other side.

"We're actually hoping our detainees *do* rejoin the fight in Iraq. 'Get in bed with ISIS, go ahead.' We *want* them to hook up with their Baathist brothers and their old army buddies. Put the bacillus back in the lab, as it were. We'll know where they are 24/7 and if we find multiple signals in any one place, bingo, that makes them legitimate targets. They automatically get a place on the Kill Not Capture list. They'll have broken their signed agreement and we can get the angry birds after them. There's definitely going to be a Hellfire missile in their future."

Magazine was warming to the topic, despite the late hour and the long day. Getting evangelical again.

"This is the huge tactical upside to Freehold. These tags, I'm telling you, Chief, they're little goddamn miracles. A deus ex machina kind of thing. They even transmit GPS and map coordinates --- they supply their own targeting data! It'll be like shooting skeet. *Pull!* Germs, meet penicillin. We have the chance to get right into the *plasma* of ISIS. Really, this is a freaky-deaky piece of technology. God, the *reach* we'll have. We're going to drink their fucking milkshake. Our detainees will be like radioactive seeds in a cancer procedure. We release them into the body, and they show us right where to aim the chemo."

Magazine pulled up a chair facing his soldiers.

"OK, last item, I promise. I'm going to keyhole it for you: As of today, there are 20 people in the world who know about this base and what we're about to do here --- six each from Defense and CIA, two from inside the White House, and one each from NSA, JSOC and Treasury."

"That's only 17, sir," said Micah, the mathematician. Magazine waited a moment for him to round up to 20: "Oh, OK, sorry sir, duh --- plus the three of us."

"Makes 20," the colonel said evenly. "Even [redacted] and [redacted] are not in the loop on this, and only one of the Joint Chiefs. Chuck Hagel knows, I can tell you that. He greenlit the thing two years ago. So do [redacted] and [redacted]. But Ash Carter and Susan Rice don't know. Obviously, and necessarily, we're in a small club. Every team during the R&D was silo'd off from all the other ones."

"Does the president know about us, sir?" Micah asked.

"Nice try, Chief. But that's classified."

9. A DEEP TUNNELY QUALITY

Being down there, down in Jungleland, it was like being inside a crippled porcelain submarine, a sub that was dead in the water and sitting at the bottom of the Laurentian Abyssal. Buried there in the desert, 30 feet down, the quiet was total and unnerving.

Nearly every surface was smooth and fiberglassy. There was no here here. The windowless cells had been lined with lead panels, so that an inmate screaming from schizophrenia or pounding on a wall from dementia could not be heard in an adjoining cell. Doors functioned more like airlocks, with a soft pneumatic shhh. And you could barely hear the magnetic locks take hold. No slamming iron gates, no jangling keys, no pings, virtually no metal on metal anywhere in the unit, nothing to interrupt the white noiselessness of the place. Even the topside generators had been rigged for silent running. What had the colonel said --- living in a mayonnaise jar? That was pretty much it.

"Creepy," said Micah.

"Yeah," said Tran.

"Yeah," said Marchand.

The three of them combined had trained for hundreds of hours in the Fort Huachuca mockup, but this. This Jungleland felt different. It had a deep tunnely quality. This place did not say prison. It said coffin.

The layout was simple, like a thermometer turned sideways. The bulb had an intake area and a door to the tunnel to the helipad annex they called Nebraska, plus two shower rooms, the control room for the guards, and Tran's clinic. The tube of the thermometer was the central corridor, 120 feet long, with a dozen single cells on each side. (The troops would come to call the hallway the Gangplank.)

Tran learned her way around the clinic while taking care of Zimmerman, and she gave Micah a rundown of its equipment and capabilities. Marchand took them through the rest of the unit, and they talked over the basic operational and emergency protocols. At the foot of the access stairwell to return to the surface, Marchand pointed up the stairs and said, "This is the only bad thing. It made my guys nervous because it's the only exit."

"One pipe in, one pipe out," Micah said. "Like how we protect our computer systems. It's great for security."

"Not so great if there's a fire," Marchand said.

"Hoo-ah that," said Tran. The Jungleland architects originally had drawn up two exits, with another stairway at the far end of the corridor. But the Kroll planners vetoed that, figuring that the single exit would keep the troops extra careful on the job, and even a little bit on edge. Tran said the idea was "some bullshit about guarding against 'accidents of variance while defeating workplace routine.' "

"Excuse me, ma'am, but I'd wager there's not gonna be *anything* routine about *this* workplace," Marchand said.

"Hoo-ah that," Micah and Tran said in unison.

Up on the surface, standing on the infield of the Freehold compound, surrounded by the high, mud-brick walls of the old aspirin factory, it felt not unlike being in a small-college football stadium. The rectangular compound was about that size. There was the one main gate --- one pipe in, etc. --- and Maggie's Airstreams were down in the far end zone. A spongy new jogging track ran around the inside base of the wall. Twenty-foot guard towers stood at the corners and were equipped with .50-cals and floodlights. The paved strip of E Street went right down the middle. The Seabees had lined up four new Quonset huts along the strip, and they held barracks, supply depots, generators, the motor pool, gym, chow hall, all that.

Tran and Micah each had their own quarters, and his bedroom was attached to a hard room called the SCIF, or Secret Compartmented Information Facility. The base encryptors, its Internet connection and the single in/out pipe --- they were all inside the SCIF.

Between Maggie's Airstreams was a small grassy area with a footprint the size of a two-car garage back home. Cammie netting was strung overhead to mellow the buzz and blare of the Mesopotamian sun. "Fertile Crescent, my ass," Magazine had said when he first got a look at the place. Even the Bedouins had absconded. Nevertheless, under the netting, the colonel had been trying to grow tomatoes and geraniums in a raised garden-bed. His own actual Farmville. The topsoil had been shipped in from the States, two pallets' worth at the back of an incoming construction container. The tomatoes were Mortgage Lifters and Brandywines, and for the geraniums Maggie had gone with the blue Renoir variety. The recent sandstorm, however, had pretty well obliterated his little adventure in botany.

The colonel's other bit of folly, sitting on a low wooden deck under the netting, was a three-person hot tub complete with underwater lights, lumbar jets and a bench seat.

Mid-morning, inside Safeway, and Micah was running diagnostics on the COP's internal computer systems. Colonel Magazine, sweat-soaked and work-clothed, came into the trailer and glug-glugged a bottle of Zamzam water from the frig. He had been trying to dig the sand out of his demolished tomato patch, and he had Corporal Posner cleaning out the spa, which, since the sandstorm, was now half-filled with Jordanian desert.

"Chief, good morning. Sorry to keep you up so late last night. That was a big gulp of medicine and a lot of new news. Maybe you felt like I blindsided you."

"No problem, sir. I will say, though, that this mission sure has gotten a lot more interesting in the last 24 hours."

"Yeah, well, let's hope it doesn't get any *more* interesting. I assume all our gauges are in the green? Which would be more than I can say for my freakin' garden out there. My *former* garden."

"The system looks fine, sir. No new personal mail, although we just got a batch of detainee dossiers from Langley. Seven in all. I haven't seen them yet. They're theta-encrypted, so you'll have to look at them inside the SCIF. When do you expect we'll start receiving prisoners?"

"A week or two, that'd be my guess, although, hell, it could be tomorrow or it could be another month. We really need to get rolling on this thing, though. If those ISIS fuckers ever figure out we're camped out in their precious desert, it's going to be more combat and less outpost around here. I'd like you to open up those detainee jackets and read them over. After lunch is fine, maybe after you get in some PT with Tran's group. I just want to get a general sense of this first bunch. I don't need you to drill down into their life stories, not unless you want to. Just enough to give me a quick brief. We can do that here, over dinner later."

"Can do, sir. Also I was thinking about your garden, if you want to rebuild it. Maybe we could, you know, requisition a truckload of dirt from down where the Marsh Arabs are. South of where the Tigris joins the Euphrates. That's supposedly where the Garden of Eden was located. That's one theory, anyway."

"Damn, Micah, that's a hell of a thought. Dirt from the Garden of Eden. Great idea. We'd probably need one helicopter for one day. Or less. I could make that happen."

"The zoos in Baghdad or Amman also might have some elephant dung they'd give you. Or trade you. Assuming they even have any elephants any more. You wouldn't need much, right? It's just a thought. Apparently it's the greatest fertilizer in the world, elephant shit. Zoo-doo, I think they call it."

Magazine just looked at Micah. Big grin, hands on hips, shaking his head. "So you really *are* a freakin' genius, eh, Chief? I guess they were right about you. Pretty resourceful for a guy who couldn't count to 20 last night."

Micah smiled. "Hoo-ah that, sir. I finally worked it out on my slide rule. Seventeen plus three."

There were no weapons allowed down in Jungleland, that was the standing reg. A gun would not solve *any* problem that might arise down there, and it would almost certainly make things worse. No detainee coming in --- hooded, shackled, un-fit, jail-shocked and all pharmed up --- would ever be able to subdue a two-man Freehold team. If a prisoner physically resisted or lashed out, any trooper could easily manhandle him into submission with a clinch, a strike, a takedown.

But with weapons in the unit, if a detainee were to grab an unsecured gun, that *would* pose a problem.

An even larger problem would arise if bullets penetrated the interior fiberglass skin of the unit: Sand would start pouring in and Jungleland would become a slowly-filling hourglass. So this hard site, in its way, was actually quite fragile. Gunplay in Jungleland would be tantamount to firing a weapon inside a space capsule: Nothing good could come of it. So, no guns.

Besides, every Freehold trooper could handle himself, thanks in large part to Tran. One of the more impressive talents on the sergeant major's résumé was martial arts, particularly close-quarters combat and hand-to-hand fighting. She had drilled the platoon nearly every day at Fort Huachuca, and each man now had serious skills. Some of them had been drawn to judo, muay thai, aikido. Others liked karate, kung fu or jiujitsu. Several guys went in for Systema. She allowed for all of it, disparaged none of it, and she brought in expert trainers in all the disciplines.

Tran herself preached and practiced krav maga, the Israeli hybrid whose plain-vanilla name in Hebrew meant "contact combat." For Certified Master Tran, krav maga better translated as "finish it." Break the nose, stab an eye, crumple a knee, then get the hell out of there. That was her approach. If you have to fight, finish it fast. Don't box, don't grapple. Even with admirable strength and good technique, women did not fare well in extended fights with big strong men. Those were just the inalienable facts and physics of fighting. One of her mottos was, "Be the first to the fight, and arrive in bad humor."

When she first began studying martial arts, as a boot corporal, Tran would find herself in any number of emergency rooms, often at night, usually after some vigorous sparring at an off-base dojo. She would hobble in with bruised thighs and a dislocated knee. Or she'd present with a torn eyebrow, a split lip, a cracked knuckle, a cracked rib. A swollen cheek, a streamer of bloody snot down her neck, somebody else's blood on the front of her gi.

While they patched her up, the ER nurses would invariably take the same gentle lines of questioning with her. A social worker would often be summoned, and they always asked the same things. *Who did this? Howsabout we call the police. Trouble at home? Husband, boyfriend? Y'all been doing some drinkin' tonight?* The word "attacked" was frequently heard. Tran would try to explain: *Karate training, things happen, see my outfit, see this brown belt, it's no biggie, really, it's not what you think*. The MSWs rarely bought it, and after awhile Tran would just have to wave them off. "OK, thank you, now please leave me the fuck alone." Then she'd limp back to base.

Physical training at COP Freehold was mandatory, six days a week, just as it had been at Huachuca. At Freehold you could run 4 miles on the track outdoors or you could spar inside, your choice on any given day, as long as you sparred at least once a week. For her first session at Freehold, Tran had 28 men gathered around the sparring mat.

At the center of the mat, Tran called out pairs of names, battle buddies who had teamed up at Fort Hoochy-Koochy.

"Swigert and Dunbar, you're up first. Then Flipper and Brown. Sumner and Brooks. Pepe and Roche. Velasquez and Buford. That should get us going. Three-minute bouts. Check your gear, gentlemen. Do what you want with your groin protectors, but I want that headgear cinched tight. Do it now. Head injuries are no joke. With head trauma, you run the risk of not being you any more. It's not a black eye or a split lip. It's an existential threat.

"The same with securing your shinguards and elbow pads. Mouthguards *in*. Do it now. I'm the only dentist within 400 miles, and I'm using major air quotes around the word dentist. Think 'Marathon Man.' Believe me, you do *not* want *me* working on your chipped teeth. Or your groins, for that matter." That brought a laugh from the men.

Sergeant Flipper whispered to Brown, "That Tran, man, she's got tits *and* balls. The girl be magnum."

"She's freakin' rebar, dude," Brown said quietly. "Freakin' Lara Croft. You fight her, you better bring a sack lunch."

Tran: "I want spirited sparring, gentlemen. Think about your technique. Counter your opponent. Hone the attacking techniques that we've worked on. You know by now that I incline toward the view that if you're seriously attacked, you should just go ahead and fuck the dude up. These will be the rules of engagement down in Jungleland. Gouge his eyes. Break his jaw. Rake his face. For now, though, let's restrain ourselves. This is still just sparring."

"Swigert, Dunbar, on my whistle. Ready! Fight!"

The troops were well into their sparring session when Micah arrived. He had been reading the new detainee dossiers and lost track of the time. As he walked up, two soldiers were upright and grappling at one edge of the mat. The bigger man, a staff sergeant named George Washington, no shit, he had the smaller trooper in a bear hug from behind.

"OK, stop right there, Washington. But keep ahold of me."

It was Tran. Micah hadn't recognized her with all the padding and the headgear.

"Now here, gentlemen, we have a couple good options. What moves can I make here? Where can I go? Any thoughts?"

Men shouted out suggestions. Tran acknowledged each of them in turn, then said, "Here's my instinct. It's not the only answer. But let's slo-mo it. Washington, stay with me, about half-speed."

As she tried to bite into Washington's right bicep, she squirmed her left arm free, then went into a slight crouch, which caused Washington to have to bend slightly at the knees as well. She dipped her left shoulder, looked downward, then semi-seriously jammed her free hand, palm down, onto the back of Washington's calf behind the knee. His leg gave way, almost involuntarily, almost like it was in spasm. He toppled onto his side and Tran was free. "Now I can pluck an eye, tear an ear, break the nose, attack the throat --- or run like hell. Washington? All good?"

"Good to go, Sergeant Major. Yes, ma'am."

"OK, who's the next pair? Flipper and Brown. Headgear and mouthguards, gentlemen. First Sergeant, can you take over for a minute?" She tossed her whistle to Marchand.

Micah had not geared up for sparring, so Tran got down to just her T-shirt and shorts, gray over black. She took him over to a side mat and they went through some of the basic fighting moves he had tried during his limited time at Huachuca. Heel of the hand to the nose, elbow throws, finger stabs, your basic streetfight attacks.

"Let's try some leg sweeps, OK, Chief? We haven't done those yet. They're easy, they're super effective and they'd be something we might use in a situation downstairs. A lot of martial arts people think sweeping the leg is a joke because it was in that Karate Kid movie. That dipshit grasshopper kick. That one-legged crane kick, or whatever it was. But leg sweeps, they work on almost everybody, even on the really skilled guys, because they usually carry the element of surprise."

She was wound up now, eager to demonstrate, speaking quickly, moving Micah into position on the mat. "Surprise and initiative, Chief. That's Clausewitz on war. Works in martial arts, too. Classic stuff. More important than strategy. We'll go half-speed, OK? OK. Just think of me as your Mister Miyagi." A wisecrack. Huh.

Even when Micah was looking for it, Tran's arcing leg sent him banging onto the mat. She was so deft, even at practice speed, he couldn't defend himself. He'd watch for one leg and it would be the other one that put him down. They were both soon dripping with sweat.

"Now you see the movements," she said. "Simple, right? Now you try."

"I know kung fu," Micah said.

"Show me," Tran said, and it took her another moment to catch his reference. " 'Matrix.' Nice. So show me, Neo. I believe your White Crane kung fu is not strong."

She defeated his first four attempts at the leg sweep and they ended up each time in a fumbly-tumble mess of pushes and grunts. She was strong, maybe stronger than him, even though he outweighed her by 50 pounds. He was thinking he wouldn't want to arm-wrestle her. Tran called a timeout, tweaked his hip-turn a bit and got him to push harder on her shoulder as the first point of attack. On their sixth spar he put her down with a thump.

"Now that was fucking *great,*" she said, flat on her back and smiling up at him. "You swept the leg, even when I knew it was coming. Can't do it any better than that. You got it, Chief. Nice."

The other troopers had stopped 10 minutes earlier to watch their two bosses going at it. When Micah finally put Tran down, they all applauded and hoo-ah'd. Micah hadn't felt that good since he fell into the Connecticut River.

10. OVERCOME BY EVENTS

Do our chains offend you? Sweetmeats of vengeance. Those eyes, and then the squirts of freon.

Micah was in his Freehold bunk, scenes from last week's torture video poisoning his sleep, keeping him awake. *Not again, not the insomnia, please, no. I thought I was past this.* This was how he had felt --- jumpy, sleepless --- back in 2013 when they were vetting him at Langley for inclusion on Magazine's team. [redacted] had kept him waiting for 2 hours the first time. Micah figured the delay was part of the test, so he walked around the CIA campus for awhile, wondering how long it would take a security team to catch up to him.

He had found his way to the agency cafeteria. Its windows looked onto a small interior courtyard that held the famed Kryptos sculpture --- four tall copper panels, joined and curving, perforated with rows of letters. The messages hidden in three of the panels had been decoded rather quickly, just a bit of three-card monte for guys like Micah. But the fourth piece, with its 97 letters, was a tougher nut --- and it had gone unsolved for 25 years now. Even the big Caltech savants and NSA brains hadn't cracked it.

He got a mug of the agency's decaf, spigoted from a chrome Farberware urn that cooked the coffee into a nasty black slurry. You could float a roll of quarters in the stuff. He walked out into the late-winter sunshine. Sat on a bench in the courtyard. Puzzled over the mystery panel. Between subtle shading and the absence of light. He drifted off. Swam out, way out, into Apalachicola Bay, all the way to the buoy.

Security did find him. "Bring your bag, leave the coffee," said a red-haired agency man wearing a tan suit and brown-on-cream saddle oxfords. He and two unhappy Marines escorted Micah back to the Robbins Room. After 40 more minutes, [redacted] and a pair of Army colonels appeared for the interview. "We were OBE," [redacted] said to

Micah, apparently by way of explanation. He seemed be the lead man in the trio, and there was no trace of apology in his voice.

"OBE?" said Micah

"Overcome by events. Got hung up at the, at the. We got hung up is all."

Ahems were ahemmed.

"On paper, Chief Ford, you clearly have the tools for nearly any task we might throw at you," [redacted] said, turning around his laptop so Micah could use it. "Your work on all these crypto and cyber teams in recent years has been quite impressive. I wonder, though, how you might perform working alone under a tight timeframe. On demand, you might say. On deadline. How about if you dazzle me with a hack or two?"

"I can only hope you're easily dazzled, sir," Micah said.

It took 11 minutes in all, including the time it took for the printer in the room to deliver three pages. Page 1: The frequency of Dick Cheney's pacemaker (408.5 kHz) and an e-mail confirming his next scheduled appointment with his cardiologist at Walter Reed. Page 2: Sasha Obama's last 20 text messages and her five most recent Snapchats. Page 3: The names, Socials, cell numbers and home addresses of the SEAL team members who took out Bin Laden.

Eyebrows were raised. Glances were exchanged. "How about something in Arabic?" said the agency man.

Micah asked for a set of headphones. Eight minutes of rapid typing later, the printer started up again. Two pages. In MSA Arabic.

"So what is this?" the second colonel asked, looking at the pages. "My Arabic isn't what it should be. For all I know, this could be the cafeteria menu."

"It's a partial transcript of two phone calls," Micah said. "The first one is from the Saudi ambassador talking to his Syrian mistress. It appears she lives in Chevy Chase, but I didn't confirm that. He is saying he can raise her allowance, but he wants to pay her in dollars from now on. She's saying she still wants it in euros. The second one is her calling the Russian ambassador, 40 seconds after she hung up with the Saudi guy. It's about her getting title to a villa in Crimea."

"This is rapid response, Chief, and impressive. But you should know that we already have this stuff," said CIA.

"I know you do, sir. That's how I got it: I hacked your phone taps. You're still using Fuzzbuster to encrypt your FISA requests and taps. I helped design that system for NSA a couple years ago. So your encryption on that gateway, sir, one might say, has been OBE."

"You can at-ease the attitude, Chief," Colonel No. 1 said, although not at all harshly. "You're the smartest guy in the room. We acknowledge that. No need to be the smartest-assed guy in the room, too."

"Roger that, sir. My mistake."

It's a damn small room, is what Micah wanted to say. *Anne Frank had a bigger room.*

"That's all I have," [redacted] said as he closed Micah's personnel folder after a few more minutes of Q-and-A. "Chief Ford, I know you've been with the agency psychiatrist and our background team. We're still waiting on their final reports. For now, I'm going to send you down to Medical for one last set of tests. Just to make sure you're fully fit for duty. And by that I mean fit for duty downrange.

"I knew your father, by the way. Only in passing. More by reputation. He was a real American hero. He had a lot of friends here at Langley."

You didn't need a cryptographer to decipher this one: [redacted] somehow thought Micah Ford was *not* fully fit for duty, at least not in the hallowed employ of *his* beloved agency. The CIA man seemed to view him as some kind of twitchy egghead Rain Man, but Micah thought there must be something else. Maybe it was something about his dad? Or something in his file? And now they were sending him to Medical? That was a clumsy dodge, even for CIA. He had punched through their flimsy Sheetrock firewalls with his hacking demo, and now this guy was hot about it.

These CIA guys could be real nitwits, that's what his dad had always said. Raised-pinkie Ivy League washouts from law and finance. These jokers had missed every significant event from Ho Chi Minh and Katanga to the Yom Kippur War and Shining Path --- and this wing-tipped old silverback was symptomatic of why. ISIS was only their latest blunder. Tet, Khomeini, the Bay of Pigs, North Korea, India's Smiling Buddha, AQ Khan, the Arab Spring. And oh yeah, that "rock-solid" WMD intel that led to the Iraq War. It all made for quite the résumé.

The CIA's so-called operatives were the very guys that Hank Ford had railed about so bitterly in private, even as they spent taxpayer-millions buying his fancy radars and overpriced ordnance. Their incompetence was endangering the country, Hank had said. The agency had become larded with seersuckered commuters, not real spies. They were all cloak and no dagger, and they were giving the espionage business a bad name. They lived in mini-mansions out in McLean, ate organic, summered in St. Michaels and made their black housekeepers clean up after their incontinent old spaniels.

"So, any questions from your end, Chief?" said [redacted].

"No, sir. Well, yes, I guess I have one question. I wonder if you might arrange a meet for me with somebody from the Crypto unit. I think I figured out that fourth panel on Kryptos. I'd like to run it past them."

"What's that? You solved the thing? When?"

"While you were, while, uh, you know, while I was waiting for you gentlemen. I went down to get a coffee and I saw the sculpture there in the garden. I had heard about it, but I didn't think it would just be out there in the open like that. It's pretty nifty. I'm usually better with numbers, but as a spastic sequestered Vernam cipher, you know, it's really, what's the word, *smooth*. Which is a lot more than I can say for the coffee in the cafeteria. No offense." He was gee-whizzing and aww-shucksing them now, the way his father had taught him. He had buried the lede just enough.

The other three men were quiet. And astonished. Just looking at Micah. As mysteries went, the fourth panel of Kryptos was like finding Jimmy Hoffa. "Write it out," said Colonel No. 1. "I mean, can you do that, Chief? Can you write out your solution?"

"Sure." Micah extra-slowly fished a book from his bag and the title caught [redacted]'s eye --- "Black Weapons," about chess openings against White. He tore a blank page from the back of the book and wrote this: LANGLEY STORMS SPIN AND SPIRAL CYCLONE ELH JUST CAUSE 333 WONDERFUL THINGS. "I have no real idea what this means, in context, but I'm sure somebody will. Maybe it's a doorway to something else. Anyway."

He left them the solution and went down to Medical with one of the Marines. A male nurse took his vitals, and he coughed while a female nurse checked his testicles. He got semi-hard at that. A doctor listened to his chest, then lubed him up and gave the finger to Micah's prostate. Then they sent him for PET and CT scans, which he assumed was the real point of this silliness. They weren't interested in what was right with his brain; they were looking for something wrong with it. Glimmers of autism, or Asperger's, maybe a brain injury, something like that.

When he got home there was already a message on the land line from a CIA woman in Crypto. Calling about Kryptos. News travels. Could Chief Ford message her back? She gave him a VPN proxy identity to use. That could wait.

Instead he hacked into the computer of the psychiatrist who had interviewed him several times the previous week. The doctor was one of the agency's regular contractors, with a practice out in Takoma Park. Micah's personal file was there in his computer, only lightly secured, and the doctor's notes had not yet been uploaded to the CIA. Under the Summary/Conclusion section it said this:

"The subject, a 33-year-old white male, an Army Chief Warrant Officer, suffers from a moderately severe case of post traumatic stress disorder, with occasional and florid expressions of same, largely the result of significant life traumas in boyhood and as an adult. He has seen an array of extreme violence, less against his actual person than against his emotional person. The subject's Glasgow Coma score is 12, with some localizing to noxious stimuli, although this contraindicates with no apparent physical history of Traumatic Brain Injury. Age 10 he lost his mother, a nurse, to AIDS-related illnesses. His father and fiancée were killed in New York on 9/11. His paternal grandparents were killed in a highway accident and the subject saw his maternal grandfather violently killed in Hurricane Katrina. Soon after that a close woman friend was brutally raped and murdered. Subject's PTSD symptoms have included binge drinking for some years, although he continues to perform his cryptography duties at a very high level. He holds a TS/SCI clearance. Subject reports some evidence of social distancing, although his interpersonal and communication skills can be exceptional. Depressive periods have occurred in recent years, although chronic or clinical depression can be ruled out. He has a low startle threshold, rated 9 on the Barris Scale, which is worrisome to this examiner. Insomnia is acute and chronic, although the subject resists medication. This examiner recommends regular and ongoing psychiatric treatment for stress syndrome, with appropriate medication for collateral insomnia and anxiety. Deployment to hostile environments, combat theaters or other conflict zones is not recommended. Subject is not seen as a security risk. His capability for significant leadership positions appears limited to this examiner."

Micah was surprised that the shrink had been so hard on him. He had liked the man and thought their sessions had gone pretty well. Huh.

It took him about 15 minutes to rewrite the report using that hackneyed subject/examiner language. After that, presto, Micah was psychologically healthy and possessed of an admirable work-life balance. Rather than an introverted math prodigy, he was well-adjusted and admirably buoyant of spirit. "Subject enjoys a good number of both casual friends and trusted intimates. He reports his sex life to be tender and fulfilling. His alcohol use is social and moderate. The subject's Glasgow Coma score is within agency parameters at 14. His security clearance of TS/SCI appears appropriate, and as a stable personality he poses no discernible security risk." (Micah was really troweling it on here.) "Subject reports that he sleeps well. He displays great optimism for further strides in his ground-breaking work in cryptography, and appears willing either to work for the agency as a full-fledged officer or as a loaner from his current tasking at Defense. Deployment to any military duty or agency posting would not be problematic, even to hostile environments, in this examiner's opinion. Indeed, this examiner recommends that his superiors find more challenging leadership positions for him forthwith."

Micah changed the metadata on the doctor's original file and scrubbed up the computer's history. Once CIA got a look at this file, they would be seeing a spit-and-polished Micah Ford. And that's exactly what Colonel Francis Scott Key Magazine saw when he later began recruiting for Freehold: a squared-away genius, immaculate skill set, the right age and the correct rank, as steady and solid as a wall of granite.

• • • •

Micah Ford, now in his bunk at Freehold, had reason to be awake and on edge: Colonel Magazine had gone to Amman for a few days, so Micah was in charge.

The head of Maggie's general-officer review board was flying in for a consult. Magazine was being considered for his first star, and that was about the only thing that still sprung him out of bed in the morning. It was crunch time for the old man: If the board passed him over for the one available generalship in the Army, he'd have to retire. It was up, or out.

The Army was Darwinian that way. The review-board chief told Maggie he would get his star as a goodwill gesture from the White House, but only if his current (and secret) assignment was a success. If the mission cratered, he could take his colonelship and fuck off back to Maryland or Jersey or wherever. He'd be just another full-bird reject.

There still had been no word from Langley on when the first detainees would arrive, although it was a promising sign that an agency contract team was coming to do a security sweep of Nebraska in couple days. In the meantime, Micah continued to pore over the prisoner dossiers. He had more than a hundred of them now, like planes taxiing for takeoff.

It was obvious from their jackets that some of these guys were real shit-heels --- and they had suffered accordingly at the hands of their interrogators and jailers over the years. All the evils that lurked in the mud hatched out. One old Baathist, Usama bin Zaid, had managed to survive Cobalt, Luda Kuca outside Belgrade, Camp 1391 in Israel, and Palestine Branch in Damascus. Zaid apparently still had all his marbles, and both his testicles, which was saying something. He was an authentic, Koran-thumping jihadi, almost guaranteed to be a recidivist and a prime candidate for ISIS recruitment. Just the kind of seed corn that Freehold was created for.

For each violent gang-banger like Zaid, however, there were a dozen other inmates who were clearly harmless. (Gitmo, too, was full of such guys.) These were the hapless saps who had been caught up in some political vendetta during the 2003 invasion. Others had been shanghai'd by Shiite bounty-hunters, turned over to the Americans as supposedly high-value detainees. The post-invasion chaos hadn't allowed for much vetting or justice. Every joker in custody was deemed to have been a "senior" something in the old regime, or "Mukhabarat," or someone from "Saddam's inner circle." So much was high value, nothing was.

One poor schnook coming to Freehold, Yusuf bin Ayyub, had been a bootblack for Chemical Ali, the maniac general who gassed all those Kurds back in '88. A dirty-handed shoeshine boy is what Ayyub was, but still the Americans had had him in the cooler for 12 years now. The CIA feared him up harsh for six whole months, but all he could tell them was about the general's bunions. And oh yeah, Ali had liked calfskin Bruno Magli loafers. Size 11. That's all he knew.

The Russians had been holding him for the past decade, moving him and three dozen other Iraqis through some of the Motherland's hardest and blackest sites --- Norlag, The Library, White Swan, Krasnokamensk, Black Dolphin, The Little School, Kitchen Creek. The group was currently installed at a work camp in Nizhny Novgorod, an arrangement that had V.V. Putin's greasy Slavic fingerprints all over it. By day, the Iraqis mined bauxite. At night, most nights, after some thin bread and potato soup, they were used as paint ball targets by vodka-soaked Spetsnaz commandos from the nearby Russian army base.

Another man coming to Freehold had been picked up by a U.S. Special Removal Team the summer the war started. A middle-aged gent. Last name: Zaza. Profession: chess player. Or so he said.

Zaza's tale of woe began when U.S. forces tracked Uday and Qusay Hussein to their hideout villa near Mosul in July of 2003. (Saddam's two boys had not been hard to find --- Uday had parked his gray Lamborghini Countach right in front of the house.) As a coalition task force was surrounding the place, a sniper element noticed three Iraqis on the flat roof of an adjoining guesthouse. The people appeared to be waving and running across the roof, as if they were lookouts signaling to someone. TOW missiles soon collapsed the main house, killing Uday, the ace of hearts in the American deck of 52-Pickup. His brother, the ace of clubs, was also killed in the blast. Two of a kind.

The missiles also brought down the guesthouse, and an hour later a forensics team was digging Abdul-Razzaq Ahmed Zaza out of the rubble. His wife was dead. His daughter was unconscious. *Is dying harder than being dead?* Zaza himself had two broken wrists and a dislocated hip.

Yes, the three of them had been up on the roof, but they hadn't been signaling to anyone. They were flying a kite. Kite runners. This is what Zaza told team after team of angry American interrogators. He told them the same story that he'd tell for years on end --- how they made the kite from one of Uday's Members Only windbreakers, the strips of pillowcase they used for a tail, how his daughter had named the kite Viktoria. He told them this in basic English and scholarly Arabic. His forearms itched under the plaster casts. His heart had shifted to the right side of his chest over the loss of his family. Hearts could do that.

Zaza said he had been at the Mosul house only because Qusay Hussein had hired him for the summer to tutor his oldest son, Mustapha, in mathematics and chess. (All the Husseins were on the run at the time, true, but they were certain the Fedayeen would soon gather themselves, the Americans would leave Iraq and the Baath regime would reorganize.) It was also summer vacation for Zaza's 15-year-old daughter and his wife, an art teacher, so they were both with him, the family trying to keep together while avoiding the tumult in Baghdad. "Adhamiyah, that is our neighborhood in the capital. People know me there. Our house is near the Baghdad Wrestling Club, by the Imams Bridge. Go there. Ask them."

Zaza explained to his interrogators that he was an international chess master with a rating of 2412. He knew Karpov. He had once played Bobby Fischer to a draw. Instead they beat him in the head with the Tampa Yellow Pages. He had played in three Chess Olympiads. Find Ali Gattea and Saad Sarsam. His teammates. They had played together just the year before in Slovenia. He had used the Nimzo-Indian to defeat Australia's first board. Instead they gave him a Palestinian hanging. He had nothing to do with the military. Instead they took his clothes and locked him in a wire dog crate. At the Al Jadriya prison, next to the polo club where he had once been a member, they chained him in the birthing stall for donkeys and horses. Checkmate, motherfucker. He was a Baath Party member, yes, of course he was, there was no denying that. But he was not active. He was not political. He just played chess. Instead they dressed him in a sateen brassiere and high heels and assigned a woman soldier to guard him. What of the three blue dots tattooed on his wrist --- the mark of the al-Himaya bodyguards of the Husseins? I had no choice.

Uday controlled the sports ministry and the chess federation, and he insisted that everyone had to belong to the party and had to get the tattooing. One did not say no to Uday Hussein. He fed troublemakers to Zena and Gambi, the lions in his household zoo. He called himself Abu Sarhan, the Wolf. My God. He killed his father's valet with an electric carving knife. Both Hussein boys were *safala.* Please. I am a cultured man. I know about George Gershwin, café au lait, Cervantes. Not a political man, no, no. I am a chess player only.

The interrogators weren't buying it. Somebody somewhere at some point had put a NTR on his file --- Not to Release --- and it stuck. A thing like that was not easily unstuck. Detainees so designated became nameless numbers on a list that was afterwards mislaid.

Finally, sleep was arriving. Micah closed down the detainee folders, secured the SCIF and went to bed. He was soon borne away by the waves and lost in darkness and the distance. He dreamed of a girl with a kite.

• • • •

The base was in good order. The weather improved. Posner finally had the colonel's spa gurgling away again. The men were getting restless, though. At their morning brief, Tran told Micah she'd set up a sparring tournament and a pistol competition. Diversions. Magazine was due back in two days.

Micah kept at his dossiers. He set up a database that collated the known knowns about each incoming prisoner: hometown, age, tribe, schools, dates and locations in custody. (These were simple compilations, more like tricked-up Venn diagrams.) Each detainee coming to Freehold had been to an average of 5.7 prisons on 2.3 continents over 10.7 years.

Something nagged him about that Zaza file.

The dossier on Abdul-Razzaq Zaza showed he had done stretches in the Salt Pit, the stall at Jadriya, Bucca, Azouli, Al-Barzakh, Bagram. C Max in South Africa, Masyaf Castle in Syria, Temara in Morocco, Al Hayer in Riyadh. He might have disappeared at any one of these places. Or somebody also might have easily nudged him over the rail on the USS Boxer or the USS Bataan.

After his first several months of confinement, Zaza became a withdrawn and compliant prisoner. Military Intelligence continued to sweat him, mostly using a regimen called Pride and Ego Down. They slapped him in the face, sleep-deprived him. Smashed his wedding ring with a hammer, on a table right in front of him, then threw the broken bits down a toilet. Zaza's strategy for survival was a simple self-contained silence. He did not retreat into the Koran or into religious anger. He did not exercise or hunger-strike. He read books when they were available. The DST warden at Temara allowed him to have a pocket chess set but then took it away after a few days, leaving Zaza with just one piece, a black pawn. The rules changed from place to place. He rarely spoke. At C Max he was allowed to smoke one cigarette a week. Guards at every prison site reported that Zaza usually seemed lost in thought. He paced his cell in a slow and very erect manner, as if he was studying each step. Sometimes he mumbled to himself. Most guards figured him for insane.

Once Zaza got to Freehold, Micah hoped, the grandmaster would simply sign his release and go. Go home. Back to Adhamiyah. Insha'allah.

• • • •

1620 Zulu and 104 Fahrenheit. Out on the jogging track, Micah figured he'd do 5 miles, then catch a shower and lunch. Roadwork was his new swimming: It helped the mind to wander. *I've seen the Atlantic, a little too frantic. About the Pacific I can't be specific. Who said that?* A mind could reel under this kind of heat. He was three miles into his run when Tran sprinted up behind him. She handed him a radio and said, "Micah, we've got a problem at Nebraska." The first time she had called him by his name.

Marchand's squad had been monitoring closed-circuit footage from inside the Nebraska annex --- this task was part of the daily humdrum of the COP --- when one of them noticed a contract worker tucking a piece of paper into the pillowcase on his bunk. It looked a little sketchy, so Marchand and Romo went over to check on it. The paper they found was a hand-drawn map of the Freehold-Nebraska-helipad layout. There were directional markings and a latitude line. A small circle marked the stairwell entry leading to the underground Tunnel of Love that connected the prison unit to the annex.

Marchand got on the blower to Tran. She told him to quietly locate the worker, a 30-year-old Bangladeshi cook, and take him out to the helipad. They should strip-search him there and cuff his wrists. After that she caught up with Micah on the track and he called on the radio for Posner to meet them with his video camera.

The cook was standing on the Nebraska tarmac in flipflops, wearing only his underpants, pouring sweat. He was whimpering in some mixture of rapid, high-pitched Bengali and a highly curried English. He had meant no harm. Good worker. Absolutely for sure. Loving America. No problem, no problem. He was nauseous with fright. He had worked at other military lockups and knew how black-site prisoners could be treated.

The man's file would show that he had been with KBR for seven years, five deployments, not married, a Hindu, from Cox's Bazar, father a shipbreaker, mother dead, nine siblings, clean work record, health good, A-negative, NKA, last vetted by the company in December 2013. Micah was telling Marchand to put the cook into one of Nebraska's holding cells when the man suddenly broke loose and began running crazily across the sand. What was he thinking, running out into the Big Empty like that? And handcuffed? In his skivvies? Taking on 200 miles of hot dry bleak? Churchill had called Iraq an ungrateful volcano, and he'd been right, especially about Anbar. Escape was never the safest path. One of the man's sandals flew off as he ran. Romo started to run after him, but Micah barked out a quick, hard no. "Just wait."

The swarthy little man got 50 yards or so before he went down. He had managed to avoid the land mines but then fell headlong into a bear pit. Each of these camouflaged holes went down 15 feet, and once its trap door was triggered, it was designed to fill itself up with sand, burying whatever was inside. It was a self-sealing casket. All chute and no ladder. The desert wins again.

It was dreamlike, and almost comical, the way the man had been swallowed up. So quickly. So quietly. Swallowed whole. One moment he was there, and then he wasn't. The Freehold troopers knew there were mines and sensors out there, encircling the base, but not the man-traps. Nobody said anything for a long minute.

Micah: "First Sergeant, hand me that map the guy drew. Thank you. Inventory the man's effects from his bunk area, if you will. Anything suspicious, personal letters, work documents, passport, anything that might be valuable, you can give those to the sergeant major. Seal his other things in plastic bags. *Clear* plastic bags. And put the bags on his bunk. Leave them out in the open. We want all his co-workers to know that he's gone. *Definitively* gone. Let's let this be a cautionary tale and a teachable moment. You good with that, Sarntmajor?"

"Roger that, Chief. Hundred percent."

"Firsarnt?"

"Hoo-ah that, Chief. A hundred and ten."

• • • •

Micah sent a brief encrypted report up the line to Colonel Magazine about Assistant Fry Cook Nazzim Uddin and his unfortunate descent into that sandy circle of hell. The subtext to the note was that there was no need for the colonel to hurry back. Magazine's entire reply was "Keep calm and carry on."

Later that night, again unable to sleep and reading more files in the SCIF, Micah laid Zaza's black-site timeline over the scant biographical information that the CIA had on Abu Bakr al-Baghdadi, the caliph of ISIS.

At first, the two charts seemed to barely intersect. Zaza was Baghdad-born and bred, while the leader of the Islamic State was about as "al-Baghdadi" as Hillary Clinton. He wasn't "of Baghdad." He hadn't moved to the capital until he was 18. Only recently had he appended the Baghdadi suffix to his name.

Ibrahim Awwad Ibrahim Ali al-Badri al-Samarra'i --- that was the caliph's given name --- and he actually did hail from the city of Samarra. So it seemed almost impossible that he and Zaza would know each other.

But they did. They spent nine overlapping months in the Waterfront wing of the Camp Bucca prison. Micah backdoored his way into Naval Military Police records and discovered that for three of those nine months, in late 2004, the two men had even been cellmates --- Bravo Compound, Section A, Row 1, Cell 13.

The CIA had missed this overlap, and Micah decided to wait until Magazine returned to Freehold to tell him about it in person. This was the sort of intel the colonel might use to good advantage in his campaign for that brigadier's star. If Zaza had been close to the proto-caliph, he might well reconnect with him on the outside --- just the kind of seeding of ISIS that Magazine had talked about. Germs, meet penicillin.

It was now close to midnight and he still couldn't sleep. Maybe a few miles on the track would wear him out. He closed down the SCIF and radioed to the towers commander that he was going out for a run.

"Roger that, Chief," Sergeant Wozzeck radioed back. He was one of the new guys. "That K-9 team went through about 15 minutes ago."

"Went through? Went through where? What freakin' K-9 team?"

"Through the tunnel. They said they wanted to run their dog around the compound a little because he had been cooped up all day. They had their badges."

"How many of them are there, sergeant? And where are they, exactly? Inside the COP?"

"Yessir. I mean, yes, Chief. I've got my NVGs on them right now. A guy, a woman and the dog. The guy's wearing BDUs. The woman's in like, like, in PT gear. They're down in the Red Zone, by the hot tub."

"How the fuck? I'm going out there, Sergeant. No way should they be inside the COP. Go set a watchman at the gate, and alert the watchmen in the other towers. When you see me reaching the K-9 people, I want all the floods turned on. Light up the whole fuckin' infield. I also need you to wake up First Sergeant Marchand and have him get two gun teams out there ASAP. Down to the hot tub. And wake up Sergeant Major Tran. Give her a sit rep. You got all that?"

"Roger that, Chief. I'm on it."

Micah strapped on a holster and a reflective belt, checked the magazine in his Glock, grabbed a flashlight, grabbed a walkie. Went out to E Street, fast-walking toward the grassy area, which was about 30 yards off. He could hear their voices, then saw a man in silhouette standing by the tub.

"Oh, Vick, yeah, baby, that's so fucking *hot.* Get it, sweetie. Yeah, baby. You like that? Aww, *yeah*, Vick. That's *so* fuckin' hot." The man was excited, but he was keeping his voice low. He was tall, lean, maybe early 30s, crew cut. On the grass next to him --- towels, a leash, a gym bag, a gray shirt, a big jar of peanut butter.

The woman was shirtless and sitting on the bench inside the hot tub, waist-high in the water, leaning back with her arms outstretched and hooked over the rim of the tub. Head back. Dark hair. Somewhere between laughing and moaning. The dog, a big black Malinois, was straddling the woman and thrashing in the water, roarking and snorting, licking excitedly at the woman's large, peanut-buttered breasts.

"OK folks, this ends now," Micah said sharply. "Vickie, ma'am, push the dog away and get a shirt on. Sir, get a leash on the dog. You guys are not area-cleared for here. Let's go."

The COP's big floodlights kicked on, and the dog stopped humping and licking. It was panting heavily, still excited, still in the water, looking to the woman for a command. The woman, wet and surprised, hadn't moved.

"Hey, easy there, pal, we're the security team out of Diyarbakir," the man said. "We're TDY here."

He and Micah were 20 feet apart in the grass and time was dilating, slowing down, thickening. The man did not seem threatening but he also did not move to leash his dog. The lights overhead threw down short sharp shadows. There was the ambient noise of the base. The generators and air conditioners.

"I know who you are," Micah said. "You're cleared for Strong Point Nebraska. That's the annex. *This* area, inside the walls, is secure. You shouldn't be in here. Police up your stuff and let's go."

Several troopers were now running down E Street, coming toward them, fully illuminated at the center of the base, 50 yards and closing.

"Who are you, if you don't mind me asking? Where's Chief Ford?"

"I'm Chief Warrant Officer Ford. Colonel Magazine is off-base. I'm the XO. None of which matters. You are moving out, right now." Micah unholstered his pistol.

"Chief Ford, all right. You're my contact. Take it easy with that weapon, will you? We're friendlies. My name's Joll. And we *are* cleared for here. With our badges. We're, you know, O-G-A. You know? We're just havin' us a little pussy riot out here in the desert. Know'm sayin'?" He was grinning a grin that Micah had seen often at Langley. Teflon-y. Veneer-y.

Marchand, Romo, Rascal and three of the new sergeants arrived at the tub. More were coming behind them, sprinting up the road. They looked like two waves of a kickoff team.

"Firsarnt, form a detail and escort these people off the base," Micah said. "Di-di-mau them back to the annex. If they resist in any way, you will cuff them both and shackle them into cells in Nebraska. Now, sir, I'm going to ask you one more time to control your dog. Leash the dog, and use a muzzle if you have one. Vickie, ma'am, let's go. Out of the tub, right now."

"Vick is the *dog*, you moron," the OGA man said to Micah. His tone had turned, and he was angry. "Vick. *Hier. Platz.*" The dog vaulted out of the hot tub and sat at the man's side.

"You are way out of line here, Chief, is one thing, and the second thing is that you need to mind your fuckin' manners and put a leash on all your little Army poodles here. Darla, stay in the tub as long as you want, honey. I feel like having a soak myself. These Army cocksucker pricks need to remember they work for *us*."

The other troopers arrived. About a dozen of them were on the scene now. The dog was antsy and growling, dripping saliva, feeling the tension, and it kept looking up at OGA. Marchand stepped forward to stand beside Micah and said, "Sarnt Farinelli, Sarnt Flipper, go fetch two Gators from the garage. Do it now. And sir, please hold onto your dog. We don't want nobody gettin' bit. Like Chief Ford said, we're leavin' up outta here. Right now."

OGA looked directly at Micah, who still had his pistol out, and called him a fuckin' faggot Army cocksucker. He knelt down, nuzzled his face tenderly into the dog's neck and whispered something. The dog sprang up quickly toward Micah. Three strides and a leap was all it would take. But then two shots rang out, and the animal was flung sideways into the grass, as if flattened by some invisible hollow-pointed linebackers. It lay still and silent now.

"You motherfucker! You killed my fucking dog!" the man shouted at Micah, although the chief had not raised his gun. Darla was still in the tub, screaming, spluttering out something.

The agency man, bigger, younger, rangier, lunged for Micah's throat. But Micah sidestepped him, swung his right leg at Joll's ankles, and the bigger man slammed backward onto the grass, right next to his inert black dog. Sergeant Washington was on the man in a flash and turned him over and rode him like a wrestler, with a knee in the small of his back and a forearm pressed hard across the base of the man's skull.

"You be still now, Skippy, or I'm gonna have to go ahead and fuck you up," Washington said, calmly, into the OGA's ear. Got him cuffed. It had all taken 15 seconds.

"Anything I can help y'all with, Chief Ford?" This was Tran, laying on a little South Texas twang. She emerged slowly into the light, walking out from the dark-shadowed area between Safeway and Piggly Wiggly. She had her favorite .45 with her, and she was smiling. It was quite the entrance.

"Why, Sergeant Major, nice of you to put in an appearance," Micah said. "Maybe you could make sure that this woman gets dressed and arrives safely at her final destination."

"Roger that, Chief. Happy to help. And if I might say, you swept the leg perfectly. *Very* nice. *Excellent* technique."

Micah gave her a deep bow and said, "Thank you, sensei."

All the cocksucking faggot Army poodles laughed and hoo-ah'd.

Washington and Rascal got OGA to his feet, and Rascal used the cuffs to guide him from behind. The bigger man tried to pull away. "Don't," was all that Rascal said, but he said it using his Vacaville voice, his inmate voice. He also pressed the CIA officer's right thumb in such a way that the man gave out a small whimper, a rabbit caught in a snare.

"Sergeant Marchand, since these folks seem rather uncooperative, please put them into holding cells at Nebraska after all," Micah said. The Gators arrived. "Have somebody bring a body bag for this dog. And treat him carefully, please. He was a service member killed in the line of duty. Let's remember that. He was killed following orders in a war zone."

"Roger that, Chief. I'll get a detail on it."

Micah then said "William" very quietly and whispered to Marchand that he should keep the man and woman separated --- and cuffed --- all night. They shouldn't talk to each other. And no cleaning them up, even the streaks of dog slobber and peanut butter. No toilet breaks, even if they piss themselves. No food or water. He'd have Magazine order a chopper from Baghdad to collect them tomorrow. This whole episode was now the agency's pile of dog doo.

Tran got Darla into the gray T-shirt, which said A-R-M-Y across the front in bold block letters. Tran perp-walked her over to a Gator, but before they got in, she took the woman's shirt off, right there in front of the men. Her boobs hanging free. Again.

"Hey Yoko Ono, you fucking bitch!" Darla shouted. "This is *not cool*." There was peanut butter in her hair.

"Shut up," Tran said. She turned the shirt inside out and put it back on the woman --- but backwards.

"You dishonor this shirt, just having it on. I don't want your sloppy tits anywhere *near* my Army."

11. MAKING MOVES

It was a week after the dog show that Colonel Magazine gathered his soldiers in the chow hall before dinner. And said this: "Gather your forces and harness your horses, gentlemen. Let the wild rumpus start. We are finally open for business."

Eight detainees were being choppered in from Amman the following morning, Magazine said, and Combat Outpost Freehold would henceforth be up and running. Full tempo. Golf tango golf. This first batch of prisoner arrivals was just the trailer, he said. The major motion picture was coming soon.

The troops hollered and applauded. Tran, also excited, gave Micah a shoulder bump when they got in line for chicken-fried steak.

"*Finally*," she said quietly.

Micah had known all about the impending arrivals, although he hadn't let on. He had been snooping on Maggie's P4 memos and private email traffic with Langley and the Pentagon. He was using a loop-encrypted oblivious transfer PIR mechanism, a little something he had built and beta'd by himself. He had described its architecture in an early draft of his thesis at Stanford. A perfect little piece of perfect secrecy.

After dinner, at a briefing in Safeway, the colonel went over the intake protocols one more time with Micah, Tran and Marchand. He also caught them up on the CIA's "zero-visibility disposition" of the runaway fry cook and the scrimmage with the canine team. Nobody asked what zero-visibility disposition meant. It sure didn't sound very good. Magazine also said he had NJP'd the sergeant who had passed the CIA contractors into Freehold. Assessed him a week's pay.

After the brief, Magazine asked Micah to stay behind to talk about Zaza, since he would be among Freehold's freshman class. Micah told what he knew about Zaza's capture, his travels through the black-site system and his subsequent overlap with Caliph al-Baghdadi, a coincidence that agency analysts still hadn't noticed.

"CIA and Defense don't seem to know very much about the caliph himself," Micah said. "He's something of a cipher. He's like Kim Jong-un in North Korea. We don't even reliably know how old he is, or if he's married. Very basic stuff we don't know. He's living in a lead-lined cave in Syria for all we know. So if Zaza will talk."

"Yeah, just some clues, any new intel on Baghdadi, the Pentagon would love that, even finding a guy who was close to him. Maybe we could even groom Zaza to re-offend. 'Induce susceptibility to re-engagement' is what the planners call it. You think Zaza will get back in the game?"

"Sir, I'm not at all convinced he was ever *in* the game. He was a world-class chess player, we do have a high degree of confidence on that. He's been treated pretty badly since we grabbed him. MI kept him for two months inside a shipping container at Al-Barzakh. I only know about the stuff that's been written down. So you can imagine. He might be pretty well bonkers by now. It might run counter to our directives, but I was thinking that we might hold off on releasing him. I could play some chess with him, chat him up, see what he knows. He might not even remember Baghdadi. He might not go for it, the soft sell, if only because he has spent the past 12 years in our kennels. Twelve years for felonious kite-flying."

"OK, Chief, sometimes the squeeze ain't worth the juice, but spend some time with the guy. Suss him out, draw him out if you can, and keep me posted. I would love to get some actionable intel, but I also don't want to make a career out of this guy. At some point we'll have to offer him the release deal. With everybody else, though, it's ABC."

"Sir?"

"ABC. Always be closing. That's our new motto. My boss got it from that Alec Baldwin movie. A --- always. B --- be. C --- closing. Always be closing. Get those signatures on the line that is dotted."

The chief and the colonel drank some coffee, talked about the Syrian crisis and the Donald Trump political hijinks back home, and Magazine made himself some toast with orange marmalade. He cued up a video of "Gladiator," which happened to be Tran's favorite, which figured, her being a gladiatrix and all. But about 20 minutes in, with Maximus telling Quintus that that dirt cleans off more easily than blood, the colonel shut the movie off, saying he was hitting the rack. He was tired, and his meeting in Amman had not gone well.

"Micah, I gotta tell you, I could sure use a home run with this prick Zaza. If Freehold works, I'm in. I get my star. They've pretty much told me that. Hell, they might even put my face on a fucking stamp. But if there are any glitches here, I go back to being an insect. I get to retire as a colonel. The autumn of the patriarch.

"My sit-down with the review-board guy in Amman, between us girls, I don't think I exactly knocked his socks off. He knows I'm on this covert op --- the White House told him that much --- but he seemed to think I was being unnecessarily evasive. Like I was fucking with him. I probably came off a little too spooky, and too arrogant. That's on me. But Jack told me to watch out for this guy."

Jack was Jack Keane, the retired four-star who still had policy sway inside Centcom and serious political juice inside the Oval. He had been Magazine's principal mentor for 20-plus years now, going back to when Maggie was J2 on Keane's staff in Bosnia. As military godfathers go, Jack Keane was as Corleone as you could get.

"I'm so close to that freakin' star, and it's all I've ever really wanted, you know, ever since I was a plebe at West Point. 'General Magazine.' It sounds craven to want it so badly. I honestly wish I didn't. The vanity of it feels so, so, so damn *vain.* Magazine Agonistes. But it's like I've always been 20 feet from stardom, you know? Playing the big arenas but always singing backup. I'm a freakin' *Pip.* Everybody knows Gladys Knight but *nobody* knows the names of the Pips. Any of them. Elvis Costello and the Attractions. Name me *one* Attraction. You can't. Nobody can. Fuck me, I do sound pathetic. The walk to the front of the big stage can be complicated --- I get that. It takes balls, ego, luck, ambition. And in the military it's a conceptual leap, too, in a way. Like that great line from Prufrock: 'Do I dare ascend the stair?' "

Magazine said he was "just an old man in a dry month, an end-stage colonel slipping from my dotage into my anecdotage. Pretty soon I'll be entering my Unzipped Trousers Phase." He had received a presidential waiver to stay on active duty past 62, but the actuarial alarm clock on his career was ticking faster now. "That waiver got me thinking for the first time about dying. Actually dying, as in dead-dead, not as some abstraction," he said. "I've outlived Jesus, Lincoln and Hemingway, and I'm closing in on Muhammad. Sounds kind of morbid, right?

"Dave and Skip and other guys in my West Point class, they were our Springsteens. Man, they were some fast burners. Marty Dempsey was chairman of the Joint Chiefs. Keith Alexander. They all lapped me about 10 years ago. They're all four-stars. And hey, I salute them. They played the game better.

"People say that after Norm Schwarzkopf hung it up, all our generals became like substitute teachers. 'First-rate second-rate generals.' But I'll tell you, those guys from my year, and the generals I know personally, almost to a man, they are fucking sequoias. Smart, politically savvy, charismatic. Great diplomats. Guys comfortable with complexity. Even Petraeus with his so-called issues. They don't see duty as some cheap idea. They see it as a demand, a requirement. Most Americans think our generals got small. That's wrong. The generals are still big. It's the fight that got small."

Micah nodded, partly in sympathy with Maggie, but he was thinking more about his father. Hank had dealt with a lot of generals over the years, from all the services, and he had had a different take on the sequoias. More like a pod of cetaceans, Hank might have said. Or stegosauruses. Slow, ungainly, self-important, too often too tubby. Massive and passive. Generals were like politicians, ugly buildings and hookers --- they all get respectable if they last long enough. Hank thought most general officers now prized obedience over originality. Iron filings obeying the magnet. They loved to push through any door marked Authorized Personnel Only, just because they could. They were always authorized, forever authorized, and they took plenty advantage of that. Their kids got married in the Temple of Dendur or up in the crown of the Statue of Liberty. One call got any general a sideline pass to the Redskins. Seats at the last minute for Streisand at Wolf Trap. They borrowed Whistlers and Wyeths from the Smithsonian to hang in their Chincoteague bungalows. *Did you know we now have serving generals who've never killed anybody? The old guys, they'd come at you full-frontal, like Ajax or Zhukov, up-armored and bloody-minded.* A lot of the new guys had Rolex wardrobes and Timex brains --- that was another Hank phrase. Their dress uniforms got gaudier and more dandified every year, and unnecessarily so --- generals have always scored plenty of gold-braid pussy. Now they could retire to phat jobs with some defense contractor or a think tank or take up a university chair. Meanwhile, so much for the meritocracy they swore by: The old crocs at the Pentagon were a year late on taking ISIL as a serious threat, and now the caliph and his hyenas were drawing up new maps of hell. Were we really going to let the generals put our heads back in this oven? Anbar was becoming a howling wilderness, Micah mused, and it was happening on their watch. The boulder of Iraq was rolling back on the American Sisyphus.

• • • •

Frank Magazine was a tough one to figure. Big tall guy, always trim, always came correct, a flat-top mostly gone gray, that drain-cleaner voice and those wolf-gray eyes. Cross him, and he could fix you with a look. He could ice you. You did not want that wind blowing your way. He sure *looked* like an officer, like a movie general. He was so physically impressive, even at 62, that one might not profile him as a scholar as well.

He was poet *and* warrior both. That was the surprise of the man. He had Master's degrees in American literature and political science, and he was closing in on a doctorate in international relations --- ABD at Georgetown. "Just an old ringknocker," he'd say about himself.

He was born in the Texas section of Freehold, New Jersey, grew up on South Street, worked nights and summers at Al's Grocery, and was an all-state tight end at Freehold High. He was friends with Springsteen and Southside Johnny Lyon, and he would sometimes work security at their gigs down the shore. Dated Southside's little sister for awhile. Introduced Bruce to Clarence Clemons. Gave Springsteen boatloads of shit in the early days because Bruce was always wearing the same pair of filthy jeans and he didn't seem to shower all that much. A real greaseball, and smelled like it for about a decade. Maggie was a character all right. Bruce nicknamed him Mission Man in "Spirit In the Night." They had stayed in touch all these years. Maggie loved Patti and the kids. He sent Jessica, the equestrienne daughter, one of George Patton's old saddles. Maggie never called Bruce "the Boss." Never called him for special tickets. Didn't go in for all the celebrity shit.

Maggie played football his first year at West Point but gave it up as a yearling mostly to keep from flunking chemistry and physics. He fell hard for Hollister Knowlton, the daughter of the academy superintendent. They dated all during his junior year and Holly came up from Dickinson most every weekend. Kissing Rock, Flirtation Walk. He laid on the full-court press. Maggie gave her a spoony button engraved with OAO. His One and Only. But then she dumped him the following summer for Dave Petraeus, his eating-table buddy who had been conducting a bit of romantic counterinsurgency on the side. *That covert little fucker.* Magazine passed Rock Math but he flunked Holly Knowlton. Holly married Dave after graduation in '74. Magazine never got over the heartbreak, and never married. After several years the comet of his Army career also went cold, as dead as an asteroid, and he wondered if Petraeus Christ Superstar hadn't been putting the chill on his promotions all along.

• • • •

The Freehold training kicked in, right from the first day of intake. The first detainees were escorted to the COP by black-masked JSOC teams that handed them over at the E Street Gate. Not a word was spoken by any of the troopers. The prisoners were shackled, hooded, gagged and jumpsuited. Everything was by the book. They were guided down the stairs to Jungleland, steered into their cells, and the hoods, ball gags and chains came off. Orange jumpsuits were replaced by anti-suicide smocks. Exit soldiers. *Shhhh* went the doors.

Micah went to each cell to deliver the regs. Some instructions he gave in Arabic, other times it was English, depending. He also gave them formal, written versions. He did not respond to questions. You will shower and shave and brush your teeth every 14 days. If you resist, we will forcibly shave you. Throwing feces or sperm, spitting, fighting with a guard, resisting an order --- these are not allowed. Do it once, and it's no clothes for a month. Do it again, you also get the restraint chair 'round the clock. No lawyers, no Red Cross. No Korans, no prayer rugs. There is no hard yard, so there's no exercise. There's no outside for you any more. It's no more sun and it's goodnight moon. If you hunger-strike, fine, we will let you. We will lock the cell door and come back in 10 or 15 days to sweep up what's left of you. Even with good behavior you will never again see the sky or the stars, never again hear children laughing. No one will ever again touch you in a tender way. No singing, no music, no books. No tea or bread or jam or sweets. Indeed, you will never eat solid food again. No chewing. You will never again converse with another human being in your own language. You will never see or hear any other detainee at this facility. You won't know whether it's Eid, Christmas or Kwaanza. You will never again know which way Mecca is. There is no parole. This is the end of pretend.

Then he told them about the deal. "There is only one way to avoid this treatment, which I assure you will be far more terrible and far more damaging to your psyche than you can possibly imagine: You may simply sign this release form and go home. It is not a confession. It is not an admission of guilt. You merely agree never to act or conspire against the United States or its allies, and you agree never to associate with any other former detainees. Those are the only two conditions. If you break either of these promises, you acknowledge that we have the right to hunt you and kill you, without a trial. If you sign the form, we give you a final medical checkup, hand you enough money for six months of living, dress you in new civilian clothes and take you back to Iraq. It's as simple as that. You can be back inside your old life within 72 hours. Drink tea, smoke, make love to your wife, have a feast, stroll in a garden, read a newspaper, go to the mosque, kiss your children, smell the jasmine, relax in a café, walk around freely. Sign the form, we let you go. You may think about this overnight. After that, the deal is off.

"I should warn you" Micah told each of them, "if you do not sign our form, you will die a slow and malodorous death in our deep deep deepest hole. We no longer object to your self-destruction. If you develop cancers, goiters, tumors, these will not be treated; they will simply erupt and explode inside you. Cry out in pain if you wish. No one can hear you. No one will come. And know this: Long before your body dies, your mind will go. The brain chews itself faster than the body does. You will be living inside your own private caliphate of horror. You will blister and fester and percolate in your own filth. You will become so deranged that you'll forget even to call out to God for help. You will *shrivel* to death. You are now a sheep in a slaughterhouse. You will not be missed. Allah will not even know you're gone. In the end, we will cut off your feet so you cannot walk to Paradise. We will burn your corpse and sprinkle your ashes in the Rose Garden of the White House. And such glorious red blooms will appear on our president's flowers!"

Shhhh went the doors.

• • • •

Abdul-Razzaq Ahmed Zaza, Dossier 643/5/19/0, he got a different sort of welcome to Jungleland.

"We know a good bit about you, Mr. Zaza," Micah said. "About your chess talents and your innocence and these last 12 unhappy years."

He let Zaza wash up before getting into his smock.

"Life here is going to be horrifying for a man of your sophistication. The physical pain you have experienced will not happen here. This place was designed to cause harm --- *atha*. Harm is very different from hurt, very different from *alam*. The damage from *atha* goes deeper, and it will stay with you. It's shameful to me that we have created this environment. But this is the world now. I think you understand me?

"I honestly don't know how you've survived to this point, but please believe me when I tell you that the game has changed. The rules have changed. Our 12-year conversation, if we can call it that, this conversation is over. Your file says you rarely speak, but it would be helpful if you could show me that you understand. My Arabic needs improvement, I know. *Assif.* My apologies for that. It's better for you in English, maybe, I think."

"I replayed Fischer-Spassky."

"Sir?"

"How I survived. That is what you asked. I replayed their games. In my head." He spoke slowly, enunciating each word. His English seemed very good.

"But that tournament was in 1972, with more than 16 games," Micah said. "It must have been hundreds of moves."

Zaza looked at him blankly, dull-eyed, resignedly. This was just another jail, with just another jailer. A white dog leaves, a black dog comes along.

"Twenty games, and one forfeit by Fischer," Zaza said, this time in Arabic. "One-thousand and one moves."

Micah handed him a paper cup and poured out a bottle of Ensure. The label on the bottle was in French. *Vanille.* Another dodge to dislocate the prisoners. Tomorrow the label might be in Mandarin. The next day Hebrew or Cyrillic.

"This is dinner. In fact, you will be having this for every meal from now on," Micah said, toneless, in English. "The water faucet is there, with a maximum of 3 liters per day. Toilet is there, in the floor. I will come back tomorrow if you want to play a little chess. That is the only privilege I can arrange for you. My rating is only 1823. Nothing like yours, of course. If you don't want to play, I won't be seeing you again."

Zaza had a sorrowful look and appeared not to have heard him. He looked like a frayed brown ribbon. After a moment he said, "Da. Shakhmaty. Zavtra."

Micah did not respond to Zaza's Russian reply, but he admired it as an opening gambit: a kind of weak-side black-pawn approach to see if he, Zaza, might somehow still be in Russian custody.

The new game had already begun.

• • • •

The following morning, Tran goosed Zaza's Ensure with enough Zoloft that the detainee was almost chatty. Micah lost quickly and reliably in their initial games, and as they reset the board each time he read out excerpts from Zaza's dossier, asking about various prison camps and torture programs. Micah didn't care about the answers. He just wanted to get Zaza talking about the custodial details so that follow-on questions about Camp Bucca and al-Baghdadi --- the important questions --- would not seem out of place. He asked about Camp 1391.

"I don't know that name."

"Allegedly you were there. In Israel."

"Oh yes. That was the name? The sky was blue and the whips were black. That's where they shaved the Star of David into my hair. I keep track of the places by their cruelties, not by their names. Other prisoners were tattooed that way on their fore, fore, how do you say it?"

"Forehead?"

"No, no. Down there. *Qulfa.*" Zaza pointed to his lap.

"Foreskin?"

"Yes, that's it. Correct. *Qulfa.* Foreskin. Tattooed them on the foreskin with the Jewish star."

"My god, that must have hurt a little. Which was the worst prison?"

"I had an unpleasant time at Petak Island. Russia. It was very cold and my hip no longer can enjoy such cold weather. I also there got tuberculosis."

Micah already knew that Bagram had been one of the worst of the horror laboratories, but he was going to ask anyway. It was all bad cop there. The guards and soldiers thought cruel meant manly. Guys playing Jack Bauer dress-up.

"What about Bagram?"

"Bagram was a lawless place. A kind of hell. Many days with water torturing. That is why I am a little bit afraid now for taking showers. That must be in your records, yes?"

Zaza spoke slowly.

"Being threatened is addictive, did you know that? When a great power like America becomes interested in you, you feel valued. At Bagram I felt very much valued. At Bagram they poured diarrhea on me. A woman guard stood over me and urinated on my stomach. They marked numbers on the back of our necks, like cattle. We became so hungry that we ate our own sperm. They sodomized me with a light stick. 'Sodomized,' yes, this word I learned very well in your language. And *dhaw kimiya'ee* --- I had never heard this word before. 'Chemical light.' The stick broke inside me and the yellow liquid came out. At first I thought it was my urine. One Afghan and one American did these things. I wonder why they did it. I had no information for them. Why does one human being want to break the soul of another? These were not human beings."

Zaza noticed that Micah's eyes were filmy with tears. The silence between them seemed to last a decade.

"They were amateur jailers and professional sadists, and their torture was the compliment they paid to my innocence," Zaza said evenly. "Is all this in your file? I think maybe not. Whatever has been written there in your records is not me. Zaza's file is not Zaza. I am not your terminology."

The next game lasted nine moves before Zaza suggested that Micah resign. Otherwise, he said, "it will be checkmate in seven."

"You play too aggressively, like Americans usually do," Zaza told him. "Driving always into the middle of the board and leaving the margins en prise. The word is what --- *mista'jil.*"

"Always in a hurry? Hurrying."

"Yes. Like guards all the time are saying to prisoners. 'Hurry up.' You are too much playing the ECO chess. Encyclopedia chess. You play White better, I think. Black, not so good."

"I play a lot of computer chess," Micah said, not looking up, as if he was absorbed in reading Zaza's dossier. "We had you in Bucca for awhile. How was that? 2004, it says here."

"I don't know the years. They are lost to me. Camp Bucca I do remember. There was quite humane. We could do socializing and exercise. I played chess every day. They fixed my bad teeth. But they punished me when they found the origami I was making. They said the designs looked like airplanes hitting into buildings. Stupid people."

"The Navy was in charge at Bucca."

"Yes. My block was called Waterfront. The guards one night showed a Marlon Brando cinema called 'On the Waterfront.' They thought that was very funny. Waterfront and waterfront. They were children, really. Big terrible children."

• • • •

Running laps on the Freehold track was becoming the PT of choice among the soldiers, and the cadences got ever more loopy and inventive.

Woke up this morning and prayed for rain,
The desert needs moisture to ease its pain.

Hot as hell in this prairie dog town,
Ain't no shade, sun beatin' down.

Fuck you Air Force, and fuck the Corps,
The Unknown Soldiers are mindin' the store.

One-pac, Tupac, three-pac, four,
Ain't gonna work on Maggie's farm no more.

Ain't gonna work on Maggie's farm no more.
Ain't gonna work on Maggie's farm no more.

Micah and Tran often did laps with the men, although they trailed behind so they could talk as they ran. Tran was not one to volunteer much about herself, and most of the time Micah felt like he was interviewing her, pulling at her, much like he was doing with Zaza, getting to know both of them, intrigued by both of them.

"So how's your potato gun working, Sergeant Major?"

"Working fine, thank you, Chief. Seventy-four tags, with just six stitches total. My *potato gun*? Really, Mister Crypto?"

In addition to sweeping each other's legs on the karate mat, Tran and Micah also were now eating a lot of meals together in the DFAC. When they were alone, they sometimes called each other "Micah" and "Teeny." The other troopers let them be. Some good-natured whispering among the men, yes, had begun.

"You went to high school in San Antonio, right? Lots of Army brats at your school, I bet, from Fort Sam."

"Robert G. Cole High School. The Cougars," Tran said. "The school's about 200 meters from the base. Or less. About 60 percent of the student body was military. The officers' kids mostly went to the private school across town. Shaquille O'Neal went to Cole. But he was like 12 years ahead of me."

Tran told Micah about being valedictorian of the Class of 2001, and how O'Neal was the commencement speaker that year. She and some other top students were invited to a small gathering with him after the graduation ceremony, a meet-and-greet at the Dominion Country Club. Shaq was charming and funny at the reception, and he was especially attentive to Tran. When she went looking for a bathroom, he followed her and pulled her into a small meeting room. She kept looking at the size of his hands, even as he was sweet-talking her. He said they had a few minutes to fool around.

"Maybe he wouldn't have hurt me or anything, and maybe I overreacted, just being 17 and all, but I pushed him right in the chest, kinda hard, with both hands, and I got the hell out of there," she said. "I *ran*. It sounds almost funny now, but I was completely fucking scared. I'd never felt that way before. He was just this *huge* human being. Really massive. He weighed like three times what I weighed. Literally. His fist was the size of my *head.* He could have subdued me with one hand."

She said she resolved never again to feel so defenseless, to *be* so defenseless, which explained her near obsession with martial arts when she enlisted after 9/11. She wanted to be the kind of girl who when she said stop, they stopped. And if they didn't, she could make them stop.

"So what about now?" Micah said. "Could you take him now?"

She thought about that for a minute, then smiled and said, "Easy. Easily. Yeah. I could fuck him up."

They both laughed and fist-bumped across the table.

• • • •

One month into the mission, 86 detainees had been eighty-sixed. Sixty-five to go. The troops had settled into a good routine and seemed to be handling the isolation from The World, from football and fast food and social media and women. Below decks, the shock-corridor horrors of Jungleland had not had enough time to get their hooks into any of the detainees: The release deal was so tempting, nearly everybody went for it right away.

Most of the arriving prisoners were stooped, bedraggled, nearly limp. They walked like 6-foot men who had been living forever under a 5-8 ceiling. Coal miners coming to the surface, blinking and bent, emerging into the light after years underground. They had strained and scratchy voices, maybe from shouting through all the beatings and the voltage. They were like packages that had been mailed in a previous decade and were just now being delivered.

But a few of them were not so docile, not so beaten down, far from it. These were the prisoners who had contracted Hepatitis J, as Tran called it. J for jihad. As Micah once told Magazine, "I see bullets in their eyes."

Only one man fully resisted being set free, a former Sadr City goon-squadder named Muhammad Hamza. He hated the Muslims who had tortured him at the other black sites, especially the Egyptians and Kuwaitis, but he loved the Americans, almost as much as he loved his daily Ensure. Magazine thought the man had acquired some variant of Stockholm syndrome, although he had his suspicions about him, too: "For my money, there's still too much Muhammad in his Hamza." The colonel called him "the guest that would not leave." No matter. They were going to evict him soon anyway, whether he signed or not.

Maggie told them in a Safeway meeting one night that the nano-tags had started showing up on CIA screens, although no two tags had connected yet, the requirement for droning. Also, no single tags had appeared in the ISIS capitals of Mosul and Raqqa. Micah hadn't seen any of this information in any of the email traffic, and that puzzled him.

"The python is still swallowing the piglets," Magazine said metaphorically, which was not unlike him. "Fully digesting them will take some time."

Micah was taking his time about offering a release deal to Abdul Zaza. If he was being honest about it, he would have said he liked practicing his Arabic and getting master classes in chess strategy. And he liked Zaza, who seemed to have kept a moral equanimity despite the inflicted loss of his family, his work and his country. As they sat down at the chessboard one day --- Zaza playing Black --- Micah asked if he recalled an inmate named Ibrahim al-Badri al-Samarra'i. He was finally dropping the hammer.

"We know you shared a cell with him at Camp Bucca. He has lately become what we call 'a person of interest.' Maybe you knew him as Abu

Dua. He had various names. We have information that he's planning a big attack on Baghdad. We'd like to prevent that."

Zaza looked at the board. He fussily tidied up his pieces in the back row. Said nothing. Stalling.

"Look, I know you're innocent and you've been treated badly, but my intelligence people think you're still some hard-core Baathist who deserves to rot away in prison. They are insisting that I stop playing chess with you. No more talking. They have a whole list of small terrors and psychological assaults planned for you. It will get so much worse, believe me. One day soon I will simply not come back. You will live here alone, forever, drinking your meals and playing Fischer-Spassky over and over in your mind."

Zaza just shrugged. He was a tough old coot, fully convinced of his psychological resilience and intellectual superiority. "Just because you have the key to my cell," he said, "does not mean that you are not a prisoner, too. You are locked into your own kind of prison. You are perhaps too young to know that you are digging two graves."

Eighteen moves into their game, Micah was up three pawns and a bishop using a conventional Ruy Lopez Breyer, an opening that Zaza clearly knew and would normally demolish. Micah had never been more than two pawns ahead in any of their games. Zaza's focus was clearly elsewhere.

"Why not just tell me what you know about al-Samarra'i," Micah said at last. "You must remember him. I suspect he's not somebody easily forgotten."

Nothing.

"If you help us, I think I can get you released. I'm sure I can. You can be back in Baghdad in three days. You'll reunite with your daughter and your life can begin again."

Zaza took one of his rooks off the board and tried to squeeze it into black powder.

"Of all the cruelty that your devils have inflicted on me all these years, this is the most terrible," he said, rising from his chair until his waist-shackles stopped him. "Worse you are than the slapping and the rapings. My wife and daughter died from your rockets, this you know." His English was breaking down along with his reserve. "I saw them dead and broken apart beside me in that house, and now you injure against me with their deaths. Evil has extended its hand over a chessboard."

"What? No! Your wife did die, yes. *Allah yirhamha.* But your daughter is alive. Didn't you know that? My God, all these years. I assumed you knew. She didn't die. *Wallah!* She was badly hurt and unconscious, but the military doctors at Ibn Sina Hospital, they saved her. Zainab."

"Do not say her name! Your heart is a shoe. You. This is, my god, the evil that you men do. My god."

"No, you mistake me. Zainab. She's alive. She's the first violinist with the Iraqi national symphony. How do you not *know* this? Zainab, yes. She's in your file. I can show you tomorrow. I can get a recording of her playing. She wrote an entire opera for the symphony. My god! She's married to a police captain and they have a baby boy. Your *grandson*! They're living in your old house in Adhamiyah. I find it impossible that you don't know this."

Zaza was weeping. He assumed Micah was lying, just to bedevil him, the good American cop having gone bad. For the first time in all these years, he felt himself about to break. "I would like you to go now. This is too terrible for imagining."

Micah packed up and left. Later that evening he downloaded some of Zainab Zaza's music, a piece from Bartók's second violin concerto, and he piped it softly into Zaza's cell as he was going to sleep. It was a clip of just 40 seconds or so, and barely audible, so faint that Zaza might have thought he was dreaming it. It entered the cell as a distant whisper, the sound of a kite breezing up, the soft sweep of a broom. Or a drone lazing overhead. The game was still on.

• • • •

Colonel Magazine joined Micah and Tran at breakfast the next morning and told them to assemble a small convoy for an overnight trip to Amman. Out and back, 420 clicks each way, good highway, drone surveillance all the way. His Garden of Eden dirt would be coming into Freehold by chopper the following week, but his zoo doo had been tactically acquired and was now ready for pickup at the Ghamadan Zoo in Amman.

Their convoy also would be bringing in a high-value detainee who had spent most of the past 10 years sweltering away in some invisible West African sewer called Fort Vodun.

"And both of you pack your dress blues," Magazine said. "Your promotions came through." Beat, two, three, four.

"Somebody seems to think you guys are officer material. 'Leadership potential' or some malarkey like that. There's going to be a ceremony at the Amman Sheraton. Nothing big or flashy, but General Thomas, the JSOC boss, he'll be in town and his protocol team will run the show." Maggie stood up, saluted and said, "Captain Ford, congratulations. And my congratulations to you, First Lieutenant Tran."

Tran bolted up from her granola, saluted, and shook Maggie's hand. While Micah just sat there, stunned-astonished. It took a whack on the shoulder from Tran to revive him. Stand, salute, thank you, sir.

"How is this even possible, sir? I mean, how?" This was Tran also being astonished.

"Jump-step promotions and battlefield appointments can be ordered by the White House under Army Regulation 601 dash 50," the colonel said formally, big-smiling them both, enjoying his surprise. "Off the record, let's just say I know a guy." Pause. "Chief, you OK with this?"

"Oh, yes, sir, more than OK. Yes, sir. I was just thinking, my father, sir. My father was a captain."

"I know he was, son," the colonel said. "I know he was."

12. PEOPLE COME APART

She kissed *him*, is how they would both remember it. Which figured, her always being drawn to the action, forcing the action, magnetized by it, punch-kick-sweep, making the big move, upstairs at the Sheraton, getting off the elevator on 5, all dressed up after the promotion ceremony, their new bars on their starched-up uniforms, fraternizing right there in the hallway, breaking some kind of Army regulation. He kissed her back. They'd both remember that, too. And then some.

The group heading back to Freehold mustered the following morning just north of Amman, in the old limestone quarry that Jordanian Special Forces sometimes used. It was the velvet hour, near to dawn, the daybreak gray and dim, the sun not yet blanching the sky over the big white city. The convoy was three thin-skinned Humvees, plus a dump truck with the load of Magazine's elephant shit. A pair of recon drones already swung at anchor overhead, launched from Az Zarqa. A Predator and a Global Hawk. When they came in close and rocked their wings they sounded like sewing machines. Drones and dung, modern warfare, can you dig it.

They were somewhere around Safawi on the edge of the desert when the explosions took hold. Terrible things were about to happen. Somebody wired you up, somebody else pushed a lever, and they crashed thunderbolts into your skull.

The first device struck the back end of the lead Humvee, whirling it like a dreidel in the center of the roadway. Tran and Romo crawled out, shaken, orienting themselves when the second explosion came --- a hard bright magnesium flash, 50 feet back, a convex of fire underneath the dump truck. The big deuce bucked hard onto its rear axles and then pitched sideways across the road, groaning, tires and rims gone, downed like a Mausered rhino, its load flung outward in a sweeping, smoking arc.

The last of the three bombs upended the front of Micah's vehicle. There was a basso thunderclap, a gigantic sound, like an elephant's heart exploding. That was the C-4 talking to the copper. A sensational column of thrusting dirt and rock went up, a nasty brown toadstool of a cloud, and then came the clattering fallout of debris. Scorch and burn and frack. Cordite and granite thunder. Lord God of trajectory and blast. Flame kissing flux kissing solder. The air wrinkled with diesel'd heat. The sky was canceled. There wasn't anything you could do, or anywhere to go. You couldn't help breathing strangely.

"I feel like I'm on safari," Micah had said to Sergeant Flipper, who was driving, as the convoy entered the hot zone of the Jordanian desert. Then the bombs started going off and the earth began to heave and breathe underneath them like an animal. Every new explosion was the music of the future, great bulges of mayhem, the sound of the wild black yonder. There was no escaping the indigenous Islamist berserk. *Who owns the whole stony earth and all this sticky blood?* The air inked. The world smudged. The world went from sphere to plane, snap-click-boom, under the full isosceles expression of the plastique.

Micah's Humvee flipped twice, end-over-end, as if weightless, a piñata whacked hard with a broomstick, a double-gainer fully 15 feet in the air, and the truck slammed back down into its crater in the roadbed, somehow upright, and facing forward, its carcass angry and steaming. The windows were gone and the doors were off. The left turn signal was clicking. The air had a heavy, ammonia smell. Sooty fires flared all around.

That third bomb was a piece of Iranian tradecraft called *Mes Shekaaf*, the Copper Splitter, and it was pure, inspired malice. The device, which had a dimpled copper bottom that glorified the rip, had been packed with marbles, toy jacks and American coins. It was artisanal, in its way, and the secondary platter charge of shrapnel raised 12 kinds of hell inside the cab of Micah's truck.

The Honest Abe pennies, the Massa Tom nickels and the FDR dimes instantly shattered under the heavy fist of the charge, and the pieces scissored and scythed through anything soft. They got busy, and they got theatrical. Inside the vehicle it was like being trapped in a spinning phone booth filled with Ginsu knives and throwing stars. Imagine being killed by spare change. (The surgeons would later dig 48 cents out of Sergeant Flipper's back and legs. They also pulled two dimes, intact and spendable, from his abdomen. Flipper planned to make them into cufflinks.)

The jacks and the marbles in the IED behaved differently: They went all lava-gooey under the focused acetylene heat, and the goo seemed to enjoy fastening itself onto any available skin, with terrible hydrochloric effect.

The Humvee's gymnastics and the knives and the stars, Micah wouldn't remember any of that. He had been thrown clear when the blast began to fasten its grip on the vehicle. Flipper survived, but in the back seat, Rascal and the detainee did not. People come apart. Part of the prisoner was found inside the demolished truck. Part of him was found outside. The bomb had cut him in half like a boiled carrot. His remains would lay smoking in a roadside culvert for a very long time that day, tumor-black and gray, a piece of spent charcoal among the stony rubbish.

Rascal, well, Rascal just plain died. The flying knives had done their worst. When Tran reached him, he had a lurid garish gash across his neck and his chest was a wet and open window, utterly red, a burst of liquid vermilion. The light of ancient stars was there in his open eyes, the dying light from a thousand years back, the light that was already gone by the time you saw it.

Tran felt something damp on her face that wasn't mud, and brushing it away she found a glob of someone's brains on her fingers.

Micah was in the road, and the road was sweating oil and tar, and he felt himself becoming part of the road. He was the gray cloud on the X-ray. The coal miner under a cave-in. He was on his left side with his cheek flush to the asphalt, nearly glued to the hot black macadam. The cracked road had gone molten beneath him, runny wax beneath krakatoa fire. In other places the bomb had plowed the road like a field, with great slabs of it turned over and shoveled apart.

The position of his body suggested someone asleep, or he might have been attempting one of Tran's yoga positions. Reverse Warrior. Preying Mantis. He was fully still, lying like dead people do, waiting for their outlines to be chalked. His Oakleys were still on, although the charge had melted and crinkled the amber lenses. His hair was singed and smoking. Mounds of the elephant waste had been flung on top of him and lay in piles all around. His new captain's bars were gone. Helmet gone. His right sleeve had been ripped away, and his father's Bulova was gone. Micah always wore it on his right hand, like Hank, and his dad's white circle was there on his tanned wrist. His nostrils were filling with smoke and ash. "I can't breathe," he thought to himself. Panic ballooned in his brain. The bomb-noise was inside him now. He smelled chlorine. When my ears blistered on that Outward Bound hike. Al Green. The cold window of the police cruiser. The churn behind Dad's boat, the color of root beer. Grandpa Jimmy's face on that hurricane morning. Micah was only thinly attached to his wits now. A man's leg, torn off at the hip, a man's full leg, was just beside him, charred and smoldering in the road.

Tran ran up, kicked the leg aside and knelt beside him. She cleared away some of the zoo shit. "Micah? Can you hear me? Micah!" She was shouting to him. He gave no response.

"Don't, don't, don't, don't," she yelled to the air. "Not like this."

Then, softly, from Micah: "Namaz?"

"Yes, yes, I'm here, I'm here. You're gonna be fine, OK? Do you understand me? Micah!"

"Teeny?"

"Yes, I'm here, baby, I've got you now." She began to cry, which surprised her. "You just lay there now. Relax. You're gonna be fine." She was half-shouting to him now, even as she was scanning the blast site. Looking for follow-on attackers, looking for help.

Romo sprinted up with Tran's CLS Molle bag. She poured water onto Micah's head and carefully worked his face off the tarry patch of hot asphalt. It was an odd thought, but it came to her: rhinoceros hide. She cut the strap off his mangled goggles and then saw his eyes, red and blazing. Like bouillon. Like boiled. "Oh, Micah, no."

"Yeah, I can't see very well, Teeny."

"I know, Micah. The Dustoff is coming. It's gonna be OK. You're just shook up is all. It's a little bit of shock. Completely normal."

She looked overhead for the escort drones --- not there, and she hoped they had seen the IEDs strike the convoy. She told Romo to find a working radio and call in their location. "Then check on the other men and set up some kind of perimeter."

The whole bangarang scene was black with creosote smoke and chaos and rubble. The debris field extended 50 yards all around --- the bite radius of the three bombs. Two roadside shops had crumbled under the shock of the blasts --- a barber's and a meat market. Two butchers came toward Romo, eyes wide, arms raised, their hands red, their aprons red. A shoeshine boy was face-up in a puddle next to a mangled dog. A meat cleaver had taken the kid in the throat and his eyes looked strange, filmed over and dim. A man who sold umbrellas from a pushcart lay dead atop a sheet of blood. A dozen of his umbrellas had popped open from the explosions --- black ones, flowered ones, a Lion King --- and they were now flipping down the road, swept away and tumbling end over end, carried along by the hot heavy wind of the afterblast.

"Teeny, are the other guys OK?"

"I don't know yet. I think so. But it's gonna be OK, Micah. You're gonna be OK."

"Could you stop saying that? It makes me nervous."

She was relieved. He had finally recognized her voice and her name, and he had even cracked a little wise. But his eyes. The memory of the tortured Private Zimmerman was on her now. Her cortisol pump was stuck open. Nothing in her training. Eyes boiled in their sockets? A life can change in the instant. Optic nerves, TBI, spinal cord, internal bleeding. Entrance/exit. Dilated. Nonresponsive. She went through her checklist. She flashed her penlight and his pupils didn't signal back. Red marbles was all. Beast mode. The Hulk. Blind. Blind. Dying. This is what was coming to her. She was crying again.

He could feel her pinching his calves, testing for feeling, and he said he thought his thigh was burning. She rolled him over and saw an umbrella stave deep in his leg.

"It's a little piece of metal, baby. I'm going to leave it there for now. The doc can zip it right out for you. When we get sterile. You hang in there now. They're coming for us. I've got you now, Micah. I've got you."

The dump truck exploded. The fuel tank went. A fireball, and more shit and shrapnel. A shovel and someone's boot were hurled their way. Gear oil, diesel, water, feces, brake fluid, jellied bits of road, sand, pieces of tarpaulin, chunks of machinery, all manner of crap rained down on them. Tran leaned over Micah to shield him. She could cover.

13. THE NECESSARY CATASTROPHE

This contraption they have Micah wearing, it's a nylon-and-leather get-up that fits down snugly on his head. The thing makes him look like a World War I bombardier or a Notre Dame wingback from the Twenties. Rounded ear cups so he can't hear. D-rings here and there, some Velcro patches. It suggests bondage more than rehab.

Micah hasn't seen the headpiece yet --- they've got him in a blackout blindfold, too, something a welder might wear.

He has been woozy and headachy since they brought him in a week ago, and he's losing track of time, not unlike Zaza back at Freehold. He's been on his back in this trauma ward in Amman, his helmeted head cushioned between two blocks of foam. His noggin is a steady bubble on a carpenter's level. They put cold packs on his forehead from time to time.

Once or twice a day they stand him up, a couple attendants on each side, Arab guys, infrequent bathers by the waft of them, as big as Big Ten linebackers. They empty his bag, change his sheets, flush the IV, perform a good all-over Baby Wiping, dry shampoo, ointments, lotions, creams. "Lunch, mister. Please to have this good Ensure now, mister." His bowels run like warm tapioca. Colonel Magazine got the Pentagon to fly in a big-time neurosurgeon from Landstuhl to handle his case. "Best brain man in the Med," Maggie said. The doctor doesn't want Micah to lose his vertical, which is how he put it, so the linebackers walk him around a little more every day. Up the hall and back, up the hall and back. The other 23 hours, the doc wants him quiet and calm.

The leg will be fine: It's a simple puncture wound from that piece of umbrella. Other than that, he came through the explosion pretty much intact, not counting the slip-knotting of a few ligaments and a cranial bruise that Brain Man keeps calling "the insult." Oh, and those parboiled eye sockets. With so many blood vessels bursting in Micah's head from the bang of the blast, it had looked like his eyeballs were floating in ketchup. Marinating. Blood-shot. Shot with blood. It had scared Tran silly, back there on the tarmac, and she isn't somebody who scares. BM's diagnosis: "No cause for undue concern." Undue.

Micah's blood pressure was the thing they were watching so closely now, keeping it up, pushing both numbers into triple digits. They wanted most of his body just this side of comatose while getting the heart to keep all the blood-trains running on time. (The doctors ordered up the occasional squirt of norepinephrine, but any serious analgesics were out. Maybe an occasional hit of liquid Tylenol, but that was it.) His body was internally cold, pharmaceutically cold, Michigan-ice-fishing-cold. The internists doing the video-consult from Walter Reed wanted him on an ice floe, and whenever a new trickle of epi arrived in his system, Micah felt like he might be bobbing away toward The Final Island.

• • • •

The subacute ward that Micah's in --- the medical staff calls it the Wreck Room --- is a wing reserved for the U.S. military as part of the new King Abdullah Medical Centre. The ward has eight hospital beds, with an American attending and some military nurses, and there's a day room with couches and two big card tables. A dozen or so enlisted guys spend their days in there, mostly Reservist trainers and Special Forces guys in from Baghdad. They come and go, a week or two at a time, reading the outdated magazines or playing Texas hold-em. A couple guys might play some chess now and then. Everybody mostly just shoots the shit, talking shit, talking nonsense, enjoying the air-conditioned break from the broil of the suck.

They're all in the Wreck Room for minor repairs, with injuries that just need some time and attention – swabbings of Betadine, tweakings of meds, the checking of sutures, adjusting trusses, rewrapping ribs. Nobody is getting shipped home for this kind of thing, but still, they'll be getting their Purple Hearts.

Some of the men go on and on about how they got wounded, trying out different versions, getting their delivery down, getting their stories straight for the folks back home. The smaller the wound, the bigger the story. Hurt guys wash in, healed guys wash out, and everybody speaks some version of MIL --- military idiot language, not unlike the dopey chatter of a second baseman to his pitcher. MIL-speak adjectives are essentially these: unbelievable, awesome and fuckin'. And then you had your three go-to adverbs: absolutely, totally and fuckin'.

What did they talk about? Sports, sex, money, music, Obama, vee-hicles, the way things were so political back home, how their entire fucked-up lives were going to be different when they got back. Wives. Old girlfriends. Jobs. Booze. Changing their MOS. Their dicks. (Oh, they talked *a lot* about their dicks.) How fucked up their officers were. They dreamed up Top 10 lists. They played Who'd You Rather? The usual. It was the American id, unsheathed.

They deconstructed their favorite video games --- any Madden, any Halo, any C.O.D., any Grand Theft Auto, Myst, Doom, Heavy Rain, Bayonetta. They planned their first perfect meals back home, with lots of sentiment for nearly any burger that was backed up with fries and a Jack-and-Coke. One recurring thread: Mickey D versus Wendy's versus BK.

From his bed at the front of the ward, the helmeted Micah had heard none of this. But yesterday, with the systolic finally obeying the diastolic, the doctors took off his headgear. He could hear better, but the blindfold stayed on. And the ice packs keep coming. He still feels like a boy pharaoh being readied for the afterlife.

He discovered that the mildly deaf are able to hear all sorts of fantastic things, some of which might actually have been said. It was a strange kind of disembodied ventriloquism. "Women are a different cut of meat." "No more booty stick." "And Magua will eat his heart." "What we do here will echo in eternity." "The Hillary Clinton vagocracy." "It rubs the lotion on its skin." A wounded guy --- the blindfolded Micah came to think of him as The Loud Soldier --- said things like Lesbyterian, opinionate, Betamax, beard farmers, lash the gash, because fuck it. The Loud Soldier said he pretty much loved his girlfriend although she did have some OCD issues: "She makes me brush my teeth --- and *gargle* --- before she lets me eat her pussy."

As Micah's hearing began to dial back in, he caught some eager talk among the men about bonuses for re-upping. With the right MOS, Loud Soldier said, you could get 20 grand.

"I'd give 20 thousand for somebody to frag my fuckin' recruiting officer, that lyin-ass cocksucker. Fuck a re-up."

This was a staff sergeant, name of Sickles, mid-twenties, military police, from Baltimore, which he calls Harm City. He lost the lower part of his right leg in Afghanistan a few years ago, in the Korengal, as part of the famed Restrepo platoon. Now a sniper outside the Green Zone has shot through his prosthesis. TARFU. Sickles didn't want to rotate home --- where he suspected there was marital infidelity afoot --- so he's waiting on a new leg to be shipped in.

"Hoo-ah that. You had me at frag." This was a Marine lance corporal, a terminal lance, doughnut-complexioned, 25, from Something-hocken, Pennsylvania. Eyes the color of Benadryl. A dog handler. The dog had tripped an IED a week earlier. The poor thing was torn to pieces and a shard of rib bone flew into the corporal's groin. Damn.

"Now I know how my wife feels, chillin' at home every day, doin' jack shit." This was commentary from Jack Wilson, 30, first sergeant, South Oak Cliff in Dallas, ex-baggage thrower for American Airlines at DFW. He was fresh off a field promotion when his FNG driver rolled their MRAP down an irrigation berm alongside a sugarcane field. The vehicle had flipped on them and a shard of cane speared Wilson in the left buttock. Deep, too. He almost bled out. Took 21 stitches to close it up. One of the American nurses in the Wreck Room has taken to calling him Sweet Cheek.

"The wife, shit, she's probably layin' up on the sofa right now, shopping online and spendin' up my combat pay," Wilson says. "Eatin' her Ding-Dongs and watching Project Runaway."

"Tell her I got all the ding-dong she needs right *here*. I seen her picture. She can run away with me whenever she wants." This was a specialist named John Fitzgerald Jackson, an 11-Bravo in Wilson's platoon.

"Bitch, please. You'd fuck a bullet wound. At least I *got* a wife."

"Roger that, Sergeant. I told you that shit, right? About my wife? My *ex*-wife. I fuck her sister one time, *one damn time,* and she puts me out the house. Bitch puts *me* out? And man, her sister is fine, know'm sayin'? Packed like a fuckin' *Samsonite.* The fuckin' *Pope* woulda rubbed up on this girl. So my old lady hits the brakes and I hit the windshield. Didn't leave me shit in the settlement neither. Even took my mixing board and sold it on eBay. There is some shit I will not eat. How'm I supposed to make a living without my board? Obama can't get a brother no job. Now I'm up in this sumbitch with all you shot-up and sugar-caned motherfuckers. Looks like a fuckin' Jerry Lee Lewis telethon up in here."

Johnny Jackson is a California kid, tall, verging on scrawny, turns 22 next week. Says he's a Crip straight outta Compton but really he grew up in a 4-2 brick ranch on Surfrider Way in a not-bad part of Costa Mesa. Two days after Wilson got stalked in the ass, Jackson was shot in the armpit by an ISIS sniper in Bayji. Got him from better than a grand away. The round went right under the gap in his vest. Getting shot, more than anything, it just scared the hell out of JFJ Junior. Really put the zap on his head, the idea that this was one-on-one and personal --- a bullet meant only for him. The sniper had seen Jackson come into the soft-green-glowing circle of his rifle scope --- "through the looking glass," was the translation in Arabic. The shooter had probably *al-hamdu lillah*'d about a hundred times when he saw Jackson go down. Most def.

After they brought him in, Junior was meowing night and day for a week, softly, curled in his bed, like a kitten. They got him on antipsychotics, which stopped the whimpering, and now they've moved him to sub-acute.

They're watching him. Could be he's faking. The nurses privately call him Cat, because of the meowing. And because of catatonic. His nerves will never again be quite right.

"I'd give my whole damn re-enlistment bonus to spend a Motel 6 weekend with January Jones," said a tech sergeant, a Reservist named Scarpia, an ex-sheriff from Tosca, Georgia. "Every time that woman lights a cigarette, ooof. Just watching her smoke gives me a hard-on."

Scarpia was a fobbit MP trainer, almost always in the rear with the gear. Keeps his old Barney Fife badge pinned to his assault pack. Badge 417073. Spends half his pay at the KFC trailer. He had come to Iraq weighing a buck-sixty. He's well over a deuce now. Twice a day he's a 10-piece, white meat, extra crispy, extra gravy, extra biscuits, hold the slaw.

"Who?"

"January Jones," said Scarpia. "She was on that show 'Mad Men.' The blonde one. She was the pissed-off mommy with the bitchy resting face. I'd be banging her like a screen door durin' Katrina. I bet she smells like Miss America."

"So, what, she smells like money?"

Scarpia was a blowhard and a bully, actively disliked by his troops and barely tolerated by his superiors. The half-clever motto of his unit was 212 Degrees --- water boils, making steam, creating power, etcetera fuckin' etcetera. One day in a briefing his colonel did a double-take at Scarpia's waistline and asked him what the fuck. "Holy shit, Sergeant, are you trying to *weigh* 212? You look like half a ton of bad veal." A week ago, on some kind of snipe hunt with the Kurds up in Kalak, Scarpia was inside a Porta-Potty when two big privates ran full-speed at the thing. Like they were hitting a blocking sled. They put their shoulders into the shitter and sent it banging over into the dirt. It might have been funny if Scarpia hadn't broken his collarbone.

"I know one thing, I'm too old for this Army shit." This was coming from a corporal, wheelchair'd, barely 22, White Horse Beach, Massachusetts. He had taken shrapnel through the fat part of both inner thighs --- "danger-close to my business district." He said his name was Roderigo Madison and his great-grandfather was John Dos Passos.

"Who the fuck is that? Sounds fuckin' gay." Army private, South Side of Chicago, White Sox fan, a bit on the deep-dish-doughy side. Lost his left pinkie in the door jamb of a Humvee. He's alopecia-bald, so his squad calls him Chemo.

"John Dos Passos. The writer. You know, the U.S.A. Trilogy."

"Didn't see it."

§ "Fuck it, motherfucker. That shit don't mean fuck to me. Fuck that. *I'm* the blood and the treasure. We all are. Fuck money. There's blood in our gasoline. *We're* the fuckin' treasure."

§ Frank Krieger, Army staff sergeant, 32, Sea-Clift, New Jersey: "I was just reading about that kid in the Boston Marathon bombing, I forget his name, Joker or something, but they gave him the death sentence. There's no way he could have got a fair trial, not in fucking Boston he couldn't. Those assholes up there. 'Boston Strong.' My ass. Four people died, OK, that's not cool, but that's a slow Tuesday morning in Syria. The whole city went into lockdown over one juvenile delinquent with a .38 pistol. Everybody cowering in their houses, scared shitless, peeking through the Venetian blinds on the lookout for this terrible terrorist. And this is the birthplace of the freakin' American Revolution. City used to have some balls. People used to bow up. But the cops tell 'em to stay inside, so the entire population throws the deadbolts and waits for the all-clear. Bunch of obedient fuckin' sheep is what. Those cops had better armor than the 4th I.D., and that kid still evaded their so-called manhunt. Their *dragnet*. Shit. Some homeowner grabbing a smoke on his back porch was how they found the kid, and he was already all shot up and half-dead. 'Boston Strong.' Paul Revere would be fuckin' ashamed."

§ "You know what I miss about America? Everything! Every. Damn. Thing. I just wanna get home, smoke a blunt and eat my Cocoa Puffs. I don't wanna see another Iraqi flag until the freakin' Olympics."

§ "I heard the VC used to make dice out of dead grunts. You know, carve up the vertebrae."

It was men's talk, the laugh and boast and yak and stupidity of unapologetic men, cut and thrust, and not touchy about race, God or politics. It perhaps didn't rise to the level of actual conversation, and it was certainly not debate, but rather the kind of talk that wasn't trying to get anywhere, just circling and circling and enjoying itself.

§ "Whatever happened to VD? You never hear about that any more. Crabs, blue balls, syph, the clap. The good old days."

§ "My drill instructor said he'd only allow two kinds of haircuts during Basic: 'High and tight, like my wife's ass. Or smooth and shaved, like my girlfriend's pussy.' He was an asshole, but I kinda liked the guy."

§ A young specialist from Dyersville, Iowa, was on the ward. Ropy, bad skin, erstwhile meth fiend. Kicked his habit with a month in a drug program before he enlisted. He was an Army dog handler, although his shepherd had attacked him while they were training with Jordanian SWAT. Dog tore him *up*. Now he's rehabbing in the Wreck Room, in the warm embrace of Sister Morphine, his nerves trying to lay back in their tracks. "I was in drug use then. Lotta K-2 and Mojo. I was confused to what my direction was. As per my parents, I felt abandonment. No insurance at all, and my gums was bleeding bad. I was drinking at least maybe a quart of Listerine every day or more. My whole life collapsed like a house of dominoes. It was the economy and all, that's why. Like pulling hen's teeth. So I enlisted. The beginning of an adventure --- that was how it felt. I guess I can't get this right, neither. Just this life, and no more. What's it going to be then, eh? What's next? No one told me."

§ Private First Class Grabstein, 36, another loud soldier who claimed to be the oldest private in the 964, and maybe in the whole Army: "I have no idea what war means any more. It's anything you can get away with, I guess. They don't give Medals of Honor for killing the enemy any more. You get 'em for saving your own guys. That seems kinda fucked-up to me. Every war we ever won, we killed our way out of it. These ISIS fuckers need killing. Ah, fuck it. In the end it's all just fuckin' real estate."

§ Guy from Idaho named Killebrew. No age, no rank. "I was all shot up, in a field hospital in Sanur Province, we'd had a big gunfight, spring of 2010, my third deployment thanks to our Surgin' General, Dave Petraeus. I was waiting on a medevac to Kabul and this doctor comes by and asks me about my last words. Like I was about to kick. Scared the fuck out of me. He said he had been making notes on guys' last words, you know, right before they died. He'd been doing it since the invasion, keeping notebooks and shit. He even talked to Afghans and foreign fighters. Said he was going to write a book about it some day and the title was going to be 'Strike the Tent,' which I guess is what Robert E. Lee said right before he passed. Anyway, we get to talking and he says everybody gets panicky and scared when they're bleeding out. He said the American guys always call for their mamas in their final moments, and the Arabs call out to God."

§ "So one day our terp comes up all excited --- we called him Hey Boo --- and Hey Boo says he has a local guy who can take us to a huge weapons cache. This is in Diyala, late oh-five, maybe early oh-six. 'Many arms, so many, too many arms,' that kind of babbling shit. So we go down about 28 alleys, completely on the X, exposed as all hell, and we come up on, you know, there's like dozens of these 55-gallon drums lined up behind this big building. We look inside and they're full of arms. Actual arms. Like, you know, *amputated.* Arms, legs, hands, feet. I mean, it was fuckin' messed up. Turns out the building was a hospital and the orderlies had been dumping the limbs in these barrels. I mean, damn. That shit will fuck you up. Believe it."

§ "What doesn't kill you makes you stronger. You've heard that one, right? Well, I call *bull*shit on that. What doesn't kill you makes you injured and wounded and fucked up. Guys talk about getting' 'pain boners.' That's a whole *load* of bullshit. But I will say this: Being hurt is teaching me that there are worse things than being hurt. That's about the only upside to all this that I can see."

§ "Guy I know with the 1/2 Marines was waiting for a refill on his meds at Walgreens. Seattle, I think it was, was where he lived. He tries to take his blood pressure while he's waiting, right, with one of those machines, and he tore apart the machine when he thought it wasn't gonna let go of his arm. You know that sleeve you put your arm in, with those machines? The cuff, yeah, the cuff. The fuckin' cuff closed up on him and he couldn't deal. The boy went all bravado and shit. Full clip. The dude was vexed."

§ Nicolas Appert, Army staff sergeant, Paris, Kentucky, a sulky brute but a solid soldier even though he washed out of Ranger School at Benning. No shame in that. Most guys didn't finish. "My old man cries like a little girl every time I call home when we're downrange. He was such a hard ass on me growing up. Cut me *zero* slack. Now it's like he's the son and I'm the dad. I went to see the wizard at Bragg one time and he said that for some guys the military is all about Daddy. He said it's one long embarrassing scream of 'Daaaaddy!' It's really just fathers and sons, and you're out there trying to prove something to him in the most intense way possible."

§ Guy named Brownie because in civilian life he drove for UPS, and also because he was a keen student of his bowel movements. Every time he headed for the shitter his squaddies would yell, "Code Brown!" He says: "So where's the *American* disease? You got German measles, Hong Kong flu, Japanese encephalitis, Spanish influenza, West Nile virus, Ebola. What do we get? Fuckin' *Lyme disease*? Is that even a real thing? Named after some place in Connecticut? That miniature-ass state. How about something big? Texas Plague. The Black Death of the Tetons. Oh, wait, yeah, we've got Rocky Mountain Spotted Fever. That's cool. And I guess we've always got Lou Gehrig going for us. So, yeah, that's cool."

The nurses stayed out of the goofball jabber and political rants. Mostly they did. But one day a middle-aged Whiskey heard a guy named Castro, a carpet mechanic from Grand Concourse, El Bronx, talking about wanting to introduce Paris Heel-ton to various tuberous vegetables. That is, to introduce the vegetables *into* her. The nurse came out from her station and said that kind of talk was disrespectful and out of line, no matter who the young lady was, so Castro should knock it the fuck off.

"Sorry, ma'am, but I believe Paris is too spoiled for her own good. I blame her parental upraising. She clearly needs some boun-da-ries. In her sub-conscience she really *wants* some boundaries. You know --- structure. I believe I could help her with that."

Castro wondered --- not knowing that Miss Hilton was an actual millionaire heiress --- whether Paris would agree to what he called "a brief veg-o-matic" for $1,000. One thing, as it always did, led to another.

"I'd give a grand to piss in Mick Jagger's mouth while he's signing 'Satisfaction.' A grand, easy." This was another Fuckin' New Guy, wheelchair, Houston, maybe 19. The kid said his mother once told him that he never would have been conceived "without that second quart of Colt .45 that night." So she named him Colt. Shrapnel from an IED had hot-sprinkled both of Colt's calves and another piece had nicked a lung, so they had run a full pulmonary toilet on him. His BP started booming and now he's on Diovan and Betaloc, plus Elavil, Flexeril, Firedryl --- pretty much all the ills in the Wreck Room pantry.

"That's fuckin' weird, man." Scarpia again. "Pissin' on Mick? How could you even think that shit up? Are you a fag, or what?"

"Your problem, Sergeant, and I totally fuckin' get this, given your senior longevitude and all, but your problem is that you think there are only two genders."

For this Scarpia absolutely and totally had no fuckin' reply. "What? Aw, *fuck* that noise. Kiss my sugar-frosted nutsack."

Somebody said he would spend two grand to give Scarlett Johansson a sponge bath. Five hundred was offered to lick Taylor Swift's eyebrows. A grand to be on a pit crew at Talladega. Another grand to spank Serena

Williams --- "just a touch of the quirt, to bring up the color." A grand to punch Hugh Grant in the face, just once, a nice clean shot. That led to a string of other face-punch nominees: Caitlyn Jenner, Billy Ray Cyrus, Bill Maher, Tiger Woods, any Kardashian, Donald Trump, Miley Cyrus, Bieber, Seacrest, Kanye, Wolf Blitzer, Axl Rose, Sarah Palin. Somebody offered a thousand bucks to be Courtney Love's tampon. That led to several men awww-shitting and grabbing their belly stitches, after which followed a long and rather serious discussion of MILFs and who exactly qualified. When some guy nominated Jessica Rabbit, there was a lot of nodding all around.

Another discussion went 20 minutes about the relative merits of songs with just sounds in their titles: Click Bang, Click Click Boom, Boom Boom Pow, Bam Thwok, and Tap-Rack-Bang. *It's only joy I ache. You da hubcaps on an Impala.*

Eventually, though, the idiot talk always bam-thwokked back to the war. The war the war the war. "At least in Afghanistan," one soldier said, "we got to fight back."

• • • •

He was sleeping, so she stood and watched him awhile from a distance, then pulled up a chair beside the bed. The ward was quiet for a change, and a nice afternoon light was sliding through the blinds.

He stirred, coughed once, stretched his arms over his head, then felt for his face --- yes, the goggles were still there. He cocked his head at an odd angle and lifted his nose like a retriever.

"I know that silence. Smells like Teeny spirit," he said to the air, speaking in the opposite direction of where she was sitting.

"I'm over here, smart ass," she said. "How did you know it was me?"

"Your soap, your shampoo, and your feminine chi. Those are three very significant aromas. My powers of smell have increased so much since I've been blindfolded in here. It's true what they say."

"What they say is that soap is the yardstick of civilization."

She sat on the edge of the bed and took his left hand. He seemed thinner and more fragile, but he was smiling. And gripping her hand.

"What are you doing here?" he said. "Did the colonel give you a weekend pass, *Lieutenant*?"

"Pretty much, yeah, a 48. There's some kind of bottleneck in deliveries to the COP so we're standing down for a few days. I saw your chart and talked to the neurosurgeon. How are you feeling?"

"You should see the other guy," he said, and she laughed. She fed him a sliver of ice.

"I feel OK, actually. I probably look pretty bad, though, huh? The urine bag is gone. I can walk around a bit. I've tried playing chess games in my head --- without much luck. I got that trick from Zaza. I'm still getting headaches at night, and weird-ass dreams. Other than that, though, not bad. Better *now*. I sure wish I could see you. Something has tried to kill us, Teeny, and failed. Will you be my girlfriend?"

"Easy there, tiger. One improvised explosive device at a time. Your hair is pretty funky, for one thing. Although I do like this unshaven thing you've got going. Very manly, even for a brainy captain. They showed me a picture of you in that Red Baron headgear thing. Brilliant disguise."

Tran found a nurse and got the OK to pull the curtain around Micah's bed for some privacy. She leaned over and kissed him lightly on the mouth.

"Did you save my life?" he asked her quietly. "Do I have a brain injury? Teeny, they haven't told me anything. The doctor treats me like a freakin' child, like I've lost my facility to understand English. When am I getting out of here? Did you get hurt at all? Kiss me again. Please."

"Micah, listen, slow down. You have to keep calm, baby. It's normal after a combat injury to get emotional and overwrought. You think you've escaped death and you start to get hyper ideas, especially in your dreams, like you said. Or you'll get Unwanted Thoughts Syndrome, which is exactly what it sounds like. And you might experience something called lucid dreaming, where you're aware that you're dreaming *while* you're dreaming. Some guys feel a sense of giddiness. Some get depressed. It's all completely normal, and the mood swings will flatten out. But you have to watch it."

"OK, OK, but how are *you*? As I recall we both got blown up. Be honest."

"I'm fine. A little whiplash and a bruised rib is all. I've had way worse just from sparring." She pulled up her shirt to show him the purpling on her side, an angry shadow that rode right across her meat tag. *O-POS. NKA. 582-02-0766.* Then she realized, duh, that his blindfold was still on. She re-tucked her shirt. "I had a checkup right after the attack, and the neuro guy looked at me again just now. He's a good man, and thorough.

"And no, I didn't save your life. The Dustoff team did that. The neurosurgeon says the insult to your brain was minimal. He's already reducing the anti-seizure drugs and the diuretics. That's a really good sign. And he showed me the results of your TBI test. Listen to me now. The test produces two metrics, the Glasgow Coma Scale and the Revised Trauma Score. And you aced them both. So it seems you're going to continue being brilliant. Seventeen and three is how much again?"

She was using a lot of specific terms and concepts on purpose, careful not to be condescending but also wanting to test his memory and cognition. She held his hand and watched his monitors and told him about losing Rascal, Posner, the detainee and the others. About Flipper's successful evac to Landstuhl. About the Freehold guys all asking about him. About Zaza's agitation over something. About the leg puncture that was almost healed. About Maggie's emotional homegoing ceremony for the dead Freehold guys, and his arranging a helo for her to visit him.

"Thank you, Sweetie. For explaining things," Micah said. "Can I call you that in private without you warning me about my blood pressure?"

"I've never been a Sweetie. To anybody. You're nice."

"I have a giddy-brain-insult-half-coma crush on you. I will forever remember the Amman Sheraton Hotel, Room 569, and the seersucker robes and the melted Toblerones. But I take your point about my possibly over-emotional state. So forthwith, there is no longer a warm, lovable person inside me. Beneath Micah Ford's cold exterior, even if you break the ice, you will find cold water. You will need an axe to break the frozen sea within me."

"So there *is* brain damage," she said, gently touching his face-stubble where the sticky road tar had been. She was encouraged by his detailed memories and the quick, nuanced joking. She didn't guess that he was doing all this on purpose because he knew she would be testing him, which was her way.

She got fresh washcloths, refilled his ice bucket, fixed his blankets and pillows.

"It feels like you're leaving," he said.

"The doctor only gave me 20 minutes, but I have another day of leave. I'll come back in the morning. He said he might take off your eye bandages tomorrow. How do your eyes feel? Can you tell?"

"They don't hurt. They itch sometimes. I guess it hurts a little when I cry. From the salt, do you think?"

"Oh, baby, you're going to be fine. I promise. You just need a little more rest, is all. You've had a hell of a shock. I wish I could kiss your brain."

She smoothed his hair and kissed his mouth, a little bit hard this time, and with intent.

"OK, Captain Ice-Man, now turn off the war and get your ass some sleep."

"Roger that. Thanks for coming, Teeny. Serious now: Thank you. I've been. I just. I just never thought I'd be touched by anyone again in any kind of tender way. With tenderness."

She put a hand on the center of his chest. "You're my guy, you know. So please take it easy. I'd hate to see anything happen to you."

"Thanks," he said, calmly, "but I think it already has."

• • • •

What was happening to Micah Ford in Amman was something close to a rigorous moral inventory. The IEDs out in the desert had shaken him in more ways than the brain scans would show or the neurosurgeon could know. Nothing like a little disaster for sorting things out. He was awake now, really awake, and maybe it wasn't too late. For the first time in a long time he didn't feel so alone.

Inside the sarcophagus of his bandages, Micah had been thinking about the CIA psychiatrist's report, the original one, the one he had doctored. The shrink really had gotten it right, and Micah was now fully aware that he had arrived in Iraq, arrived at Freehold, with a legitimate case of stress disorder. This realization was not especially unnerving to him. More like a problem-set to work through, an equation to balance.

He considered what the man had written: For most of his life, Micah had been smacked around by the monstrous tragedies of modern America --- the AIDS that killed his mother when he was 10, the sexual assault on Namaz at Michigan, the terrorism of September 11 that took her and

Hank, Hurricane Katrina taking his grandfather, the BP catastrophe that did in Apalachicola and the Sangarees, and the nativist racism that led to Beni's torture and murder. And now, here he was, caught up in the tragedy of Iraq. His biography matched his country's.

This is what he told Tran when she came to the hospital the next day. She had expected an easy late-morning chat with her banged-up colleague and possible boyfriend. No.

Micah's eyes were still bandaged, and maybe that helped him to talk, which he did for several hours, in a clear, unbroken and unrelenting way. Tran let him go, sitting there on his bed, listening to his history, his inventory, taking in the stories that she felt it would be important for her to know and understand. Micah talked about his mother dying from AIDS in the plastic tent, and he talked a lot about Namaz and Hank. About the psychiatric diagnosis that he had hacked and rewritten. He told her about the work-secrets he had been keeping, about Zaza's innocence and about Jimmy's bloody pyjamas. His mom's bike. Drinking so much in Apalachicola and Voncy's attempt to rescue him. Beni, too. About how he had been in full emotional retreat when he joined the Army. *The past is so much in me, Teeny. I can feel it beating sometimes, like a second heart.* The long swims and the tidal turbulence and his famous thesis and the math prizes and the millions he had made from his programs. That call from the man from the fund. The miraculous escape at Reichenbach Falls while he was in language training at Dartmouth. The Alabama murder. The Arlington mud.

He unpacked his fears and sadness, hidden for so long, so unspoken, so hidden even from himself since 2001. Things unsaid. He was coming clean. He told her about what had come to him in the night, the idea that the violence of the IEDs had unshackled him from all the violence he had already endured and stored up. He called the IEDs "the necessary catastrophe," and felt he had somehow been frightened into the present. *Where is the real desert? Not where one might think.* It was a reversal of the usual story, with soldiers contracting PTSD in a war zone, then returning home to suffer with it. It was the opposite with Micah: He had arrived in Iraq with stress disorder but it was the extreme violence he had found there ---

the detainees' tales of torture, the vile rationale for Jungleland, those three bombs in the road --- this was what was curing him. It made no physical sense. It was like falling sideways off a mountain.

All this just swam out of Micah like rivers of code, swirling fractal packets of ones and zeros, his history and ideas reeling out, with no big theatrics, almost no adjectives, him groping now and then for Tran's bedside hand, unashamed of his account, far from it, just giving her the truth as best he knew it, his best available truth, the best available truth. Maybe 5 percent was seduction; the rest was confession and submission. Everything was different now.

Tran got it. She did. And she wanted him to know that she knew something about where he had been, where his mind and soul had been. She told him about a former patient at Fort Benning, a Cavalry Scout named Dave Gamelgaard. Big tough guy from Erie, Pennsylvania. "Erie, P-A," he said. He got sepsis after a spider bite went nasty on him, and Tran had treated the wound.

"So I ran into him a couple days later at Home Depot," she said. "I needed some paint and I was checking out the color samples. Fan decks, they call them. You know, 10,000 freakin' colors. Anyway, this guy was in the aisle just staring at this color sample in his hand, staring down at one of those little cards, and he was bawling and starting to hyperventilate. He went to his knees and his whole body was shaking. It was a real panic attack. I reminded him who I was and that he should take really deep breaths and that I would stay with him. He looked right at me --- but it was more like he was looking through me --- and he said he had killed a kid in Ramadi, shot the kid in the face, and this was the color of the little boy's brains. That *card*, he was saying, it was the same color, and it had brought everything right back to him. 'I did terrible things,' he said. I stayed with him for a couple minutes and he collected himself. I never saw him again. The card said 'Dutch Boy B13-2, Family Tree.' That was the name of the color. I'll never forget that. Some wounds, I think, are never going to heal. Maybe some of them aren't meant to heal."

Micah was feeling her face and wiping away her tears when the neurosurgeon suddenly appeared. He was ready to take off the bandages.

"So, are we ready for the big reveal?" the doctor said. Tran, sniffling, closed the blinds against the afternoon sun. She faced the clock on the wall. It was 3:11. At 3:13 the doctor said, "There we go. That's better." Tran took in a deep breath, then turned and looked at Micah.

The red tide of tomato bisque in which his eyes had been swimming after the attack, that was gone. Micah blinked up at her and smiled. "I know you," he said.

He still looked a little bloodshot, but no worse than a decent Roseate Spoonbill hangover. His eyebrows were growing back. The doctor, a young major named Robert Gregory, scoped Micah's eyes for several minutes --- no retinal swelling, no corneal abrasion, no edema. He squirted in some artificial tears and some Prolensa.

"Things are going to be a little fuzzy for another day or two, Chief. And you might feel like your eyes are playing tug-of-war on you. That's normal. No reading or TV yet. But one more week, give or take, and you're going to be out of here. You're doing fine. The internal medicine guys have already signed off on your release, and your colonel somewhere has been pressing us to get you back to duty. He didn't want you shipped home. Said you were too important to his mission, or something. And for some reason my boss took more than a passing interest in your case.

"Anyway, I just want your numbers to stabilize a little more. Like I said, about a week. Meantime we're going to get you some good physical therapy, plenty of active walking around, get out in the sun a little. Lieutenant Tran is it? Maybe you can help us with that? You seem to have a palliative effect on Chief Ford's condition. I might even say a medicinal effect."

"I doubt it, sir," Tran said, managing a smile. "And it's Captain Ford now. He just got a battlefield appointment."

"Oh, my apologies, Captain. Congratulations. Chief to captain, that's pretty unusual. Somebody up there must like you."

• • • •

Colonel Magazine arrived nine days later to take Micah back to Freehold. He had a Black Hawk, two Cobras and an F-16 escort on the tarmac at Az Zarqah. Micah signed a release form, thanked his nurses and the Brain Man, and they were Oscar Mike. The embassy had sent a few up-armored Escalades for the ride to the air base, and Maggie began briefing him on the way.

While Micah was recovering, Maggie said, Freehold had continued to tag and release a steady stream of black-site detainees. The mission only had six more prisoners to process, after which they could strike the tent and quit the desert.

Trouble was, Centcom's computers back in Tampa had just been hacked by some group of anarchist code monkeys claiming to be the Islamic State. (One taunting message had read *Je Suis Zinzana*, or "I Am the Gulag," which had sent the heckles and jeckles at Langley into lockdown spasms.) Sensitive ops like Freehold --- and a companion base that was busily processing Yemeni detainees --- had gone immediately to condition red. A re-start would depend on new firewalls and a system reboot. The crypto engineers back home had put patches in place, but they wanted Micah to run simul-diagnostics before they brought Freehold back on line. If everything went to green, the final inventory of prisoners could start arriving again.

"I'll get on that first thing, sir," Micah said, sounding weary already. His head was aching from the venusian sunlight in Amman and the bouncing of the Escalade on the deeply pot-holed roads through the capital.

"Also, Zaza has been in a damn tizzy," Magazine said. "Tran has been cooling his jets with some extra meds. I don't know what you told him before you left, but he looked like he was ready to checkmate himself. Nobody has said a word to him --- regular protocol --- and he doesn't know about your accident --- I just figured you were gaming him somehow. God *damn* these fucking roads!

"You might make Zaza your second priority once you get settled in, Micah. He's going to have to shit or cut bait about Baghdadi. My boss is tired of waiting on his ass, and we're down to our last batch of prisoners."

"Roger that, sir. I think I can turn him."

Micah would also have to read, censor and archive a month's worth of backlogged mail, intake dossiers, agency directives and Magazine's P4 letters before they could get the COP up and running again. In the hospital, he thought he had figured out how Maggie had been receiving information that was bypassing him. Yes, he'd soon be having a look into the colonel's secret sharing.

14. RUST AND STARDUST

Romo was there when they landed at the Nebraska helipad, waiting with a Gator to drive Micah and Magazine over to Freehold. It was unusual, damn near unthinkable, for a young sergeant to hug an officer, but Romo couldn't help himself. Salute became handshake became bear hug.

"Hey, hey, uh, nice to see you, Sergeant. Nice to see you alive. How you doing?"

"I got my battle rattled, but it's all good now. All the way, sir. It's great to see you back. Can't believe. You know. You had us wicked scared."

"Me, too, Romo, I must admit. At some point I want you to explain to me what the hell we ran into. The physics and the chemistry of those IEDs."

"Roger that, sir. They were some nasty ones all right."

They had arrived in time for lunch and Magazine led the way into the DFAC. "Stand and salute, there's Army officers in the house!" the colonel shouted as they pushed through the double doors, and nearly every man on the base ---- already assembled by Tran and Marchand --- began cheering Micah's arrival. What was it? The honest camaraderie, the after-emotions from the blast, seeing Tran again, Romo's spontaneous hug, Micah's own new clarity? The fundamental metaphysics of euphoria? Whatever it was, Micah broke down, head lowered and eyes flooded, which caused the applause, table-banging and hoo-ahs to last several minutes.

Maggie walked him to a small riser among the cafeteria tables and the men quieted down. The colonel made a brief, heartfelt speech about Micah's recovery, his importance to the Freehold operation and how he had lasted 13 hours as a captain before the moozh decided they needed to blow him up. The colonel made a show of pinning onto Micah's blouse a Combat Infantryman's Badge, a Purple Heart and a new pair of captain's bars.

"Captain Ford, this is the last set of these bars we have on base, so try to keep track of them, will you? We also found your old ones --- the ordnance guys dug them out of the dashboard of your Humvee. Unfortunately, they got a little melted. For my money, they oughta pin *these* babies on you." He handed over two globs of misshapen brass. "We're damned glad to have you back, Micah. I salute you. We all do."

The whole room ten-hutted and held salutes, and Micah, eyes stinging, snapped one off in return.

• • • •

Micah got the comms and computers back online after lunch, then reported to Colonel Magazine for a briefing at Safeway. Tran was already there.

"I got you this when I was in Amman, as a get-well gift," she said, handing him a brown MRE bag. "I didn't want to make a big thing about it in the DFAC. But here. I'm glad you're still with us."

Inside the bag was a big fat yellow watch with a black face and three dials, like something a deep-sea diver or a fighter pilot might wear. It was the size of half a lemon.

"Oh, it's a G-Shock, nice," he said, smiling at her. "Thanks. I appreciate the irony."

The colonel, perhaps anticipating the imminent closing of Freehold, was in an expansive and reflective mood. He gelled his hands a couple times, made espresso, offered them ice cream and began to roll out memories of West Point, his previous commands, stories about the Joint Chiefs, lots of inside-Centcom gossip. An old soldier running over his splendid résumé. Magazine Unplugged: The Desert Sessions. At some point Tran excused herself, but Micah was happy enough to settle in for awhile to listen to the colonel. Zaza could wait.

"You and Tran finally found your stride, I see," Magazine said. "It seemed a little bumpy there at first, am I right? How do you find her?"

"She's different."

"In what way?"

"In every way."

Magazine laughed and said he was in favor of getting more women into Special Forces and frontline combat assignments. He knew plenty of fine women officers who certainly would have made general --- or made general faster --- if they'd been able to get combat patches. "Women these days, I'll tell you, they're better hung than the men. They really just need to get a bunch of us old fucks out of the way. Good riddance, they should be saying, and I kind of agree." He had enjoyed his Army career, he said, but he'd be happy to retire after getting that single star. "My star," he called it.

He wanted to have a real tomato patch after so many years of inconstant gardening in suburban rentals, base housing and living abroad. House plants. The daily paper thumping onto his porch. Might get a dog, maybe a Dalmatian. He'd name it Spot. Simple pleasures, you know. Once you don't have to be perfect, you can get down to just being good. He wanted to try his hand at restoring mid-century Buicks. Roadmasters, Wildcats, boat-tail Rivieras, LeSabres, Skylarks, the Invicta, the Electra 225. Crank-window Buicks with VentiPorts, the tri-shield medallion, the Nailhead V-8, Dyna-Flow transmissions and that wide, wicked Delta fin. He said he liked Pontiacs, too, and they had been popular when he was growing up in Jersey, especially the LeMans and the GTO. "Buick, though, oldest active brand in America, big and bad and classy, at least up to 1990. Then they went to shit, of course, like every other American car. But I like the idea of restoration in general, as a concept, as a kind of moral code, rehabbing stuff. That's why I liked Rascal so much. Now there was a kid *worth* saving. I was really sorry to lose him. Anyway, Buicks. Could be fun. Ah, what the hell, it's all going to be bullshit after this. The rest is just rust and stardust."

"Rust and stardust. Wow. That's nice. Is that from something?"

"Yeah, good catch, I did steal that one. Nabokov. 'Lolita.' I taught it one semester when I was TDY at West Point. Almost got Article 15'd over that. Too much s-e-x, you know."

Magazine told a story about being on Rick Sanchez's staff in Baghdad after the U.S. invasion. One day he took a meeting to make a payment to the Iraqi minister of culture. Payoff, more like. Some kind of bribe, a large one, but not unusual given the millions in cash that were sloshing around the Green Zone back then. It was an ordinary piece of grift or graft that had been approved by Jerry Bremer's baby mafiosi. In turn, the appreciative minister handed Maggie a 1983 National Geographic with Iraq on the cover.

"You pick," the man said, and opened to a photo spread showing the collection of Iraq's National Museum of Art and Antiquities. Assyrian gold jewelry from the Nimrud treasury, Sumerian alabaster vases, gold and jasper rings, ivory combs, the copper Bassetki statue, cuneiform tablets from 3000 B.C. Magnificent stuff. Some had already been circled and then crossed out with an X. "You pick, make your circle and I get for you."

"It took me a minute to figure out what was going on," Magazine said, "but the guy was auctioning off the fucking museum. Only the very best pieces. It was like he was burning the library at Alexandria. My interpreter, an older guy, an Iraqi national, he just shook his head. You could tell he was really sad and pissed. But he said it would be a huge diplomatic insult to refuse the offer. I'll never forget what he said to me: 'An answer of no is not possible.' So I circled *that* little guy."

Magazine pointed to a small bronze ibis, maybe 3 inches high. Handsome, elegant, hand-crafted seven centuries before Christ. "It arrived at my office two days later, wrapped in the minister's monogrammed handkerchief."

Micah and the colonel talked about the sad course of the recent wars, about September 11, about Micah losing Hank and Namaz that way on that day. Maggie said he had known only one person who died in the attack, a West Point graduate who had been a year behind him and Petraeus. The man had gone to work for Monsanto after the Army. Just before 9/11 his wife had killed herself, a terrible punishment of a death, by drinking weed-killer. "Poor guy," Maggie said, then paused and added, "Poor *woman,* I should say. Imagine being that sad."

Colonel Frank Magazine was largely unacquainted with the most profound declensions of sadness, but he did know a bit about the wider world, the world beyond soldiering and military politics. There was his immense and florid vocabulary, which reinforced a combative debating style. He had a fascination with Malevich and Pollock. He knew the plots of all the big Italian operas. He knew Moby-Dick was hyphenated. Curious stuff like that, he knew. That Emerson had dug up his wife's coffin and his son's coffin after both of them had been long dead. That the novelist Richard Ford had fired bullets through the book of a female critic who had slammed his work. He knew that a pitcher named Candy Cummings had invented the curveball but was just 21-22 lifetime. He knew far less about matters of the heart, too true, although he did allow this to Micah, harkening back to his unrequited romance with Holly Knowlton: "It was a great freedom to give up on love, and get on with everything else."

• • • •

Tran was in her Jungleland office when Micah arrived to see Zaza. He hadn't been alone with her since arriving back at Freehold. She grabbed him and kissed him a long time. There were no troops in the Jungle at the moment, she said, and Zaza was the only detainee in-house. The last five prisoners were due within the hour.

"Should we try it?" Micah asked, and she pouted a no at him. But she pressed herself into him and they held each other. She turned around, rubbed her bottom against him, and he held her hips and kissed her neck.

"L.T. --- limited time," he said, doing some pouting himself.

"Later, Toots," she said, moving away, eyeing his erection and smiling. "You're different from most guys. You're not *always* thinking of Topic A."

"Uh, yeah, well, about my prisoner," Micah said. He pointed to a bank of monitors and the closed-circuit feed from Zaza's cell.

"He's *my* prisoner, thank you, Captain. I've had him in pharmaceutical detention ever since you left. He was very agitated. I've got him on Ativan, 4 milligrams twice a day, breakfast and dinner. That's an anti-anxiety med, and it seems to be working. He's pretty calm now. I could always double the dose if you want to beat him at chess."

In his cell, wrapped in the gauze of the medicine, Zaza barely gave Micah a nod of hello. Tran came in, wearing a black balaclava and blue neoprene gloves. She set up a table and chairs for chess, and short-shackled Zaza's ankles to an iron bolt in the floor. She nodded to Micah and left.

Micah gave a non-apology for his long absence --- "Overcome by events," was all he said. He asked if Zaza had considered his previous offer of release.

"Yes," Zaza said glumly, his brain silky with the Ativan. Then he asked, "White or Black?" Even doped up he wanted to play.

Micah said Black but didn't move to begin setting up the board, so Zaza did. "I've read Mandela and Orwell, mister, so I know about silence and isolation. I know about your mortuary here. You people are like a baby with a hammer."

Micah did not parry these thrusts. Zaza opened with his customary Modern Benoni, and this was not unlike Tran with her karate: Micah saw Zaza's leg sweep coming, knew it was coming, and still had no defense for it. But Zaza was less than sharp now, almost certainly from the meds and perhaps from the blunting effects of Jungleland. He blundered badly in the mid-game.

"You use the same old opening, and now you've played Qd4, just like Spassky in Game 3," Micah said, a bit meanly, looking to provoke. "You know this ends with the bare king. You're playing like a prisoner."

"So you know that game? That means you must play Bd3, like Fischer did, and it also means I must resign." He gently tipped over his king. "I lose, therefore you win."

"Have you thought any more about your daughter? The offer remains. I can arrange your release."

"Ah, the *other* game. You have played the one gambit I cannot decline, so I agree. I tell you something about al-Samarra'i. Then you let me go, yes?"

"Then I let you go."

Zaza gave a deep sigh and began to speak, slowly, carefully, correcting his mistakes in English as he went. He was alert enough to have remembered the intricacies of the Fischer-Spassky game, and Micah wondered if maybe he hadn't lost on purpose. Qd4? A crafty diversion?

At Camp Bucca, Zaza said, Samarra'i was known as Abu Dua to the prison guards. But in the privacy of their cell he told Zaza and the others to call him Abu Awwad. He came from a small family, not very religious, and he moved on his own to Baghdad to study when he was 18. He was quiet, scholarly, articulate, restrained.

"This is not information," Micah said abruptly. "This is *journalism.* It's nonsense." He stood to leave.

"Wait," Zaza said quickly, a touch of panic squeaking into his voice. His bluff had been called, and so easily. "Did you know Abu Awwad has a younger brother in Paris? Living in the rue des Ardennes. In the nineteenth.

"He uses the name Muhammad Sa'im al-Dahr and he calls his brother Abu al-Hul. When they spoke on the telephone they used a code --- a 'marriage' was an operation, 'books' were guns and 'the library' was the weapons supplier. They planned some attacks together by telephone, even from Bucca they did this. We could call family once a week from there. The little brother worked in an animal shop in the rue du Bac. I do not know the English. *Mahal tahneet.*"

"Taxidermy. He worked in a taxidermy shop? What did he say about Al Qaeda?"

"He approved of Osama bin Laden and the 9/11 operation. But the violent Qaeda operations abroad were not so interesting to him, as I remember. He talked often about a movement --- a program, maybe you can say? --- to create a caliphate in the Levant. He watched your soldiers very closely and listened to their military ideas. He liked the strategic of clear-hold-build. Holding territory for making a country. Many young believers came to our cell for talking jihad every day, and Abu Awwad always spoke about this. He called it 'Remain and Expand.' He said there should be a large *hijrah* --- I think your word is exodus?"

"Migration. Immigration."

"He preached about a migration to Dabiq, in Syria, and this town should become the capital of the new caliphate. Even at that time his brother was already sending money from France so their parents and cousins could move there. To Dabiq. They were building it up with tunnels and water-wells and weapons. Quietly. They planned to use Raqqa as a decoy for the Israelis and the crusaders. 'Decoy,' you can say this? Raqqa would be advertised as their new center but Dabiq was to be the real beating heart."

"Was Awwad in good health?"

"Oh, yes, he was very much exercising. Strong. Not fat. Very big man. He had to sleep always in the low bed of our cell or maybe he could crash onto me from the top bed. He often had a pain in his big toe. And I think you know that he is diabetic. We always carried sugar cubes out of the eating area in case of his weakness."

• • • •

Late that night in the SCIF, still sorting through the backlog of messages and dossiers, Micah found the hidden cache of e-mail traffic between Magazine and his bosses Stateside. [redacted]

Their messages concerned an operation called Skip Trace and each carried the header, TS-SCI//BEYOND//NOFORN//SEC DEF HAS SEEN//[redacted]//13-422//S-21. The early memos congratulated Magazine on the rapid processing of prisoners while Chief Ford was recovering. [CIA OFFICER No. 1 REDACTED] from Langley called it "releasing that invasive species back into the wild." And the faked signatures, the man reported, "would certainly stand up legally, come what may."

More recent messages centered on the Disposition Matrix, the Kill Not Capture list that charted those Freehold detainees that the agency considered drone-worthy. That was the term the secret circle was using now: drone-worthy. But even at a quick reading Micah could see that all the Freehold alumni were on the list, identified by name, dossier number and nano-tag designator. The final six detainees, still in-house, unsigned and unreleased, they were on the kill list, too. One general joked that all 151 detainees "need to share the same DNA, as in Dead, Not Alive."

Micah could scarcely believe it. They were killing detainees outright, almost as soon as they were released. Reading these cables was like falling into a graveyard.

There was no discussion in the cables of waiting for the signals from two nano-tags to connect. Presidential authorization also was not mentioned. This wasn't predictive policing. It was first-degree murder.

Several of the more recent messages in the thread complained about a scarcity of drones available for Skip Trace air strikes. "Fuck the drones," said [redacted] at one point. "The whole damn government is drunk on drones. We'll do it ourselves with fast movers." F-16s with FLIR-N pods had already proved effective, he said, with 16 kills and acceptable collateral damage. [CIA OFFICER No. 1 REDACTED] from Langley dispensed with the bureaucratic syntax and said it outright: He wanted all the Freehold detainees assassinated by early fall. "I want them removed from the battlefield. I want to start using the past tense on this mission," he wrote. "It sounds arbitrary but let's make our completion date the first game of the World Series. Our *other* national pastime."

Micah's head throbbed, a hard angry steady beat behind the eyes. He copied all the Skip Trace messages onto a USB drive, then pried open the drive and took out the chip. He unscrewed the back of his new watch, removed the battery, put the USB chip its place, and closed it all back up. Come what may.

15. 'I COULD PEEL HIM LIKE A PEAR'

Colonel Magazine, a full-platoon brief in the DFAC, after breakfast, 0830:

"So, gentlemen, we're down to cases. We'll be closing up Freehold the day after tomorrow and I don't want any last-minute aneurysms. I want the closing to be done in a smooth and military manner. Well, in a smooth manner, anyway." Laughter all around.

"Lieutenant Tran has posted everyone's work assignments for the next two days. You all need to have your personal gear packed, only what you can carry, no exceptions and no fucking around. Muster at the gate at 0900 and we'll have two Chinooks and a Black Hawk waiting. We'll put the last six detainees on the Black Hawk with a JSOC escort, leaving at the same time. The last flight of Con Air. Firsarnt Marchand? William, you'll need to have two transfer teams ready by 0700 to final-prep the prisoners."

The final disposition of COP Freehold would go like this: Romo and his EOD squad would detonate explosive charges to seal off Jungleland once the prisoners were extracted and Tran's clinic had been emptied. One big underground grunt-groan and the desert would reclaim everything downstairs, like the collapsing chambers of an Egyptian tomb. Agency and DOD cleaners would arrive with Chinooks the following day from Amman, and they would haul off Safeway, the Pig, and the Humvees. Engineers would use Semtex charges to blow Freehold proper, and B-1 incendiary strikes would handle the final demolition of Freehold and Nebraska from the air. Leaving no footprints. The desert wins again.

"Our immediate destination from here is classified for now, but trust me," Magazine said, "you should all be home inside of a week. The lieutenant has drawn up a schedule for each of you to come down to Safeway and have a word with me sometime tomorrow. You guys mean a lot to me, as does our mission here, and I want to speak with each of you individually before we close it down. Let's keep it to 5 minutes or so, each guy, max.

"You probably know that we officers love to go on and on about after-action reports and lessons learned. And takeaways. Oh, man, we *do* love our takeaways. Hoo-ah that? So here's your takeaway from *this* briefing: You ain't gonna work on Maggie's farm no more!"

The chow hall thundered with applause, shouts and table-banging. The man could work a room. Mission nearly accomplished.

• • • •

Before the closing-up chores began, most of the men turned out for a final few miles of PT on the track. The heat was incendiary, even at mid-morning, and boonie caps were the order of the day. The sun hit you like a hatchet. You could get a four-alarm sunburn inside of 400 meters. The cadence went like this:

Good old Rascal, one helluva bro,
Sure was sad to see him go.

From the Hoochy-Koochy fire to the cast-iron pan,
Nobody harder than L-T Tran.

Sweep the leg, swing the sword,
Nobody better than Captain Ford.

Marchand, Romo and Flipper, too,
They're the brave, the proud, the few.

Classified for now, but you might guess,
The Unknown Soldiers are headin' west.

Ain't no secret, that's for sure,
Ain't gonna work on Maggie's farm no more.

Ain't gonna work on Maggie's farm no more.
Ain't gonna work on Maggie's farm no more.

"Here's an algorithm for you --- Six tags to go / Ain't gonna work on Maggie's farm no mo.' " This was Tran, chanting alongside Micah, playfully bumping him off the track. "*Seis más*. Nip, tuck and adiós."

"Teeny, I need to ask you something."

When he didn't say anything else right away, she stopped running and said, "Micah? What?"

"I want you to not put a tag into Zaza."

"What? Get out. You're not serious. What do you mean?"

"Look, the guy's innocent, and he just wants to see his daughter again. He's nothing, Teeny. He's *empty*. You've seen him. He's like every other detainee we've had here. Their brains are all broken, and we know this because we're the ones who broke them. This guy is no threat whatsoever. You know what he told me yesterday? He said, 'Now I can't see my face in the mirror. I've lost my skin. I can't feel my mind.' I'm telling you, this guy is *cooked*. If you tag him, there's no telling what could happen to him. Just by accident."

Washington and Marchand came up behind them with, "From the fire, to the pan, nobody's hotter than L-T Tran."

"At-ease that shit, gentlemen," Tran said, fake-angry, over her shoulder. "Carry the fuck on."

The big sergeants laughed and passed them in a half-sprint.

"Micah, I don't get it," she said. "Why wouldn't we tag Zaza? We tag him, he goes home to his daughter and he doesn't backslide. Just like all the others. As long as he stays a civilian, he's got no worries. That's the deal. Besides, all these chips are assigned and tracked. You know that. They're like plutonium fuel-rods or something. They have to be accounted for. I can't just *lose* one."

"I can't tell you why I'm asking. Believe me, you don't want to know. You just have to please trust me on this."

"I don't know, Micah. I trust you, but something like this, Jesus, I could get court-martialed. Or worse. We both could. What about the colonel?"

"I'm going to talk to him after PT. I've been summoned. He wants to meet in Safeway for a 'special lunch.' This guy and his fucking crab legs. He calls me his Sherpa but I feel more like his Tonto. Anyway, just please, Teeny. Please don't tag Zaza yet, OK?"

"All right, OK, I can hold off. But it sounds pretty spooky. You'll need to keep me posted."

"I will. Thanks, Sweetie. It means a lot to me. I know it might be asking a lot."

"So you'll talk to the colonel and we'll go from there. Hoo-ah?"

"Yeah, agreed. Although why do I feel like Fredo getting into the rowboat with Al Neri? Or like Luca Brasi's sitting behind me with a length of piano wire."

"So, you're suggesting Colonel Magazine is like some Mafia hit man? Or the godfather himself? Will you have to kiss his ring like the undertaker did? Speaking of which, I could go for some more kissing. I'd love to get you down to my clinic for a thorough pre-release checkup. I've still got some of those roofies left."

"At ease yourself, Lieutenant. I am unaware of any such activity or operation, nor would I be disposed to discuss such an operation if it did, in fact, exist."

"You're in a very Hollywood mood today. Martin Sheen, 'Apocalypse Now.' Nice. And hey, *you're* a captain and he was *playing* a captain in that movie. Very nice."

• • • •

Inside Safeway, Maggie was working his way through a major glop of sanitizer. Lunch was waiting. Steak, crab salad, succotash, Zamzam water. "The perfect meal," Magazine said. "And Cherry Garcia for dessert.

"So what's the dope on Zaza?" he said, digging into the crab. "Did he give anything up on Baghdadi or not? This fucking guy. Fucking diva. There's not been a trustworthy sonofabitch in the entire bunch."

Micah laid it all out for Magazine. Baghadai's family details, the likelihood of gout in the big man's big toe, his use of Abu Awwad as a nom de guerre, the brotherly connection in Paris, the doctrinal divergence from Al Qaeda, the secret plan to build up Dabiq as the seat of a new caliphate while Raqqa served as a diversion. Some of it was boilerplate, but a lot of it was new, and it would fill in some of the blanks in the CIA's dossier.

"That's outstanding, Micah, holy shit," Magazine said. He was up now, and pacing. "Is Zaza fucking with us, or do you believe him? Jesus, if this is for real. Names and addresses even."

"I believe him, sir. It'll be easy enough to check. Somewhere along the way he must have heard about Baghdadi's emergence with ISIS. Maybe the Russians told him, or he heard about it on the gulag grapevine. He just never had any impetus to reveal what he knew. Now he does. Have that impetus, I mean."

"Which is."

"Which is he thought his daughter had been killed along with his wife when the Hussein boys were taken down in 2003. That's when we detained Zaza, if you remember. But his file shows that the girl survived, and I checked her out with MI in Baghdad. I was surprised that he didn't know. I thought one of our guys would have told him at some point, if only to fuck with his head. But he went crazy when I told him. It was legit. He was completely surprised."

"So the girl's alive? Do we know where she is?"

"She's the concertmaster with the Iraqi national symphony. First violin. She's kind of famous, at least among the new Iraqi elite. It's pretty incredible. She's recorded CDs and everything."

"This sounds like a damn Disney movie. 'The Violinist.' So, that's how you turned him --- using the daughter?"

"Yes, sir. After that it was easy. 'Always be closing.' He jumped at the deal. He even let me beat him at chess. Once."

Micah had two bowls of the ice cream. What came into his head was this: *The condemned man ate a hearty meal.* Magazine fired up some espresso.

"I'll head over to get Zaza to sign his release form," Micah said. "He'll be on that final helo, obviously, but I think it's important to get his handwritten signature, if only because it's our protocol."

"Sure. Fine. Makes sense."

"Because I saw where you've been releasing guys without getting their actual signatures. You were stuck, I guess. While I was laid up."

"Yeah, well, we had to cut a few corners for operational reasons. Our jigsaw puzzle needed a pair of scissors to finish it off. And what do you mean you *saw* that I was releasing prisoners without signatures?"

"Well, I saw the ongoing message traffic between you and [redacted] and [CIA OFFICER No. 1 REDACTED] and General Fields and General Platt about you forging signatures and the agency's Disposition Matrix. And I've seen the list of successful drone strikes against the guys we've already tagged. This thing called Operation Skip Trace. As you know, sir, they're killing *everybody*, whether their tag signatures are linking up or not. Even the guys we're still holding are on the hit list. Two or three days after a guy gets released, he gets whacked. It looks like the F-16s are getting in on it, too, coming out of Kuwait, Saudi and Diyarbakir, under the guise of hitting ISIS targets. It's not just the drones. It's indiscriminate, sir. If you're tagged, you're dead."

"You shouldn't have seen that stuff, Micah. Those messages were classified as Beyond Secure. How did. There's no. Not even the president is authorized to see those messages."

"I didn't go rooting around for it, sir. It's just information. It just comes to me. It's just *there.* It's absolutely none of my business who's been getting droned."

Magazine looked uncomfortable. The frother gizmo on his espresso machine was making one hell of a racket in the rear of the trailer. He didn't say anything, but he fixed Micah with a hard stare. In conversation, typically, the colonel's silences were not prompts, but Micah spoke anyway.

"I hope this information from Zaza guarantees you that general's star, sir. I know you've earned it. You've been very good to me, and to Tran, and to all of us here. The men are crazy about you. It has felt like Jonestown around here sometimes, in a good way, I mean, you know, part cult, part FOB. It hasn't been an easy mission, and it probably wasn't easy to manage. I can't imagine all the politics and the pressure."

"No, that's right, you can't imagine. But you've been a good XO, Micah, a helluva fixer, and I was proud to have gotten you that promotion. And Tran, too. We've had a good team here, top to bottom, under rough conditions. But now ISIS is breathing down our necks. Lord willing, we'll be back to our real lives soon enough."

"Thank you, sir, thank you. I do have a final request, that we release Zaza without his being tagged. If he's tagged, he'll be killed, that's pretty clear now. His daughter could be killed, too, if she's with him when the drone arrives. He's innocent, sir, and he always was. His value-add from Day 1 has been zero. Everybody who has ever interrogated him knows it. His story has never changed, not once in all these years. And now that he's helped us with Baghdadi, I think we should let him go clean. Get him off the X. Take the target off his back, so to speak. There's no *need* to kill him, and Skip Trace can remain a secret."

Magazine jumped from his chair. "You're fuckin-A *right* it remains a secret! Why wouldn't it? [redacted] and General [redacted] are the only ones who know about this thing, top to bottom. They're the ones driving this op, and they've made a warrior's call. On the battlefield. Which you've got to make sometimes. That's their job, Micah. To be ruthless and definitive. You can't go into a trance to make decisions on the battlefield."

"But it's a violation of our signed deal with the detainees. I'm just recalling your speech about our generals being sequoias and all."

"My *speech*? You're forgetting your place, Captain! This is still a goddamn *war*, you know. Now more than ever. You should know that better than anybody after losing those men in the convoy and getting your own bell rung. It's hard, ugly, shitty and anonymous. Maybe it isn't glorious, but it also ain't number theory. It's warfighting, Micah. Everything else is just stamp collecting."

"Yes, sir. Sorry, sir. I was absolutely out of line. My apologies."

"Don't bullshit me, Micah. Are you honestly messing with me over *Zaza*? That dried-up little gleet? You're defending *him*? He's a no-good leprous fuck. I could peel him like a pear and Muhammad the Prophet himself would call it justice. I've read every single file on every one of these characters, even if you think I haven't. These guys are *transactions*. You might remember that Zaza was an associate of Uday The Fucking Mass Murderer Hussein. And after that he was roomates with this Muslim maniac who's tearing up the Middle East and slaughtering thousands of innocent people. They've reinstated *slavery*, for God's sake. That makes Zaza guilty by association in my book. In *anybody's* book. We could hang him in the town square in The Hague and nobody would squawk. If there's one guy we've tagged who might actually reconnect with Baghdadi, it's Zaza. If there's *anybody* who's drone-worthy, it's him."

Magazine walked back to the hissing coffee machine and shut it down. He also switched off the nervous little table fan.

"There must be a why," Micah said. He said this to the air, apropos of nothing.

"There's no why here," snapped Magazine. "This drone stuff is the kind of ethically ambiguous shit that happens on a battlefield. Things go asymmetric and it just *happens.* We've all wrestled with it on this mission. You make policy in black and white, but you fight the battles in gray. It's asymmetric, always and everywhere. And now you're insinuating that something might leak from here? That has the odor of betrayal to it, Captain. In fact, it *reeks* of an Article 134 violation.

"Look, I like you, Micah, I think you know that, but I'm not fucking around here, and here's why: This might be a piss-ant little COP in the middle of the fuckin' desert, and we might be in charge of some crazy-ass mission dreamed up by three generals, a half-dozen spooks and some chickenshit D.C. lawyers, but this thing affects our entire national security. I shit you not. I know more than a little bit about geopolitics, young sir, and any disclosures about our operation here could well affect the image of our country, the standing of our military and maybe the future trajectory of this whole region. That sounds lofty and think-tanky and apocalyptic, I know. But news of this gets out, and it's a *thousand* Abu Ghraibs. Believe it. Torture, war crimes, lying to Congress, lying to the president, crimes against humanity, Christ Almighty, it'd be a fucking holocaust. There'd be *centuries* of payback and blowback out here. This is not, believe me, something that a new captain in the United States Army should be tampering with. Not in any way."

"No, sir. No, sir. It's a dirty piece of political business, and I know it needs to get done. And done quietly. I fully grasp the calculus of that. I can appreciate the damage we'd suffer if our mission was exposed. But we also have the chance to do one very small thing here, sir, in the correct and honorable way. I'm not blackmailing anybody. Zaza means nothing to me personally, but in a way he does stand for something.

"We're shredding all the other evidence, sir, and that's really what these detainees are --- they're the evidence. We're basically fitting all these guys with suicide vests. We're better than that, or we ought to be. Untagging one harmless old chess player doesn't hurt our mission. It doesn't fight the mission. In fact, I think it *ennobles* the mission. It's one blue geranium growing up through a huge mound of elephant shit."

"Don't be so fucking delicate, Micah. This is the job. We all need to see a bit of hell now and then. At times we're *required* to be violent. We can't apologize for the violence. I mean, come on, we traffic in it."

"No offense, sir, it's just. It's just that I thought I'd be doing something bigger than me. And this feels smaller. This feels small. What we're doing now is just this side of custodial murder. We're not so different than that racist idiot in Charleston, killing all those people in church. In cold blood."

"Please. Bad analogy. That kid was off his rocker."

"I meant the cold-blooded part."

"Have you told Tran about any of this? Anybody?"

"No, sir. Not a word."

Magazine walked to the back of the trailer, used the toilet, washed his hands, then poured himself a glass of water.

"OK, so let's, let's keyhole this thing. It'll help me with the timeline if I say it out loud. Zaza signs the form and leaves untagged, like you want, and we deliver him and our last remaining deets to Baghdad. The agency will probably assume that Zaza's tag was a dud. You scrub everything you have on the Disposition Matrix and Skip Trace. And you *forget* everything, too. Everything and forever. I take the Zaza intel to Centcom and shake hands with the president in the Map Room. You get a Bronze Star, so does Tran, and you take a month's leave in Hawaii or somedamnplace. Zaza goes back to his daughter, lays low, *stays* low, and it's happily ever after. That's the endgame. I guess I can live with that. Can you?"

"Roger that, sir. Thank you, sir. It's a good result."

Magazine went over, shook Micah's hand and said, "I'm a man of my . . ." He left it there. Just globbed a bit more gel into his hands and appeared lost in thought for a long moment. Micah began to feel uncomfortable, and said, "Permission to leave, sir?"

"Yes, of course, Micah, on your way. We've all got a lot to do. Thanks for the conversation. And I want you to say nothing at all to Tran or anybody else about this. Not a thing, you got me? This is Beyond Secure. *I* will get with Tran about Zaza's tag. Not you."

"Understood, sir."

• • • •

Micah got with Tran that evening at dinner. They took a small table and sat outside the mess hall. No sign of Colonel Magazine.

"He's going to talk to you directly about Zaza," Micah said. "He agreed not to tag him. I made my case and he said OK. No tag. But you can't let on that you and I have talked. Serious now. Absolutely no way can you say that we've talked about this. So look surprised."

"I *will* be surprised," she said. "I've thought about it a lot, too, and I'm trusting you on this. Micah. Serious now. It's only my career, is all."

"I know, and I appreciate it. He said he'll talk to you. We talked it out."

After that they ate quietly. They looked at each other in the warm evening air. Not a word was lost between them. Romo and Washington came by the table and yakked for a few minutes. Then they were alone again.

"So I was thinking," Micah said, "should we take some vacation after this? Together, I mean. Or am I jumping the gun? I'm getting six weeks off. They promised me before we deployed."

"That's a sweet idea. Thank you for asking. I've got five weeks. And not that I was expecting or planning anything, well maybe I was, but I was thinking we could go to Paris and Washington. And then to San Antonio to see my parents? If you want to. I'd love to see Arlington with you. Meet your parents, kind of, if that's not too weird."

"Now this is *me* looking surprised. And as Sergeant Washington might say, I'm in complete agreeance."

"My French is pretty rusty," she said. "Maybe we can practice before?"

"Moi je n'étais rien, mais voilà qu'aujourd'hui," Micah said. *"Elle a dû faire toutes les guerres, pour être si forte aujourd'hui. Je t'aime à mourir."*

"I'm not entirely sure what all that means, Monsieur Captain Showoff, but I think I got the *je t'aime* part."

16. DIFFERENT KINDS OF DEAD

The closing-up chores at Freehold went well enough, and the COP suddenly had an industrious, ant-colony feel to it. Micah disabled the computers in the SCIF and stored the hard drives in Colonel Magazine's safe. Technical manuals, hard copies of anything, keyboards, a portable chess set, the computer monitors, anything paper or meltable, all of it went into the 55-gallon drums that burned throughout the day. The prisoner dossiers went in, too, the last of the evidence, and they flared like cremation fires, sending up sparks.

Magazine gave farewell attaboys to each man in the platoon, as promised, and the visits were jokey but genuine. Most of the troopers had never been inside Safeway. It was their first glimpse behind the curtain.

Maggie had brought his Callaway 60-degree lob wedge with him to Freehold, figuring he could maybe work on his short game while deployed in the Big Sandy. He never used the club, though, and after awhile he even forgot that he had it. He found it (along with four dozen black Titleists) while cleaning out a back closet in the Pig. When each soldier dropped by, he had them hit a ball over the wall of the compound. He promised a thousand-dollar bonus to anybody whose shot cleared the wall and detonated a device in the minefield on the other side. Nobody collected.

Tran spent the day packing up the Jungleland clinic and tagging the remaining prisoners. Only one man in the very final group resisted vaccination, Mohammad Mazgouf, a former Mukhabarat informant, a greasy little horror whose time in rendition had left him mute, paranoid and incontinent. His agency file had categorized him since 2007 as a "non-viable person." He constantly slapped at the imaginary wasps attacking his face and the nightmare-spiders that never stopped crawling on his body. Handcuffing, as a result, terrified him. Tran had to vape his cell with fentanyl, which dropped Mazgouf into a nice REM sleep for 40 minutes. His nano-tag went right in, a quick *tsiss* into the fleshy back of the left arm, and she used a dollop of SurgiSeal to close up the tiny hole.

Nobody could sleep.

When morning came, they would set their explosives in Jungleland, lower the flag inside the base and haul out their gear to the two big Chinooks. They would put the last of their prisoners into the separate bird, and it would not be clear to any of the soldiers, not clear or imaginable in any way, that all the detainees would soon be dead. The same as those who had gone before.

• • • •

Moving day. The Chinooks and a stealth Black Hawk had been on the helipad at Nebraska since before dawn, throwing off dry scours of heat and black plumes of diesel. Loadmasters got to work at sunup, packing in the heaviest matériel, crates of weapons and ammo, and the colonel's big safe.

By mid-morning the final six prisoners were lined up on the pad, trussed and goggled but dressed now in black civilian suits and loafers. Hitchcock's crows on a wire. Black was the new orange. The Iraqis would be dropped at the airport outside Baghdad, and after that they'd be on their own. Those from Baghdad, with any luck, might be home by dinnertime. If home was still home.

Marchand's team was getting the last of the detainees into the Black Hawk when Micah came over. Already there was no slant to the sun. He pulled Zaza aside to say goodbye, to say godspeed, or *something*. But when he grabbed Zaza's arm, the prisoner flinched.

"Mr. Zaza, what, are you hurt?"

"Not so hurt, mister. Not so harm. Some small stitchings. The lady gave me medicine in my arm last night."

What crashed down onto Micah then was something dark and complicated and unknown to him, a black reek of anger, betrayal and dread, a draining-away of hope. It suddenly occurred to Micah that Zaza didn't know his name, his rank, nothing about him at all, really, at least nothing personal or important. *Nobody knows anybody, I guess, not that well.* He just stood there with his hand on Zaza's shoulder, trying to keep the world from coming apart. The Black Hawk started to throb and whoomp.

"Good to go, Captain?" This was Marchand, anxious. "The pilot says he's ready to roll."

Micah looked as if he was about to speak. But he just nodded.

Five minutes later, the detainees' helicopter was lifting off, into the air, up and up, then gone.

Twenty-three soldiers were strapped into webby seats on either side of Micah's helicopter. It was as big inside as a Quonset hut, cavernous and loud. Colonel Magazine walked up the back ramp, a black Pelikan case chained to his left wrist. He stood there, outlined and backlit, and silently saluted the seated men. Magazine thought to himself: "The road is cleared. We are going back to the world." He then about-faced and walked back down the ramp to his own chopper. It was a striking and cinematic gesture, that final salute, and it registered deeply with the troops. Micah couldn't even look at the man.

They were only waiting on Tran and Romo now, and after a few minutes the two of them arrived on a Gator. They drove right up into the barn of the helicopter, and the rotors and engines began to rev as the Gator was tied down. Tran buckled herself into the seat next to Micah. The noise was tremendous, and sand and grit and exhaust blew up through the open hatches in the floor of the Chinook. The back ramp closed up slowly with a hard hydraulic whine, and the chopper rocked and staggered as it shook free from the helipad. Then liftoff. The roar diminished. Then a heavy push through the oven of Anbar.

Micah leaned over, half-shouting over the noise. His mouth was close by Tran's ear. He could smell the Ivory. "Teeny, what happened, didn't Magazine talk to you? I saw Zaza and you tagged him! Now they'll kill him for sure. I mean, I thought . . ."

She turned to interrupt him and they bumped foreheads. "Colonel Magazine talked to me last night, Micah. He said you were against it, but he ordered me to chip the guy. He was very explicit."

"But he agreed that Zaza wouldn't have to be tagged. We shook hands on it. In his trailer. He *agreed*."

"That's what I figured," she said. "Like you told me."

Just then the helicopter bucked, went hard to starboard and dropped sideways through the air, like it had been punched, or shot. The interior lights flickered, and even the door gunners looked startled. But just as quickly the Chinook gathered itself, righted itself, and the pilot came on the intercom to say it was just a random shear of overheated air. One of those things that happens out here in the desert, he said. *No worries.*

Tran again: "That's what I figured, that you guys had worked something out. But he was so definite about me putting in the tag. I wanted to talk to you, but he told me not to. He was very clear about that, too. He kind of threatened me, actually. He asked if I understood his orders, and then he said this weird thing: 'An answer of no is not possible.' "

They rode for 15 minutes in silence, the dunes passing beneath them, the land a hot-shadowed blur, visible through the open hatch. Micah was back on the rockface, stuck, back on the X, unable to move, unable to imagine a river. No one would miss him. So there were two different kinds of dead after all.

"It really bothered me," Tran finally said, "how hard-ass he was being, like almost mean. I'd never heard that tone in his voice before. He talked about a court-martial if I disobeyed his orders by speaking to you. He actually said it would be *treasonous*. That's the word he used. There was no need for that. I know we just got our promotions, but still, I'm a fucking officer in the United States Army. I'm a fucking *Ranger*, Micah. Even as a sergeant I lived by the code. I *was* the code. I *am* the fucking code. So where the fuck would treasonous come from?"

"I don't know, Teeny." He didn't turn his head. He didn't try to speak up so that she could hear him over the chopper noise. More like he was talking to himself. "I don't know what to say."

"So listen to me, Micah. It was so squirrely with Magazine, I knew something wasn't on the level. Because. You. I just." She was choking up.

"So I thought about it some more and I decided not to tag Zaza. Like you asked me. Instead I gave him a flu shot last night, a real one, and I messed it up on purpose. It must have hurt like hell, 'cause I did kind of gouge him with the needle. But he didn't complain. I had him pretty doped up. I needed a reason to put a couple stitches in him. Just for show."

She reached into an inside pocket of her body armor and pulled out a test tube, heavy-looking, faceted, green, like a crystal sleeve of emerald light.

"This right here is your Mr. Zaza," she said, trying for a smile, holding up the tube. She read from the label. "Nano-Tag Designator V.K.96/W/9-3H."

Tran looked around at the other troopers in the helicopter --- nobody was watching --- and she broke the seal on the tube. She pulled out the tag itself, not even the size of a kernel of corn, and then, as casual as could be, she tossed the tube and the tag through the open hatch, one mile down, down down down into the desert.

"There lies Grandmaster Zaza, may he rest in peace," she said into Micah's ear. "They can drone him out here if they want to. They can Hellfire an acre of sand and call it a victory."

Micah took her hand, leaned back and closed his eyes, and the big helicopter began a slow arcing turn through the hot brilliant rescuing air of the morning.

ACKNOWLEDGMENTS

A thrilling correspondence with William Styron encouraged me to follow through with the writing of this book, and to approach it as a meld of fiction and journalism. Bill sent me an appreciative and complimentary note about a story I had written upon the reissue of "Nat Turner," a letter which, to a young reporter, was something tectonic, unthinkable and precious. From then on I pestered him with letters and queries --- stalked him, really --- for writing guidance and career advice.

Over the past 15 years, my deployments to more than a dozen conflict zones inspired and informed most of the combat situations in the book. Notable among these incidents was a Taliban ambush in southern Afghanistan, during an embed with Task Force Saber, of the Army's 3/4 Cavalry. Along with a squad of Army Scouts, the men in Alpha Troop who came under a withering crossfire that day were exemplary in their courage and wholly professional in their conduct. Among them were Captain Brian Peterson, Sergeant First Class Doug Bishop, Specialist Nick Plummer and our wheel man, Private Matt Ruhnke. They had my six.

I have profited beyond measure by working in the field alongside some of the finest reporters, photographers, interpreters and fixers of this or any generation, and they were especially valiant in war zones, conflict zones and under fire. Foremost among these is Abbas Fadhil Lutfi al-Bayati --- friend, eccentric, calm counsel, university professor, sidekick, brother. Abbas saved my life any number of times during the early and vicious fighting in Iraq, and he was resolutely brave and professional under pressure.

An absolute master of at least seven languages, Abbas supplied most of the Arabic translations in this book. Roxana Shirkhoda was helpful with the embroidery and nuances of Farsi. Koranic citations come from N.J. Dawood's translation (Penguin Classics). For Biblical passages I used the new international version of the Quest Study Bible (Zondervan).

Major General Robert C. Hughes Jr., former head of the Army's Human Terrain System, patiently answered many of my meddling questions about military politics, West Point, the career arcs and the personal motivations of senior Army officers. Colonel Magazine is a more substantial character because of the kindness, intelligence and forbearance of General Hughes. I salute you, sir.

Likewise, almost unfailingly, American troops and foreign commanders have been generous and accommodating to me --- in Iraq, Afghanistan, Pakistan, Turkey, Indonesia, Chechnya and East Timor. (In Cambodia, Myanmar and Sri Lanka, no.)

Marine Colonel Tim Nye was particularly helpful to me in Tbilisi, Georgia --- he was a major then --- and we ran into each other later, by coincidence, on the day that Mosul was captured from Saddam's forces during the 2003 invasion of Iraq. Thanks, too, to General Walter (Skip) Sharp and Admirals Dennis Blair and Joseph Prueher. Speaking instructively with me on background were numerous CIA and NSA analysts; desk and political officers at State; administration and Defense lawyers, and civilian contractors and military intelligence officers. Unless identified elsewhere in these Acknowledgments, they will remain unnamed, per their wishes.

U.S. ambassadors, politicians and senior diplomats were generous with their time, notably Pete Peterson, Sandy Vershbow, Ryan Crocker, Rep. Charles Wilson, Zal Khalilzad, Chris Hill, Tom Leary, Kent Wiedemann, Sen. Trent Lott, Priscilla Clapp, Shari Villarosa and Robert Gelbard. I profited from many hours with Sérgio Vieira de Mello, an especially fine U.N. diplomat. Losing Sérgio in Baghdad in 2003 was a terrible blow.

The Freehold section of this book owes much to Charles Swift, Eric Columbus, Alberto Mora, Jack Goldsmith, Carol Rosenberg and the Gitmo librarian Abu Saleh. Along with the detainees' lawyers, they have done courageous work at Guantánamo Bay, notably on the thorny issues of trials, tribunals, habeas corpus and national security. A grateful nod, as well, to the Joint Detention Operations Group: Its service members and officers are often forced to work under troubling and trying conditions.

Some of the protocols and conditions at Freehold and other black sites and secret prisons are echoes from the Eyewitnesses Office and Archive at the Hohenschönhausen Remand Prison in Berlin. The Stasi's methods aren't gone; they've merely changed languages and locations.

My appreciation to the diplomacy and foreign policy section of the National Archives in Washington; [redacted] and [redacted], staff historians at CIA; the Army War College, Carlisle Barracks; Kori Cioca and other veterans affiliated with the Service Women's Action Network; the Rafik Hariri Center for the Middle East; the Imperial War Museum, London; Saad Eskander, director of the Iraq National Library and Archives; Magnus Ranstorp at the Center for Asymmetric Threat Studies at the Swedish National Defense College; the SITE Intelligence Group; the Center for Constitutional Rights; Stratfor; the War Studies Group, King's College, London; and the Documentary Service of Sciences Po in Paris.

Shukran to the librarians at Al-Azhar University in Cairo; Salahaddin University in Erbil, Iraqi Kurdistan; Trinity College, Dublin; the George C. Marshall Research Library; Upjohn Library at Kalamazoo College; the National Security Archives of The George Washington University, and the Shaw and Himmelweit libraries at the London School of Economics. I have spent many happy hours under the Shaw's Fabian window: "Remould it nearer to the heart's desire."

Global security experts Christine Fair, Bruce Reidel, Bruce Hoffman and Peter Galbraith have been more than obliging with their replies to my interview requests over the years. I am also indebted to Brigadier Mowadat Hussain Rana in Pakistan and Hassan Abu Hanieh in Jordan, two of the great experts on Islamist groups, jihadis and suicide attackers.

Former Iraqi President Jalal Talabani and Foreign Minister Hoshyar Zebari were gracious in granting me substantial interview time. Likewise, Abdul Salam Zaeef, the ex-Taliban ambassador to Pakistan. (He would later become ISN 306 as a prisoner and for a time was known as "the president of Gitmo.")

I have much admiration for the King Abdullah II Special Operations Training Centre in Jordan and the officers who introduced me to the rigors of three KASOTC courses --- Basic Ranger, Adverse Action and Air Insertion. (Adverse Action taught me a lot about writing this book.) Likewise, my thanks to Brigadier General Fadhil Jalil al-Barwari, now head of Iraq's Counter Terrorism Bureau, and his Special Operations branch.

As I prepared to sneak into Iraq in late 2002 (as the United States seemed determined to go to war), Knight Ridder managers insisted that I take the Hostile Environment and First Aid Training courses given by Centurion Risk Assessment Services outside London. I was resistant then; I am grateful now. Would that all journalists could take this or a similar course, especially as more freelancers, contract journos and amateur adventurers find themselves in jeopardy in combat zones.

The principal characters of Ford, Tran and Magazine filled themselves out in any number of unexpected ways. Details, angles and edges came from benefactors far and wide: the Bloodworth, McLeod and Sangaree families of Apalachicola; General Tony Zinni; the Austin writer and martial arts instructor Susan Schorn; Karim Wasfi of the Iraqi National Symphony Orchestra; the Patriot missile team at Raytheon; forward-deployed members of Blackwater, Titan, CACI and Triple Canopy; the Dartmouth Mountaineering Club; the El Cap speed climber Ammon McNeely; the Unclaimed Baggage Center in Scottsboro, Ala., and the Alabama Bureau of Investigation.

My special and extraordinary thanks go to the staff and service members at Arlington National Cemetery, where my mother, stepfather and paternal grandparents now reside.

Micah's interests in advanced mathematics, cryptography and computer science were illuminated by iSIGHT Partners and ThreatScape; the Clay Mathematics Institute in Providence; the Hirzebruch Collection at the Max Planck Institute in Bonn; the XDATA, XG and MeshWorm teams run by [redacted] at the Defense Advanced Research Projects Agency; the All-Russia Research Institute of Technical Physics at Snezhinsk; the Bibliothèque Mathématique d'Orsay; the Institut Henri Poincaré; and the Mathrice Network and Groupe Calcul at the C.N.R.S. in Paris.

Dr. William H.R. Rivers was crucial to my own recovery from post-traumatic stress disorder. (So, of course, Pat Barker, thank you.) Appreciation, too, to Dr. Jonathan Shay and Dr. John Tremaine of Meredith Hospital, Dover Parade, London. I would also award oak-leaf clusters to Dr. Charles Hoge at Walter Reed, Skip Rizzo, Karen Perlman, Virtual Iraq, and the Program for Anxiety and Traumatic Stress Studies at Weill Cornell Medical College in New York. Doing the Lord's work, all of them.

Forever and with little prompting will I raise a glass (as will other conflict reporters) in the direction of the Ochberg Fellowship from the Dart Center for Journalism and Trauma; the Committee to Protect Journalists; Reporters Without Borders; Investigative Reporters and Editors; the Norman Mailer Center; the Iowa Writers' Workshop; and the Guggenheim, Arthur Vining Davis and Robert Wood Johnson foundations. And not to forget the MacArthur Foundation, whose Big Macs keep a lot of journalists, writers and other artists going.

Professor Susan Douglas at the University of Michigan handed me a rare and priceless gift --- the Howard R. Marsh visiting professorship in journalism --- and my seminar students redoubled that gift with their energy, attention, friendship and purpose. Earlier, also at Michigan, Charles Eisendrath helped me to turn the battleship of my career under the compass of a Knight Wallace Fellowship. How ever to repay all these generosities?

I am equally indebted, of course, to countless colleagues, so many, and of such gleaming quality and unfailing integrity. As a foreign correspondent I have been blessed to have worked with first-rate managers and world-class editors: Dan Sneider, Jerry Ceppos, David Yarnold, Michael Winter, Rebecca Salner, Jay Harris, Susan Goldberg, Kim Fararo, Jonathan Krim and Sarah Lubman at the San Jose Mercury News. My heartfelt thanks to Clark Hoyt, Kathleen Carroll, Steve Butler, Frank Greve, Linda Epstein, Tish Wells, Lee Stern, David Montgomery, Beryl Adcock, Renee Schoof, Ray Walker, Judy Treible and countless others at Knight Ridder. Our Iraq war reporting was getting it right when nearly everybody else in Big Journalism was getting it wrong --- alas, this was recognized and acknowledged far too late. Still, I was honored to have been involved. Taking the point on the KR team were John Walcott, Warren Strobel, Jonathan Landay and Joe Galloway. They should all get the Medal of Honor.

I offer the deepest of kowtows to Mort Rosenblum, Philip McClellan, Len Apcar, Bob McCabe, Charles Mitchelmore, Charles Sherman and Walter Wells at the International Herald Tribune (now The International New York Times). Likewise, at The Times, Marty Gottlieb, Susan Chira, Fern Turkowitz, Kim Fararo, Ian Fisher, Arthur Pincus, the late George Kiseda and Joseph Prisco, Frank Litsky, Paul Winfield, Harvey Morris, Marcus Mabry and the international desk editors. Finally, and verily, there is no better newsroom worldwide than the INYT bunch in Hong Kong. Ladies and gentlemen, I could buy the next 88 rounds at the FCC and it still wouldn't begin to repay your expertise, kindness and cool.

Thank you to colleagues and friends in Iraq: Eddy van Wessel, Ashley Gilbertson, Warzer Jaff, Tim Grucza, Peter Bosch, Hannah Allam, Tom Lasseter, Anna Badkhen, David Filipov, Dan Williams, Pauline Lubens, Michael Goldfarb, Don McCullin, Jim Muir, John Simpson, Lynsey Addario, Mick Ware, Marcus Stern and Jane Arraf. *In Jordan*: Eric Seals, Nancy Youssef and the late Ed Bradley and his '60 Minutes' team. *In Sarajevo*: David Leeson, who enlivened our stay at the "Holiday Inn" and our breakneck trips down Sniper Alley --- and whose generosity allowed me the use of his stunning photograph of Iraqi prisoners on the cover of this book. *In Chechnya*: Paul Starobin, the murdered Anna Politkovskaya and the two FSB escort-minders who saved my life under perilous

circumstances. *In Afghanistan*: David Gilkey, Soraya Nelson, the Reuters/Kabul staff whose body armor I borrowed, and the superb Qais Azimy. *In Pakistan*: Rahimullah Yusufzai, Syed Kabir Ali Wasti, Peter Tobia, Javed Rana, Imran Khan, Prof. Dr. Chishti (who warned me off a clandestine meeting with Lashkar-e-Taiba), Nic Robertson, Lyse Doucet, Kathy Gannon and the floridly flame-bearded Muhammad Manzoor.
In Myanmar: Seth Mydans and Greg Constantine. *In Sri Lanka*: Thomas Fuller and Sanath Malalgoda. *In Moscow*: Lyudmila Alexeyeva, the late Paul Klebnikov, Sergei and Galina Blagov, the splendid Vitali Lagutin, Sabra Ayres, Rebecca Santana, Jill Dougherty, Susan Glasser and Peter Baker. *In Seoul*: Fiona Bae, the great Choe Sang-hun, John Delury, Simon Martin, Sebastian Falletti, Jasper Kim, Christian Oliver, John Glionna, Andrei Lankov, Douglas Binns, Jacquie and Ian Smith, Paula Hancocks, Doualy Xaykaothao, Jean Lee, Sohn Jie-Ae, Krys Lee, Don Kirk, Steve Herman, Sujin Chun, Soo-mee Park, Sei Chong, Woohae Cho, Jean Chung, Kent Davy, Kevin Kim, Andrew Salmon, Lucy Williamson, Tony Spaeth, and that most splendid Bukchon pair, Jade and David Kilburn.

The legendary correspondent David Lamb was a wonderful sidekick and colleague in Vietnam and throughout Southeast Asia. I owe him a lot, along with an equal dose of appreciation to his wife, the documentary filmmaker Sandy Northrop. Also in Hanoi were Simon Redington, Donald Berger, Nhu and Tom Miller, Ambassador Peterson, Andy Soloman, Michael Mathes, Jim Laurie, Anya Schiffrin, Catherine Mckinley and Thuan Thanh Tran, David Brunnstrom, Bob Schiffer, Greg Torode, Owen Bennett-Jones, Thích Quang Dô, Jeff Richardson, Jay Ellis, Chau Doan, Richard Vogel, Suzanne Lecht, Freddie Balfour, "Muoi Hanoi," Kay Johnson, the late General Tran Do, Messrs. Quynh and Khanh, the swell crew at Au Lac Café, plus Tony Nong, his mother Ann and their most generous family in Saigon. There are so many other Vietnam friends and colleagues, too many to list, and please pardon my AWOL Rolodex and my failure of memory. *Xin cam on.*

A deep and impressive roster of friends has buoyed me through the long writing of this book. Thomas Maurstad has been an important co-conspirator, and his timely consults in Dallas led to many mid-course corrections. The INYT editor David Moll was a major help as he voluntarily suffered through two readings of my early drafts, and his repairs and edits are everywhere throughout the book. I've also drawn inspiration and energy from Bill and Helga Block, Johnette Howard, Jerry Caffey, Ken Hancock, Drew Brown, Richard West and Dena Timm, Phil Karber, Michael and Ruthie Precker, Raad and Karena Cawthon, and Leslie Baggott. One could never overlook Eddy van Wessel, Bobby

Chinn, David J. Bratt, Scott Busby, Rod Davis, Delia Rios, Eric Moyé, Wesley Drent, Estelle Olivia (and her splendid cover of this book), Robin and J.P. Stephenson, and the Clarence and Titovets families. Nicholas Sherman of Bizrazzi Books was massively helpful with his publishing suggestions and the hands-on formatting of the book, essentially guiding the manuscript into actual print. Nick's gracious intervention at the 11th hour quite literally made the book happen.

I was lucky enough over the years to have been pulled occasionally into the marvelous whirring orbits around David Carr, Stanley Karnow, Don Coburn, Frank Rich, John Leonard, Seamus Heaney, Hal Drake, Wole Soyinka, Chinua Achebe, Zhenya Yevtushenko, Billie Fischer, Conrad Hilberry, Chris Hitchens, Anthony Shadid, Blackie Sherrod, Alexander Solzhenitzyn, Richard Ben Cramer, George Kiseda, Red Smith, Dave Anderson, George Vecsey, Jim Murray, Mark Nepo, Richard Hoffer, Stanley Elkin and James Church.

Finally, even at the remove of three decades, I owe much to my fellow *salonistes* at No. 15, rue du Cherche Midi, Paris 6eme. In the early days of my career, in the Paris years, they prodded me to dream big and to think bigger about my life, about journalism and about the actual accomplishment of a book. Their urgings, it seems, finally took. Thank you: Cynthia Pigott, Fred Hughes, Pierre Bergé, Andy Warhol, Dan Dixon, Lisette Figueroa, Lionel Poilâne. And most affectionately, Loulou de la Falaise, now gone, *je t'embrasse*.

Mark McDonald is a veteran journalist, foreign correspondent and bureau chief. He has worked for Knight Ridder Newspapers, The New York Times, the Los Angeles Times, the International Herald Tribune, the Dallas Morning News and the Boston Globe. In addition to foreign postings in Paris, Moscow, Hanoi, Seoul and Hong Kong, he has reported from more than 100 countries plus a dozen combat theaters and disaster zones, including numerous deployments to Iraq, Afghanistan and Pakistan.

At the IHT and The New York Times he won several Publisher's Awards, Human Rights Press awards, and he shared the 2009 Osborn Elliott Prize for Excellence in Journalism on Asia. While recovering from injuries sustained while embedded in Afghanistan, Mark served as the Howard R. Marsh Professor of Journalism at the University of Michigan, from 2005-2007. He previously held the Knight Fellowship in International Business as a Michigan Journalism Fellow. While at the Dallas Morning News he worked on a team that went on to win the 1994 Pulitzer Prize for International Reporting. He also won a Dallas Press Club Katie Award, APME and GLAAD awards, and the Charles Green Headliner Award as Sportswriter of the Year in Texas.

Mark's sports journalism, foreign reporting and essays have appeared in a number of nonfiction books, including most recently Eddy van Wessel's prize-winning memoir on war photography, "The Edge of Civilization."

Born in Washington, D.C., and a political science graduate of Kalamazoo College, Mark did post-bac work at Columbia University (history), New York University (fine arts) and the Monterey Language Institute (Vietnamese). He is a 2002 diplomate of Lomonosov Moscow State University in Russian language studies. He lives in New Mexico, Texas, Mexico and France.